JONATHAN ABERNATHY YOU ARE KIND

# JONATHAN ABERNATHY YOU ARE KIND

/// A NOVEL ///

# MOLLY McGHEE

∧
ASTRA HOUSE
NEW YORK

Astra House
A Division of Astra Publishing House
astrahouse.com
Printed in Canada

Library of Congress Cataloging-in-Publication Data

Names: McGhee, Molly, 1994– author.
Title: Jonathan Abernathy you are kind : a novel / Molly McGhee.
Description: First edition. | New York : Astra House, [2023] |
Summary: "A piercing critique of late stage capitalism and a reckoning with its true cost,
JONATHAN ABERNATHY YOU ARE KIND is about a man who takes a job as a dream auditor
to pay off an insurmountable student loan debt"—Provided by publisher.
Identifiers: LCCN 2023009230 | ISBN 9781662602115 (hardcover) |
ISBN 9781662602122 (ebook)
Subjects: LCGFT: Fantasy fiction. | Novels.
Classification: LCC PS3613.C458 J66 2023 | DDC 813/.6—dc23/eng/20230426
LC record available at https://lccn.loc.gov/2023009230

First edition

10 9 8 7 6 5 4 3 2 1

Design by Richard Oriolo
The text is set in Bulmer MT Std.
The titles are set in Karrik.

*For the forgotten who have been worked to death*

*They entered—and he suddenly felt that this day which he had been looking forward to with such fierce longing was passing much too quickly—was going, going, would be gone.*

—VLADIMIR NABOKOV, *PNIN*

*If you cannot bargain with the gods because they already have everything, then you certainly cannot bargain with the universe, because the universe is everything—and that everything necessarily includes yourself.*

—DAVID GRAEBER, *DEBT*

# CONTENTS

I. JONATHAN ABERNATHY FALLS ASLEEP

1

II. JONATHAN ABERNATHY IS SLEEPING

75

III. JONATHAN ABERNATHY DREAMS

143

IV. JONATHAN ABERNATHY WAKES

219

ACKNOWLEDGMENTS
281

ABOUT THE AUTHOR
285

# JONATHAN ABERNATHY YOU ARE KIND

/// **I** ///

# JONATHAN ABERNATHY FALLS ASLEEP

**JONATHAN ABERNATHY STEPS INTO THE** office and death is there. Death is not alone. A redheaded attendant named Kai looks up from her paperwork as Jonathan Abernathy walks through the automatic doors. Neither Abernathy nor the attendant feels death, sees death, hears or touches death, but death is there. Death is watching them both. Though it will take three years, from this moment, for death to act, Jonathan Abernathy will never live a life unmarked again. Death will be tethered to him as a shadow.

His will not be a good death. When he dies, it will be slow.

The poor dumb son of a bitch is, of course, oblivious to this. His oblivion makes him human. He is sweeter for it.

Except for Jonathan Abernathy and Kai, the attendant, the empty office is located in a strip mall just off the highway. The only signage is a weather-beaten brass plaque that reads—

**THE 508TH**

**ARCHIVAL OFFICE**

**FULL SERVICE & RECORDS**

A piece of white printer paper is taped to the bottom of the plaque—

**INQUIRE FOR EMPLOYMENT OPPORTUNITIES WITHIN**

The interior of Archival Office 508 is no more specific than the exterior. The waiting room is Abernathy's spiritual cousin: chairs of vinyl, cluttered secretarial space, carpet that's almost as downtrodden as he. There is a damp aura. It is the type of room a government official leads you into to execute you, financially. In such rooms, there are always contracts to sign. Ballpoint pens. With the tips of his fingers, Abernathy can reach above him and pop any of the Styrofoam ceiling tiles out of place. As if the visual similarities between Archival Office 508 and the purgatories of our modern world (IRS rooms, liminal spaces, notary offices at large) are not glaring enough, the waiting room even has a jingle that loops.

Last night two people visited Jonathan Abernathy in his dreams and told him to come here. In this place he could find forgiveness: of his loans, they said, yes, but also of other things.

Though Jonathan Abernathy is not usually the type of person to listen to dreams, voices, or "signs from God," today he is desperate. Today he has defaulted on his debt.

The debt of Jonathan Abernathy is large. Myriad. His loans, IOUs, and bills so diverse ecologists would be within their jurisdiction to classify the collection as "an ecosystem." Despite the diversity, the two main life forms are fairly simple: (1) a series of unpaid credit cards inherited after the death of his parents, and (2) the legal culminations of the decisions he made as a seventeen-year-old kid, also known as private, American nonsubsidized student loans with an APR so lethal it can kill in a week. Jonathan Abernathy has student loan debt in the quarter million. His inherited debt is in the low six figures. Even though it is illegal to inherit debt from your deceased family members, this will not stop debtors from attempting to collect. Combined, Abernathy's debt is one of the most prosperous ecosystems in the world.

Jonathan Abernathy does not make good money. What is illegal when done to some people is not illegal when done to him. He does not have the money to prove the illegality of other people's actions in the court of law.

So, yes.

A voice in Abernathy's dream told him to visit this tiny, miserable office, at the outskirts of the city, and he went.

Crazier things have happened.

In time Jonathan Abernathy will believe himself to be in love. There's nothing crazier than that.

Kai, the redheaded attendant, sits at the far side of the room, at a reception desk separated from the waiting area by a plexiglass partition. To get her attention, Abernathy walks up to the partition and taps on the scratched screen.

"Hello," Abernathy says.

He looms above the sitting woman. He avoids eye contact with both her and his reflection. His shirt is depression-wrinkled. His hair sheening with sweat. He will never have a deathless moment again, yet all Jonathan Abernathy can think of is his appearance: the dampness of himself, the slouch.

"I think I am here about loan forbearance?" The word "forbearance" feels strange in his mouth. "I received . . ." Jonathan Abernathy hesitates. "I received a call from your office . . . just yesterday, about a government . . . ah, forgiveness program? Does that sound right?"

The attendant looks him up and down. Her bottle-red hair and green eyeglasses contrast with her skin and make her look like a beetle. Her name tag reads: KAI, DREAM COLLECTOR 265.

Kai rolls her eyes. Without verbally acknowledging his presence, she points behind him with her ballpoint pen.

Abernathy turns away from the attendant and his reflection in the plexiglass. If the walk here had not ruined it (his outfit), he might have looked nice. In his dream he was told to look nice, otherwise resign himself to suffering.

Jonathan Abernathy does not wish to suffer.

He takes a clipboard from the caddy labeled APPLICATION: DREAM AUDITOR. At the far wall, against a window, he settles into one of the polymer seats.

He's never liked his looks, despite how charming others perceive his appearance to be. He has to live in his body. Others don't. Perhaps if Abernathy knew people found him charming, he would like himself more. As it is, he knows nothing about the perceptions of others. He has wavy hair. A roundish face. Nice shoulders. Kind eyes. This morning he tried to look storkish: stately, regal, destined for greater things but currently resigned to standing in wait for his proverbial big catch. Instead, he looks like a pigeon. Dirty. Beaky. Wide. Behind him, on the sill, there it is—a dying plant standing in as a metaphor for his life.

✓ Yes, Jonathan Abernathy is in financial peril.

✓ Yes, he is a former student of the public education system of the State.

✓ Yes, he feels like a failure in all things, but still somehow wakes up each morning feeling hope.

Does he sleep at least eight hours a night? As unbelievable as it is—

✓ Yes, he does.

Returning to the window, he slides the clipboard beneath the barrier. The attendant ignores him. She clacks away at a keyboard, huffing and sighing, before finally, in her own good time, turning to his application.

In silence, Kai's buggy eyes quickly sweep down his writing. Abernathy bounces on his heels with anticipation. She hits a red buzzer on her right. A chute opens in the floor. She drops his paperwork in.

As if nothing out of the ordinary has happened, Kai does not acknowledge Abernathy, though he is right in front of her, separated by only the thinnest, most scratched layer of plastic imaginable.

Kai pulls an orange from a desk drawer. The chute seals. The carpet is intact again. Still ungreeted, Abernathy stands in front of the barrier now at a loss for words.

On the other side of the plexiglass, Kai presses a long nail into the crown of the orange and begins to pull down the skin.

The room is flooded with the asynchronous smell of citrus.

Abernathy raises a finger. Goes to say, "Excuse me, Kai, the two-hundred-and-sixty-fifth collector of dreams, hello," but he is too nervous. Instead, he says nothing. He tells himself lies.

✓ Jonathan Abernathy you are kind.

✓ You are competent.

✓ You are well respected and valued by your community.

✓ People, including your family, love you.

Abernathy clears his throat. What did the recruitment voice in his dreams say? He can't remember. Something about appearance being the end-all-be-all of both this life and the next.

As far as Jonathan Abernathy is concerned, he always says the wrong thing. So Jonathan Abernathy says nothing.

Instead, he turns. Walks away. Gets to the automatic doors. Is proud of himself. Only then he remembers: he is no coward.

Or, at least, he does not wish to appear cowardly.

On this updraft of consciousness, Abernathy turns from the exit and dashes back to the counter. He exhales a rush of words in the dream collector's direction. His sentence follows an emotional trajectory that goes something like, "What the fuck?"

Kai stops. Mid-peel, she leans forward. Onto her elbows.

"Yell at me again," she says.

Abernathy had thought her to be, like him, the type to take shit.

He sees his mistake.

Abernathy blushes. Steps back.

"Ah," he says.

Kai looks at him.

He repeats, this time with words, instead of feelings, his inquiry. "You, uh, threw my application away. Just there."

He points.

Kai sets the orange down. She says, "Right there?"

"Yeah," he says, then corrects himself, remembering his manners. "Yes."

"Uh-huh. And this gives you the excuse to talk to me that way because . . . ?"

Abernathy mumbles an apology.

"What was that?" Kai leans forward. She cups a hand around her ear.

Abernathy starts again. "I haven't been able to pay back . . ."

"No, please. You clearly have a good reason. Keep going. Go ahead."

He falters.

Jonathan Abernathy wants to say that he is desperate for forgiveness. From the government or otherwise. He hasn't been able to pay back his loans. He's looking for an end to—or at least a break from—his suffering. He would like to one day have a life. Live with another person. Be successful. Now, as he defaults on his education, a great machine he could never get to work for him, those loans are actively ruining his one shot at life.

He needed—he needs—help.

He says, instead, "I just really need this job, man."

Kai stares at him.

"I, like, really need it."

More staring.

"You know?"

"Look," Kai says, not without patience. She has a deep southern accent and a stone face. She wears a hoodie and a pair of slacks, which contrast with the richness of her makeup and hair. She points at the place in the floor where the chute in the carpet opened. "That's the file drawer."

"Oh," says Abernathy.

"It takes your application and digitizes it, so that our somnambulatory officerial force can review and assess your capabilities."

"Ah." Abernathy does not understand any of this, but he wants to sound smart, and competent, and all the other things employers look for in new hires. He repeats the biggest word, "So-nah-em-bew-la-tory?"

"Somnambulatory."

"Doesn't that mean . . ." —he tries to remember— "something about sleep walking? Like when you're sleeping but walk around?"

Kai rolls her eyes again. "Yeah," she says.

Abernathy is starting to think he did not hallucinate the men in his dreams who told him to come here.

Still, this place is not what he expected.

He leans into the partition separating him and Kai. His nose just touches the surface which is, like him, weirdly damp. He looks into her tiny reception office. The chute in the floor has closed. The floor is beige carpet patterned with feeble green infinity signs. "So in the dreams . . ."

"Yes," says Kai, patience wearing out. "We come to you in dreams. That was us. Is there anything else, Mr. . . . ?"

"Abernathy," he says, realizing too late that an office that recruits their workforce through dreams may have an architecturally unconventional infrastructure. Their workflows might not align with the workflows of, say, other, more traditional workplaces.

Not that Abernathy has ever worked in a traditional work space.

"Jonathan Abernathy," he says. "But only my parents called me Jonathan. Nobody calls me Jonny, or Jon. Everyone just calls me Abernathy."

"Is there anything else, Mr. Abernathy?"

"Just Abernathy is fine."

Kai looks at him.

"How does the dreaming stuff . . . how does it . . ."

"Work?"

"Yeah. Sorry, yes. That."

Very slowly, with exaggerated, buggy blinks, Collector Kai the Two-Hundred-and-Sixty-Fifth begins to speak to Abernathy as if she is speaking to a child. Abernathy is a child, though he won't admit it. Just a really tall child masquerading as an adult. To his credit, he tries hard not to be. Jonathan Abernathy wants to be self-sufficient. He wants to grow up. One day, he wants to have children of his own. In short: he wants to enter the great American employment and leave behind his vast forest of debt. This is his dream.

"Have you heard of the Archive of Dreaming Act, Mr. Abernathy?"

Abernathy stares blankly at her.

"Several years ago," the attendant sighs, "the founder of the Archive discovered that humanity shares a consciousness while it sleeps." She sounds very bored, as if she has said this a million times.

"There are ways," Kai continues, ignoring Abernathy's disbelieving stare, "of tending to this . . . shared consciousness . . ." She pauses. Abernathy thinks it is because she cannot find the right word, but he is wrong. Kai is actually pausing in disgust. "We partner with the government, who then sell our services to employers whose workforces seem"—she closes her eyes and takes a deep breath—"depleted."

Abernathy has a hard time following this. "Wait, so, what are you saying?"

"I'm saying that in this job—*if* you get this job, and I'm not sure you will get it—you'll be going into the dreams of American workers and cleaning them up."

"Cleaning?"

"Cleaning. Them. Up."

"What does that . . . I mean . . . how do you even . . . ?"

"We will review your plea," Kai says, interrupting him. Abernathy realizes he has unconsciously crossed his arms across his chest, as if hugging himself. He unfolds. "If we feel like you're the right candidate for the program, we will get back to you."

"But," says Abernathy, lips dry, "what about—"

"Hey," says Kai. She taps on the smudged barrier, where Abernathy's nose once was. "I'm only here filling in. My actual pay grade? Not enough to put up with this shit. OK? So, please, if you'll just—" She waves at the door. Her nails, a rhinestone set in the center of each, are painted an immaculate emerald.

This must be what the recruiters meant when they spoke in his dream of appearance. Be like Kai. Appear to be confident. Appear to be competent. Appear to be good. Abernathy takes a mental note: develop appearances and, in the process, solve your life.

## 2

**THE NEXT THREE DAYS ARE** a panic.

Abernathy thinks: *They won't like me.*

Abernathy thinks: *I'm not likable enough.*

Abernathy thinks: *If I become likable, they'll hire me?*

Only two out of three thoughts are true.

To assuage himself of doubt, Abernathy ruminates over Collector Kai, whose personality seems to be that of a wood chipper, but whose confident appearances have already wholly endeared her to him. Abernathy spends his last remaining $66.60 on a cheap suit to impress her. As attractive people often do, especially attractive people who are oblivious to their looks, Jonathan Abernathy equates looking good to being good.

He desperately desires to be good.

To develop a more robust sense of self, Abernathy wears his suit while in his room. His small apartment is located in the basement beneath his landlord's house. In its past life, his room was a mother-in-law suite. The mother-in-law died, the ruination of her son's marriage shortly followed, and to pay for the subsequent divorce, the dead woman's room was rented out to Abernathy. The homeowner, Kelly, got the house in the divorce and Abernathy with it. At the time of the viewing, Abernathy billed himself as "a new graduate looking for his start in life."

Technically he never did graduate, but Kelly did not need to know that.

Abernathy moved in five years ago.

His life has not progressed much since.

The room (his apartment is only a room, though it does have a small bathroom attached, as well as an open kitchenette equipped with a microwave, a hotplate, and a sink) is wide enough that should Abernathy lay on the floor with his feet against a wall, he could just touch the other side with his fingers.

This depresses him.

He does not do this self-harm.

Instead, he sits in his sixty-six-dollar suit on the edge of his bed, his knees almost touching the kitchen counters in front of him, and eats ramen out of a Styrofoam plastic cup.

Above him, he can hear his landlord—*Kelly*—entering and leaving the house. As the sound of her heels fades, Abernathy thinks, not without envy, that she must be going somewhere where someone will tell her what to do. Then, in exchange for this, they will give her money. Jonathan Abernathy would like to be told what to do in exchange for money.

LATER THAT NIGHT, the ramen's excess sodium causes vivid, surreal dreams. Jonathan Abernathy doesn't know if it's a consequence of the dehydration or of submitting his application to the Archival Office three days before, but representatives appear as he is dreaming of a trip to visit his parents in Heaven.

In Heaven, he is wearing his sixty-six-dollar suit. He does not clock that in this dream, he is wearing the outfit he fell asleep in. This should be his first clue that this dream is no ordinary dream at all.

Abernathy sits upon the upper deck of a tour bus. His parents sit in front of him. He can't remember their faces, in this dream, and they won't turn back to look at him. Still, he knows they are there, and that gives him a dual sense of comfort and calm.

The tourists are being shown gates of pearl. Very pearly indeed. Lots of sheen. Exactly the type of retirement community one aspires to find for their parents' eternal lodging. The only regrettable flaw in the design is that the gates swing outward, not inward. Eager patrons are often injured at the gate's threshold. The dead are too excited. They've been waiting for salvation for too long. They don't think to step back.

A woman and a man join Abernathy on the tour bus. They wear matching jumpsuits that look like space suits from the seventies. The suits are white, a bit plasticky. Not unlike ski suits, actually. There are a lot of zippers. There are round logos above the left breasts: a brown box embroidered onto a blue background. The two newcomers even wear white, bubble-like helmets with reflective visors. At first Abernathy thinks they are strange tourists, like him, on a jaunty trip to visit their lost. Oblivious, Abernathy is only vaguely aware that he is dreaming. In dreams, anything is possible. But that also means events and people can be possibly anything.

Among the silent crowd, Abernathy and the new tourists watch God explain Their choice of topiary. God claims to have hired an expert landscaping operation, but to Abernathy, Heaven looks suspiciously like his backyard: brambles, fallen fences, trees that refuse to flower, wild mushroom patches that dot the landscape in Rorschach-like patterns. Abernathy lives in the outer city, where things are not exactly green, but not *not* green, either. Brownish-green and greenish-brown and sidewalk-colored, mostly. God waves Their hand across the stubbly yard of Their creation, drawing the tourists' eyes to Their glory-work. God is not who Abernathy supposed Them to be. In this dream, They wear zinc sunscreen and a toga. They speak into a flesh-colored mic that is wrapped around Their ear, the kind celebrities wear on stage. They seem like They have a sense of humor. Abernathy likes that. He did not expect humor from God.

The two new tourists take a seat on either side of Abernathy.

"Some dream," the woman says under her breath.

Abernathy is rapt in his admiration of the gates that border his neighbor's yard. They really are that pearly. What a wonder that is! What a relief!

In his waking life, Abernathy desperately desires to believe in an afterlife. He does not.

It takes Abernathy a moment to realize the woman sitting on his left has turned away from her partner and is now peering into Abernathy's face. Somewhere, there is a horn blowing. Abernathy cannot tell if the horn is traffic (does Heaven have traffic?) or Angels (does Heaven have Angels?).

The woman presses a small button at the base of her helmet and the reflective visor becomes transparent. Big eyes stare at him framed by green glasses and wisps of red hair. He recognizes the beetle-like woman as Kai, The Two-Hundred-And-Sixty-Fifth.

"Jonathan Abernathy?" she asks.

"Oh," Abernathy says. "It's you."

"Yep," says Kai. She smiles with her lips tightly closed. "It's me."

"What are you doing here?" Abernathy asks.

"Do your questions ever end?"

"Is this about what I think it's about?" Abernathy asks. If so, he is excited.

Kai gives the man on Abernathy's right a "see what I mean" look.

The man chuckles and passes a clipboard over Abernathy to Kai. The man has made his helmet transparent as well and Abernathy is surprised by how devilish his good looks are. He has dark, swooping hair. Chiseled cheekbones. A chin that anyone would envy.

The man realizes Abernathy is looking at him and winks.

Kai flips through the printed sheets, frowning. "Great. Perfect. Before we proceed—we're going to need you to take a standardized test."

Abernathy looks to the man to confirm this.

"Don't look at him," snaps Kai. "Look at me."

Abernathy realizes what they are holding is his application.

"Wait," he says. "Does that mean we're doing this now?"

He looks quickly between the two. The man shrugs the shrug of a person who, believing they've seen it all, no longer gives a shit.

"Yes," says Kai. "We're doing this now."

"So, I got the job?"

Kai breathes through her nose. "We are considering your application."

"And I need to take the test before I move on to the next step? Why?"

Kai groans. "The questions never end."

"We need to make sure you know how to behave," jokes the man.

"I know how to behave."

"Look," says the man. He is smug. Serious-ish. "Don't tell me, tell her." He thumbs to Kai, who rolls her eyes. "She's the one who doubts you."

"Is that true?" Abernathy asks. He sounds more hurt than he would like to.

Kai holds Abernathy's eye contact.

As They speak about the process of creating this yard, God walks up and down the aisle.

"I guess I can take a test," Abernathy says. "What's the harm in that, right?"

The clipboard Kai shoves into his hands is a run-of-the-mill clipboard. Abernathy flips through stacks of slightly crumpled paper and realizes he is wearing only his underwear—white boxer briefs covered in little printed hearts.

Despite his lack of clothing, his nerves, his erect nipples, his general and pervasive feeling of unwellness that stems either from the increased circulation of sodium in his bloodstream from the ramen or his quickly diminishing sense of self now that he faces A Task, the test is pretty easy. On each piece of paper: a small moving scene. Per the instructions, Abernathy circles everything that could cause (or be caused by) anxiety.

- ✓  A child crying.
- ✓  Money burning.
- ✓  Teeth falling from a mouth.

When he finishes, he watches Kai flip through his answers with a frown. God directs the bus through the pearly gates into the yard of Abernathy's neighbor, a single mom named Rhoda whose child frequently hovers at the fence line to ask Abernathy for advice. Abernathy loves to be asked for advice.

Kai takes her time reviewing his answers. The plants in Jonathan Abernathy's dream begin to wither, die. God looks around, confused. As the group trundles through a section of the yard filled with overgrown chanterelles, a mushroom with a particularly labial frill, Kai informs Abernathy that though his approach is not necessarily the most creative or interpretative she's ever seen—in fact, it's abysmally cliché and shows a complete ignorance to the complexities and processing power of a mature human psyche—their team is regrettably short on hands, so he (and his astonishingly low emotional intelligence) passes. On a trial basis. For now.

"Congratulations," Kai says as if reading from a script long memorized. "You now have a government job that pays twenty dollars a night with a per-pay-period hundred-dollar incremental loan forgiveness component. Health care will not be included. Any government-issued liens placed against you due to outstanding debts are now frozen. Third-party lenders who have taken legal action have been sent a notice that you are now employed by the State

Department. Should those third-party lenders be contractors of the TSD, their legal pursuits will be delayed."

Like earlier, when she spoke of "somnambulatory officerial forces," Abernathy doesn't understand a single word that comes out of Kai's mouth, except for the word "lien," which he is intimately familiar with. When a lien is placed on a bank account, money is automatically withdrawn by the bank and placed in the lienholder's account. Aka, the person who gave you the loan in the first place gets to go into your bank. They get to take your pay, even if you only have enough money to eat. This has happened to Abernathy multiple times.

Not wanting to seem ungrateful, he nods along.

He suspects Kai might be on to him. She gives him a stern look. "A piece of personal advice," she says, "Don't blow it all at once."

The flowers in the garden shoot cannons of golden pollen at the bus of passing tourists. Midair, the pollen becomes celebratory confetti. Abernathy is ecstatic. His dead parents in front of him do not turn around, but he senses they are pleased. Angels, somewhere in the yard of his neighbor, blow their horns.

"Jesus," says the handsome man. He picks confetti out of his hair. "Don't get your panties in a wad on our account, Abernathy."

Abernathy stops crying with joy.

The man roughly brushes the golden windfall from Abernathy's shoulders as he explains (perhaps not exactly with patience) that siphoning away the petty depressions of America's white-collar workers isn't all "stardust and shut-eye, Bucko."

"We're at the forefront of technology," the man says. "We're exploring frontiers that no man"—Kai coughs—"has ever explored before."

"I'm crying because it's exciting?" Abernathy says, wiping his eyes.

"You should be crying because it's important," the man corrects. "This is a role that has an impact. What we do here is integral to a lot of shit, OK?"

"What . . . type of shit?" Abernathy asks.

The man explains that the job is a key component in the contemporary capitalist model that governs America's economic sector, mostly in that it keeps the public from doing bad stuff.

"Like murdering each other," he offers, "or having poor workplace performance."

The poor workplace performance especially.

"It's not just dream monitoring for dream monitoring's sake. American workers face an unprecedented crisis of mental health which transcends the personal into the professional, OK?"

"We," he says, pointing to himself and Kai, "are tasked with helping people stay at work. We help them do more work. No matter how stupid, trivial, pointless, low paying that work may be—bottom lines need saving. That's where we come in."

The man can't see her, but Kai rolls her eyes.

"How does someone even do that?" Abernathy asks. "How do you even save a 'bottom line.'"

"All right!" interrupts Kai. "Enough. OK? Believe it or not, this is a job. We have work to do."

This little reality check doesn't get Abernathy down.

Abernathy's life? It's looking up! Though Abernathy has more than $250,000 in loans with more than a 10 percent annual interest (that's raw growth of $25,000 a year in *debt that is owed* (so far he has accrued $100,000 of this debt (his interest collects interest))), no career prospects, a tenuous-at-best living arrangement, untold debt inherited after his parents' death (precise amount not yet calculated due to the illegality of the inheritance, though based on the never-ending phone calls it is *substantial*), Abernathy is happy.

Bankruptcy? Put on hold, baby.

Paychecks (should he receive them in the future)? No longer being automatically confiscated by the US of A.

This? This is the stuff of life itself.

In the land of Nod, Abernathy plans to shake hands firmly and introduce himself as this: Jonathan Abernathy, dream auditor, honored to be here.

## 3

HOW, EXACTLY, DOES ONE AUDIT anxiety and/or depression in the average white-collar American worker? Good question.

The welcome packet that arrives later in the week is laminated. The work is supposedly pretty easy stuff, described as "unskilled labor for America's legions of unemployables." Of which, if that's the group Abernathy is thinking of, he's certainly a (self-consciously) card-carrying member: current and former workers of fast-food joints, dying malls, general stores, long-shuttered factories. University and nonuniversity students alike who, upon their 'failure to launch' slide back into the routines of their hometowns to take jobs as baristas, gas station employees, grocery restockers, clerks. The salt of the Earth. The foundation of American wealth. Abernathy has had more of these jobs than he can count.

The recruiter who appeared in Abernathy's first dream said that they, the benevolent government, are considering all such down-on-their-luck people for candidacy at their archival centers. If you could hold a clipboard with feeling, then the title of auditor was as good as yours. And boy, could Abernathy hold things with feeling. Though he does not know this about himself, having feelings is pretty much the only thing Abernathy does.

As for the dreamers—those whose minds the Abernathys of the world step into—the procedure is paid for by their corporate employers through tax subsidies. In other words, it's complimentary, baby. Consider dream support one of the many ways America values public health.

Abernathy had no idea such opportunities were available. He feels quite moved by the thoughtfulness of the whole system. It seems like things are finally heading in the right direction. Who knows, maybe one day this job will lead to another job, and that job could lead to something corporate, and then if he's employed by a corporation, maybe one day it will be his dreams that are complimentarily maintained. Abernathy would love to join a legion of employees. Imagine something like that: stability so common eventually even the most hardened schmuck takes it for granted.

There is a reason Jonathan Abernathy has not heard of this process before. The archival services are not marketed to consumers. The pamphlet he's browsing does not say this, but the procedure itself is closely guarded. The secrecy is intentional. The folks who have their dreams processed do not have to consent to the processing. They are opted in by their employers. Most Americans have not heard of the Archival Act for the simple reason that it is more beneficial to use the languages of bureaucracy, difficulty, and redundancy to reduce public accessibility. The job of "experts" is always easier when they have the luxury to make decisions in private, without scandal or coverage.

Abernathy will never understand the scope of the Workers' Archival Project or the bill that made it legally viable. When he learns of the motives of the Archival Office (why they make money, how they make money, who they make money for), he will have already lost everything. It will be too late.

But for now, Abernathy is not worried. Like many, throughout his life he has ignored the fine print.

Outside, in the sun, on an old plastic lounge chair he often drags into the driveway, Abernathy reads through the packet. He is unbothered. He is pleasantly warm. His legs are crossed at the ankle and he feels proud of himself. He relishes the process of learning about something he didn't know existed a week ago. Learning about something like that is a wondrous, hard-to-replicate feeling. The world becomes a vast curiosity to be transversed rather than cowered from. Abernathy intends to luxuriate while he can.

Abernathy's neighbor Rhoda sees him reading as she's taking out the trash. She calls out to him and leans against the fence, holding garbage bags in both of her hands. The black bags leak into the flower beds.

"What's that?" she asks.

Abernathy grins and sits up. "Work stuff," he says, waving the packet at her. He feels grateful for the opportunity to say he has work. He rises from the chair, pushes his sunglasses up into his hair, and ambles over to where Rhoda stands at the fence line.

Rhoda has short black hair that ends crisply at the lobes of her ears. Rhoda always keeps her hair in a blunt cut, a bob, with sharp, well-maintained bangs. She is tall and covered in lots of tattoos with faces. She wears a bathrobe and a matching pair of stained Uggs.

Abernathy quickly looks away when he catches sight of her footwear. He doesn't know why, maybe to preserve her decency. The stains on the Uggs cause a bit of feeling to rise up in him when he looks at them, though what type of feeling is rising up or what it means, Abernathy is unsure. What rises up when he looks at the sorry state of Rhoda's shoes could be best described, perhaps, as wobbly, and in the throat.

"I've never seen you read before," Rhoda says.

Abernathy laughs.

"No," she says, tucking a piece of hair behind her ear, "seriously. Like, never."

Although Rhoda's face betrays no hint of humor, Abernathy knows she is joking (*Right?*). Rhoda always looks like that. Humorless. She is very funny, but she is not a person to whom expression comes easy.

Unlike Kai, the redheaded two-hundred-and-sixty-fifth dream collector whose steady stream of green judgment feels palpable despite how few times they've met, Rhoda's lack of laughter means nothing to Abernathy. Rhoda never laughs. Rhoda never smiles, either. Rhoda is thirty-two, Abernathy's senior, and should be in class over at the community college. She is hardly ever in class. Today, like almost every day, Rhoda skipped class because her ex-husband did not pick up their child. She could not find last-minute childcare.

In addition to the smell of old milk that's wafting up from the trash, Abernathy can also smell her perfume. It's piney. Slightly floral.

The combination is confusing.

"What does that mean, there?" Rhoda gestures toward the left side of the pamphlet with her chin.

"There are levels," Abernathy explains. He holds the pamphlet so she can better read it. "I'm gonna start out as a dream auditor. See, that's right here, at the bottom. While we sleep, instead of dreaming our own dreams, we go into the dreams of other people. Our bodies are still sleeping, but our minds are somewhere else."

Rhoda looks skeptical. "Is this real?" she asks.

"Yeah, of course it's real."

"Are you pulling my leg?"

Abernathy shakes his head. "No. It's a thing."

"And what is it, exactly, that you'll be doing?"

"Observing stuff, mostly. Noting stuff that 'goes wrong.'"

"What can go wrong when you're dreaming?"

"Like, nightmares and stuff. I just have to guess about it, like, the stuff causing, uh, they call it disruption. Then I submit a report and the dream collectors are dispatched (that'll be my boss) to supervise the removal. After that, it goes to archivists to preserve, but I don't really know what that means. Um, and then there's something here about an operator. But I won't be working with them. Auditors are entry-level. Mostly we just move through dreams. I guess we don't always get to see how it works. Anyways, then see here there's managers and executives and stuff." He points to the top of the org chart in the middle of the foldout pamphlet where this is all color coded. "They call the really important people officers."

Abernathy beams.

"Like, as in, police? Police officers?" Rhoda asks.

Abernathy ignores her. Rhoda does not like the police. "It's supposed to be, like, really, really easy. It's a pretty sweet gig."

Rhoda catches a glimpse of her daughter, Timmy, out of the corner of her eye. "Oh honey," Rhoda calls, turning behind her. Timmy has crawled beneath the deck. "Come on. Don't do that. You'll get muddy. Come out of there."

Timmy squiggles on her stomach. She has dark hair like her mother. Her hair is braided in two. "That's the point, Mom! I have to get to the good ones."

"She's obsessed with them," Rhoda says to Abernathy, referring to the mushrooms beneath their deck and the ones that speckle their yard.

"It's cute," Abernathy says.

"Yeah, real cute until you step on one at three A.M. You try thinking it's cute then."

"I bet I would still find it cute."

Rhoda looks him up and down. "You know, actually, you probably would. You're a sick fuck like that."

Abernathy laughs. Rhoda's mouth twitches.

"All right," Rhoda yells to her daughter, "but don't complain when I hose you down later!"

"I won't!"

"Yeah right," Rhoda says under her breath. Abernathy grins. He has always liked Timmy. When he met her, she was three. Just as nonplussed then as she is now. Very small. Mostly scrappy. Crawled all over everything. Actually, come to think of it, Timmy doesn't seem upset about her paternal non-pickup, like, at all. She is about eight or nine, if Abernathy remembers correctly. She is obsessed with mushrooms, and big old trees, and mossy patches of grass that, she says, when you squint, look like faces. Does she care that her father is not here?

As Rhoda reads more of the packet, Timmy talks to herself beneath the deck, making up a little story about the mushrooms and their friends. She thinks mushrooms communicate underground. When one mushroom suffers, she claims, the rest of the mushroom colony experiences the pain as well. She is not necessarily wrong.

Instead of roots, mushrooms have mycelium systems, tiny strings that extend from the base of the fungi and travel deep into the ground to gather nutrients. Mycelium connects individual plants into a larger organism that can work together instead of alone. Often the mycelium doesn't just benefit the mushrooms it's attached to—the fungal root will also attach itself to a tree's root. The two plants begin to meet the needs of each other. This means that the threads that connect mushrooms to one another are good for the forest, the mushrooms, the moss, the trees.

Timmy has only a childish understanding of roots and their fruiting bodies. She's never heard the word "mycelium" in her life. But like most children, she understands something that the adults around her do not.

Individuals within a species are interconnected in hidden ways. Humans are not immune to this phenomenon. The main difference between mushrooms and humans is that our systems are activated as we sleep. We cannot see them. The roots that link us to one another are not visible. But in dreams, we are interwoven. We share a local consciousness. In slumber, we bind ourselves to those around us in delicate and invisible ways. Because of the delicacy of such systems, they are easy to ignore in waking life. Most humans do. Abernathy and Rhoda do. It is not included in Abernathy's pamphlet. But as he sleeps, Abernathy's body will remain at rest and his mind—his mind will travel the root systems of his community, repairing, sure, but also taking sustenance for himself.

Abernathy has no idea what he's getting into. No one in their right mind would volunteer if they knew how the work is done or what the work entails.

Abernathy can see the soles of Timmy's teal rain boots clipping merrily away at the mud as she pushes herself farther beneath the house.

Rhoda frowns and sets the garbage down, crushing a few August coneflowers.

"What?" Abernathy asks, pulled out of reverie. He searches her face. "What is it?"

"Kelly know about this?" Kelly is Abernathy's landlord. He prefers to think of her as a nameless, looming figure who takes all his money without having a personality, let alone personal needs.

Abernathy shrugs and looks away.

"I think if you would just talk to Kelly. If you just told her what was going on . . ."

Kelly and Rhoda are friends. Used to be friends. Through their husbands, maybe, both of whom are now gone. Not dead. Just divorced. They are not really friends so much anymore, but certainly they wave as they pull out of their respective driveways every morning for work. They are negatives of each other. One brunette, one blonde. One with child, one without. The only thing they have in common is that they are young ex-wives who had not planned to live alone. If it weren't for work, if there were still time, perhaps, then yes, friends.

Friendly.

Neighbors.

There's that feeling of throatiness. Maybe it's sadness? Guilt of some kind? Anxiety?

Rhoda rubs her brows with the back of her sleeve. Some of her black makeup smudges off. She changes the subject. "Pretty sure my ex got into this crap," she says after a beat.

She licks her thumb and rubs at the black stain on her sleeve. She wipes her thumb against her robe pocket.

"Don't think they treat people very well over there," she says. "You ever heard of a pyramid scheme?"

Abernathy asks, "Like King Tut?"

"Basically it means all the shit? It pools at the bottom. And you just signed up to shovel the bottom. The shit pool."

The laminated pages (shining! beautiful! luminous! full of promise, not to mention potential! no sign of shit!) illustrate that the auditors do all their auditing during their own personal REM cycle. The auditor is then assigned to identify inner turmoil as it manifests in the dreams of American citizens who have been opted in to the program by their corporate lieges. Noncorporate workers are not welcome to participate, allegedly. This type of procedure is strictly emotional management for the white-collar.

Rhoda is good at understanding jobs. That's how come she's had so many.

Currently Rhoda part-times as a bank teller. She hopes to go full-time soon, for the benefits. Health care, you know? But she's not so sure they'll hire her. Her manager, a Christian, hates Rhoda's tattoos. The manager thinks tattoos make people look poor. Which, though not generally true, does apply to Rhoda at this moment in time—she is, in fact, poor—so Rhoda can't even get all self-righteous and fault her manager for the belief. Abernathy loves it when she gets self-righteous. He frequently tries to provoke her into doing so.

Abernathy has had many part-time gigs. Dream auditing certainly won't be his first. So he gets it, the struggle. The cynicism. Whenever they talk about the prospect of going full-time, Rhoda ends the conversation with a dry not-smile and always says the same thing. Abernathy can't tell if she means it or not. "It's in God's hands."

But Abernathy doesn't think Rhoda knows much about this job. For example, the part that seems complicated—how turmoil is removed—won't be Abernathy's job at all. That's the duty of dream collectors, the next level up. Abernathy's job will be to observe. To pay witness. To prep for interference. To note Things That Might Cause Issue. Things like (and this is what the pamphlet says) obsessive preoccupations, anxious yearnings, worryings, sadness, or malaise. It's written in all caps, to emphasize its importance. OBSESSIVE PREOCCUPATIONS, ANXIOUS YEARNINGS, WORRYINGS, SADNESS, OR MALAISE.

Such emotions—so says the pamphlet—often prevent workers from meeting their quotas and can take many forms within the subconscious. What forms such preoccupations manifest as is up to Abernathy, as an auditor, to discern. That doesn't sound hard, or pyramid-like, or awful at all. All told, it sounds downright kind.

Abernathy is excited. He has never had this level of responsibility at a workplace before. He anticipates the feeling of being needed with the same fervor that he looks forward to arriving at a destination with air-conditioning after a long heat-soaked walk. That first step into the blast of cold, after crossing long stretches of steaming pavement—the relief is euphoric. Addictive.

Plus, when the client does wake up, they are in their own bed, oblivious to the operation that has taken place. The memory of the dream slips from them as all dreams do. Thus, all their client-y unconscious turmoil? Miraculously healed! Their life? Made much better! Productivity? All-time high.

When the auditors are effective, workplace performance in the client's waking life is boosted, and thus, in turn, at least hypothetically, so too does the economy rise. Voilà. Productivity Magic. American Magic. All thanks to folks like Jonathan Abernathy, the humble working-class salt of Earth.

"You'll see, Rhoda. Just watch." He grins. She can't help herself. The corner of her mouth ticks a bit upward, too. "This is going to be the best thing to ever happen to me."

Abernathy does not think it sounds like he will be treated like shit or handling shit. Abernathy thinks he will be treated like a valuable asset whose work is integral, important, and good.

ABERNATHY SPENDS TOO LONG SCULPTING oven-bake clay into miniature mushrooms for Timmy's collection. With his hands he builds slender *Armillaria tabescens*. Abernathy likes *Armillaria tabescens* because they grow together huddled close. They're also called friendship mushrooms. The largest living organism on Earth is a species of friendship mushroom. They have white stems, bulbous honeyed caps, tiny pink gills. When they die—and the *Armillaria* he picked from the yard will soon die—it will be like a tiny family dying. Unlike mushrooms that grow from the ground, Abernathy hopes his sculpture will last a long time. Will last forever. Will last past then.

Because of his sculpting, Abernathy is late for his first client's dream.

He smells embarrassingly like mushrooms, and there are crescents of dirt trapped beneath his nails, but that does not stop Abernathy from hastily changing into his sixty-six-dollar suit. He hopes his colleagues will think thoughts like "That Abernathy? He's got character," or "Jonathan Abernathy? Talk about a man with enviable skill!"

With great aspiration, Jonathan Abernathy falls asleep.

As he drifts into himself, Abernathy realizes he stands in an elevator. The walls are chrome. His reflection stares back at him, wearing his suit. Hold music plays. He doesn't have time to look around. The elevator rumbles to a stop. The doors whir open. He sees green. Brown. The blue of another person's sky.

Just like that, Abernathy steps from his sleep into someone else's.

It's a strange feeling, stepping out of yourself into the self of another. He is decanted. He feels it immediately.

The dreamer dreams of a bog. Or maybe a mud pit? Abernathy's not sure. There are a lot of spindly trees, like a forest. In the middle of this landscape there is a pit of frothing mud, surrounded by ferns. The mud bubbles and creeps toward Abernathy. Abernathy must step into it. At first, the mud barely covers the soles of his shoes. He lifts up his wingtip, to better see the substance. Thick, dark brown. He hasn't seen mud like it. Can earth be so brown it appears purple? By the time Abernathy takes his next step forward, the mud has filled his loafers.

Abernathy tries to go back to the elevator, but the elevator is gone. When he looks down again, the mud has risen to his ankles.

A train whistles.

Abernathy turns toward the sound.

There is no train. But there is a child. A bloated dead kid with matted hair that floats face down in the mud, limp limbs lame on the water. Abernathy is surprised how real it looks.

Stomach cramps?

Nausea?

A sweeping feeling of regret?

✓  Yes

✓  Yes

✓  Yes

In the bog, Abernathy is sick.

Another person, a woman, presumably the dreamer (*has she always been there?*), fumbles with the kid's shirt. She attempts to turn the child right side up.

Abernathy's half-digested stomach contents float downstream.

A dead thing like that has got to be heavy. Right?

Abernathy feels both very far away and very close. The crying dreamer, combined with Abernathy's first-day-on-the-job anxiety, does not help his sweating problem.

The dreamer does not appear to have seen Abernathy and is talking to it. The kid.

For all Abernathy knows, she could be saying something quite touching, like: "I love you." "Don't leave me." "Come back to me." "I'll miss you for a thousand lifetimes." "Without you, I am doomed." Every time the dreamer opens her mouth, what he thinks must be a train engine drowns her words. Not so much talking as revving. *RRRRRR. RRRR. RRR.*

This is Jonathan Abernathy's first time seeing a person dead.

Though his parents' deaths were almost ten years apart, he did not look upon the dead face of either of them. Both times Abernathy refused to go into the hospital room where his progenitors sunk into their eternal rest. Both times other people took his parents beneath the hospital to smolder away until they were ash. When Abernathy did, finally, pick up their bodies, the two people who had created him were reduced to dust. Their remains fit inside of a small ziplock bag.

Unsurprisingly, Jonathan Abernathy is more than a little scared of death. Jonathan Abernathy does not understand death at all. The things we don't understand are always the things that scare us.

The mud rises. The woman stands in front of him, pleading with the child for one last embrace.

Dead people? To Jonathan Abernathy, they are mostly frightening.

Dead children? Ha ha.

Abernathy's watched enough movies to know that he should be terrified. And he is! He is terrified. He is also, right now, sad in a floaty, indistinguishable way that he keeps thinking could just be nausea but is actually something deeper and, you know, more in his soul.

Not that he has time to think floaty thoughts about souls and purpose and what it means to be alive. The mud has filled the only loafers he has left. He can feel the earth on his legs as it crawls up the cuffs of his slacks.

The mud is ruining his sixty-six-dollar suit.

Vomit, somehow, is in the crease of his arm.

Despite his suit, he looks like shit. His disappointment at his appearance almost eclipses his terror. He did not expect the interior of this dream to be so lifelike. It feels very lifelike. Disorientingly so.

Thus, Abernathy becomes quite certain. This is it.

He is about to die.

Jonathan Abernathy has never felt like he was about to die before. The fear catches him off guard. Now that his parents are dead, he thinks of death as a type of contractual obligation. A debt, if you will, whose collection won't come until Abernathy reaches an age far away—like fifty. After fifty seems logical enough to Jonathan Abernathy. Fifty, he reasons, is still young-ish. So not too selfish of him. Not too desperate. For Jonathan Abernathy, fifty is only twenty-five years away. He is in the prime quarter of his life.

Abernathy wildly pats his suit pockets and tries to even out his breathing. He's not hyperventilating. But he's not *not* hyperventilating, either. With an honest-to-God desperation, he searches for the clipboard Kai gave him.

In the background a phone rings. Like he is a fish on a hook, Abernathy feels a tiny jerk, right behind his heart.

The dream rushes away from him.

Something is reeling him in.

In the elevator, the hold music picks up exactly where it left off. His reflection in the elevator doors looks surprised. But then, in a flash, his visage is gone, and he awakens in bed. His bed. The comforter, an old ratty thing from before college, is wrapped tightly around his legs. On the nightstand, his cell phone buzzes.

The moon light daggers beautifully through his curtains in a way that suggests this is reality.

His reality.

He knows because it is oppressive. It smells like mushrooms. He doesn't want to be here. Upon waking, he immediately feels twinges of hopelessness up and down his limbs.

He picks up the phone.

The hopelessness alone is enough to realize he is awake.

"What are you thinking, moron?" It's Kai on the line. Though he's only met her twice, her accent is unmistakable to him. It's hard to hear her through the static. "Are you *trying* to get fucking cancer? Wear the safety gear we sent you. Jesus Christ."

Kai hangs up before Abernathy can reply.

Abernathy throws the tangle of covers from his body.

Opening the large cardboard box in the corner takes a bit of time and brute force. There is a blobby white mass inside, which, upon picking up, Abernathy realizes is a type of suit. A space suit.

Well, kind of. A kind of space suit.

He frowns.

The suit is . . . it's not very good looking. He has to peel plastic protectors away from the fabric, which is light and squeaky in his hands. Bold. And too shiny. A horribly bright white. Abernathy has to shimmy and squeeze into the thing. The new suit is slightly sticky on his skin.

Despite the suit's ugliness and unwieldiness, wearing it does make Abernathy feel important. After peeling the plastic protector from the visor, he puts the helmet over his head and lays back in bed.

The suit is warm. A staticky sound emits from the helmet. In order to lay horizontal with the helmet on, Abernathy has to hold his neck at an inhuman angle. For several moments Abernathy is uncomfortably aware of his body. His left elbow itches. His neck hurts. Sweat is dripping down his brow and every time he moves his chest hair catches on the plastic.

The suit is firm and slightly inflexible. It squeaks against itself.

Before he has time to wonder how long it will take him to fall asleep, he finds himself standing in the elevator. The return to the dream is smoother than his initial ascent. The elevator plays its cordial music until it jolts to a stop. The doors whoosh open and Abernathy steps back into the cold mud.

Abernathy looks like he is wearing a bad astronaut costume. The gear is just as white and unwieldy as it is in waking reality. A really, really ugly astronaut costume.

Abernathy sees his clipboard floating serenely on a stream of mud. He struggles toward it. The helmet makes his breath feel hot and claustrophobic against his face. At least now he is wearing the right shoes.

The dreamer is still crying. The train engine has stopped. The child who floated face down is now floating face up. Its eyes are off-white, rolled into its head. Puffy, bloating face. Mouth open. Mud pouring out.

Abernathy does not want to die. In his opinion, to die ugly is the worst death of all.

Abernathy manages to grab his clipboard. He fumbles for a pen. The mud flows quickly. More mud comes. The river has risen past Abernathy's waist. He can no longer walk. He must swim. He treads water—*mud*—by kicking his legs swiftly back and forth. It's hard to do in the plastic suit. Keeping himself afloat seems impossible. There's a moment where he almost goes under.

Does his life flash before his eyes?

More or less.

He sees himself in all his various homes, alone. He sees himself as a child, looking out a car window, pastures and country land rushing past. He sees all his dead family members and his college years where panic filled him. He sees Rhoda, leaning across the fence line to laugh at him. Jonathan Abernathy does not enjoy thinking about his life.

Instead he tries to think:

*I can do this!*

*I deserve this!*

*I will prevail!*

It is within his right to tell himself such comforts. We all do silly things like lying, praying, hoping, breathing. Don't judge him for the things you yourself would do.

Jonathan Abernathy purses his lips tight and fumbles for his paperwork. Thank God, he finds his pen attached to his sleeve. On the clipboard he tries to write down the disturbances as quickly as he can while the dreamer swims around the body, crying.

Dead friend?

Sure.

Strange silence?

Yup.

Mud?

A lot of mud.

Trees all looking skeletal and sad?

You betcha.

Weird trains never coming?

All that seems like the by-products of anxiety and depression to him.

Check, check, check.

Abernathy turns circles to get everything. He holds the clipboard above his head to keep it from ruin. What life could yield this subconscious? He has no idea.

Abernathy tears the paper from its sheet. Though he is, at this point, oblivious to the inner mechanisms of the Archive, when he drops his report he actually sets off a complex system of notifications that deploys collectors to handle the removal and repair work. This isn't relevant, really. Mostly it's just cool.

Anyways, Abernathy drops his report. When the paper touches the mud, it vanishes.

At the tree line, four officers appear in clean white jumpsuits. Their suits are the same as Abernathy's: white, sticky, sheeny, obscene. They don't seem to mind this, however. They slap one another on the back.

Abernathy struggles toward them. He has never been very good at swimming. He brutalizes the black water and long-strokes toward the shore. As he gets closer, the river begins to shallow out. He is relieved to see one of the collectors is Kai, the two-hundred-and-sixty-fifth.

The collectors wear small packs on their backs. They disengage the hoses attached. As Abernathy nears, they begin to joke with one another.

Now that Abernathy isn't facing all this horror alone, everything seems much more manageable. He feels silly getting himself worked up. Yes, he looks horrible. Sure. Fine. But at least he's alive. Not everyone can say that.

As he stands and splashes his way toward his colleagues, mud schlicks off him in great slopping globs. He raises a hand to wave at the three newcomers, but they don't see him.

Well, Kai does. It's only that she's busy pretending not to.

Abernathy reminds himself: This? This whole experience? Just a job.

A glorious, beautiful job that has nothing to do with his actual life.

The materials of his suit are quasi-waterproof. Or maybe the suit isn't waterproof. Maybe it's just very, very shiny. Either way, the mud drips off him.

The collectors look competent, congenial. Nowhere near as terrified as Abernathy. (They have formed a circle. Small groups always form circles. Why? It is the hardest social configuration to join.) They are laughing. It's unclear whether they're laughing because Abernathy is wearing an idiotic suit or because Abernathy is idiotic. Period.

Inside the suit Jonathan Abernathy sweats. He is sweating? He is sweating. It is hot.

"Hey guys," he says.

The group does not hear him.

Abernathy tries to join them in their laughter, but it's too late. Once he starts laughing, they stop.

The group gives him a long, bewildered look.

This is when Abernathy realizes: *Ah*; the group is making fun of him.

Abernathy steps back.

The next joke seems to be about Abernathy's laughter itself. Apparently it sounds like a horn.

*Honk*

*Honk*

*Honk*

This is, at least, how Abernathy perceives the event. And to be fair, his perspective is horrible to endure.

However, from the perspective of the collectors, they've arrived at their second job, a night shift. They are tired. They don't really want to be here. Two of them have kids and are worried they're not going to get a full shift in before they have to wake up. The collectors stand in a loose circle making small talk when a handsome, lanky man we know to be Jonathan Abernathy but who they only know as a stranger interrupts with an obnoxious, too-loud laugh.

Jason was telling a story.

He was right at the good part.

The silence that follows the new arrival's laughter is awkward.

The group consists of Kai, Jason, Kim, and Mike. They work together pretty regularly. They do not know who the stranger is. Well, Kai pretends not to. What they do know, as a group, is that the dream is going a bit haywire. They have a quota. Surely this guy can't be the new auditor? What's the district playing at?

When the young man doesn't leave, the collectors meet his laughter with nervousness. They look around at each other with eyes like: *Is this guy for real?*

Yes, Abernathy is for real.

Abernathy's coworkers are of average height. Most are smaller than Abernathy, yet to Abernathy their laughter makes them appear bigger than they are.

To Abernathy, the mirth of the officers doubles and with it they grow.

"Jesus," Kai mutters.

Abernathy winces, tries to be brave, stumbles forward to shake Kai's hand, but trips. He manages to catch himself and stops just short of his reflection in Kai's helmet. Tears prick his eyes. Jonathan Abernathy doesn't know why. He pulls back. He blinks. He can't help but notice his suit is perfectly split in two by the mud line. Half of him is glimmering and plasticky and new. Half of him is streaked with the fading remnants of guck.

Next to the suits of the collectors, his is brown.

Like he has been dipped in shit.

Abernathy is humiliated. He is also ignorant to the fact that his humiliation is self-actualized.

No one else notices. No one else cares.

Abernathy comforts himself by thinking that he gets their joke, a little bit: he does not look good. He believes he does not look good.

Meanwhile, Jason is thinking that the stranger is very awkward, sure, in a bumbling imbecile type of way. But also? He's kind of hot.

Mike is worried about her daughter.

Kim hates Jason and doesn't want to be working with him.

And Kai? Kai frowns. "You've let it get out of control, Abernathy. Haven't you?"

Kai doesn't give Abernathy time to reply. She palms a gray button on her tool belt.

Abernathy feels that familiar hook behind his heart. He's pulled backward, out of the dream, once again a fish on the line. He falls into, and seems to be suspended in, the gray elevator. He hears the jingle. The elevator stops.

He expects the doors in front of him to open. They don't. The doors open below.

Abernathy plummets.

He wakes himself, screaming.

His white suit is shining and brand-new.

Jonathan Abernathy knows that this is his reality.

How does he know this? His reality blows ass. In his reality he is always alone.

Abernathy can't tell, but a part of him hopes that Kai sounded sympathetic. Full of sympathy, goodwill, and hope. Just like him.

## 5

THE FIRST DAY ABERNATHY DOESN'T hear back from the Archival Office is cruelty. The third day is misery. The first week is torture. The second week is hell and the third week is a brutish inferno of suffering he barely makes it out of alive. By the fourth week he realizes he might not have gotten the position at the Archive. This is when Jonathan Abernathy decides he needs a "real" job.

This is how Jonathan Abernathy, wearing his sixty-six dollar suit, comes to be on his knees in the food court of an open-air mall, hat in literal hand. The falling orange and red leaves of a sycamore tree batter him as he kneels. Some leaves stick in his hair, like a crown. Taking into account the press of the suit and the smell of swiftly approaching autumn in the air, a generous person might find the image of a dapper young man begging for his life enthralling.

Others might look upon him and think, "Who the fuck is this guy?"

Neither perspective is incorrect.

"Adam," Abernathy says to his former manager. His kneeling draws a crowd. "Please."

The wind is crisp and tousles Abernathy's hair, which makes the scene particularly pathetic to behold. Abernathy's former coworker stands in front of a person-sized aluminum box painted white. The box is covered in yellow-and-cream bunting. A menu praising the box as "the best place to get a hot dog in all of America" is hand-drawn with chalk, hanging from a cutout where orders are taken. A sixteen-year-old boy stands at that window. On the grass, in front of the box and standing a few paces away from Abernathy, the manager of the establishment—the aforementioned Adam—crosses his arms.

The box isn't so much a "restaurant" as it is a glorified food cart, a franchise, that sells "upscale" hot dogs on an expanse of open greenery that separates the outer city from the suburbs. An outdoor mall surrounds the space. (Can hot dogs be "upscale"? This is the pressing question the box hopes to answer.) Patio tables litter the sidewalk. A wall around a fountain hosts a series of customers who have stopped eating their chili dogs to gape.

"Get up," hisses Adam. His uniform matches the cart. "You're embarrassing me."

"Hire me," says Abernathy.

Abernathy and Adam went to high school together.

"No."

Abernathy tries framing his demand as a question. "Hire me?"

"No. Abernathy, seriously, get *up*."

The folks perched along the fountain's edge seem to be enjoying the afternoon show.

"Please?" Abernathy begs. Half begs. Only sort of begs. OK, definitely he is begging.

Adam closes his eyes and takes a deep breath, in through his nose. He is only a few years older than Abernathy. He wears the customary yellow-and-white outfit of a cart employee. The yellow button-up and crisp white slacks haven't changed since they were in high school. The outfit still makes the wearer look like an old-fashioned ice cream server, complete with a stupid, striped paper hat folded into the shape of an inverted boat.

"Fine," hisses Adam, marching over to Abernathy where he kneels in the grass. "Jesus Christ, fine. Fine!" He pulls Abernathy up by the arm (a few of the watching customers clap, whoop. This is the most action they've seen in decades). "Never say I didn't do anything for you."

Adam drags Abernathy around the cart, to the back where a small metal door hangs open.

Abernathy's smile is broad despite Adam's vise grip.

"You," says Adam to the sixteen-year-old kid scooping chili in the aluminum interior. "You're fired."

"Wha— But I—"

"You start now," Adam says, ignoring the kid and handing Abernathy a button-up shirt, an apron. He takes the yellow hat from the kid's head.

Abernathy starts to strip and change, oblivious to the older women at the fountain who lean back to get a better look. The kid in the cart is saying stuff like "This isn't fair!" and "How is this legal!" as Abernathy strips to his boxer briefs.

"Go home," says Adam, dragging the kid out and shoving Abernathy, still shimmying into the pair of slacks, inside. Adam steps into the cart and closes the back door as Abernathy puts on his shirt.

"Thanks, man," says Abernathy. "You don't know how much I appreciate this."

The cart smells overwhelmingly of boiled meat. Relish. American cheese.

Adam turns to Abernathy and crosses his arms. "I'm only doing this for you because orphans are pathetic."

Abernathy, who is, technically, yes, an orphan, grins.

Twenty hours a week. Minimum wage. The same job Abernathy had when he was sixteen.

"Well," says Adam, flapping his hands. "Don't just stand there."

The labor is not challenging, really, as long as Abernathy doesn't have to factor in the effort it takes to keep a firm chokehold on his indignity. All he has to do is serve people their lunch. That's easy enough. Especially when you consider that the only people who have real lunch breaks are over the age of fifty. People over the age of fifty hate Abernathy.

As long as things go well, Jonathan Abernathy won't even have to make small talk.

As the lunch rush weans and Abernathy falls into the old rhythm of customer service, he tries to keep a pleasant spin on the situation. There are people who might find the prospect of falling a decade backward into a job humiliating. And, yes, Abernathy *is* humiliated. But a job is a job is a job. He denies the humiliation. He denies the self-judgment. The most he is willing to acknowledge of his discomfort is the tight fist forming in his chest.

A powerful fist. A big fist. The fist of a man who will prevail. The fist of a man who has no other option but to prevail. The fist of a man fighting for his life.

Right?

Right.

He has been in this position before, so knows relief is soon incoming. All Abernathy must do is await a DEATH OF THE SELF to kick in. DEATH OF THE SELF is a type of thing his brain does whenever he has to keep on keeping on. You know, despite it all. Once his self dies (the ego-y, embarrassed part of him that feels things), he can do anything. He can work sixteen doubles, dumpster dive at midnight, walk three hours home in the rain, you name it. Experience tragedy. Homelessness. Loss. If there is no one inside him, if he vacates his own body's premises, there is no one to experience the humiliation that goes hand in hand with poverty.

Not that Abernathy would call himself "impoverished." We would, of course. We know he's impoverished. He often skips meals, is unable to pay rent, and lives his entire life on credit. But Americans are very prideful. Would Abernathy consider himself impoverished? No. Absolutely not. He is only Experiencing a Hard Time. Actually, even that makes it sound bad. And it's not too bad, he thinks! His life. He gets to wear a costume at his job. That's kind of fun. Boat hat. Frilly sleeves. Buttons of yellow shaped like miniature hot dogs. It's not so ugly, the costume. It makes him feel like a more uniformed version of himself. Nostalgic for his teenage life of structure and hope. Mostly, he misses his mom. The uniform reminds him of her. She used to think it was so stupid. Every time Abernathy went off to work, she would laugh. Cackle, really. Abernathy loved her cackle. "Ha!" she would say. "HA." He wished he could hear it again. He will never hear it again. She died a little bit ago. Not a big deal, he would say. Happens to everyone, he would say. A fact of life, he would say. People? They die. All the time. It's what makes them human.

Still, now that Abernathy wears the uniform, time slows down. He can travel back to a different period of his life, when he felt better, more competent, less doomed. Wearing the stupid thing is like wearing the past. Jonathan Abernathy would much rather be in the past. He would spend all his time there, if it were possible. That's why it's dangerous for him to linger in it. For Jonathan Abernathy, the past is an addiction. A way to escape the future. And the present. He would do anything to escape.

The truth is this: Any day Abernathy's landlord (Kelly) could issue an eviction, legally. He knows this. He doesn't disagree with this. He is ashamed. He has no excuse. He has tried his best to make rent. He has failed. He owes his landlord. At any moment she could file against him and it would be within her legal right to do so. His home is not *his* home at all.

So—because of this job—Abernathy will now make enough money to have options. Options-ish.

Abernathy does the math later that day while Adam watches him close the stand. ("You missed a spot." "Fuck you." "That's the spirit.") After the liens eat 15 percent of his paycheck, Jonathan Abernathy will make $115 a week. That $115 is Jonathan Abernathy's to spend.

And what choices he has! A cornucopia of choices! For example: Abernathy can now spend his salary on rent, debt, or food. Though he *can't* have all three, he *can* choose any two he likes.

This level of control over his own life is unprecedented. Jonathan Abernathy isn't sure what to do. The choice is almost suffocating.

As he's strolling home after his first double shift, worry floats to the top of his thoughts like debris rising to the surface of a polluted ocean. He knows it's not enough money. It's more than he had last week, but it's still not enough. It's barely anything, to most people. The math seems impossible. The question seems suffocating. How to eat, how to shelter, how to appease the government—he doesn't know. He is forced to live in the past (his debt), the present (his hunger), and the future (his housing) all at once.

He berates himself ungenerously:

*Fuckup.*

*Incompetent.*

*Generally hated piece of sludge.*

*As soon as someone meets you,* his brain tells him, *they know you're a waste of time. You are so bad at being alive, you couldn't even afford to save your own life, if you needed to. You will die destitute, unknown, and unloved. And when you do—*

*It will be your own fault.*

That last thought, particularly, hurts.

Abernathy does not realize that choice without freedom is harder to bear than the usual combination: a lack of both choice *and* freedom. At least before his employment, there was no illusion of control. He did not have hope.

One hundred fifteen dollars may be meager, but there is no way to deny the truth: $115 a week is raw, unfiltered hope.

Abernathy does not consider this, though. He gives himself no grace. His interior landscape is not a hospitable place. The more the ecosystem of his debt flowers, the less hospitable his mind becomes. It is a wonder any thoughts can grow at all.

Abernathy turns into his driveway. He feels hot, and suffocated, despite the mild weather and the cool breeze. He unbuttons the collar of his shirt. Pockets the stupid hat. Fucks up his hair. He smells like mustard and drudgery. He is in desperate need of a shower.

*Deep breaths*, he tells himself. *Deep, slow breaths.*

"Hey!" calls Rhoda from across the fence line. "Abernathy!"

Abernathy pretends not to hear her. He doesn't even look at her. He keeps walking down his driveway, speeding up a bit. He smells like sulfur, boiled hot dogs, the sweat of dead pigs. A part of him would rather die than have Rhoda see him like this.

"Rough day?" she calls. He hears her crossing the yard.

Abernathy slows, and then stops. *Don't look back*, he thinks, and then immediately looks back. A part of him withers up in humiliation, dies on the vine. She stops just in front of him. She's wearing a pair of skate shoes she stepped into without flipping up the heel. Her shorts are black and she's wearing a too-large hoodie. Her hair is pushed back behind her ears and her bangs are all over the place and she has large circles under her eyes.

While a part of him does die, another part of him sprouts to life. No matter how embarrassing he smells, it always feels nice to talk to Rhoda.

Abernathy is not sure why, but a simple, slow relief begins to fill him. Like gas leaking from a stove to displace all the oxygen in a room. He is light-headed. He turns to her—she's only an arm away—and there's that small uptick at the corner of her mouth.

"Like you wouldn't believe," he says. Up close she smells like pine. Cigarettes.

"What's with the costume," she asks, picking at his yellow collar. "New gig?"

"Oh. This old thing?"

She won't let him dodge her question. She stands there waiting.

He doesn't know what to say.

She is persistent in her silence, which is neither judgmental nor impatient.

"Yes," he says, looking away. "A new job."

"What happened to all that stuff about 'auditing' and 'dreams'?"

Abernathy shrugs. Looks into the sun on the horizon where it languorously sets. The garage light has come on and they stand both in dusk and the warm hue of electricity.

"Did you decide not to take it?" she asks.

He hesitates. Then confesses, "They haven't offered yet."

He doesn't want to admit to his fear: that the Archival Office will never be in touch again. That he will be evicted. Then houseless. Then insolvent. Not necessarily in that order. Any order is plausible. What he does know to be certain is that he will live the rest of his life in a pit of melancholia, shuffling from one dumpster to the next. He doesn't even have a car to live in. He is so desperate, he now serves hot dogs to the professional suburban class. Just as he did when he was six-fucking-teen.

How can you communicate something like that to another person?

Rhoda squints at him. Abernathy is trying not to read into her squint, or her silence. He holds his ground. He tries to look nonchalant. He shrugs.

"All right," she says. "It's decided. You're coming over for dinner."

"What? Rhoda—no—"

"You're coming over for dinner," she says firmly. "Nothing fancy," she says, as if she isn't talking to a man in a hot dog costume. "You just have good timing, that's all. I already started cooking."

INSIDE HER HOUSE, Abernathy sits on her settee. This is his first time inside her home. It is . . . very . . . clean. Not like his room at all.

The front room of Rhoda's house is open concept. There is a stumpy hallway on the right that leads to two bedrooms and the bathroom. On the left a patio door opens to an unfinished deck. In the living area there is a lounge chair. A settee. A rug. A TV cabinet. Everything is neutral, mostly gray, and noticeably worn. Behind the pale leather sofa is the kitchen, the stove, and a vinyl-covered island where a couple stools are tucked.

Abernathy is not in other people's houses very much, so he's not sure if Rhoda's house has a standard or substandard level of cleanliness. He felt the same way about his parents' house, which, at the end of their life, was run over with dust bunnies that rolled from room to room like tumbleweeds. The rest of the house remained otherwise unscathed by clutter and debris.

The dust bunnies of Rhoda's house—which is to say, the element that calls into question the otherwise structural spotlessness—are these towers of colorful laundry, stacked on almost every surface. The towers both threaten to fall at the slightest gust of wind and also seem as if they will withstand the test of time. Abernathy imagines that one day the piles of laundry will become a ruin. Long past Rhoda's occupancy people will gather to worship the totems and ask, "What happened here?"

After they discover what happened, naturally they'll also want to know, "What did it mean?"

Timmy, Rhoda's daughter, is on the floor, trying to explain the book she's reading to Abernathy. Her two long braids are frizzing out of their holders. Her hair is deep, inky black and, like her mother's, almost blue. She is covered in freckles all up and down her body. Whenever Abernathy sees her, she's wearing a pair of overalls. This is true for her today, as well.

"They go into space," Timmy says, as Abernathy stoops down to hear her. She is a soft speaker and he is *just* a bit too tall to sit comfortably on the couch. His feet are on the floor, but his knees are up to his chest. To hear, he has to lean forward.

"Or something," Timmy says. "I don't really get it."

"Right," says Abernathy, nodding. He tries to forget that he smells like boiled meat. "I would like to go to space one day."

"It doesn't seem fun," Timmy says, nodding like the brilliant but gap-toothed sage she is. "I'm not sure why people are so obsessed with it. Everyone in my class is. But what's even out there? Seems like it's all dead things. And quite chilly. That doesn't sound like a fun place to visit at all."

"Exactly," Abernathy agrees. "I would probably feel right at home."

Timmy rolls her eyes.

Despite Timmy's charm (her double braids! her gap tooth! her freckles! her affinity for yellow dungarees! her insistence on adult qualities (namely: sarcasm, like her mother)) Abernathy can't help ruminating on the Archival Office now that he's said out loud the thing he's trying desperately to ignore. The Archival Office has not contacted him in almost a month. Though he's been going to sleep in his suit, squeaking his way through the night, it's only the terror of his own dreams he experiences.

The dream officers have not invited him back.

"You're not dead, dummy," Timmy laughs. "So it wouldn't feel like home to you at all." She pokes him in the gut.

"One day I will be."

"What?"

"Dead."

"Yeah, right," says Timmy. "Boo-hoo."

"Shows what you know." Abernathy flops backward, onto the sofa. His hat falls out of his pocket, onto the floor. Lying down, he crosses his arms across his chest. Pokes out his tongue. He pretends to be gone.

At the stove, still in her slip-on sneakers-that-are-not-slip-on-sneakers, Rhoda gives the saucepot a dreamy one-two stir. She is making pasta. Infinity-signing the spoon back and forth through red sauce. Still, she's not so much paying attention to Timmy and Abernathy as she is looking intently at the backsplash, working over a problem in her mind's eye.

Timmy, very diplomatically, shimmies over to Abernathy on her knees. She rests a hand on his head as if taking his temperature. Her fingers are *tiny* tiny. Abernathy feels sick at his first thought, which is that he could crush her fingers easily. On accident, even. Just walking. Abernathy moves very delicately around her, just in case, keeping his feet far away. Timmy moves her crushable hand to his cheek.

"Just as I thought," Timmy declares. She is feeling his temperature. "Not cold at all! You're faking it." Confident Abernathy is alive and merely staging his death for sympathy, she laughs as she peels back his eyelid, as if to peer into his soul. Not much there to peer into, but Abernathy humors her until Rhoda interrupts. Her thought has finally surfaced.

Rhoda asks, "How would you know?"

Abernathy sits up. Blinks away the dryness that comes with someone else opening your eyes. "Know what?" ("Hey!" says Timmy. She hangs over the sofa arm, her plans to jump on Abernathy's cadaver now paused.) "Know that you're dead?"

"Know if your employer opted you into the program?"

It smells very much like tomatoes and that childhood smell that is always hard for Abernathy to place, but which he associates with safeness. Garlic, maybe. The smell of someone cooking garlic for you.

"What program?"

"M-o-o-oo-o-o-m," whines Timmy. "Stop interrupting. It's rude."

"Sorry, honey," says Rhoda. Then, to Abernathy, "Dream monitoring. Like when they're in your head and stuff." This is delivered in a monotone. It's hard for Abernathy to tell if she's joking or genuinely is asking. Her tone suggests Abernathy is a moron for not understanding her initial question. But the thing about Rhoda is her tone always sounds like that. Not that it matters, really, if she thinks he's a moron. Lots of people call Abernathy dumb. Adam, his new boss, did so just today, in fact. Abernathy tries to assume it is with affection. Merely a loving observation of his inherent disposition.

Abernathy swoops Timmy into his arms before she can topple backward ("Let go!"). She squirms and one of her braids gets into Abernathy's mouth. He splutters and lets her free on the floor.

"Ha!" she says, elbowing Abernathy in the gut. The wind blusters out of him and he has to take a few seconds to cough. "Take that!"

How to tell. Have his dreams ever been audited? Probably not. He's never really been "suitably" employed. As such, he's not sure what employers who might opt their employees in to such a system even do. He turns to Rhoda. She stands at the stove, holding a wooden spoon, watching him. Abernathy is struck by how comfortable she looks in her home. Her hair is tucked behind her ears, which are a bit too big and pierced almost all the way up on both sides. She wears an overlarge hoodie and a pair of black basketball shorts. Her feet are dirty and she's still wearing the beat-up slip-ons. Her nose piercing is crooked. She seems comfortable. But her eyebrows are pulling in and she has a look of disconcerted curiosity. Like she has asked a question that's been worrying her since they stood together, talking over the fence line.

Abernathy words his answer delicately. "Perhaps," he suggests, "Your *esteemable* employer might send, through the U.S. Post, a letter on company letterhead?"

This feels right. Abernathy has never had that type of job (he's never even worked in an office), but in his head the types of employers who can partner with the government to bolster internal productivity have things like letterhead.

Rhoda snorts without smiling. "Yeah," she says. She turns back to the sauce and her solitary dreaming. "Right." Even in rooms of people, Rhoda likes to be alone.

Timmy flops onto the couch and puts the book in front of her face again. She has slightly outgrown the overalls. Her ankles are exposed. Once she was small. Now she is still small, just bigger. Weird how life works that way. She has the energy of a child in their prime years of childhood, which is to say their last. She rests her head on Abernathy's leg. Her elbows, poking into his side, feel too pointy to be fifth-grade elbows.

He can see what she is reading, over her shoulder.

*This can't be normal death.*

"Where did you get this?" he asks, plucking it out of her hand.

"Hey! Give it back, what the hell!"

"Timmy!" reprimands Rhoda.

"Sorry, Mom. He started it!"

Abernathy flips through the book then hands it back. Timmy takes it with a withering look.

"If you must know," she says haughtily, clutching the book tightly to her chest, "I got it from the bookshelf."

"Should you be reading this? Should she be reading this?" he asks Rhoda. "It seems kind of dark. What's it even about?"

"She's allowed to read anything she can reach," Rhoda shrugs. She doesn't turn around from the pot on the stove.

This doesn't sound like a good rule to Abernathy. Like her mother, Timmy is tall.

"Besides," says Timmy, completely unimpressed with Abernathy now that he's shown himself not only to exert his adulthood unfairly upon her, but also to be the type of plebeian who questions her reading, "it's about *friendship*. Are you saying I can't read about *friends*?"

She climbs off the couch, taking her book with her. Before Abernathy can answer, she bounds toward the backyard, down the porch steps, all the way to the fence where the mushrooms sprout in solidarity at the edge of Rhoda's yard. Timmy likes that patch of mushrooms best. She claims it is the best patch to ask questions.

## 6

BUT ABERNATHY BELIEVES ALL IS not lost! All cannot be lost. Please, God, don't let all be lost. For sixty-four more days, he wears his Archive-issued suit to sleep.

One late night three months after his initial application, on a particularly crisp November evening, sleep is slow incoming. Winter has already become relentless in its oncoming approach. The day was long. And rather cold. The stand had a holiday lunch rush. Mothers buying gifts for their children. Fathers buying gifts for themselves. Shimmying into the white suit for what he believes to be the last time, Abernathy feels drunk with the hopelessness of it: employment, life, time. The pointlessness makes him dizzy. *Why why why* repeats in his head alongside his heartbeat. *Money*, he thinks, *has to have a reason for existing, right? Other than its usage as a constant source of shame?* The white suit is easier to zip tonight. This is the last time he will wear it, he tells himself, and that makes the process almost sacred. Special. Like a last prayer.

✓ Deliver me from this.

As Abernathy drifts to sleep, beneath a mass of blankets that do not warm the chill in his heart, he finds himself wading through a long, low swamp. He is in one of his own dreams. Of course he is. A checklist appears, already filled.

✓ Not good enough.
✓ Too stupid.
✓ Unloved.

The usual stuff.

✓  Pathetic.
✓  Pathetic.
✓  Pathetic.

The swamp breathes in and out as if it agrees.

Will Jonathan Abernathy ever make enough money that his day-to-day existence stops being so embarrassing? It's hard to say.

As Abernathy walks aimlessly through the marshes of his mind, he finds himself in a particularly swampy grove, covered in low-lying yellow mushrooms that sprout from pools of tepid, brown water. The mushrooms are swamp beacons, tiny fungi with a bright yellow, almost wet-looking cap. The caps look like amorphous blobs of light.

As Abernathy bends to examine the beacon, the water, which is shallow and full of leaves, ripples around him. As he gets closer to their lighthouse caps, the mushrooms seem to get farther away. He lowers himself and lowers himself, attempting to bring his face close enough, but the beacons are out of reach. With the slow logic of a dreamer, Abernathy realizes the pond is caving in.

When he reaches out to catch himself, he sees that he is not in a swamp at all, but a long dark tunnel. At the end of the tunnel is a light.

Sluggishly Abernathy thinks that the light must be the swamp beacon. He is drawn to it. He has the urge to capture it and swallow it. He tries at first to walk down the corridor, but the corridor lengthens. He breaks into a run. The corridor is not a corridor at all, but a long dark tunnel illuminated only by a lantern bobbing many yards ahead.

As Abernathy focuses on the light, he begins to hear a faint jingle in the background. It is a jingle that loops.

Before he can gather his bearings, catch his breath, lights flicker on and the tunnel is not a tunnel at all. He stops running. There is nowhere else to run. He is in an elevator. The thing he previously thought to be a swamp beacon is the reflection of his suit in the chromatic doors. The blue patch is bright. He looks strange and distorted in the reflection of himself.

Before he can become too accustomed to the shift, the elevator whirs to a halt. The doors open and Jonathan Abernathy stumbles out, amazed, onto a winding path lined by chaffs of wheat. He reaches out a gloved hand to touch their swaying golden tops. When he turns back, the elevator is gone.

He is wearing the white Archive-issued suit.

This dream is not a swamp at all.

This dream is not his dream. His mind would never dream of something as pleasant as this.

Above him: a motherly sun tends to her innocent clouds. The wind is cool. The sun just warm enough. Temperature perfect. Toward the end of the path he can see a large tree, and for the most part, the path is downhill. The incline steep. Not so steep that you have to pick your way along it, balancing as you go, but steep enough that Abernathy has to jog a bit as he descends. His heartbeat stutters. For months he's been trying to ignore the tiny thudding in his chest. It's with genuine surprise that Jonathan Abernathy realizes being alive can feel good.

He is, thank God, employed. It is Abernathy's first time in a dream since the incident with the dead child. And overall the dream is sweet, quiet, warm. Among the grassline, a row of six cows chew cud alongside five calves. He yearns to take off his suit and feel the sun on his face. He rounds the bend and slows as the path flattens out. His good mood feels infectious. Abernathy waves to the cows.

They do not wave back, but Abernathy does finally see that under the large oak tree, a nice-looking woman sits on a swing, lazily kicking air.

"Hey!" he calls out to the woman. "Howdy."

She does not return his salutations, nor does she turn to greet him. Abernathy has forgotten that dreamers largely cannot see the Archival staff. Her shoulder is to him, the side of her face just visible. The sun's light, dapple-like and pretty, falls gently through the oak's royal crown to rest upon her lap. She looks slightly familiar. Black hair.

What about this dream is bad, exactly, Abernathy can't tell. Looking around, he spots his clipboard in the grass, at the base of the tree. He jogs over to pick it up. Though he desperately wants to do a good job here, the dream is so pleasant he's at a bit of a loss what to mark. He looks to the sky for guidance.

Though the sky has no answers, it seems to be saying: KEEP GOING, YOU GOT THIS.

As much as he would like to stay here, chitchatting with the sky and the woman and the cows, he tells the swinger he's going to have a quick look around. With his hand he mimics a small fingery man taking a stroll. Does the woman understand him? He squints. Abernathy can't really see her face. He assumes she understands. The pink of her dress reflects upward on her chin in a very "I understand things" type of way.

Abernathy strolls around the tree. His suit really does seem unneeded here. Nothing appears to be wrong. But, trying to show gusto, leadership, ability, competence, trying to prove himself a competitive employee, the sure-fire choice, he marks the swing set (*made of rope?? Like a hanging??*) on his crumply paper—trying to be quick—and draws a couple of cute question marks next to the words.

On second thought, he scribbles out one of the question marks. This way it looks more official. Two question marks look absurd. Better to be aloof than friendly, he remembers being told. It's certainly true at the hot dog stand. The ruder he is to Adam, the more Adam seems to like him. It's only when he's nice that things get weird. And take Rhoda, for example: always removed and yet he is filled with nothing but goodwill toward her.

Abernathy looks around for a clue. He wants Kai and the other officers to think of him as good, talented, God-given. Brought to this chaotic Earth expressly For This. The ears of cows fall below and rise along the grass line as they eat their fill. The movement reminds him of ships bobbing along soft ocean swells, in and out of view. Wheat is oceanic. In the novels he read at his state school, before he dropped out, it was frequently described as such. Abernathy sees why. Not because of any aesthetic similarity. Rather, the likeness can be found in wheat's expansion outward, seemingly forever, on all sides, roiling and dipping mysteriously with the wind. Like the ocean, it is vast, unknowable, infinite in its ability to both contain and destroy life.

Abernathy thinks this for a second, and then decides it is a stupid thing to have thought.

Besides the wheat—and he's pretty sure the problem is not the wheat—there's not a whole lot to cast his judgment upon. Woman on the swing set.

Pebbly path that leads bucolically into the setting sun. Cows being cows in the fields.

Surely there should be more than just *one thing*? He can't just write down *Rope???*.

Unless being in this dream is like taking one of those trick pop quizzes that ask you to make a list, even if the answer is singular. This could be Abernathy's chance to prove that he does not overthink things. Something he is desperate to prove. Since his last foray into dreams, he has listened to enough motivational podcasts to know overthinking = the death of ingenuity.

Abernathy drops the page with his report onto the ground and it evaporates in a puff of air. Rope (question mark, singular) it is.

Only Kai appears this time. Redheaded Kai, in all her green-accented glory, who respects him and realizes he is destined for great things. Kai, who fought to bring him back into the field of dreams because of her sheer belief in his ability. Or that's what Abernathy assumes. She stands among the wheat. She holds his report. The page has turned silver. Kai does not turn on her vacuum pack.

"Dude," she says as greeting, her glasses glinting. "You can*not* be fucking serious. The *swing set*? We bring you back for the holiday rush after like four months of hiatus and you think it's the motherfucking *swing set*?"

"Did I go too far?" Abernathy asks. The sunlight looks strange on Kai's suit. "Perhaps the dreamer is afraid of heights?"

Kai's eyes bulge. A hiss: "*Heights*."

"Or perhaps the rope indicates desire to perform a suicide? A hanging? People do that, you know. People kill themselves."

Abernathy starts to get the feeling Kai is not exactly pleased. Her mouth is a twisty frown.

"Never made much sense to me, either," Abernathy agrees, "Hard concept to wrap the mind around: Why would someone leave this world for one that is unproven? Maybe they hope for a better life beyond this life? I don't know. I have a feeling that after this, it's probably the big nothing for me. I mean, I hope not, but I figure that's probably what comes next. Anyways, as far-fetched as it may sound, it does happen: people thinking something better lies on the other side. Of death, I mean. My parents, for example. They thought so. I mean, not at the same time. That would be a lot. But eventually they did come to the same conclusion."

Abernathy is reaching in his assurances, talking a little bit too much, afraid to lose this job which is maybe why he is telling her about his mom's death (and his dad's death, when he was a teen) sort of against his will, word-vomiting, as one of his bosses used to call it, before he fired Abernathy on the spot (the personal being the most embarrassing of all anecdotal types, even if his anecdote *does* prove his point that people sometimes die on purpose, even the people you would not expect. Your parents, for example). Anyway. All this is just to say that Abernathy really does not see how anything in this dream could be bad.

"It's hard to know the logic of another person," Abernathy tells Kai, mimicking wisdom to cover for his earlier blunder of vulnerability. "Hard to know the logic of another person even when you're within them. *Especially* when you're within them."

*There,* he thinks. *That sounds kind of like something a smart person would say.*

Kai physically takes him by the shoulders and turns him to face the cows. They are beautifully dumb-faced, the white tops of their bodies spotted with honeyed-brown splotch. He sees why religious people might worship these animals. The whole pack of cows graze with leisure in the grass like stupid entitled gods, hunger nonexistent to them.

Abernathy feels that throatiness again. Sadness? Perhaps beauty.

"The cows?" he asks Kai. He is confused, but does not admit to it. He tries to sound competent, wise, a little condescending, very much how he imagines people with authority to sound when they are questioned. "The cows." No question mark.

"I looked at them," Abernathy says to Kai, a little bit of whine in his voice. "I've been looking. I don't see anything wrong."

With a gloved hand, Kai rubs her temples. "How many cows?"

He counts the cows slowly, moving his mouth as he does so, just to make sure. "Eleven," he says. He tries to sound confident.

Kai narrows her eyes.

"No," she says. "How many *cows* and how many *calves*."

"Six cows, five calves, that's what I said."

"Why," Kai asks, "are there only five calves when. There's. Six. *Six*. Cows."

Abernathy decides to be defensive. "So what? The cows are uneven? How is that relev—"

"It's a *fertility* dream, idiot. It's basic arithmetic, you fucking moron. I *literally* don't have time for this. Have you ever heard of the subconscious? Symbolism? The interpretation of dreams?"

He looks at her blankly.

"Jung?" she asks. "Freud? You know what. Never mind."

Abernathy does not have time to reply. Kai hits the button on her pack. He feels the fish hook in his heart. He is not ready to go home. He calls out, "Wait— Don't—"

It is too late.

He plummets through the floor of the elevator and lands, quite hard, on his back. He is overflowing, like a shallow basin.

Jonathan Abernathy has fucked up. He believes he will never have a real job again. He will wake up and once again go to the hot dog stand, where he will serve lunch to people who look at him without seeing him at all. One day, against his will (and Abernathy cannot imagine anyone going willingly), he will die.

Abernathy stares without seeing the ceiling above him. He blindly, desperately grasps for any thought that might make him stop thinking. Two-by-fours loom above him.

Slowly an important realization unfurls within him.

This ceiling is not *his* popcorn ceiling. Abernathy flings his arms out. There is concrete around him. Dirt. Yes, he is in a basement, but it is not *his* basement. He has no basement.

Jonathan Abernathy is in another person's dream.

Tears prick the corners of his eyes. He will get it right this time, he thinks. He will get it right.

But the remainder of the night's dreams proceed in the way of the first.

When he crawls out of the basement covered in the blood of a stranger, someone the dreamer cherishes, the officers greet him with unimpressed looks. When Kai does finally send him home, shaking her head as she does, Abernathy staggers from the final dream's quicksand into the elevator. He is so tired that he struggles to stand up straight.

His blinking slows until he finds himself awake, in his bed, in reality, his alarm clock chirping.

Unbelievably, eight hours have passed.

He feels as if he has not slept at all.

It is time for him to start his next shift.

The sun coming through his window is not the same sun that dotted the first dream's sky. This sun is lazier and stupider. Not benevolent at all. Very real.

His room is just as small and cramped as it was before he fell asleep. His bed takes up most of the room. The small cupboard at the foot of his bed that doubles as his sink is full of dirty dishes and cups. The ceiling above him is a popcorn ceiling and there is a stain at the corner. Beneath the window, on the left side, there is his desk shoved haphazardly against his wall. There's no room for a chair. He uses his bed. The bathroom door is creaking a bit as a draft moves through the room.

In the early-morning silence, he listens to his landlord vacuuming above. *Kelly.* He can't stop calling her by her name. She probably doesn't know his. He's desperate to forget her personhood and thus absolve himself from the onslaught of guilt that comes when you cannot pay a bill to someone you know.

Jonathan Abernathy is certain that if he were to die, no one would notice until Kelly clomped down the stairs to collect that month's late rent.

**WE CARRY OUR FEELINGS IN** specific parts of our bodies. Or, at least, this is what Abernathy once heard.

**SOMETIMES ABERNATHY STOPS** what he is doing to discover where his feelings reside. Is it his knees? His shoulders?

**COMMON PHRASE WOULD** lead one to believe human beings carry feelings primarily in their heart. Yet no matter how many times Abernathy searches the chambers of his chest for the source, he finds the sadness that pervades his life originating not in his heart, or his gut, his elbows, or his mouth, or his hands.

**SOMETIMES, IN MOMENTS** of desperation, he thinks he must carry despair in his blood. How else to explain the fact that though he tries his best to be happy, anguish moves so fast inside him, everywhere. Everywhere and all at once.

**ABERNATHY RECEIVES A LETTER IN** mid-November, as the trees in his yard lose the last of their leaves. The letter requests he return to the outer city offices immediately. This time, the request comes on official letterhead through the U.S. Post. In the small space between his kitchen cabinet and bed, Abernathy stands reading.

> DEAR MR. ABERNATHY,
>
> IT HAS COME TO OUR ATTENTION THAT YOUR PERFORMANCE, WHILE PROMISING, IS WANTING ON THE WHOLE. AT THE REQUEST OF YOUR SUPERVISOR, WE CORDIALLY INVITE YOU TO ATTEND A SEMINAR ON IDENTIFYING EMOTIONAL STATES. THE SEMINAR WILL TAKE PLACE IN THE CELLAR OF OUR OUTER CITY OFFICE TODAY AT 12:00 P.M. SHOULD YOU CHOOSE NOT TO ATTEND, YOUR CONTRACT SHALL BE TERMINATED.
>
> WARMLY,
>
> MANAGEMENT

Abernathy arrives at the office late by three minutes. A harried woman leads him through the cold foyer, down a set of carpeted stairs, into a small basement recently refurbished. The woman deposits him next to a table of bagels, pastries, and the like.

The room is low-ceilinged and has green industrial carpet. In the middle of the room, forty folding chairs are broken into five rows. A white projector screen has been pinned to the wall.

A group of dream collectors, looking superior, chat in the opposite corner with their arms crossed. There's about ten of them. They talk conspiratorially amongst themselves.

The other people in the room are dispersed in depressed clusters and, like Abernathy, are there for training. They clutch plastic cups of water, murmuring. There are fewer than twenty of them, the auditors. They do not resemble the officers. Most look like Abernathy—dark under-eye bags, rounded bad-posture shoulders. The whole group appears to be stooped low by a potent, subconscious self-hatred. Their lives are too compacted by work (or the search for work) to contain skin-care routines, yoga practices, self-maintenance, or pride. They wear uniforms of varying colors or, if they are not uniformed, they wear ill-fitting clothes that indicate thrift. Most of them carry weight around their gut. They look nice but outdated. These are Abernathy's people. Immediately, Abernathy is filled with love for them.

There are about thirty souls in the room, total.

"The holidays are our busiest season." Kai says, coming up behind Abernathy. She surprises him, and to his horror, he jumps, knocking into the table of bagels. A few plastic forks go wonky.

"Kai," he says, attempting a smile as he straightens the forks. "You surprised me. Hi. How are you?"

"'Why am I here again,' you might find yourself asking." She reaches over Abernathy to take a strawberry. "'Why call me back at all?' Any guesses?"

"Your team couldn't resist my charm?"

"No," says Kai, popping the strawberry in her mouth. "Not your charm. Try again."

"Your love for me?"

". . ."

"I have skills the company values?"

"Holiday cycle," she says. "noticeable uptick in depressive episodes across the country."

"Ah."

"Depressive episodes mean a downturn in productivity. Downturn in productivity means an increased demand for our services hither to unprecedented during other fiscal quarters. Hence"—she takes another strawberry—"why *you* are here."

Simple stuff like saying "hello" would be beneath her, Abernathy thinks.

This, like most of Jonathan Abernathy's assumptions about other people, is incorrect.

Abernathy does not understand Kai, Kai's personality, Kai's life, what Kai has done to get here, or what she has lost to be in this room, standing on a Tuesday morning next to a bagel platter with a lanky new recruit whose doe-eyed excitement just about stabs her in the gut every time she gets near him.

Jonathan Abernathy has no idea how he comes across.

It might not look like it, but Kai is putting in a lot of effort right now. She is trying her best, despite the fact that Abernathy shouldn't be here at all, really, and that dumbasses like him are shipped in every year by the Archive in an attempt to replace Kai, who, so far, has proven to be irreplaceable. None of these dudes last more than, like, nine months. Do you know what that does to a person? Having to train a new guy exactly like the last guy every *nine* months?

Abernathy's lucky Kai remembers his name.

"Right," he says. "Who doesn't get a little blue this time of the year. I know I always feel worse." Abernathy decides not to take her rudeness (it's not rudeness, but we'll let him have this one) personally, even though he thinks her eyes are a little too glinty and aggressive for his comfort.

Mostly, he tries to feel lucky to be here.

"That's why we bring assholes like you back into the fold." She takes a sip from her tiny cup of water and smiles, tight-lipped. "Even though it's apparent to anyone who's met you that you've never understood another human being in your life."

"I'm grateful for the growth opportunity you've provided. I know I've only completed two night cycles, but both were an honor to audit."

Kai snorts. "Do you always talk like this?"

"Like what?"

She stares at him.

Abernathy doesn't understand what she means.

"Are you always so"—she gestures up and down his figure—"*earnest*?"

They stand next to a beige and buttery pastry platter, a sin of croissants and stale scones. Abernathy has been eyeing the precut bagels and their exposed bellies with some interest for several minutes. There is silence, which Abernathy spends deciding whether or not the platter is only there for show. Is it socially acceptable to disturb the platter by touching one of the croissants? Having skipped breakfast to make it here on time, Abernathy is hungry. No one else has disturbed the platter of bagels. The same is not true for the fruit plate, now mostly melons. Abernathy does not want to be the first to break the pastry seal.

"Can I ask you a delicate question, Kai?" He turns with regret away from the bagels. He is hungry, but not hungry enough to risk shame.

"Fine."

"Are you paid a salary? You mentioned pay grades, when we first met. I'm just wondering if now that I'm being brought on . . . that I might . . . well . . ."

She looks at him as if he is a silverfish. Examining him. Determining whether she should stomp on him or help him escape. He is very stompable. Abernathy's comfortable acknowledging that.

"You don't understand *what* this is, do you?"

"What?" Abernathy has, against his will, reached for a bagel and is now spreading butter across the top. Except the butter is not soft, so it really takes elbow grease to cover the bagel's surface. He is destroying the bagel he did not consciously decide to eat and he feels horror, a sort of grim defeat and resignation, as crumbs fall like little pebbles from a cliff face to scatter across the table and the floor.

Kai watches him. She chooses her words carefully. "This isn't corporate employment."

"Yeah," says Abernathy. He corrects himself: "Yes. I get that."

Kai is at the precipice of realizing Abernathy is not the person she expected him to be, either. She baits him. "It's not an internship to collect on your way to your big-boy job."

Abernathy is confused. Does she think this is just a first step for him? To him, this is the final goal. The big break.

"I don't think of this as an internship," he says. He tries to sound earnest. He is earnest, but he tries to sound earnest, too. He tries to make his eyes sparkle. Usually women like when he does that. "I take my work here very seriously. I'm honored to have been chosen for training."

Kai stops watching him attack the bagel. She pulls her eyes up to his. "I'm incarcerated," she says. It's more like a confession. A very blunt confession. "Formerly, once I finish this program. My pay grade is my freedom."

Abernathy straightens up, trying to figure out where this conversation is going. The mauled bagel looks less appetizing now.

"Oh," he says. "That's cool?"

Kai raises an eyebrow.

"I had a cousin," Abernathy says. "It took him like twenty years to get out. I met him as a full adult only after I had heard all these stories about him. I bet your family is really relieved."

Kai stares at Abernathy blankly. In the silence that stretches out awkwardly between them, Kai appears to realize something about him—

"You know what this is, right? I'm working off the remainder of my sentence. Everyone in this room is working something off." She gestures to the group of people scattered and small-talking throughout the room. "It's not," her voice is firm, like she's explaining something really important, "like, a 'feel-good' opportunity—this job."

"Right, right," says Abernathy, not sure if this is the appropriate thing to say. He must have hit a nerve.

He smiles at her gently, trying to placate her. Comfort her. "Well, it's no wonder you're so good at this," he says. "You really want it, I bet." He takes a bite of his bagel. It's not good. "Do you think," he ventures, "you might be paid . . . afterward? Like after you finish working off your sentence?"

"Oh my God," Kai says. Her eyebrows have ascended even higher. They are now closer to her hairline than Abernathy thought possible. She sounds almost awed. "You are being completely serious."

"I have a lot to learn still, yes," Abernathy agrees. He doesn't want to lay it on too thick, but he wants her to understand he really needs this. "But I am really excited to take on that challenge with you! I think our working relationship has so much potential."

Before she can answer, the lights dim. A projector light flickers. The screen on the wall is illuminated. So that's what it's for.

"Ope," says Abernathy. "And that's our cue."

He salutes her, hand to head, and Kai looks—frankly—astonished. That or completely disbelieving. Hard to know the difference sometimes. Abernathy's not sure why he saluted, but no time to think about that now. Quickly he shuffles toward one of the empty middle seats, excusing his way across the legs of those already sitting. He comes to rest comfortably on a metal chair positioned between a very angry-looking man and a teenage (or maybe not teenage; Abernathy has a hard time telling) girl in a fast-food uniform.

Kai believes Abernathy to be entitled. Full of himself. Destined to swoop in and boss her to death. She does not realize, yet, that he is a well-meaning dumbass, and that he has no idea of the risks he agrees to by being here and working in this office.

Abernathy, on his part, does not realize the severity of the situation he is in. Nor does he realize that for Kai, as for him, this job is life or death. He thinks she is rude and blunt. He panders to her in an attempt to ignore these elements of her personality, which in turn exacerbates Kai's assumption that he is a kiss-ass who will throw her under the bus at the first moment of inconvenience. To Abernathy, Kai is simply saying the things everyone thinks about him out loud. Though he finds her honesty grating, he also finds it comforting. In his heart of hearts, Jonathan Abernathy believes that he is a waste of human life.

The projector flickers.

Abernathy settles into his seat.

A black-and-white man in a much better astronaut suit than Abernathy's struts onto the screen. He looks . . . very strapping. He takes off his helmet like an aviator returning from war. Hair shake. Gleaming smile. Very "Ta-da, I am here." I am here, I am a man, I will get things done. Abernathy would like to have a smile like that. Abernathy thinks it is very easy to trust a man whose appearance is that beautiful.

The man on the screen begins to talk.

"So you're the brave souls who wish to colonize"—the fast food worker next to Abernathy snorts—"the next great beyond. Man's final frontier: *his dreams*."

"Wowww," says the could-be teenager. The food worker next to him is the youngest in the room by far. Nineteen, maybe? There's something sad about her that seems nineteen to Abernathy. She is one of maybe four women in the room, including Kai. Her hair is in two long braids and her mouth is set into a hard, unfavorable line. The food worker keeps glancing over at Kai. She's not the type of teenager who starts smoking due to social pressure. She's the type of teenager who starts smoking because she wants to die early and soon.

Will Timmy carry this sadness herself in ten years? That's hard for Abernathy to imagine. Like, hard as in actually painful. He was a smoker, at that age. He desperately wanted to fit in, to have an excuse to stand in little groups. He never inhaled, but it became a habit anyway. He gave up at the request of his first college girlfriend. They dated for three months. She said his mouth tasted like ash. Ash reminds Abernathy of crematoriums. Crematoriums are where dead people are taken. Like his family. It's not hot to think about family members while you kiss.

The fast-food worker has a notebook and isn't even looking at the screen.

The man in the projection is walking toward the camera now. He's saying stuff. (Abernathy is having a hard time turning off his thoughts long enough to pay attention, but the informational video thing has been going on for several minutes now and the man on the screen is talking very assuredly about things like "futures" and "employment" and "personal growth." Really boring stuff.).

The girl is writing with determination in her notebook as the projection plays. A bunch of dangly bracelets on her left wrist click together as she does so. *Click click click click.* Of everyone in the room, she's making the most noise by a pretty big margin. It is very distracting. The rest of the would-be auditors are hushed. What's the guy on the screen saying? Something about safety. Safety and self-protection and liability. Boring stuff, still. In the dim glow of the projector, the people in the room are simply a bunch of shadows together, upright in the dark.

Abernathy can't help himself—he tries to look at what the food worker is writing. He manages to catch a few words at the top of the page before she shoots him a nasty look and scooches as far away from him as she can. The chair seats are not wide at all, so Abernathy decides this must be more for show than an actual desire to get away. Abernathy's not sure why she does this. In her notebook she only wrote one phrase and it wasn't exactly illuminating: *government sponsored indentured servitude.* Very foreboding, except she has doodled little hearts around the sentence.

♥♥♥ *government sponsored indentured servitude* ♥♥♥

What does that even mean? His neighbor closes the notebook before Abernathy can get a better look.

Was he like this when he was nineteen?

Not really.

He mostly just felt bad for his parents. They were really poor and had outsized personalities that could swing high and low without much notice. As a kid he was too busy navigating their moods to have much of a personality of his own. Jonathan Abernathy never doodled hearts on anything.

In a whisper he asks the teen what she's writing. The teen ignores him. Another auditor-in-training shushes them from behind.

Abernathy has no choice. He must watch the informational video. The film is boring, in a twentieth-century way. A lot of glamour shots of employees talking about the importance of their job in that slow "I am teaching you" voice. Very official language. Not like how people actually talk at all. Dolly shots as they walk down long corridors. Rigid smiles of enthusiasm from all in the production. A dedication to a false idea of reality that isn't realistic. Merely set pieces. Abernathy suffers through the film, bouncing his leg and occasionally glancing at the food worker, who has since put her journal away. Abernathy has never been one to excel in applying prolonged attention. From what he could gather, the video can be summed up as basically this:

What the dream auditors, officers, and servicemen do in the dreams has real-world impact on their customers. Like any service job, one should conduct oneself with the utmost integrity in the assistance of one's client. While the technology is still new and there are some difficulties, it is important that one takes every precaution to . . . yadda yadda yadda; Abernathy stopped paying attention at this part.

After what feels like the third excruciatingly long segment about personal liability, which would be particularly illuminating if Abernathy chose to listen, the room's lights turn back on. The projection whirs off. Abernathy is not really sure what it is he's supposed to take away from this whole thing. Maybe: be confident in all that you do and you will go a long way to improving your dreamer's life and, by extension, the economy, and thus yourself.

Abernathy's colleagues stand up and begin to stretch. He stands with them, cracks one shoulder, then the other. The customary post-video mingling begins. An opportunity to network means it is now the time where Abernathy can assuage his curiosity. Abernathy turns to his seatmate to ask about her notebook again, but she is gone. Quickly he scans the room and sees she's already at the exit shrugging into a jacket.

Abernathy knows this is ridiculous, but he hops over a chair to reach her—not trying to be dramatic, just trying to be efficient—but in the process he knocks the chair over.

Lots of folks turn to look at him.

"Hey," he calls to the service worker, righting the chair. He is flushed red. "Hey, wait!"

She is already out the door. He rushes to follow, ignoring the stares, but Kai grabs him by the arm. Her grip surprisingly firm.

"Did you pay attention?" she asks him, searching his eyes. Her glasses are the greenest of green. Something about the way she looks at Abernathy makes him think that her question is important. Maybe, like, *really* important.

"What?"

"Did you pay attention to the film?"

"Oh," he says, "right. Right. Very informative. It's just that I—"

"Good," she says, relieved. "Follow me."

She lets go of his arm, turns, and exits through a small door at the back of the room that swings shut behind her. Abernathy did not see the door before. It is hidden partially behind a half-full rack of metal chairs. He hesitates.

All the other folks are putting on their jackets.

A few of the more impressive dream collectors even mingle with the new recruits.

Abernathy looks toward the exiting crowd. Right now really is the perfect opportunity to show his worth to his colleagues, to prove himself capable, to shine, but the fast-food worker is already gone, and besides, Kai has a task for him. A task is good. A task means she must trust him. If she trusts him, that's a good sign, right?

Abernathy opens the door.

A long hallway awaits.

## /// **9** ///

KAI WALKS AT A PRODIGIOUS pace. The click of her walk is like a Morse code to be deciphered. Though what her stride across the tile tells Abernathy, he doesn't know. Maybe: *I am difficult to like because I protect the softness of my heart.* Or: *Follow in my footsteps and I will show you the path to stability.* The hallway is long, dark, and narrow.

"Hey," Abernathy calls, "wait up!"

Kai recedes ahead of him, always at the cusp of disappearing into the shadows. He can see the white button-up of her shirt, but as Abernathy jogs, the hallway stretches out like hallways are known to in dreams.

Kai does slow a bit, her back to him, and Abernathy finally manages to reach her. He can't see her face in the gloomy darkness. The only light is thin and flickering, coming from an old-fashioned halogen at the end of the hall.

"What are we doing here?" he asks.

Kai stops mid-gloom. She turns to him, slow-motion-like. Her face looks normal. That's a relief. For half a second Abernathy expected the shadows to turn with her. Things are that spooky, here in the hallway.

"Be honest," she asks in the dim light. "How much have you thought about this?"

"Thought about what?"

She exhales slowly through her nose, the way fitness instructors do when centering themselves and fathers do when they are trying not to yell.

"Have you thought about why we appeared to you in your dreams?"

"Oh," Abernathy says, laughing, "that."

Kai looks at him, her eyes searching his face for an answer. She has a soft, boxy face. Red hair, a wig or a weave. Dark skin. Eye glasses. Wide, sharp cheeks. Beneath the collar of her shirt he can just make out the gold of a necklace. She wears matching hoops. Her demeanor is scaring him. She looks worried.

There are a few alcoves in the hallway, but otherwise it is long and skinny, and the only point of interest is the door at the end.

"What? Is it important? I thought I was here because of my stellar candidacy." Abernathy is only half joking.

Kai rolls her eyes. That feels more normal. She turns from him. She takes a few steps forward, but then the shadows of the hallway begin to move, and the same man that appeared in Abernathy's initial recruitment dream steps out from an alcove. What's-his-face, from God's garden. The devilishly handsome guy who passed the clipboard to Abernathy that first time around. Mr. Panties-in-a-wad. Where did he come from? He has a smug and arrogant face.

"Kai," the man says. He looks perfectly disheveled. Some people spend a lot of time disheveling themselves to look the way this man looks. Abernathy attempts to be this person himself, but he never knows how other people perceive him and thus can never tell if he's pulled it off. Abernathy can't tell if this man is one of those people who try or if he possesses a natural dishevelment. Which is probably the point and also the exact thing Abernathy can never achieve. The man pushes dark hair out of his face and smiles a slow, languorous smile. "A joy to run into you here, Kai."

"Penn," she says curtly.

"I didn't know you had archival access."

"I'm just showing Abernathy the archives. New recruit. Abernathy, Penn. Penn, Abernathy."

"Nice to see you again," Abernathy says.

"Of course," Penn says, not taking his eyes away from Kai. His face changes abruptly. He looks concerned. "Actually," he says, still only speaking to Kai, "you know what, from what I recall, you're not supposed to be down here—are you?"

"Cute," she says.

"Am I wrong?"

"Like I said, just showing the new guy the ropes." She says this in the manner of professional women everywhere who often need their neutral statements to double as daggers.

"That's me," says Abernathy. He gives a wave. He can't tell if he needs to be as enthused as he is, but it's always better to play it safe than sorry when it comes to potential employment opportunities. "You gave me my onboarding packet on the bus, remember?" He tries to give a dazzling smile. "Thanks again for recruiting me! Very excited to be on board!"

Penn doesn't acknowledge Abernathy's speech.

Instead, with dark eyes, he watches Kai. She turns her back to him. There is now a door in front of her which was not there before. She inserts her key into the lock. Abernathy thinks he sees her hand shake. But that can't be right. Kai is the type of woman who is scared of no one.

Over her shoulder she asks Penn, "Do you mind?"

Lipless smile from Mr. Hot and Terrifying. "Oh, I'm sorry," Penn says. "Am I disturbing you?"

"Yes," says Kai.

Penn puts his hands in his pockets. Rocks back and forth on his feet. The exact type of man Abernathy wants to be. "Well," he says, "I suppose I should just . . ." he sighs, turning on his heel, "leave you alone then. Ropes to show, and all."

"Thank you," Kai says stiffly. "Yes."

Kai waits until the hallway swallows Penn's receding figure to exhale the breath she has been holding. She mutters something under her breath.

"What?" Abernathy asks.

This time Kai says, "I hate that guy," and turns her key in the lock. "Destined for the executive table and an absolute cunt about it, the dumb dick." She shoulders open the door. "Anyway, whatever. He's not in charge yet. He's still in the outer city offices, just like us. And besides, we're not here for him. We're here for this."

She steps into the room. Abernathy follows. He stops, surprised by his own fear which rises within him like a many-headed beast. Goose pimples erupt on his arms.

The shadow of Jonathan Abernathy's death flutters around him, as if awakened.

"The Archive," Kai says, "of Dreams."

**WHAT LAYS BEHIND THE DOOR** is dark and hushed as if filled with the shallow breaths of one hundred sleeping children. The room itself rises and falls as if a chest. From floor to ceiling, the Archive is lined with shelves of small, square cardboard boxes. The lights above are off. Faint light from the hallway trickles in.

It is a cramped, tall room. If Abernathy squints he can see the top.

"Nothing like the city offices, of course," Kai whispers. "Shittier than the city and nowhere near as well funded as the suburbs." She crosses her arms on her chest. "We're a tiny operation. Underserving the underserved."

"What *is* this?" Abernathy asks, indicating all the boxes. And the creepiness. He's not sure why he feels terror.

He doesn't want to show Kai he's scared. He wants to seem strong, competent, smart, good. He tells himself:

- ✓ Jonathan Abernathy you are strong.
- ✓ You are brave.
- ✓ You are doing exactly what you need to be doing at the time you need to be doing it.
- ✓ There is no such thing as fear.
- ✓ There is nothing in life not meant for you.

He walks over to a shelf.

Squinting, Abernathy can just make out names scribbled in pencil across the lid of each box. The room is damp. On each wall, between the shelves, is a black door. Shelf full of boxes, black door, shelf full of boxes, black door. Four doors in total. As he gets closer to the boxes, the gloom seems to shimmer around him.

Kai watches him. "Any guesses?" She's speaking in her nice voice again, which is freaking Abernathy out.

"No." Abernathy clears his throat. "No guesses."

But that's not exactly true. Abernathy has a bad feeling. He thinks of all that mud in the first dream. A bad feeling like that, actually. A feeling you might feel if you had not yet realized death stands behind you, gently breathing upon your neck.

Abernathy does not want to open the boxes and he certainly does not want to know what's inside them. He wishes he had paid more attention to the film. He is starting to feel like he is involved in something . . . abnormal. Of the film all he can remember is a guy walking toward him. The constant refrain of safety. Responsibility. Personal liability.

Abernathy shivers. He steps back from the shelves, closer to the light from the hallway.

Into all that apprehension, Kai tells him, "This is where we keep the runoff."

She walks up to the rows of boxes. She runs her finger along them. They're alphabetized. She pulls one box down from the sixth shelf. It is tiny. The size of her two palms. She holds it out to Abernathy. He takes it. The box is light in his hands, barely weighing a thing.

"Go ahead," she says.

"No, thank you." Abernathy tries to give the box back.

"Open it."

"I don't want to."

She says, "You need to know."

He gives her a low look, a terrified look, and she grins a bit.

"Prove you're not just another pretty face. Go ahead. Don't let yourself get eaten like the rest of them."

Her joke works. Abernathy's distracted. For a moment he frowns. "Are you calling me dumb?"

They stand in the dream archive together. Abernathy holds the box. Kai looks at Abernathy.

"There's nothing to be scared of," she whispers. Is she making fun of him? "Yet."

She reaches over and pulls off the lid.

The box is empty.

Her showmanship confuses Abernathy. But then he realizes—what he thought? It's not quite right. The box is *almost* empty. The corner of the box holds a shadow that does not look right, almost like a smudge. Abernathy can only tell that the shadow is there because the smudge moves. The smudge struggles. In the corner of the box, the smudge wriggles as if it were a tadpole. A tadpole of darkness.

The runoff, Abernathy wonders, of *what*?

Abernathy stares inside the box and then closes his eyes abruptly.

He holds the box out to Kai.

"Please," he says, "I don't want it."

"Even though it's yours?" Kai asks. She puts the lid back on.

He sees now that the box is labeled. In thin, scratchy pencil, the label reads: JONATHAN ABERNATHY, DREAM AUDITOR, 100030008003.

"I'm trying to warn you," Kai whispers. She's urgent, fervent, as if someone could interrupt them at any moment. "I thought maybe you were just full of yourself—that you knew what you were getting into. I thought you wanted to best it, or conquer it, because it's unknown— like the rest of them. But that's not what you want, is it?"

"What are you talking about?"

"You don't understand how this works. You don't know what this is or how jobs like this *work*. Try to really *critically* think about why they offered a job to *you*. Think about what you may be giving up or why you may be stuck here. I didn't get to, but everyone—even *you*"—she gives him a look here, which even in the dark Abernathy can tell is scathing—"should get the opportunity to know what they're getting into."

Abernathy shudders. He feels that he is committing some great cosmic wrong by holding the box. That saying in all the movies? That if you travel back in time and come across yourself, you may create a paradox? That the world would prevent you from encountering your own existence, otherwise you'd risk contaminating time, life, the natural order of being? Abernathy kind of feels like that. Like he is somehow corrupting reality by holding this . . . this . . . *thing*.

"Take it, please." He holds the box out to Kai, desperately, in the dark. "Just take it."

Kai takes the box from him. Delicately, she places it back on the shelf.

Not all the boxes in the room are empty, is what she's saying. And what they're filled with? It is not good. It is very not good.

Abernathy understands what Kai means by runoff.

He could feel it in his hands when he held the thing.

The boxes in this room are filled with all the nightmares that are not had, the anxieties and yearnings and depressions and hopes that have been collected from their rightful dreamers. Those fears and desires have to go somewhere, once they're removed. So too do the dreams of the auditors and officers who sacrificed their sleep to assuage the nights of others. Those dreams have to go somewhere, too.

Abernathy wants to ask Kai if her box is here, but he already knows that it is. There are two of her breathing in the room. He can feel it. One version of her breathes slightly slower, as if asleep. Her box is probably filled with more than a tadpole of shadow. At this point, her box must be full of horrors.

All the officers, their boxes are here. And it's the boxes, not the room, that breathe. Whatever it is that's kept inside the boxes is alive.

It's only—Jonathan Abernathy's box hasn't been filled yet.

# /// II ///

# JONATHAN

# ABERNATHY

# IS

# SLEEPING

**THE THING ABOUT DREAMS—AND,** coincidentally, this applies to work as well—is that once the dream ends you can no longer recollect what happened. You feel that something has happened. A vague memory remains. The exhaustion is there. You are changed. But the nature of both dreaming and working is infinite, and thus incomprehensible. We can try our best to explain it, to understand it, to conceptualize it, compartmentalize it, or track it, but in the act of dreaming time is stolen and made unreal.

**IN THE INFINITY** of slumber—and labor—life disappears.

**EVERY DAY OF** your life, you will dream. You will work. Today, yesterday, tomorrow.

**TO WORK AND** to dream is to forget.

**TO FORGET IS** to live.

AFTER KAI SHOWS HIM THE Archive, Abernathy stays up all night. When he does sleep (and he must sleep), he does so in twenty-minute segments. He refuses to sink into dreams and instead sets the alarm on his phone to ring every quarter hour. He does not put on the Archive's suit. He does not get into bed. When he does allow himself to doze, he must do so sitting upright between his bed and his wall, his back pressed against his night stand, too scared to drift off.

For the entire week, he dead-eyes his way through his shifts at the box. He shuffles home in a fugue. He segments his nights. Twenty minutes asleep. Twenty minutes awake. Twenty minutes asleep. Twenty minutes awake. After a double spent with Adam serving lunch to the last minute Christmas shoppers ("Are you sure you're OK, Abernathy, you don't look so hot." "Of course I'm OK. Why wouldn't I be OK. I'm always OK."), he arrives home. The winter night is dark, and Abernathy practically collapses beneath the night as he lets himself into his small basement suite. He does not want to fall asleep. Not yet. He can't. He won't. In dreams, the boxes await him. Rows and rows of boxes. He falls forward onto his bed, still holding mail. He pushes his shoddy quilt aside to press his face into a pillow and take deep, slow breaths.

The seeping, spreading feeling of insomnia stitches him closer to the mattress. He lies sprawled-eagle, limbs increasing in weight. His body desperately tries to pin him to a sleep uninterrupted, his mind fights to remain awake.

Abernathy tears into his mail.

One piece of correspondence is his pay check.

One is a notice.

45 percent of his ($7.25 an hour) twenty-hour-a-week paycheck has been repossessed (court-ordered) into the account of a multi-billion-dollar corporation Jonathan Abernathy signed his life to before he could even legally drink or go to war.

Such practice, which is perfectly lawful in America, thank you, is known as a lien. It is a form of state-sanctioned wage slavery poor Americans stumble into.

In other words, Abernathy *must* pay.

To realize there is no choice is almost worse than thinking there may be one.

He fumbles his phone open and dials his bank account to dispute the charge.

He is on hold for an hour and fifteen minutes exactly when Rhoda approaches his screen door with a full face of makeup, a long green coat, and one of those blousy work shirts that always form a small gap between the second and third button. The sun is completely gone from the horizon. She catches his eye as she raises her hand to knock on his screen door. Her hair is tucked behind her ears. She gives a wave instead.

It's an instinct, is the only way he can explain it. As soon as he sees her he closes his phone. The call ends. His place in the hold line is lost.

By now Abernathy should be familiar with his country's banking systems and other monetary bureaucracies, as well as intimate enough with the pattern of his own personality, to know that as soon as he closed the phone, the call would never be made, the complaint never lodged.

With the willpower of a thousand suns, Abernathy pulls himself to greet Rhoda and thinks, *I can always call them back.*

Rhoda smells nice. Piney. Like some mysterious forest brought to life. She's taken out most of her earrings and her septum ring is tucked into her nose. The blouse and the pants hide almost all her tattoos. She can't hide the tattoos on her hands, however. A dagger tip emerges from her sleeves. Across her knuckles ink still reads: **SHIT LUCK.**

"Rhoda!" Abernathy says through a tired smile. "To what do I owe the pleasure?"

"Oh," she says. Deadpanning, but with the thinnest hint of apology in her voice. "You're tired. I should let you sleep."

"No, no," he says. He has already decided not to tell her about what happened with Kai, the boxes, the archive. He doesn't want her to know about the lien. He doesn't want to seem like a failure. He doesn't want to seem like he's given up. Jonathan Abernathy never gives up.

"What's up? What's going on with you on this glorious day?" He gestures widely.

Outside, in the dark, clouds blot out the stars. It looks as if there will soon be rain.

Rhoda blushes. Barely blushes. The color across her cheeks doesn't change, but her ears do. They become pink. She hesitates. She explains—her ex, he didn't show up (again). And it's just, well. She has a holiday party she meant to attend. She should go. She asks Abernathy—could he, would he be willing to please watch Timmy?

"Maybe in exchange for dinner later this week?" she asks. "We've already eaten tonight but there's leftovers in the fridge. Does something like that sound good?

Abernathy squints into the gray backyard, weighing his aches and pains. The trees are looking very mighty despite the shadows. For a moment, he thinks he sees two white-robed landscapers fighting the crisp December chill to consult the ivy at the fence line, like they had when he was dreaming of Heaven the night of his recruitment. When Abernathy blinks, they are gone.

Abernathy does not take the workers as a sign that his work and his life are not as separate as they seem.

He should.

Right now, all Abernathy can see or think about is Rhoda, who stands in front of him smelling like struggle and pine. He can tell Rhoda is desperate. Trying not to push it on him, but desperate all the same. So he slips his phone into his pocket and says, "Sure! My pleasure! Give me a moment!" And steps back, invites her inside, people pleaser until the end.

As she steps into the room, her heels stick to the tile. Abernathy had hardly noticed the sticking before. He must have spilled something and forgotten to clean it up.

"You can sit here," he says, pushing the ragged quilt farther off the bed. Not that there's much choice. It's the only place to sit in the entire room. Rhoda hesitates. And then she sits—lowering herself onto the edge of the mattress, slowly, by putting her weight on her arms. She has a firm, unyielding posture. Abernathy realizes she is nervous. She is nervous to be sitting on his bed. He is nervous, suddenly, too. They stare at each other. She looks absurd against the background of his ratty and tangled sheets. Such proper posture. Prim and mean. She also looks . . . something else.

He takes a step toward her.

She looks up at him.

Abernathy can't figure out what it is. The something else.

"Nice place," she says to break the silence. Sarcastic, as always, but this time awkward, too. He's never thought of her as awkward before. He can tell she means it. That is: she means, in that moment, to pay him a compliment. No one in their right mind would think his room was genuinely nice.

"I built it myself," he says.

"Really?"

"Ah . . . no. That was a joke."

She smiles, a bit. Or at least he thinks she's smiling. Inside. Her eyes are sparkly even though her mouth, dark pink with a freckle just to the left, remains the same. "I knew that—friends with the *landlord*, remember?"

"Right," he says. But Abernathy's too distracted to register what she's said. In the moment he's realized he left the letters on the bed, right where she can see them. He is flooded with two distinct feelings. The first feeling is a dull sense of dread. He begins to sweat at the thought of her reaching out to read those letters. The second is a sudden realization. He knows what the feeling he cannot name is. The feeling of something else in his body that accompanies him every time he gazes upon her. He can't believe it took him so long to understand. "Thanks," he says, leaning down to swipe the letters into his hand. There is a brief moment when his arm is inches from her arm. The inches are electric. "For the compliment. I'm not sure if I agree." He tucks the mail safely into his desk, an absolute disaster of used cups, coffee rings, and unopened mail. "But, thanks."

Rhoda looks around and shrugs.

Can she see the realization unfolding within him?

Abernathy clutches the desk for balance. He does not wish to fall over. His back is to her as she says, "I wasn't just trying to be nice, it's . . . cozy. In here. I can see you here. You know, living."

Abernathy clears his throat and resists the moment. He turns his head. Unlike Rhoda, Abernathy's blush is bright red and spreads from his cheek to his nose to his neck.

Wobbly. In the throat. His heart loud and in his mouth. He feels heat spreading. From his cheeks. His neck. His chest. Below.

Abernathy is almost swept over by the intensity.

Not only is he broke. To Jonathan Abernathy's surprise, attraction has snuck up on him. Already, attraction was deepening into adoration, care.

"I'll just—" He sounds strangled.

Rhoda looks at him, confused.

He coughs.

"Bathroom," Abernathy says. "Only be a moment." He just about sprints the three steps to the small bathroom. Shutting the door behind him, he slides down onto the black and white tiles.

Abernathy's whole body is hot. He groans and puts his head into his knees.

"Everything OK in there?" Rhoda calls.

*Stupid. Stupid. Stupid.*

"Yes!" Why does he sound so stupid? "Just washing up, then we can go."

"All right," Rhoda says, and the other side of the door goes silent. Abernathy can hear her stand up. She must be walking around his room, examining things.

He's not sure what's worse, Rhoda examining his room, or his sleep-deprived recognition that he . . . that he . . .

Ah.

God.

Abernathy stands up from the tiles slowly. He avoids eye contact with the mirror.

This is his realization: Jonathan Abernathy thinks Rhoda is beautiful, special, and good.

He has thought this for some time. Yet he had not realized it was a thing he thought. How was that possible? To both be thinking of a person and unaware you were thinking of them at all?

He has . . .

Just say it.

He has fallen for his thirty-six-year-old, single mom, divorcée neighbor.

What's worse: now that the feeling has come to his attention, he also realizes the simple truth that must accompany it.

There is no way Rhoda thinks these thoughts about him.

Who even *is* he?

He is twenty-five. He is $100,000 in debt. He has, according to his bank statement, exactly seventy-two dollars to his name.

What does that mean for their friendship, if he is here, staring into the white bowl of the bathroom sink, gripping porcelain, heavy beneath the realization that he adores her, and that she—she does not—

Abernathy does not want to look at himself.

He runs the tap as cold as it can get.

He plunges his head beneath.

AT RHODA'S HOUSE, she has decorated for Christmas. There's a tree, decked out in old wooden ornaments. There's garland. Two stockings are pinned to the wall. Four presents are wrapped neatly in green foil beneath the tree. Beneath the colored Christmas lights, in a sweater and a thick pair of fuzzy socks, Timmy lies on the floor, reading a book. Abernathy forgot it was Christmas. Time has been passing so quickly he hasn't been able to keep up.

"Miss Timothy," he says in greeting. Abernathy bows low in reverence. If he had a hat he would sweep it from his head. Instead he must make do with his still-wet hair as it sticks to his brow.

Rhoda snorts and pushes past him to collect her things for work. Now that Abernathy has realized what those feelings of throatiness are (and how hopelessly, pointlessly stupid he is) he can't stop looking at Rhoda. She flirts—flits—around the room.

Timmy says, "Shhh, we're getting to the good part."

Abernathy straightens. "Of course," he says, still in the haughty voice of a play actor. "How silly of me to disturb a young woman's reading." He winks at Rhoda. Rhoda shakes her head (in mock exasperation, right? Or is it in kinship? Adoration? Mutual interest?). She collects wallet, keys, phone. She works an earring into her ear.

Abernathy cannot stop watching her.

Can she tell?

What he thinks?

Did she know before he did?

For some reason, Abernathy feels as if his bank balance is printed in red across his forehead. He adjusts his hair so that his bangs covers the imaginary sum.

(How did he have time to grow "bangs"?)

Rhoda bends down to kiss Timmy's cheek. It could be the exhaustion, but Abernathy is pretty sure he feels drunk from the proximity of her and her life. The life she lives that he is allowed to participate in. Watching her kiss Timmy on the cheek, Abernathy is overtaken with the powdery imagining of Rhoda's skin pressing against his skin. He pictures what it might be like to have her hair fall into his face. The slow motion of her shoulder pressed firmly against his shoulder, her cheek against his cheek as she uses her mouth to make the sound of a kiss.

"How is work going?" she asks from her seat on the floor. She tucks a braid behind her daughter's ear.

"Mom," Timmy says, pushing Rhoda's hand away. "Stop."

". . . Good." Abernathy says. "Very good."

Rhoda smooths Timmy's hair (Timmy makes a face) and turns to Abernathy. She looks pleased.

When was the last time Abernathy felt like he belonged to something?

Looking at Rhoda, he could see how he could belong.

For a moment he is overtaken with a powerful vision of the future, one where he is successful and competent, where he makes money, where he supports her, where she quits her job, where they drink tea together, where they weed the garden, where they grow a mushroom patch for Timmy in the backyard.

Abernathy, slightly swooning and still recovering, sits down.

He has always had this tendency. When he falls, it is hard. Fast.

He takes his mushroom sculptures out of his pocket, intent on working on them with Timmy. As he fiddles with the clay, forcing it into proper shape, he wonders how he might ask the mother-daughter duo what they're doing for Christmas dinner.

"What are those?" Timmy asks.

"A surprise," he says. "For Christmas."

"A surprise for me?" she asks.

Before he can answer, the doorbell rings.

Rhoda frowns and gets up.

"No, don't tell me," Timmy says, fussing with her hair. She turns back to her book. "I like a good surprise."

"Well, in that case." He zips his lips and throws away the key. She rolls her eyes and flips a page. "What should we do today?" he asks. Maybe the insomnia is why he feels the way about . . . about . . . He has to clear his throat. "Since it will be just the two of us. The mortal world is our limit."

Timmy squints up at him. "*You* can do whatever you'd like. *I* will be reading."

"Oh, don't tell me you're still hurt about last time, Timmy."

At the peephole, Rhoda peers. When she opens the door she does so slowly, not all the way.

Timmy turns her nose up at him. "Hmmph."

"I'm sorry I questioned your reading choices," Abernathy says.

Timmy gives him a look, then nods, as if they understand each other, and turns back to her book. "Good," she says, and she definitely is holding back a smile now. "Don't let it happen again."

Abernathy crosses his heart and thinks, *She's remarkably like her mother.*

At the door, the tension in Rhoda's voice is thick.

"What do you want?" she asks.

There is a man at the door.

A *man* at the door.

Abernathy can't quite see him due to the way the angle of the door is communing with the night. The man is cast into shadows. A cool front bullies its way into the house. The man speaks in low tones. Abernathy, in his whole *life*, has never spoken in tones as low. Tones that low imply kinship. Secrecy. Shared knowledge between two colluding parties.

This must be Rhoda's ex-husband.

"You're two hours late," Rhoda says. She tries to shut the door, but the crisp air finds its way. Abernathy sits up straighter. The man puts his foot between the door and the jamb to prevent Rhoda from having her way. Men have been putting their feet into doors women are trying to close for time immemorial. The ex-husband doesn't even let out the tiniest yowl of pain as Rhoda shuts it—slams it—against the shining patent leather of his shoe.

The porch light's glare hides his face.

Rhoda pushes against the door with her shoulder. Not aggressively enough to break the pretense of cordiality, but firmly enough to say: No. No, you cannot be here. No, I won't allow it.

There is a standoff. Neither of them say a word.

Abernathy is impressed. He tries to imagine himself in such a standoff. Would he push out his chest, firm up his legs so that he had a good base he could maintain for hours? Yes. Probably. And then, once he felt like he was properly anchored to withstand a strong attack, he would, on principle, immediately give in.

Rhoda looks toward Abernathy. Abernathy sits on the couch, doing nothing.

If Abernathy were a different sort of man, he would intervene. However, to his immense disappointment, he will always and only remain himself.

Timmy seems used to these antics. She continues to read on the floor beneath the multicolored lights of the Christmas tree.

Rhoda relents first. A surrender that—in its heart—is less of a surrender and more of a rebuke. A very polite, but clear: Get fucked.

"I've already hired a sitter," Rhoda says. Is she talking about Abernathy? Is he the sitter? Was he *hired*? The bank statement flashes in his mind and he feels as if someone has dumped a bucket of cold water down the back of his shirt. Has she seen it? Did she intend to pay him? Does she *pity* him?

Rhoda sounds firm, but she looks tired, which is how Abernathy knows she will lose. His mom had the same problem. Abernathy knows from personal experience: men just have more energy for this sort of thing. For them there is simply less to do. They can afford to keep pushing when a single mother has to give in. Abernathy would keep pushing if it were his kid. Even Abernathy could probably win in a situation like this. Just thinking about all the stuff Rhoda has to do in a day—even Abernathy could probably outlast her in one of these standoffs.

Thinking that makes him sad. So he takes it back. He would let her win.

Rhoda glances at her watch. Timmy does not look up from her book.

In his lap, Abernathy's mushroom sculptures sit incomplete, and they are going to stay that way for some time yet. He returns the sculptures to his pockets. He tries to look unbothered, but also supportive. Certainly not *disappointed*. He is, after all, exactly as he said earlier: *tired*. A long day at work! No reason to be disappointed.

The cold air makes him feel warm in his jacket and a sinister drowsiness crawls across him. Abernathy could lie down right here, right now, and fall asleep.

"A sitter?" The man laughs. "Sweetheart, please."

Rhoda's mouth, a hard line, trembles at the corners.

There are principles, and then there are outside forces that cause you to sacrifice your principles. Rhoda's outside force is her job. Though maybe it is also the trajectory of her life, which she can feel pressing down upon her at all times, in all dimensions. Out of respect, Abernathy averts his eyes at Rhoda's next words. Timmy seems to sense them, too. With a resigned sigh, the child is already closing her book.

Abernathy already knows that when he gets home, he will put on his Archive-issued suit.

This is not the life he wants for them. Any of them.

Not Timmy, not himself, and definitely not Rhoda.

It is a powerless, dull life.

All three of them deserve better.

"Timmy," Rhoda says. It hurts to hear her say it. Abernathy didn't expect it to hurt to hear her say it. It hurts him because he can see how it hurts her. "Your father is here to pick you up."

## /// **13** ///

THIS IS JONATHAN ABERNATHY'S FIRST time wearing his plastic suit in a week. The chemical smell of the plastic is hard to stomach. The metal elevator is cold, chromium, sheeny. A smudge of handprints warps his reflection. Above him, from a tinny speaker the size of a quarter, a jingle is looping. *La la la.* As if all this is not offensive enough, the elevator smells like bleach.

Compared to Rhoda, what does Jonathan Abernathy have to offer?

Not much.

Still, he's doing what Kai told him to do. He's making an active choice. He's choosing.

Unfortunately, what he's choosing is . . . well . . . *this.*

The elevator doors open with a ding. Jonathan Abernathy returns once again to the realm of sleep.

In the dream, it is nighttime. Balmy. The sound of rushing water comes to him first as he steps out of the elevator into a creek bank. The doors whoosh closed behind him, and are gone. The pebbles beneath his feet are smooth, wet, slippery.

He stumbles, picking his way along the bank. The insomnia of the past week seems to be affecting him. He is slow and sluggish in the dream, his limbs weirdly weak. At a particularly sloping part of the creek, he trips over a dark log covered in waves of oyster mushrooms and falls into the rushing water. He slides across the algae-covered stones, attempting to regain his balance. He lands, ass first. His head hits the stones, water flows across his helmet and he can see only light moving across his vision, watery and cold. It is a strange feeling, falling, because despite the water rushing over him, he remains dry. And unhurt.

His suit has kept him safe.

Jonathan Abernathy gets his footing. A coyote howls. His head rings. Falling always reminds him of childhood. How one minute you are oriented to the world, and the next you succumb to it. Abernathy's breathing is heavy as he stumbles out of the creek, water sloughing off him in great sheets. His vision is dropletted. He has to open and close the visor to clear it.

The log on the bank is no longer a log at all. Now the log is a woman.

Throughout all this, trees whisper nightsongs to one another through their leaves.

Dreams are, it turns out, horrifying, strange beings that make Jonathan Abernathy feel both totally outside himself and completely eclipsed by his life.

The irony that today is Christmas Eve is not lost on him.

It has been a week since his time in the archives with Kai.

She warned him, and did he listen? Sort of. Not really.

He pinched and bullied himself into a waking fugue state. He didn't wear his suit or show up to work. He tried to outrun it. And yet he's still back here, all the same.

Maybe Kai's right and there isn't much of a choice after all.

Abernathy stops himself. He tries not to think of the bummery stuff.

Stuff like the constraints of his circumstances and the limitations of his ability.

As he plows through the creek-wound forest, Jonathan Abernathy resolves to think of this work like so: he will try his best to use it without letting it use him. Like every American, he believes this is feasible, and like every American, he is wrong.

What Abernathy tells himself is comforting enough: What a good opportunity! A great opportunity to delve into the unknown. How many other men are given the opportunity to explore both the depths of themselves and the depravity of humankind?

This, Abernathy decides in the cold chill of another's dream, is a calling.

Working here? This is *his* dream! His passion! His life!

Talk about an opportunity other people would kill for.

Abernathy is exploring man's final frontier. He is a discoverer. An innovator. One small step for man, one giant leap for mankind. Jonathan Abernathy is simply happy to be here. Jonathan Abernathy is simply astounded by his luck.

Plus, now he can show Rhoda that he sticks to stuff. He will overcome his age, and his limitations. He sticks to stuff and he's good at stuff. He's capable of employment, and thus, of other things too. Commitment? Romance? Stability? Life?

On the bright side, the fact that Abernathy has no choice means this must be his destiny.

Jonathan Abernathy has always wanted a destiny.

(By the end of the week, as his food was running out, the Christmas cheer intensifying, strangers bundling into heavier marshmallow coats, everyone holding hands and looking bright-eyed at one another, Rhoda herself looking bright-eyed, Abernathy had all but forgotten the faint light of the hallway as it shimmied across the archives' tile floor. His brain is good at protecting him from stuff like that.)

✓ Yes, he is in financial peril!
✓ Yes, he is a former student of the public education system of the State!
✓ Yes, he feels like a failure in all things, but still somehow wakes up each morning feeling hope!

Does he sleep at least eight hours a night? As unbelievable as it is—

✓ Yes! Thank God! He sleeps ten.

On the pebbled bank, the log that is now a woman has her eyes closed. She is curled into herself, her hands are tucked beneath her cheek. Slumbering like a child. Knees folded to her chest. Aqua rain boots on her feet. Black hair falling into her face. Abernathy doesn't want to disturb her. The creek gurgles and Abernathy imagines the stream is disappointed it didn't manage to swallow him whole. Ignoring his chill, and the slight squeaking of water and plastic as his suit rubs against itself, Abernathy looks around.

It is dark, which, in its own right, is sort of spooky, yes?

The dark and the unknown are pretty much the same thing. Both have terrorized human beings since the beginning of mankind. Both will continue to do so until the end.

In some cultures, it's God you find in the dark. In Abernathy's culture, it is only fear.

Very carefully, with great and astonishing care, Abernathy pulls his clipboard out of the air. He turns in a three-sixty circle.

It is a shadowy world. But he reminds himself of Kai's instructions: Do not think of the shadows. Think, instead, of what the shadows mean. The symbolification of the shadows.

Should the shadows be taken away?

Crickets and bullfrogs chirp chirrupy chirps. Big vines hang from trees. The woman in rain boots slumbers on, oblivious to him. Slumbering even in her slumber. Perhaps, Abernathy hypothesizes, this denotes an exhaustion heretofore unexplored? Lots of shadows could mean lots of night. Nighttime when one sleeps. Lots of sleep. On his sheet of paper, very slowly, Abernathy writes *exhaustion, excessive.* Though he's not sure how Kai might go about cleaning that up, it's better than nothing. Abernathy listens hard to the creek bank: all murmurs and gentle turns. He pulls the sheet from his clipboard, but then pauses. As contradictory as it is (given the speech that Kai gave about choice and Abernathy's own repressed hopelessness) all Abernathy really *really* wants, when he thinks about it, is to do a good job.

"Are you there?" a strange voice, accented and sweet, calls from the tree line. "Hello?"

Abernathy pauses in the act of dropping the paper.

Okay—well, that's got to be it, right?

This voice blunders through the forest, just past the trees. The sound emerges from the soft undergrowth behind the shrub line. The sound of the blundering (heavy, loud) does not match the sound of the voice (delicate, sweet).

Quickly, before the person in the trees can emerge from the forest, Abernathy crosses out his previous entry and writes *TERRIFYING PRESENCE*, under-line underline underline. All caps so anyone who may read the paper will understand that Jonathan Abernathy is an authority who, now that he's chosen this, knows what he's talking about, is destined to be here, will do a good job.

He drops the form into the creek water. It floats lazily downstream before *poof*ing out of existence. Meanwhile, in the forest, the footsteps grow louder.

At this point Abernathy has figured out that the more things he lists in his audit, the more officers arrive. Just one perfect thing and it is guaranteed that only Kai will come. Exactly how he prefers it. Kai is the best.

Kai arrives before the thing can get too close. Just Kai. Kai in her knockoff astronaut suit with its blue circle patch. She has arrived to remove the things that terrify. This is her destiny, too.

Abernathy doesn't want her to see the log that became a woman, in case he's wrong. He takes her arm and steers her away from the person in the teal rain boots still asleep on the shore.

Kai shakes her arm from his and pushes him away.

"What the fuck?" she says.

The sound of footsteps grows louder.

"I came back!" Abernathy whispers, to break the awkwardness and maybe to charm her a little. As if it could work. "Ta-da?"

Kai continues to look at him. Abernathy and Kai are now standing with their backs to the sleeping woman. Kai makes her visor transparent and gives Abernathy a mean look that reeks of disappointment.

"Don't look at me like that."

"Like what, dumbass? How am I looking at you?"

"Like you're disappointed."

Silence, from Kai. Disappointed silence.

"You are disappointed, aren't you?"

"Your life, your choice." She unhooks her hose from her pack.

"That's right," Abrenathy says and tries to mean it.

"OK," she says. "Just don't get me killed while you're playing pretend."

"I'm not playing pretend!"

"Oh, I'm sorry. I must have been mistaken. I thought you were pretending to be an intelligent person."

"I am intelligent!"

"All right."

"I had to come back."

"OK," Kai says, rolling her eyes. "Roger that."

Abernathy huffs and blows his hair out of his face. "You don't think I got problems?"

". . ."

"I got problems!" (This sounds stupid even as he says it.)

The sweet voice calls from the treeline, "Are you there? Hello?"

Kai changes the subject. "Should we head in after it?"

"What! No! Can't we just stand here, and, you know . . ." Abernathy mimes vacuuming the voice up into a pack and then catapulting out of the dream.

"You're the one who wants the job," Kai says. Abernathy hears the anger in her voice, definitely there's anger. Whether she acknowledges it or not—she is angry. She is angry with him. She is angry with herself. She is angry that two people like themselves could end up here, trapped. She is angry that the world is a trap.

She holds out her hand for him to go first. "Go ahead."

Abernathy hesitates before he steps across the bank of the creek. Large deciduous trees loom over him. Looking around, he realizes they're not at the edge of a forest at all, but rather they are stepping out of a small glade into the middle of a dense copse of trees. They are in the middle of a forest (never good) in the middle of the night (definitely not good) in the middle of a stranger's subconscious (terrifying combination). They have no idea which way to go. There is no sign of either exit or entrance.

Kai is right.

Abernathy is here and he agreed to do the job.

He steps farther into the woods. He can hear the voice moving near him, a few steps away. Though he is only one foot into the tree line, he whisper-yells to Kai, "Are you coming?"

Already beside him, Kai rolls her eyes and motions for him to keep walking.

As they walk, the voice grows quieter, as if they are walking away from it rather than toward it. "Are you there? Hello?"

"I really do have problems," Abernathy whispers.

"OK, I believe you."

"Like, lots of problems."

"Yeah," she says, "and one of them is being a pain in my ass."

"You love having me as a coworker." There is a sarcastic edge to his voice, which Abernathy realizes must mean he feels hurt. He brushes that thought away. It is unprofessional to feel hurt. It is bad to feel hurt. He never feels hurt. He is *a man on the job.*

"You are *constantly* doing shit like this."

"Doing shit like *what*?"

"Like this!" Kai swats a branch out of her way.

"What does that even mean?"

"It means you make everything about you."

"I am *not* making this about me right now. Hello! You're the one who said I shouldn't be here."

"Can you just chill, please? Everything I say you take as, like, either some great affront or a God-given symbol of affection. I. Do. Not. Think. About. You."

Abernathy knows Kai is just saying this. That she doesn't mean it. She thinks about him. She is his boss! She must think of him. At least sometimes. Right?

The two of them walk in uneasy silence. The trees above them sway, though there is no wind. The forest floor is covered in leaves, grasses, roots that reach blindly toward other roots. Mushrooms cluster together in circles, some of the caps as big as Abernathy's palm. As they walk farther in, the silence becomes more encompassing, as if the trees themselves emit the hush. There is no wildlife. No bugs. No rabbits to dash out in front of their path in an attempt to forestall their doom.

"I didn't want to bring you on in the first place," Kai says after a while. She is whispering, but it is *angry* whispering. "This shit is dangerous, and you absolutely don't have the constitution. It puts me at risk, taking care of your ass."

"I can take care of myself."

"I did my moral duty and told you to get the fuck out. Obviously you considered yourself too important to listen. This," she says, gesturing to him, "is not my problem anymore."

"Kai," he says. It's his turn to be whispery and exasperated. Maybe a little desperate, too. "I just want to do a good job. Just tell me how to do a good job and I'll do it."

This is the wrong thing to say.

Jonathan Abernathy should have said some poetic bullshit like "I tried to leave but you were right. How do you live with it, knowing you have no choice?"

If Abernathy had said this, Kai would have paused. She would have taken a deep breath, surprising Abernathy and herself. She would have said, "Is that true?"

To which Abernathy would have responded, "*Yes*," in a sullen, self-defeated tone.

Because of his tone, Kai would have felt, for the first time since meeting Abernathy, that he was not lying to her, that he had taken off the overconfident, entitled bullshit persona he wore to cover up his own (obviously crippling) self-consciousness. There would have been a bloom of empathy within her.

She would have said, "I don't?"

"You don't?"

"Live with myself. I don't live with myself."

Abernathy would have been silent.

Kai would have dropped her anger, let her hopelessness and desperation show. She would have said, "Every day I wake up on a tide that pulls me farther away from the person I want to be, and I am helpless to it." Or actually, she would have gone with the simpler: "I don't recognize who I am anymore."

They would have reached an understanding, the two of them, standing in the forest. The next time Kai saw Abernathy she would have softened to him. She would have opened to him. A little. Told him that she ended up in this position due to a series of unforeseeable events, and that she has discovered that the Archival Office is doing some seriously bad shit. Like evil shit. She struggles, because she does not want to be complicit, but from what she can gather, she has no option but to, on the surface, give in.

She would confess that her cousin is trapped in wage slavery to the Archive as well, and that the two of them can see a future where the scourge of this work spreads across their family. Kai believes eventually all but the wealthiest will be swept into the Archive and indebted to it.

After several weeks, she would tell Abernathy of her small act of rebellion: though she believes herself to be trapped, she does not believe herself to be powerless.

If Abernathy had humbled himself, in this moment, Kai would tell him that she plans to stop it, or at least do all she can. Abernathy would listen. He would reject this at first, and struggle against it, until, eventually, he would see the error of his ways and assist her in her plan.

If all this were to happen, this dream would go differently. The world would be a different world, the story would be a different story, Abernathy would be a different Abernathy, and the two young workers would form an alliance that could save both of their lives.

As it is, they do not.

Death will remain tethered to them, because Jonathan Abernathy instead says, "I want to do a good job. Just tell me how to do a good job."

To which Kai scoffs.

It is not their fault for responding this way. They are only human beings, mired by the pride and habit of being themselves, incapable of seeing all the people they could have been and the lives they could have lived. If the world were more generous, perhaps, then yes, life would be different.

As it is, the two coworkers walk among the trees of the dream for some time, following the voice, until the ground beneath their feet hardens. Abernathy kicks away the leaves and sees that they now walk across a parquet floor. He looks up. The treetops are still there, towering above them in the dark, but the forest floor has been replaced with high-polished hardwood. "Kai?"

"Hush," she says.

"But—"

She holds up a hand. "I hear something."

A faint rustling from behind them.

"But—"

She holds her hose out in front of her. She's crouched low, concentrating on the noises in the forest.

"What?" she asks.

"Dream switch," Abernathy says out of the corner of his mouth. This is the code they use when the dream landscape changes unexpectedly and they quickly must orient themselves to a new, unfamiliar territory.

"No shit, moron."

Now that Abernathy looks around, the two of them stand in a grand ball-room. The parquet floors are covered with leaves and overgrown roots. Trees sprout from the ground, split through the unpolished floor, and tower above them. If Abernathy squints hard enough, he can see windows glinting with moonlight at the corners of the room.

A dark, amorphous thing staggers across the tree line in front of them. Its body is a shadow and the shadow is big.

Is this what had spoken?

Kai flips a switch on her pack. The whirring noise of her vacuum is like a cat purring. The shadow turns and the dark black expanse that should be its face is turned to them. Crouched low, the beast locks in on them as if it has caught their scent. If the thing had hackles, they would be raised. Instead, the air around the shadow vibrates in agitation, shimmering as if the thing itself were emitting a haze of heat and horror.

"Be careful," Abernathy whispers to Kai. "Please."

"Oh, shut up."

At the sound of their voices, the shadow lurches backward, takes off. It crashes through the tree line in the opposite direction. Kai runs after it.

Abernathy's moment of hesitation is hardly longer than the time it takes to sharply inhale, yet it is enough time for Kai and the shadow to disappear into the darkness.

Abernathy is left there, standing alone in the shadow of ancient trees, in the light of an even older moon, hesitating.

The rustling noise grows louder. Abernathy can hear Kai breathing and crashing about until the clogged noise of her pack rumbles through the forest. The darkness bends as if being consumed. Things around Abernathy cave in on themselves and pull toward Kai. The dream is a dark star collapsing into itself.

This is a good job, Abernathy reminds himself.

You are valued at this job.

In this job, you are loved.

## 14

IN THE AFTERNOONS, BETWEEN HIS lunch shift at the stand but before he wanders the dreams of his fellow men, Jonathan Abernathy sometimes watches Timmy for Rhoda. Sometimes, if things line up right—if Rhoda can manage to leave her shift on time, if her boss doesn't insist she stay late to mop the floors without pay, if she doesn't get held up at the pharmacy or isn't stuck at the utility branch haggling with the girls who turn off the water—the three of them (Abernathy, Timmy, and Rhoda) eat dinner together.

Tonight the mother and daughter crowd the kitchen island as Jonathan Abernathy stands at the stove in one of Rhoda's aprons. Across his chest, emblazoned in red, is the phrase: WORLD'S WORST COOK.

"Breakfast . . ." Timmy asks, squinting as Abernathy fusses with the stove, ". . . for dinner?"

"Yep," says Abernathy. He is making pancakes.

Timmy does not look convinced.

"I don't think it's a thing."

"Oh, it's a thing," says Abernathy.

Rhoda is reviewing her mail while they speak. She wears a pair of reading glasses that make her eyes look a bit bigger than they are. Her hair is up in a messy pile on top of her head and she scrawls on a notebook next to her, doing figures. Her T-shirt has a phosphorescent green skull on it that melts into advertising for a death metal band. She wears a pair of purple basketball shorts.

"Mom," Timmy says, turning to Rhoda. "This can't be allowed."

Rhoda looks up. "Hmm? And why's that love?"

"Dad would never—"

Rhoda loses her dreamy look of concentration. She interrupts her daughter, terse. "Are we at your father's house?"

"Well . . ." Timmy says. She looks around the kitchen like this might be a trap. Abernathy turns to the stove. "No. But—"

"Then," Rhoda says, as if that settles that, "I don't see why it should be a problem. Breakfast for dinner sounds perfectly good to me."

Timmy still looks skeptical, until Abernathy pulls her over to stand with him at the burner. She is tall for her age. He hands her a spatula and attempts to teach her how to flip pancakes. This wins her over a bit. She burns the first two, but by the third dollop of bristling batter the tension between her mother and herself is forgotten.

"It's all about the bubbles," Abernathy says. He points to the surface of the batter in the pan. "See?"

"Like this?" Timmy asks. She shimmies the spatula beneath the frying dough and flips with a twist of her hand. It is a rare moment that Abernathy becomes the teacher. It is satisfying to see the perfect golden color of the pancake. More satisfying than if he were to have flipped it himself.

"Just like that," he says. "Amazing work."

Timmy rolls her eyes, but Abernathy can tell, though she is trying to play it cool, that she is immensely pleased.

Rhoda, at the table, is muttering slightly as she adds figures. She has a pile of bills before her and keeps scratching things off on the notebook and trying again.

"That won't work," she says to herself, scratching out the fifth row of sums.

"Let's take a break from this," Abernathy says, gathering up the bills.

For a moment Rhoda seems displeased, like she might snap at Abernathy for interfering, but then Timmy brings a plate over to her. The pancakes are sloppily stacked on top of one another, and a few of them are burnt. The eggs (badly scrambled) and the bacon (crispy) are plated haphazardly in the center of the plate. There are a lot of crumbs.

"I made this for you," Timmy says, setting the plate down in front of her mother.

Both blush.

Timmy clambers up onto her stool.

Rhoda picks up her fork. "Thank you, Timmy baby," she says, blinking quickly. She smiles. If Abernathy didn't know better, he might say Rhoda's eyes look tear-capped. "They're lovely."

"Yeah, sure, OK," says Timmy, pleased.

Abernathy serves himself and Timmy. He draws a smiley face on his eggs with ketchup.

When dinners happen, they're nice. Mostly because they're calm. And serene. And funny. And really very normal. Abernathy aspires to be as really very normal as humanly possible. There is a great satisfaction that comes with being really very normal. The type of satisfaction one gets when finishing a test or marking off a to-do list. That feeling of: *Finally! I have done something right.*

Timmy is on Christmas break and the tension between her and Rhoda—both spending more time together than normal—is high. But it seems like here, at the kitchen island, the tension is scraped away by an onslaught of syrup, bread, bacon. Abernathy pours all three of them orange juice. Outside it is snowing tiny, barely-there flakes.

When dinner is over, Timmy insists on wearing a tinseled headband and a pair of big white sparkling glasses. The three of them gather around Rhoda's old square television to watch the ball drop. Timmy is splayed out on the carpet. She barely makes it twenty minutes into the broadcast before the sugar crash hits and she is asleep, dozing on her crooked arm.

Rhoda stands and goes to the kitchen quietly. She plods back to the couch with a bottle of white wine.

"How's this?" she whispers.

Abernathy sits on the right side of the couch. Rhoda settles into the other. She tucks her feet beneath him. He can feel the coldness of her skin through his clothes. On the television, a newscaster stands in the city, eons away from them, surrounded by a bustling crowd of strangers who all have their own dreams.

"Perfect," Abernathy mouths.

Rhoda grins. Twists off the cap of the wine.

"Cheers," she says. She takes a swig and passes the bottle to him.

"Cheers," he agrees.

The wine is syrupy sweet and not at all to his taste, but Rhoda seems to like it.

"What do you want out of the new year?" he whispers, passing the bottle back.

She reaches for it eagerly and takes another drink.

"World Peace," she whispers.

"Impossible."

She laughs through her nose, trying not to wake her daughter.

"OK, fair enough," she breathes. Her voice is soft and tenored. She smells like syrup and forests. She is trying to be quiet and this gives a husky edge to her speech that Abernathy likes.

"How about a break, then?" she says. "Is that possible? I would like to catch a break."

Rhoda moves closer to him. She adjusts her shorts and her feet beneath his thighs.

"That seems more doable," he agrees. He takes the bottle as she passes it to him.

Timmy stirs on the floor and both adults quiet.

Here are two of the secrets they are keeping from each other, as they sit, hushed, huddled closely together on the couch.

We know Abernathy's. He has tripped and fallen into love. He fell fast and hard and now he is scared, so he is denying that he is here. He feels drawn to Rhoda on the level of one soul being drawn to another soul, an unexplainable process that has plagued and blessed the human race since its creation. It is more than just a physical attraction. It is a deep appreciation for who she is. He feels grateful that she is alive, on this planet at the same time he is alive on this planet. He cannot imagine his existence on this planet without her existence. This terrifies him. It is his first time feeling this appreciation for another human. For Abernathy, to look at her is to feel a new type of heartbreak. Once you appreciate someone in this manner, you always then realize how tenuous their existence is. At any moment, two lives can untwine. Abernathy cannot bear to be drawn further *in* or pushed further away. He can't seem to find balance.

Of course Rhoda has a secret, too. More than one secret, but the one she is ruminating on tonight is not so much a secret as a fact undisclosed. She is familiar, already, with the push and pull. Are both of them actively keeping something from the other? No. Not exactly. But, out of shame, out of hesitancy, out of humanity, out of a lack of language, out of worry, they each have parts of their lives they're unwilling to share.

This is the secret Rhoda is thinking of right now: She is not divorced. The paperwork has not been finalized and will never be finalized, though of course she does not know this yet. She worries over the finalization, returning and returning to the quandary. Her legal husband (emotional ex-husband? Whatever. His name is Derek. (She knows it is a stupid name.)) refuses to sign the papers and therefore the proceedings cannot move forward. At first she pushed Derek, but recently Rhoda has stopped pushing.

It is a sad thing to confess, but she no longer believes in things like "romance," or "passion." She does not believe that souls are drawn to other souls. She believes that type of shit happens when you're young and that it happens once, if you're lucky. She believes she is incapable of ever harboring such feelings again, and to some extent, she is correct. Her own self-loathing will prevent her. We cannot appreciate others if we do not appreciate ourselves.

She met her husband when she was sixteen years old. They grew up together. They were best friends. They were in love. And while she does not always like him, she will always love him, and will always be tied to him, on some type of spiritual level. There are only so many people we meet in our lives who have the privilege of knowing us the entire duration, beginning, middle, and end. For Rhoda, her ex-husband is one such person. Derek desires to know her until his end, or hers.

And it is very likely he will get his way. What she first loved about him was his will, so strong and so sure, but she did not factor in that one day his will and her will would diverge, and when they did, his desires would overpower hers until she was eclipsed.

She has small things she has won for herself in the proceedings, even if she cannot escape him completely. She refuses to live with him, for one. She refuses to be with him. But she reasons: Why fight for a right you no longer have faith in? And besides, who, she wonders, would be capable of loving her now?

This line of logic underpins most of her existence. What if she were to reveal her inner heart, her inner person, her truest loves and biggest losses, the most disgusting, pitiable, contemptuous elements of her existence, and be rejected? Pushed aside and stepped on? Eclipsed by old and new love alike? Would that mean that she was inherently eclipsable, as a person? Could she live with herself if this proved to be true? No, she could not go through it again: the loss and grief of being unseen, of being subjugated to another person's desire, of being in love and being possessed, of failing, over and over again, the roles others assigned to her. As such, she keeps herself to herself, plays her card close to her chest, refuses to reveal her soft underbelly no matter how calm the hand that is reaching out.

Yet it is also true that here she is, in her living room, on New Year's Eve, sighing and sinking into the couch next to a twenty-six-year-old boy who reminds her of her younger self, her better self, when she had not made so many decisions, and those decisions had not gathered to direct her life. It is ridiculous, of course, to think that he might be thinking the same thoughts, suffering the same worries, hesitating over the same lines, so she does not speak them. She is older than him. Poorer. A single mother, thirty-five and already, she believes, ruined by a failed marriage more than a decade long, among other unspeakable things. What would even be the point?

It's best, she reasons, to stay exactly like this.

When the ball drops, she looks up at Abernathy and wonders if he can see all this brewing inside of her.

He cannot.

Yet he still brings his face close to her face. For a brief, heady moment, Rhoda thinks they will kiss. But then Jonathan Abernathy presses his cheek to her cheek. His mouth is against her ear.

He has not shaved. She feels the prickling of his jaw on her jaw.

Is he fucking with her? She's not sure. Is this a game to him? What is it, she wonders, that he wants?

His palm is firm on her back and he holds them together. His breath is hot on her neck.

It is Rhoda who speaks first.

"Happy New Year, Jonathan," she says. She does not recognize the hoarseness of her own voice. "I hope you have many more."

She feels him swallow. The crowd on the television is cheering. Music leaks out of the speakers. Her daughter is asleep on the floor, sparkling brightly. On the TV, the same song that plays every year hums to them. There is a weight to the melody that is created through its repetition. Rhoda feels all the years of her lives lining up behind her, bumping into her, as she sits here on the couch. Her life is pushing her forward, pushing against her, urging her to fall. But she refuses to move. She refuses to go.

Abernathy's breathing stutters.

For a moment Rhoda's whole body is alight, angling toward his body of bony elbows, freckles, slender hands. She can feel him hesitating. His other hand almost reaches out, almost touches her, almost pulls her in.

Does she want to be pulled in?

Neither one of them is sure.

In the end, she wants it to be his decision.

Abernathy does not bring her closer. He can feel her right there, *right there*, but he hesitates. There it is: something within him he can't overcome. Instead he drops his hand and whispers as he pulls away, "Happy New Year, Rhoda."

For now, Abernathy thinks, this is enough.

This will have to be enough.

## 15

THE NIGHTS ARE LONG AND boring, full of tiny epiphanies that escape before Abernathy can wake. Strangers running. Strangers burning. Strangers experiencing the end of the world.

Tsunamis, plagues, operations where the patient is trapped in their body, awake.

Women crying. Grandfathers giving birth. Children erupting or exploding or dying or lost.

In the inevitable continuation of his life, Jonathan Abernathy steps from dream to work. Then he steps from work to dream.

Tonight he enters again into the forest, though this time there is no sleeping woman resting on the bank. The same voice calls to him from the woods. The shadow is not so terrifying now that he knows what it is. *Unexplained presence*, he writes, and then adds a little winking face next to it: *;-)*. In his own very professional way, it's kind of like telling Kai, "We've been down this road before."

When Kai comes, she greets him and rolls her eyes. "This again?"

"Never boring!"

"Speak for yourself. And Abernathy?"

"Yes?"

"Don't ever wink at me again."

This time they walk down the creek bank. It is the early days of February and Abernathy feels déjà vu over his déjà vu. In the dark he realizes what escaped him the last time he visited this dream, on Christmas. It is the same dream as the first dream he ever entered. Though this time, the creek is not muddy, or flooded. The trees are not waterlogged. There is no dying and dead child. He does not have to swim to get to shore.

That means he has been here three times.

"Is it normal to repeat dreams?" he asks Kai.

She gives him a side look, shrugs. "Anything about this job seem *normal* to you?"

OK. Talk about a nonanswer.

Like last time, when it was Kai, the sleeping dreamer, the shadow, and himself, a voice beckons them into the forest. The voice is eerie and light. This time, Abernathy isn't scared.

He walks into the trees and the moon above is obscured. The trees are massive, their tops disappearing into the dark. It smells like vole and pine. As they walk, the floor is cushioned by a layer of fallen leaves, needles, branches. Mushrooms glitter white in the dark.

"Do you think," Abernathy asks, "that we ever end up in the dreams of people we know?"

Kai doesn't answer—probably because she is pretending not to hear him. Though it's hard to know if it's pretend or not with Kai. Maybe that's what being a coworker is: spending all your time together and knowing nothing about one another. Not knowing who someone is but instead knowing how they will act. It's a strange and unique intimacy. It means nothing and it means everything. Abernathy doesn't know if he likes it or not. He's never been very good at wrapping up and putting parts of himself into hiding. Being able to compartmentalize yourself seems like a requirement of almost every job he's ever worked.

They follow a small beaten path until the trees grow less dense around them. Soon the forest floor gives way into a grand ballroom. The floor is covered in roots and leaves. This time, he and Kai go deeper in, following the voice. The farther in, the less the parquet floor is broken up by thick roots of trees. Leaves scatter. A grand staircase opens upward into nothing. Large windows frame sparkling darkness on all sides.

As he and Kai near, Abernathy sees that the glass of the windows has been smashed.

In this room Abernathy feels very small.

The voice, this time, seems to be coming from the field on the other side of the windows.

"I don't know about this, Kai," Abernathy says. The two workers step through the shattered frames, careful to avoid the jagged glass of the sill.

"What *do* you know about?" Kai grumbles, but Abernathy detects a hint of humor in her voice.

The field is empty, except for a magnificent oak tree. The grass covers the tops of their boots and sways in the nonexistent wind. As they near, Abernathy slows. A swing on the other side of the tree comes in and out of view. A dark creature sways back and forth.

Abernathy stops.

"You're such a baby," Kai says.

Abernathy is too scared to argue.

"Nothing to say to that?"

"Not at this juncture."

"Have it your way, then. Wait here."

Kai crouches low. As she moves in and out of the full moon's light, she disappears and reappears, like a magic trick. The swing stops swinging.

For a moment Abernathy's fear is muted. Instead, a kinship with the tree swells inside of him. It's as if the tree is part of him and he is part of the tree. He can feel the rough bark, the creaking of the swing as it pulls at a sturdy branch, thousands of leaves fluttering for him and only him. He thinks, maybe, this feeling? Maybe it's peace.

He hears Kai's pack turn on. The darkness begins to wobble. The tree warbles as if resisting the force.

But unlike last time, something has gone wrong.

In bursts of light from the moon, he sees that Kai is running toward him, across the field line, in and out of the shadows. It is a neat trick of light, and for a moment Abernathy is stunned by the beauty and the strangeness of his life. As Kai passes him, she shouts.

"Run, you idiot! Run!"

"Wha—"

The shadowy man staggers out from behind the tree, into the clearing. From what Abernathy can see from the light of the moon, the man looks rabid and angry. Except the shadow is not a man. He is now a woman. He is now Kai. Or a doppelgänger of Kai. Wispy blackness bleeds in strands from the doppelgänger's figure. It is getting closer, disappearing and reappearing in the shafts of light. Abernathy can see its face.

The doppelgänger runs on all fours.

Abernathy does not have to be told twice. He breaks into a sprint for the abandoned house. He can hear Kai in front of him, the real Kai, as she trips through the window and curses, but he can't exactly see her. Just the white of her pack as it recedes inside.

Abernathy is close behind. He vaults over the window sill. His hand gets caught in the glass and it wrenches him back. He pulls hard. The beast is nearing. His suit splits at the glove and he is running again, his hand savagely cold now that it is exposed to the night air.

Kai is just ahead of him. He can see the white of her pack weaving through the forest. The other Kai is behind him. Abernathy can hear it breathing. He is too scared to look back. Never has he run this fast in his life. He is almost at real Kai's side.

"Grab on!" she says.

"What?"

"Grab ON!"

He reaches out, takes hold of her elbow with the hand now exposed. Stumbling, running, staggering. The other Kai is behind them. Wisps of black escape her. The false Kai reaches out. Abernathy can feel her hand on the back of his shirt. The tips of her fingers graze his lower back.

"Stop," the other gurgles, and it sounds like she is speaking from very far away, or perhaps from beneath some vast chasm. No longer is the voice high and lilting. It is as if the voice is Kai's. "Stop."

Her fingers feel *real*.

She feels *real*.

In front of him, the real Kai heaves her palm against her teleport. The two of them, Kai and Abernathy, the real Kai and the real Abernathy, are catapulted out of the dream, into another, where they lay flat on their backs, gasping, gasping, gasping. Gasping for breath.

THE STARS ARE bright. All around them is darkness. Empty gray expanse dotted by tiny blinkering lights. Abernathy sucks in air. Pushes air out. They lie on their backs on a gray rock. His heart is really going inside him. His hand is painfully cold, the tips of his fingers prickling. On the horizon, a white horse stands idle and alone. They are on the moon. A horse on the horizon of the moon. Behind the horse, Earth looms emerald and blue.

Here's Abernathy's big question: "Why did we run?"

"What?"

"Your pack. It didn't work. Why did we run?"

"Oh."

Abernathy can't stop mouth breathing. Just heaving oxygen. His hand *hurts*. He sits up to better look at Kai. Real Kai. There is red on her suit where he grabbed on. He looks down at his hand and realizes that he is bleeding. A wide dark cut has opened in the center of his palm. It stings. Around the cut his skin has turned the dark, fuzzy purple of frostbite. He pulls his ruined glove carefully around the hand, but that doesn't do much to lessen the buzzing pain.

Eyes closed, Kai breathes delicately: in through her nose, out through her mouth.

When Abernathy looks down at his torn glove, the plastic is healed. His suit is whole again.

Inside his suit, his hand still stings. The stabbing cold has abated. The inside of the glove is slick with blood.

"Don't we usually, you know—here he makes the sound of a vacuum— "*rrrrr*?"

Kai shakes her head back and forth. She hasn't opened her eyes yet.

Abernathy takes the moment to look around. There's nothing behind them. Only the horse in front. Earth in the distance. Whose dream was this?

Kai is still on her back. She holds her breath, opens her helmet, and pushes the green goggles up into her hairline before closing the visor again. Her eyes still closed, she inhales deep.

"Are you ignoring me?" Abernathy asks.

"Sorry," she says. This is the first time she apologizes to him. Despite the adrenaline, his stomach flutters. Abernathy decides he will treasure this apology. She respects him after all. "It's just," she says. Is she upset? She clears her throat. "I wasn't expecting to see myself so soon."

"Ohhhh," he says, as if he knows anything at all. He asks, "Well, do you have a sister? Maybe it was her. Can you know the people who are dreaming?"

After a pause Kai says, "That's the weird thing." Her voice trembles. She clears it.

"Oh?"

"My mentor—my officer, before I was an officer—she said she saw—well. In a dream, she said she saw herself."

"Ah. OK, so, we know it happens. No big deal. It's like a rite of passage. It's cool."

"No, Abernathy. It's not cool."

"Sounds cool to me," he says, trying to cheer her. "I mean, scary. Definitely scary. But also? Doppelgängers are *Cool*."

"My mentor is dead."

"Oh."

Abernathy is uncomfortable. It seems slightly inappropriate to bring up a dead mentor at a time like this. Like a trick. How was he supposed to know her mentor was dead? Should he comfort her? She doesn't seem like the type of person who needs comfort, but surely everyone must need comfort of some kind.

He forces himself to ask: "How did she die?"

It's, like, seriously cold on the moon. Nothing lives. Yet on the horizon the lone horse lifts its head and chews its mouthful of gravel looking wistfully into the distance.

Abernathy scooches over to Kai to be ready—should she need comfort, he *will* comfort her. From this angle her face is soft, her eyelids shimmery with green eyeshadow. He can see flecks of dried hairspray or gel or whatever it is that she uses to lay her edges. To him this is very sweet and his appreciation for her as a friend and a person grows.

"It's not that I didn't try to remove it," Kai says. "I tried to suck it up. But it wouldn't budge. Everything around it kept disappearing, the trees and stuff. But whatever that thing was, it stayed put."

"Is that bad?"

"Yes!" she says. She covers her visor with her hands and takes a deep, rattling breath. "Yes. That's only supposed to happen to the dreamer. You can't suck up the dreamer. Yet it couldn't be the dreamer, could it? It's shadows. But then my pack started to shudder and the shadows transformed into . . . well, *me*."

Kai removes her hands from her eyes. The first thing she sees is Abernathy's face. He is peering down at her, into her, trying to show he cares.

"Eugh!" Kai says. "Jesus!" She breaks eye contact. Rolling over, she stands up. "Forget it! What would you know about any of this." She dusts off her knees and looks around.

Abernathy scrambles to stand, too.

"I know about things," he says.

"Oh yeah?" she dusts off her suit. Hoists her pack back onto her shoulders. "Like what?"

Abernathy knows enough to know that she doesn't want him to actually answer the question. They stand on a stranger's subconscious moon. Kai, arms crossed, stares at Earth. Abernathy stares at Kai.

He squints but cannot tell: Are those tears in her eyes or the magnificent beauty of Earth, reflecting?

## 16

RHODA IS LATE GETTING HOME. She wakes Abernathy just as he steps, ill prepared, into a dream. He comes out of the dream and it is as if he is being wrenched from many lakes. Panic has filled his lungs like water. He does not know where he is. He is surprised to learn he is on the couch, although he does not have a couch. Where has the couch come from? The TV is whirring: ugly men who sell other people's precious items for a profit debate among themselves. Abernathy does not have a TV. In those first dregs of waking, it takes him a moment to realize he is not in his home, but Rhoda's. Timmy is in bed. Abernathy fell asleep while watching her.

"Rhoda!" Abernathy sits up. He is groggy and his voice is full of sleep. His hand is still stinging. Even though it has been two weeks, his cut will not heal. "What time is it?"

Rhoda looks at him funny. In the thin light of the TV, Abernathy realizes his shirt has come unbuttoned. His collar is exposed. Parts of his chest. The skin over his heart. He fumbles with the tiny buttons. He tries to comb down his hair (he's sure it's sticking straight up). Rhoda reaches out to him. Abernathy freezes. She hesitates, then pulls her thumb softly beneath his eye.

"Sleep in your eye," she says.

"Ah."

The two look at each other.

Is she drunk?

"Did you have a good night out?" he asks. Her makeup is a little smudged, which makes her look beautiful. Sort of like the way painters add error to paintings so that the human eye mistakes it for movement. Movement implies life.

She asks, "Were you dreaming?"

"What?"

"Were you dreaming?"

"I . . . was about to be," he says.

"Ah," she says. "I'm sorry for pulling you away."

Abernathy laughs. "Never be sorry for pulling me away."

"Does it feel like work now? Sleeping?"

Abernathy frowns. "Very much so."

There is a small pause. They are talking in hushed voices. The TV is still on. She asks, "What did you used to dream about? Before you dreamed for other people?"

"Oh," he says.

The conversation is so strange he wonders if *this* is a dream. Rhoda sits close to him. He can feel her blood moving through her and heat moving through her and her life. Her life is touching him. The feeling of her life makes Abernathy dizzy, as if he were the one who had been drinking.

"A very personal question," he says.

"Do you have a very personal answer?" Her leg touches his leg.

"I—"

"No, no," she says abruptly. She must be drunk. She stands and begins to take off her shoes, wobbling on one foot and then the other as she removes strappy heels. The buckle snags on her panty hose and a tiny tear forms. Definitely drunk. "Don't answer." She smiles a laughing smile and falls back on the couch with a sigh. Is she making fun of him? Is she actually smiling? Has he made her smile? Abernathy feels warm. Her eyes flutter close and her breathing deepens. She says, "I wouldn't want us to be too personal."

She must be making fun of him.

Abernathy is very confused. He starts to get the feeling that there is a conversation beneath the conversation that he has somehow missed. He has the feeling that this happens to him a lot. That things happen and then he doesn't notice and then they are gone before he can enjoy them. Conversations taking place beneath the conversations taking place. Who knows what all he's missed. He could see how, to someone else, he may seem like a completely different person.

"I like being personal with you," he blurts out.

He thinks about moving closer. He doesn't.

She laughs. "We have very different definitions of personal, don't we?"

She holds out her hand, the one with LUCK tattooed across the knuckles. He takes it. He helps her up from the couch and now they both stand. "I got you something, at the restaurant. If you want it." She hands him a tiny box.

He takes it with his uninjured right hand. The cardboard reminds him of the dream archives, where black tadpoles of the subconscious breathe alone in the dark. It is not too heavy. His box in the archives must be heavier than this by now.

With the way she's looking at him, Abernathy knows he has definitely missed something. Either an opportunity that he was supposed to take or some other stupid thing he's probably forgotten. If he were to open the box, he would know. Inside is a small cake, for Valentine's day, shaped like a heart.

Rhoda is looking at Abernathy with great specificity. He doesn't know how to describe it. Back into his eyes, she says, "Open it when you get home."

"What?"

She turns her back to him and begins unhooking her earrings. Her voice is back to normal. "Thank you again," she says. "For watching Timmy."

Walking across his driveway he has that feeling. But for the life of him he can't figure out what it is. After all, there is more work to do.

In the morning, though he searches everywhere, he cannot find the box or the heart shaped cake within.

There is always more work to do.

BUT INSTEAD OF doing more work, Abernathy drags a folding chair onto the driveway. He wears a puffy jacket still, but the spring sun is bright and covers him in a warmth he hasn't felt in months. Occasionally Abernathy lifts his head to sip red-can Coke from a straw. The sugar moves through him like a marching band, cymbalically lifting his twanging spirits. All the leaves are green and newborn above him. They dance with the wind in celebration. Life returns! The flower buds—pink, white, yellow, orange—emerge.

It is mid-March and the cut Abernathy received on his left hand several weeks ago still has not healed.

He keeps gauze wrapped around it, a thin white cloth that he must change every third day. His cut will not scab, and continues its slow oozing of almost-but-not-quite-clotted blood. On the third day the gauze develops a red dot of color that, throughout the day, spreads. The edge of the cut is the color of the frostbite: dark purple, almost black. If it didn't hurt so much, he would think the colors looked like the colors of a painting.

Abernathy believes his cut will not heal because it is on his palm, a part of his body constantly in movement. A scab cannot form when the hand is in motion, he reasons.

But if he were to cut his right hand now, as he sits in the uncharacteristic warmth of the March sun, he would see the two cuts were not the same caliber at all. If he were to cut his right hand, the wound would heal in less than a week.

He does not do this, of course. Why should he? To him, all is right in the world. His body is not worth worrying about. Today is his birthday. He is one year older, twenty-seven, which means Abernathy has worked at the Archive for exactly one year and two weeks. This birthday is Jonathan Abernathy's second to last.

Our sweet boy raises his head to sip from the can and tells himself the trees above him are dancing for him.

In the corner of his eye, beneath the dancing trees, a shadow seems to move of its own accord.

Abernathy sits up. The shadow stills.

He sits watching the shadow for several minutes.

A trick of the light, he decides, and lays back down so the sun can move through him as it desires.

He thinks of those small boxes holding impossible tadpoles of darkness within. For a brief moment he believes there is probably no point in celebrating himself or his life. No point in celebrating because there is more work to do. Always more work to do, more work to do. More work to do, more work to do, more work to do. To do more work. There will be work every day and every moment until one day death moves inside him as death moves inside all of us, breaking us from the branches of our life so we can be free.

This thought? Abernathy pushes it away. He focuses, instead, on the present. The sun is nice. The wind, fresh and crisp, ushering the world back to life. He sees Rhoda's curtains rustling behind the windows and he thinks, maybe later, he will drop in and say hello.

Abernathy shuts his eyes. On the back of his eyelids he can see the imprints of leaves moving in and out of the light.

## 17

**TONIGHT KAI ARRIVES WELL AFTER** Abernathy summons her. Over the last three months, she has become less and less talkative. In a parking lot plagued by birds, he greets her with enthusiasm and excitement. Kai will not make eye contact with him.

Things have grown increasingly tense since their time on the moon. Lately, when he submits his paperwork, Kai does not come. If she does come, it's in a team of four or five people. Abernathy has been working with the pompous blowhard, Jason. Abernathy does not want to express how relieved he is to see Kai in case she decides to go away again.

She looks like she has lost weight. The dark circles under her eyes have grown. When he makes a sudden movement, she jumps.

"Kai," Abernathy says, swatting away a swarm of chittering long-winged birds. This dreamer must be ornithophobic. The birds circle him. "How are you?"

It is sunset. The parking lot is empty, desolate, and gray. A tornado of blue-black crows volley around them. If Abernathy half closes his eyes and squints, the crows look like dark clouds forming and breaking apart in the sky. For a moment, the crows seem to form Kai's face above them. But then, in a blink, the formation is gone. They are once again just crows.

Kai squints into the sky. "I hate birds," she says.

"They're not too bad, when you give them the chance. Quite beautiful. Sometimes."

Kai gives Abernathy a scathing look, and does not deign to answer him.

The birds do not look like normal birds. They are very wispy indeed. Black tendrils curl from their wings, smoky at the tips. As the birds career through the air, the black wisps disappear upward, and fade into the clouds.

"I'm surprised I haven't seen you recently," Abernathy begins conversationally. He slots his hands on his hips and rocks back and forth on his toes. "Been a bit lonely without you around. I've had to work with Jason. Total idiot. Not cool at all."

Kai watches the birds tornado for a long time. Her eyes follow their eddying as their blackness slowly fills the sky. The birds bring the night.

"Kai? Hello? Earth to Kai. You still there?"

Slowly Kai slides her eyes over to him. Darkness is falling. The way she looks at him is unexpected. From behind those deep-circled eyes is a look of anger, fury. A great, unknowable sadness. The look of someone who knows they will never, truly, be free.

"Kai . . ." Abernathy starts. It's been less than five minutes since she's arrived, but something is different. She carries with her a weight. He asks, "Are you OK?"

Kai does not look okay. Kai looks haunted. Kai looks like she has seen a ghost.

"You'll probably have to get used to working with Jason," she says dryly. Her smile is taut and forced and more than a little mean. She turns on her pack and the thrumming fills the lot.

"Oh, don't say that. I like working with you."

Her laugh is scornful and echoed by the crows.

"Is this about the time in the field?" Abernathy delicately asks. He hesitates, then decides it would be okay to say what he is thinking, maybe. "I am really sorry about the other you. I am still kind of confused about what happened, but I can tell it really upset you."

Kai frowns, then laughs again. But this time it is a sort of wet choking sound. Actually more like a sob than a laugh, now that Abernathy thinks about it. Abernathy *is* confused. Though he has sensed something was off between them these last few weeks, he did not know anything was wrong until just now. He had gone on with his February fine. He had dutifully arrived in March. He can see time has passed differently for Kai.

This is the first time that Abernathy realizes time can pass differently for different people, and the shock of it makes him mentally stagger.

That one or two months can go by between friends and completely change the terms of the friendship was, until this moment, unfathomable to him. Time works on two people in unique, incongruous ways. Sometimes the incongruity is enough that the dual perception cannot be repaired.

Kai's eyes are frenzied, looking frantically across the birds as if she could read in their formation some type of answer. She points her hose into the sky and the birds dive toward her. They disappear into her pack, but instead of the sun returning, the darkness grows deeper. The cars begin to shudder. Soon they are folding in on themselves, devoured by Kai who removes the birds, the cars, the asphalt, the trees, the paint, the sky.

"Whoa!" Abernathy says. "Slow down."

The dream is disappearing around them, revealing nothing but murky shadows underneath.

Kai's face is desperate. But only for a moment. When the moment ends, she is contemptuous, and far away, and cold.

Her look is scathing. Without answering, Kai catapults Abernathy into the next dream.

THE DREAM STUTTERS upon the elevator's opening. Abernathy stumbles and falls to his knees. The two figures in front of him glitch in their walk, but moments after resume their pace down the hallway beneath the outer city office which leads to the archive of dreams.

The two figures wear the white jumpsuits of dream workers and walk briskly ahead of him. Abernathy stands quickly, calls ahead and asks them to wait, but they seem not to hear.

He's never audited a dream with other dream workers. He doesn't know what to do. He tries to speed up, to get to them. He reaches them just as they near a door.

"Thanks for waiting," he says as he catches his breath. "What is it about dreamers and hallways, you know?"

"I think this one will be a good asset," says the small one. She doesn't seem to hear Abernathy. She has a clipboard and is flipping through it. "Pled guilty for a B and E when she was seventeen. Seemed like a relatively harmless break-in, but the older lady whose house it was died while she was there. Poor kid got convicted on manslaughter. Seems like a case of terrible luck."

The taller one, who Abernathy recognizes as the man who followed him and Kai down the hallway of dreams the last time they were here—Penn, the same guy who had recruited Abernathy—sighs. He sounds dreadfully bored, "I'm *so* tired of criminals. You would think management would bother recruiting more interesting people."

"You forget who you are talking to, Penn."

The taller man gives her a lazy smile that makes Abernathy feel sure he has not forgotten who he is speaking to at all. In the dark of the hallway, his smile is just as terrifying as it was before.

"Have I? Don't you think they're just so expendable? They seem to have no . . ." Penn searches the air for a word. "Staying power. I'm always replacing them."

"Well, maybe if you didn't give them the most draining—"

Before she can finish, Penn holds up his hand in interruption. "No need for us to bore each other further with politics."

The smaller woman bristles but falls silent. She straightens the clipboard's papers.

Abernathy peers over her shoulder. Her clipboard contains the same test that they asked Abernathy to take when he was recruited: full of hypothetical dreams and potential audits.

Penn opens the hallway door and gestures to the woman in a parody of politeness.

"After you," he says.

She brushes past him. Abernathy follows.

The room is small. A tiny bedroom lit only by a lamp covered in many ruby scarves. It is dark and stuffy. There is an old lady asleep on the bed, cocooned within many quilts.

Kai sits beside her, holding her hand.

"Kai!" Abernathy exclaims, mostly out of surprise. Neither the auditors nor Kai hear him. Kai seems lost in thought. When she does look up, it is because the smaller officer has cleared her throat.

Kai jumps up from her seat at the old lady's side and steps in front of the woman as if to protect her. "What are you doing here?"

Penn looks around disdainfully. "*This* is what you dream of?" He gives the smaller woman a meaningful look that she intentionally does not see.

"Hello, Kai," says the woman. "We are here to help you."

"Help me?" Kai sounds skeptical.

Now that Abernathy is looking at her, she does look younger. Maybe by a few years. Not young enough to be seventeen, but definitely not as old as she is now. Was this her memory? Is this how she was recruited? Maybe this is just a false version of her, not the real her at all, and this is some type of test.

As if on cue, he sees his own clipboard and pen on a dresser.

"We work at a special section of the government—"

Kai interrupts, she sounds hateful. "I don't want anything to do with the government."

If Abernathy had any doubt as to who this dreamer was, they are immediately dispelled. This is definitely Kai. No one else can sound so proud in so few words.

"See? There you are," says Penn to his coworker. "Let's go."

The woman gives Penn an exasperated look, not at all friendly, and then smiles at Kai. "I think you will quite like our offer, once you hear it."

Abernathy jumps when a gloved hand touches his back. It is Kai as he knows her, his coworker. She is older, and compared to her younger self, she looks much harrowed.

"Kai!" Abernathy looks between her and her younger version. "What's going on? I haven't summoned you yet."

Her face is hardened and her eyes are cold. Her hand is at the button on her belt. Abernathy realizes that she is going to catapult him out.

Before Abernathy goes, he sees her turn to Penn. Penn cannot see her. He must be part of the dream. Still, Kai musters up all her hate and looks him in the eye. She says something that confuses Abernathy. She says, first to Penn and then to Abernathy: "I won't let you take this from me. It's *mine*."

## 18

RHODA FINDS OUT ABERNATHY HID his birthday from her and she is livid. It is the first time Abernathy ever sees her mad. Which is sort of confusing. He points out he didn't *hide* his birthday from her so much as he just didn't tell her.

"It's the same thing," she says.

"No, it's not."

"It's called *lying*."

He is carrying a cooler to her car for her. "I wasn't lying," he says, "I just . . . wasn't saying."

"That counts as lying."

"Nothing wrong with having different philosophies, Rhoda."

"I would say it's a matter of ethics, not philosophy, *Jonathan*."

"Well," he says grinning, "I reject your fundamental premise. This is a problem of perspective."

"Yeah," says Rhoda, "and I'm just supposed to agree that your perspective is best? Are you saying my claim isn't worth considering?"

"I would never lie to you," Abernathy says.

"You're so full of shit."

"That," Abernathy says laughing, "we can agree on."

Rhoda is directing him with monotone anger: "Put that here," "Lift this up," "Move this." Eventually she tells him, "Oh, just let me do it," and he goes to stand over by Timmy, who has been leaning against the deck rail reading for some time now. Rhoda, fussing with the hiking boots, and the cooler, and the bags, has a small smile on her face, though she is attempting to hide this smile. In belated celebration of Abernathy's birthday, the three of them are going to the lake.

Timmy looks up from her book at Abernathy and makes a face. Abernathy realizes suddenly she must be older. There is something leaving her. Childhood wisdom, maybe. She is becoming more real, an awkward and painful process that had certainly not been fun for Abernathy when he went through it. He hears that's how it is for everyone.

"Don't worry," Timmy says, mistaking his shock. "She's like this a lot, she just pretends not to be around you."

"Like what?"

"Flustered."

Abernathy doesn't understand what Timmy means, but it's too late to ask. She has gone back to her book. Abernathy has been around long enough to know better than to ask Timmy questions when she is in a book.

THE LAKE IS more of a pond than a lake, but it is beautiful. The water is murky and green. The trees are large. It is late April and flowers are in bloom. Petals drift down from the sky to land with gold and white glory upon the pond's surface. On the edges of the pond, turtles slide from rocks into deep water. Their spelunking sounds like a tiny audience applauding as Abernathy, Rhoda, and Timmy pull up.

The cabin is one Rhoda often went to as a girl and belongs to a family friend. Timmy immediately begins to make herself at home. There are two rooms, one with twin bunk beds and one with a double mattress. Timmy goes straight to the back room with bunk beds and closes the door. Abernathy lugs in his sleeping suit and places it in the living room. Soon Rhoda and Abernathy hear music from Timmy's room.

Rhoda and Timmy have come to the pond house often, but strangely Abernathy also feels at home, as if he has been here before.

"She's at that stage, huh?"

Rhoda gives him a long look. "Yes," she says. "She is very much at *that* stage."

He does not have to know Rhoda as well as he does to know exactly what she means.

The pond is nice, and though they are only there for a day and a night, Abernathy feels deeply special that Rhoda would bring him here with her daughter.

When he, Rhoda, and Timmy pull a small paddle boat out of the weeds and paddle out into the middle of the lake, Abernathy realizes that he is living one of the best and most pure moments of his life. The sound of the water, the petals drifting down upon them, Timmy's laughter when a bug lands in Abernathy's hair, the way Rhoda turns to the back of the paddle boat and smiles so radiantly. Abernathy has never seen her smile before. Before her smile, Jonathan Abernathy never experienced anything so pure and golden. It is so much good feeling, in fact, that his heart is close to catching in his chest. His blood is moving very fast. He feels a surreal disconnection from the mother and daughter. Like this life is too good to be his own.

As the three of them make dinner, Rhoda refuses to turn on the lights and instead unpacks a small bag of tea candles that she lights and places around the main room. All they make is a frozen cheese pizza, but in the candlelight with the owls hooting softly in the distance and the frogs plopping lightly into the mud for their nightly slumber, the frozen pizza feels like the best meal of Jonathan Abernathy's life.

What do they talk about? They talk about nothing. They talk at one another, and to one another, and of one another. They repeat their inside jokes, and rehearse their long-loved bits.

Abernathy feels, suddenly, that these are his people and that these people are his life.

When Timmy sequesters herself in the back room for the evening, Abernathy begins to unfold his ratty comforter and pillow to make up the couch. Rhoda sits on the floor, with the bottle of wine they are drinking. She watches him, amused.

"What are you doing?" she asks.

"I'm making the couch."

"And why would you do that?"

"What?"

"Stop doing that and come sit by me."

Oblivious, Abernathy stops unfolding the blanket and sits down next to her. She pours him another glass of wine. Her hair is longer now. Abernathy realizes his is, too, though he doesn't remember that being a conscious decision. The edges loop around the bottom of his ears, and curl into his neck. Abernathy is so giddy with contentment that he doesn't feel drunk at all. Or maybe he does. He can't tell. The only thing he can tell is that he is flooded by total, serene happiness.

He believes this moment of happiness to be the first time of many, and the thought excites him.

"You don't need to go to work yet," Rhoda says. She scooches over a bit, so that their knees are touching. She is sitting cross-legged, and the green of her socks are peeking out from beneath her jeans. Her socks are one of Abernathy's favorite part of her wardrobe. They are, unlike the rest of her dark outfits, colorful. Yet they are rarely revealed. It's always a surprise to see which pair she is wearing. He is never able to guess.

"Did you have a good late birthday?" she asks. The wine is almost piney, and reminds Abernathy of Rhoda's perfume. Though maybe he is drunk and what he's tasting is the smell of the woods floating through the open screen door.

He looks into his wineglass (a coffee mug) for a moment. He is suddenly overcome by a sweeping wave of feeling that he can't quite put his finger on. Like he is going to cry out of sadness, but not really out of sadness, actually, more like out of the inconceivability of life. Like life is an infinity of beauty, and he is only just now realizing it. Except, in realizing it, the beauty and the happiness are suddenly hurting him.

This is the first time Abernathy has ever been happy in love, which means that he is realizing, for the first time, that this type of happiness must end. It is a bittersweet feeling, holding both truths at once.

The thought of losing this moment, when he has only just received it, causes his vision to double.

Rhoda must not think he hears her, so she repeats her question. "Did you have a good birthday?"

Abernathy clears his throat. "I had," he says, and maybe this is too intense, but he means it and it feels important to say, "the best birthday."

"Oh, shut up," she says.

"No," he says, and he is very serious. "I mean it. The best."

"Really?" She is looking at him, searching his face. Her face is more open than usual, more readable. He drags his eyes to her eyes, though it is suddenly very hard to do so. He feels like he is seeing her—like, actually really seeing her—and it feels sort of like looking directly into the sun.

"Really."

"Thank you for saying that."

She sets her wineglass down and puts her head in his lap. He freezes. Her hair pools against his knee.

"Is this OK?" she asks. It is very unlike her, and thus touches him immensely.

"Yes," Abernathy says. He clears his throat and this helps him unfreeze. A warmth spreads through his body and he feels his hand being pulled toward her shoulder, and then her neck, where he traces a finger up the small vein that runs from her jaw to her ear and then back again. The world's smallest traced infinity. It feels incalculable to him.

## 19

IT IS QUIET IN TONIGHT'S dream. Abernathy arrives in a small house on the outskirts of a town he is unfamiliar with. As Abernathy stands in the yard (his plastic suit already stiflingly hot), an older woman opens the front door of the house and slowly descends her stairs. Her car is in the driveway, gleaming beneath the hot afternoon sun. The woman stutters a bit as she comes down the front steps, but then she catches her stride and a young woman exits behind her.

"Who is it today?" the girl asks. She sounds young. She is locking up the house. The grandmother has made it to the walk now. Abernathy begins looking for his clipboard.

"The Richardsons." The grandmother has a strong, honeyed voice.

"Oh, God."

"Don't take The Lord's name in vain, please, ma'am."

The girl laughs. "OK then, have it your way. How's this: I'm praying for us. We're going to need a miracle."

"Amen."

The girl bounds down from the steps and loops her arm through the woman's. Abernathy cannot see the girl's face. "Maybe it won't be too awful."

The older woman snorts.

"That bad, Nan?"

"Worse. They're having some type of *event*."

"Tonight?"

"Uh-huh."

"For Halloween?"

"Yes, ma'am."

The girl sounds shrill, almost panicked, in her reply. "Well, how long do we have to clean, then?"

"Four hours, baby girl."

"For that whole house! Oh my *God*. We are *fucked*. We are totally and completely—"

"Watch yourself, now."

The girl lets go of her grandmother's arm and jogs to the car and opens the passenger door for the older woman. As the girl swings toward him, Abernathy sees that the girl is a younger Kai. This startles him.

Abernathy looks closer and sees that the older woman Kai is with, is the woman from her earlier dream who lay in bed under the red-silk-covered lamp. Abernathy had already started to think of things to take away—the older woman? the house? the car? This did not seem like a nightmare to him. But when Kai turns her face to him, Abernathy drops his clipboard to the side.

Kai looks young. Seventeen. Or maybe younger. Younger, certainly, than she had been in the last dream. As her grandmother ambles down the walk, Kai bounds around the car to get in the driver seat.

Abernathy makes his decision.

"What are you doing, old woman, pick up the pace, we got places to be!"

Instead of auditing the dream, Abernathy gets in the back seat.

YOUNGER KAI IS a good driver. She pulls the car up in front of a large house surrounded by countryside. Abernathy realizes the large house is actually the mansion with the parquet floors. Abernathy has never been in a dream this long. There is already another car in the driveway. Kai gets out and pops the trunk. When the grandmother gets out of the passenger side, another young woman gets out of the other car. She is visibly pregnant.

"Nice to see you today, Rhoda!" the grandmother calls.

"Oh, Mrs. S.T., you know I always feel the same."

From the trunk where she is gathering cleaning supplies, Kai calls to her grandmother, "You didn't tell me Rhoda was our *backup*."

The grandmother laughs. "I wanted to scare you a little, honey. You were taking forever."

Rhoda is pale and a little older than Kai. The two women are inside the house by the time Abernathy manages to get out of the car, stunned and slowed by confusion. He fumbles with the handle of the car door only to open it and find himself in the large, grand ballroom. Rhoda and Kai, wearing kneepads, are scrubbing the floor with a bright orange bristled brush and a bucket of soapy gray water. The two women are laughing and talking to each other, not candidly enough to be close friends, he assumes, but certainly they must be coworkers in some capacity. They are comfortable with each other, but there is a divide there. The same way there is a divide between himself and Kai, though the kinship between the two young women seems more amicable than his own with Kai.

Abernathy is nearing them when he hears a group of voices behind him. He turns and it is the family of the house. A much older woman is being helped up a grand staircase by two young men. Kai watches them out of the corner of her eye as they go. Rhoda keeps scrubbing. She does not notice Kai's gaze.

"How much do you think one of her necklaces alone could buy us?" Kai asks.

Rhoda laughs, a louder laugh than Abernathy has ever heard. He realizes that's what is so off. In this dream, Rhoda has emotions. She is smiling. She is frowning. She is side-eyeing, and sighing, and rolling her eyes and laughing with her teeth.

"Oh, probably a few souls." Rhoda says. "Definitely my soul at least."

The two girls smile at each other.

Abernathy crouches down next to them, but they appear not to be able to see him. This close, their faces look strange. Less hardened, but still tired. "Hello?" he asks them, but they do not hear.

"Being a maid sucks ass," Kai says.

Rhoda shrugs and twists a sponge into the soapy water, bringing it down to the floor. "What would you be otherwise?"

"I want to be a florist."

Rhoda raises her eyebrows. "A florist? *You?*"

"Yeah," says Kai. "I want to do weddings. I'm good under pressure and I like it when people are in love."

"I wouldn't have guessed that about you, Kai St. Clair, not in a million years."

Kai grins.

"Well tell you what," says Rhoda, throwing the bristle pad and sponges into her bucket. She gets laboriously up to her feet, her belly impeding her movements. Kai stands, too, and the two girls move toward the stairs. "I'll be your first customer."

Kai frowns. "That son of a bitch finally asked?"

Rhoda blushes happily and puts her hand on her stomach. "Is it a shotgun wedding if I'm showing?"

"That man does not need a shotgun held up to his head to marry you."

Rhoda laughs and they begin to ascend the stairs.

Abernathy is about to follow the women to the upstairs bathroom where they have to clean the floor-to-ceiling glass shower. His new officer, Jason, appears as Abernathy reaches the second landing. The hallway opens to the grand foyer and the girls are off to the side. Jason's voice is nasally as always and echoes in the ballroom's expanse: "Why haven't you called me yet? Where's your paperwork?"

Abernathy jumps. The women have already rounded the corner. He has lost sight of them.

"What?"

"Your paperwork, Abernathy? Where is it?"

"Oh," Abernathy says. Come to think of it, the floor is incredibly shiny, the sun is setting through the large windows, and the women did say they only had one area left to clean before tonight's festivities. Abernathy is still listening hard to the girls in the bathroom, even though he can't make out what they're saying. He decides to lie. "I deposited a while ago. In the foyer? The two sons with the older woman. They need to go."

Jason looks at him for a long moment. He is a bad-postured middle-management type. His hair is ashy blond and his elbows are dry as hell. On principle, Abernathy hates him. But, Abernathy holds eye contact and eventually Jason buys the lie.

Abernathy keeps trying to listen to the women even as Jason starts to file the paperwork. It is too late. Abernathy can't hear a single word.

## 20

ABERNATHY DOESN'T WANT TO ACCOST Kai, but he decides tonight is the night for answers. It has been almost a month of working with Jason (awful, weirdly quiet all the time). May is ending and the heat of June is moving in.

He and Kai are in one of those dreams where an adult is reliving their childhood humiliation. Kai does not immediately catapult Abernathy out as she vacuums up children blowing raspberries, though this has been her favorite move lately: to eject him before he can say a word. Abernathy wants to ask Kai how she knows Rhoda, why he keeps visiting her old dreams, and if it has anything to do with their time with the doppelgänger. It has been impossible to talk to her.

Tonight Kai can't send Abernathy away early. There are too many children demanding too much attention and she needs Abernathy's help.

The children are mostly boys. They compress their cheeks with their hand so that their mouths look like wet, puckered assholes being split by a tongue.

Despite this holy sight, Kai still catches Abernathy looking at her.

"What do you want, Abernathy?"

Like the first day they met, her tone punctures his gusto.

"Oh, nothing," he says. "Nothing really. Just thought I would stick around and say hi. Hi, Kai."

"Hi."

"It's been awhile since we've chatted," he tries. "You know, like motto et motto."

"Mano a mano."

"That's what I meant. Mono e mono."

Lately, most of the dreams they have been assigned to have been dreams of expansive scale. Dreams which required the deployment of full retrieval squads to properly sanitize. Kai could ignore Abernathy in those dreams.

When Abernathy wasn't assigned to one of those big, sweeping nightmares, Kai always sent Jason. Jason sucked.

"Right," Kai says. One of the kids tries to run away, but Kai catches him by the heel of his bell bottom. The kid trips and struggles. His body folds into her hose.

"Jason couldn't work tonight?" Abernathy hedges.

Kai frowns. "He had some dumb wedding apparently."

"Lucky him!"

"You could say that. Or you could pray for his poor wife."

"I'm glad he's getting married," Abernathy tries. He's going slow with the conversation, because he doesn't want to scare Kai and she looks more scareable than usual. She is thin and moving slowly as the kids run in tight circles. Her glasses don't hide the circles under her eyes.

"Oh yeah?" she asks, mind clearly not on Abernathy at all. "Why's that?"

"Well, because I get to talk to you again, for one."

"Yea, OK."

Now is the time to conversationally strike. To strike and to strike with precision. Like an eagle. Eagles are very regal. Nothing at all like pigeons. To strike like an eagle amongst all the whining children, that's what Abernathy wants to do.

Abernathy clears his throat. He looks around the playground to make sure no other officers lurk at the corners. But no. Just children. Lots of children running in terror from Kai and himself.

"You know," he says. "As two adults who do things like participate in talking smally among themselves, I feel as if I should share one of the more recent topics that has plagued my mind. Perhaps this will be an ideal conversational topic for our time together today?"

He tries to make himself sound as friendly as possible. There is an implied smile in his words, like so:

♪ :) ♪

Kai closes her eyes and lets out a pained groan. "Please, God. Don't do this to me. Not today."

She speaks quietly, almost to herself. Abernathy pretends not to hear her.

"I'll go ahead then, unless there is protest?"

Kai grunts. A kid fights to free himself from Kai's hose without any luck. Abernathy identifies with this child who is pulled into her pack, screaming as he goes.

Abernathy treads lightly. "Lately, I have . . . well . . ."

He stops. Begins again, "I have found myself lately wondering at your level of job satisfaction, Kai?" He tries to play it like his formality is a joke—because of her ignoring him—but mostly he is just nervous. He hasn't felt comfortable telling Rhoda he saw her and Kai together in a dream.

Is Rhoda right?

Are omissions lies?

If so, Abernathy is a liar.

Kai looks murderous. She takes this anger out on a child who sneaks up behind her. She elbows the kid in the face before the kid can execute his plan of attack. He goes down, hard. Kai sucks him up face first. Two bloody knee prints remain on the gravel.

Abernathy quickly amends.

"On a scale of one to ten," he asks, "how satisfied are you? Ten being immensely satisfied. One being, well . . ."

"Abernathy?"

"Yes?"

"Shut up."

She ejects him into the next dream.

Blackness crushes around him. Abernathy arrives at a hospital room. A makeshift hospital room in what looks to be an old Faulknerian parlor. A man is being operated on. His eyes, clamped open, dart around the room with panic.

Abernathy doesn't look around much or really address the situation. He mostly wants to talk to Kai. And what does it matter, anyway, what the officers take from the dreamers? Kai took the entire dream of crows and no one complained about that. It's not as if there's some rubric to compare the before and after of their removal. As far as Abernathy can tell it all goes into a tiny box of absolute doom and then that doom is stored in a moldy broom closet of terror.

He writes *spooky surgeons* with his signature winky face and drops the paper to the floor.

Kai arrives, takes a quick look around, and seems less than impressed.

"This is your worst read yet," she says.

At the operating table, surgeons wear costumes and put their heads together. Their concave mirrors clink.

Abernathy tries to be gregarious, so Kai doesn't realize how desperate he is.

"Kai! How magnificent to run into you once again. How—"

"What did you say the problem was here?"

"Spooky surgeons," he says, straight faced. "But Kai, listen, about this talk. It's been a while since we've seen each other, hasn't it? You and me?"

"I saw you last night. And the night before that. And the night before that. I see you more than my own wife."

"Right," he says. "But, I mean, *really* see each other. Like, *you know*."

"I'm not trying to fuck you, dude."

"Wow! OK. No. *No*. What? No! That's not what I meant. I just mean—"

Kai has already turned from him. Abernathy gets the feeling she just said that to shut him up, but still his whole body is bright red with embarrassment and it takes a second for his heart to chill out.

Kai uses this time to look around the room. Abernathy does the same (mostly as a pretense for taking deep breaths). Chintzy armchairs upholstered in pink velvet rest against the baseboard. If he were to look closely, he could see the wear. Golden tassely curtains frame a window whose glass is punctuated by a low white moon.

At the operating table, a man being held down begins to scream as, in the corner of the room, a small black shadow ripples at the wall.

"Maybe we should catch up?" Abernathy offers Kai. "Talk about the old jobs we've had together. Relive our highlights. Really get down to the good stuff. Like, for instance, maybe our run in with your"—this part he whispers, realizing that if he doesn't say it now, he may never get the chance—"*lookalike*?

"This isn't a surgery room."

"Aw, don't change the subject, Kai. It's been months. I want to talk to you. Can't you tell how hard I'm trying?"

"This isn't a surgery room. You were wrong to label this a surgery room." Abernathy steels himself.

✓  Jonathan Abernathy you are charming.
✓  You are intelligent.
✓  You are a very good friend.

"How would you know that?" he asks

"Because," she says. "It's not my first time here."

She throws open the doors and she's right. They are, in fact, in a Victorian house, decorated lavishly to host a Halloween party. There is music. And chattering. The clicking of glass as punch is served.

As if in a dream (ha!), Kai and Abernathy are at the ground floor, in a ballroom-like setting, fenced in by grand windows, panes glittering with their reflections. Suddenly they are surrounded by men and women in costumes. A stranger puts Kai and Abernathy's hands together. A stranger lifts Kai and Abernathy's elbows into right angles. The group begins to swirl. And much to Kai's dislike, Abernathy and herself are part of the group.

So they are dancing. And it is quite funny. Mostly because of how uncomfortable it makes Kai and how often she keeps trying to pull away.

Two or three steps into the waltz, Kai manages to push Abernathy back. He falls on his ass, catching himself with his hand as he skids across the parquet floor. Abernathy ignores the guests, who look down at him in shock. He sees a young woman go up the stairs while everyone else is dancing. He does not recognize her, she is wearing a mask. But then he thinks, *no, that's not right.* It is the younger Kai, from the dream with Rhoda. The same young woman who cleaned these very floors. She is here, sneaking upstairs.

The Kai who caused him to trip stands above him. Her hand is at her belt, already moving to catapult him from the dream. He grabs her arm.

"Wait!" Abernathy says. He drops all the bullshitting and the false gusto and tries to just be really, really earnest. "Please," he says, "I want to talk to you."

"Let. Go."

Abernathy does not let go. In fact—and this surprises him—he tightens his grip. "*Don't*," he says. Her suit crinkles in his grip. "I don't know what's going on, but I can tell something's bothering you. Kai—I want to help. Please, let me help."

On the other side of her visor, Kai frowns. Her green eyeglasses glint off the glass.

"What did I tell you? I told you, you shouldn't have taken this job. You took the job anyway. Live with it."

"Why?" he asks. He is still sitting on the floor, reaching up to hold her in place. "Why not take the job? Because of a couple boxes in a small room? So what. They can have my dreams. I wasn't doing anything with them. I have every right to work, same as you."

"It's not about *rights*," she says, trying to shake him off. He tightens his grip. "God, it's like every time I start to like you even a tiny bit you say something astronomically dumber than before." Kai looks Abernathy in the eyes. She never looks him in the eye. "Listen close. I'll only say it once: People. Do. Not. Come. Back. From. This. Line. Of. Work. You fucking moron."

"Don't come back, like . . . ?"

"Yes," she spits. "Like that."

For a second Abernathy just sits there. He sees the younger Kai at the top of the stairs, and then she is gone, having receded into a room.

Abernathy won't see this, but in that room the younger Kai will find a pearl necklace worth $5,000. She will pocket it just as an older woman, the owner of the house, walks in. When the older woman walks in, she will confront Kai. The two will get into an argument. The older woman will be advancing when she collapses, a heart attack. Kai will rush toward her, but the woman won't be breathing. She will be entering cardiac arrest. The younger Kai will attempt to perform CPR. It is the younger Kai who will call the ambulance, and when the ambulance comes, so too will the police. In one hour they will be here and this young version of Kai will be in the back of a cruiser. The old woman will not live.

There are people in this world, Kai will later tell herself, who have sold themselves for less than $5,000.

(Still, a voice in her head says. Is that really all her freedom is worth? (Another voice answers that she would have done it for a thousand.))

Abernathy, merely a worker, in a dream, standing in the ballroom of another person's memories, talking to his boss, will never learn any of this.

The Kai in front of him looks murderous.

Abernathy knows what he says next is dumb as he goes to say it, but to be fair, he is in shock—"It doesn't say that in the welcome packet."

"It wouldn't, would it?"

Abernathy searches Kai's face, but it is hardened to him. Is she fucking with him? He doesn't understand the meaning behind her look. He is so busy searching her face, he doesn't catch her in time. It is only when he looks down, to break eye contact out of shame, that he sees her other hand at her waist, closing around her exit button. This is when he realizes what has been wriggling at the edge of his consciousness since they entered this dream.

Among all the dreamed dancers, Kai is the only person who is not marred by a black, elongated shadow. The parquet floor beneath Kai is unmarked. Abernathy looks around the room, but the black mass that should be attached to Kai is gone.

Her shadow has detached.

He looks up at her in horror.

Judging by her grimace, she already knows.

With a start, Abernathy realizes they are in *the room*. The ballroom that previously held a forest.

Was this, Abernathy finally wonders, Kai's dream?

"Kai . . ." he says.

"Don't say it," she says. "Don't you dare say a goddamn fucking thing."

As if summoned by his gaze, at her feet black swirls of shadows and wisp accumulate. The mass darkens, then detaches. Behind Kai, it begins to stand upright.

Abernathy's realization is too late. As usual, everyone else knew what was happening before him.

The shadow stands upright behind her. It is the shape of a human. As Abernathy watches, it warps and begins to morph. From the darkness, it grows a face. Kai's face.

"Kai," he says. His voice cracks. "Your shadow."

She shakes her head at him as the shadow behind her reaches out. "You can't help me, Abernathy. And please don't try, because you'll probably just fuck that up, too."

Kai catapults him out of the dream.

He is standing in the elevator, staring at himself in the reflection. When the doors in front of him finally open, his popcorn ceiling is above him. He is lying in his bed. Even though it is barely morning, his landlord above is vacuuming. Dust falls onto his visor and speckles his vision. Wrapped in sheets, he's awake.

And then he is thrashing.

"Goddammit," he says. *"Goddammit!"*

And then the thrashing is over and he is tired.

Maybe it's not his landlord vacuuming above.

Maybe Kelly has a maid.

# /// III ///

# JONATHAN
# ABERNATHY
# DREAMS

**DREAMS ARE SORT OF STUPID** when you are not the dreamer. The arc of the dream is too personal to be conveyed, as dreaming is one of the few mediums wholly reliant on abstract interpretation. Strip the dream from the life of its dreamer and the dream itself becomes devoid of meaning. Without context there is nothing. Merely a series of clichés and irregularities stitched together.

**AND YET WHEN** Abernathy thinks of his own dreams, whose meanings he could not interpret even when he dreamed them, he is filled with tenderness.

**THERE WERE FARMS,** in his mind. Creeks in his mind. Large homeplaces full of people living inside of him, somewhere, no longer accessible. School rooms of children laughing and laughing at him. Attics of books. The ordeal of growing older. His parents. People he loved.

THIS DREAM HAS A ONE-STORY house, painted white, with four windows across the front. The home is a squat ranch built in the 1970s. Bushes with blossoms sit out front. The driveway is concrete. The middle of the driveway is marred by a stripe of blood that trails from the sidewalk all the way to the center, where a woman lies bleeding in a puddle of rainbow oil. Despite her legs being crushed, she is still alive. She is trying to pull herself to the top of the driveway. Her lower half makes a scraping sound as she drags it across the pavement.

Abernathy is standing beneath the divot of the open garage door. He does not lower the mirror of his visor, but he does take a step toward the woman. She pulls herself forward, bare hand over bare hand, periodically turning to check the road behind her. The dream is filled with a loud, distant rumbling. It sounds like a truck is tearing through the streets several blocks away. Abernathy assumes, as one must in dreams, that the truck is coming for the dreamer.

Abernathy steps back into the shadow of the garage, and a fiddly tune erupts beneath his heel. He has crushed a plastic toy.

The woman on the driveway snaps her head forward. She looks at Abernathy. Directly at him. Wisps of hair fall into her face and cover her gaze. She looks familiar, just like the dreamer who emerged from a log in the creek. Before he can look closer, the dream freezes. The woman glitches, and then is gone from the world. A silence drops over the house. The toy stops blasting its tune and Abernathy can no longer hear the rev of an engine. Even the trees being buffeted about by the wind have frozen midway through their arc.

The dreamer has woken up mid-dream and the dream has stalled. The connection is broken.

Instead of automatically being ejected from the dream into the elevator, the lift comes to Abernathy. The silver apparatus hovers over the grass, then lands gently among a small patch of button mushrooms.

The doors open without making a sound.

Okay.

Not weird at all.

Abernathy hesitates, then steps into the elevator. As the doors are closing, he looks at the house in front of him and he recognizes it. Of course he does. It's amazing it's taken him this long. He's lived next to it for five years.

The house is Rhoda's.

Before Abernathy can think further upon this, the elevator's floor drops out and he sits up in his bed. His phone is ringing. In the shadow of 3:00 A.M. moonlight, the sheets are wrapped around his legs. His suit is plastic and hot on his skin. He feels disoriented and sick and doesn't know where he is.

The drop from the dream is abrupt and shocking. A monotonous white noise fills his room. Several seconds pass before he realizes it's not white noise, but the sound of a torrential downpour falling upon the house. Through the black glass of his window he sees the rain. The downpour is so heavy the water looks like waves. Outside, someone is knocking fervently on his door. Insistent. He can barely hear it over the rain. A pounding.

Is he terrified?

Oh. Definitely.

Definitely he is terrified.

Abernathy's limbs are leadened and heavy. He has difficulty moving his body. The knocking intensifies as he lurches toward the door, unsteady on his feet, tripping over the blanket. He has to untangle the fabric. He is still wearing his suit. He opens the door and rain pelts him through the flimsy screen separating him from the night. He thinks, momentarily, that he must be in a dream. He is not. His vision is dropletted with all the rain sloshing down from the sky. He can barely see who is on the other side. The porch light is out. The rain is thunderous. A puddle collects at the door's threshold.

As soon as Abernathy steps forward, the person on the other side screams and steps back into the rain. She almost loses her balance and trips, forward, into the pale light of his doorway, before stepping back into the rain again.

"Rhoda? Jesus. OK. It's just me. Hey, it's just me."

Rhoda is drowned. Her hair is plastered to her forehead. Her overlarge T-shirt clings to her shoulders and she isn't wearing pants. She's wearing her stained Uggs. The green metal skull has warped and soaked. She has a wild, terrified look in her eye. He reaches out to touch her but she flinches and steps back.

"Whoa," he says. "What—?"

"Jonathan?"

Her hair is half up in a bun but the bun has been drenched through and is collapsing upon her neck. Her bangs have separated into several clumps. She keeps wiping water from her eyes.

"Jesus, yes," Abernathy says, remembering he is still in his work clothes. He fumbles with the button at his collar and his visor retracts. "Yes, come in. Fuck, come in."

"Ah," Rhoda says. She sounds so uncharacteristically small. "I thought— but no—sorry," she says. The rain is relentless. "I had—I was— and then—"

Her teeth are chattering.

"Jesus," Abernathy says. She's in shock. He steps outside to wrap his arms around her and pull her in.

"What is going on?" he asks. "Are you OK?"

Rhoda shakes her head.

"Where's Timmy?" he asks. "Rhoda, where's Timmy?"

He doesn't mean to, but he shakes her a bit, when he asks.

"At her-her-her dad's."

Rhoda's sleep shirt has stretched beneath the weight of water and now almost hits her knees. Abernathy's suit takes up so much space that he can't get them both through the doorway. Each time the plastic of his suit touches her arms she jumps.

"I had a dream," she says. She puddles. "And then I thought—it sounded like—oh God—someone in my house—someone in my—garage—trying to—get in—I ran out—the back door—I— but no one there— and then—came here—"

"What?" Abernathy says sharply. He pulls her farther inside and casts one more look at the driveway before pulling the door shut and clicking the lock into place. With the door shut, the rain is muffled though still loud. "Someone in your house? *Who?*"

"But I—what if—couldn't tell if it was-was—was"—she shudders—"or just —"

"Do we need to call someone—Rhoda, what is going on—?"

"I had a bad—" she says, but then shakes her head, she seems like she is about to cry, like she can't get her breath. "I was—and Derek was there—he—"

Derek is her ex-husband. At his name, Abernathy stiffens.

"Rhoda," Abernathy says. Her shoulders scoop inward. Her hands tremble. Her wet hair lies flat on the clammy, paling surface of her skin. "Take a deep breath for me."

She closes her eyes. She shakes her head. The trembles have spread. Her whole body is shivering, shaking. He has never seen her like this. Seeing her as weak, instead of strong, seeing her vulnerable, seeing her here . . .

"OK," Abernathy says, starting to panic himself. "OK. It's gonna be OK." He's fumbly and weird and his brain isn't working because she clearly needs some type of help but he doesn't know what to do. He keeps bumping into shit with his suit. He almost knocks his lamp over. "OK, I am going to warm you up. I gotta warm you up. How am I going to warm you up? Then we're going to go to your house and we're going to—"

"N-n-no," Rhoda says, at the word "house." "No."

Her teeth are clattering and she's trying to take deep breaths but they're getting caught in her throat before she can start again. He gets her into the bathroom and closes the door. He turns on the shower. Steam begins to fill up the room.

"All right." His suit takes up most of the room. The back of his knees press against the toilet. "OK. We won't go anywhere. We're just going to warm up," he says. "Just gonna warm you up."

He fumbles with the shower and awkwardly bends down to remove her shoes. She is covering her face. "I'm sorry," she keeps saying. She says it on loop, which is disturbing and unlike her and makes Abernathy feel ill. "I didn't know where to go, I'm sorry, I'm sorry." He holds the curtain back, helps Rhoda in.

The shower is a small box. Beneath the warm water, Rhoda looks like a wet city rat. Her hair is plastered, her clothes are at maximum absorption, the fabric clings. Jonathan steps out of his suit, the plastic sticky against his skin. He almost trips in his desperation to get it off of him. He enters the shower with her. He is tall and awkward. His head goes above the shower curtain. The water is hot. She is keening, gulping deep breaths.

"It couldn't have been real," she is saying to herself. "It felt so real. Could it be real? Do you think it was real? I don't remember—I don't want it to—Derek wouldn't do something like—unless he—or—"

"Shhh," Abernathy says. He tries to wrap his arm around her and bangs his elbow into the wall. "Fuck." Beneath his arms she is warming up. "Shhh. It's OK. It's OK." Steam billows around them both.

He tries to stay soft.

He rubs his hand up and down her back. His boxers cling to his thighs. "It's OK. It's OK."

After a few minutes of this her breathing starts to even out. She begins to blink and look around her confused, which is probably for the best. The water is going to run out soon. "There we go," Abernathy says, trying to remember what his mother used to say to him in these moments of overwhelm. "Why don't you try to take some deep breaths?"

Rhoda looks at him and then begins to do as he says.

"Yes," he says, "just like that. There we go. In. Out. Uh-huh. Good job. You're doing so good. Just follow me."

They breathe together.

He has the urge to laugh, and he surprises himself by doing so.

Rhoda pulls back and looks him in the eyes.

*Are you looking at me?* she's asking. *Do you see?*

He can't stop laughing, yes.

Yes, he's looking at her.

Yes, he sees.

Cramped in the small shower that barely has enough room for both of their elbows, they stand there. And miraculously, Rhoda begins to laugh, too.

WHATEVER STRANGE INTIMACY passed through them in the shower is fleeting. Abernathy averts his eyes as Rhoda dresses in his clothes. He sits on his bed in a new pair of clean, dry underwear. His suit waits for him on the floor.

Rhoda had a nightmare. She believed the nightmare was real. In the nightmare, she was in the driveway of her house. Her ex-husband had just left the house with Timmy. As he took Timmy, her husband ran her over with his truck.

"I know it's stupid," she says quietly. She steps into his sweatpants. "But it felt real. Then I woke up and I thought—I thought I heard . . ."

"What did you hear?" Abernathy asks. He is very tired.

Rhoda shrugs and pulls the hoodie over her hair. She mumbles her answer.

"What?"

"I thought I heard him opening the door," she mutters, averting her eyes. "I thought I heard him calling my name. And then I thought I heard someone in my garage."

Abernathy's eyes flicker to the window where he can see her house, but the lights are not on.

Abernathy's pretty sure he knows what happened. But he also doesn't want to tell Rhoda that he was there, in her dream.

He whispers, "Do you think he was in your house?"

She doesn't look at him. "I don't know. I thought someone was, maybe. But now it seems . . ." She sits on the other side of the bed and sighs.

Abernathy has slowly sunk into repose. He's propped up on one arm, to disguise his injured hand. The wound is no longer open, but there is still a small purple spot in the middle of his palm that stings whenever someone touches it.

"I don't know," Rhoda says. Her fingers are twined in her lap. SHIT LUCK (or, as it says now, TLIUHCSK). "It seems stupid now."

"Is he the type of guy that would . . . you know . . ." Abernathy hesitates. "Do something . . . like that?"

Rhoda shrugs. Her old self is back. The locked-away self. Her eyes dart out the window, behind Abernathy's head, then to Abernathy's face, then to her hands, which she holds in front of her, clasped. "I should go back," she says. She tries to sound indifferent. "I don't know what got into me."

This makes Abernathy angry. "Rhoda, don't be stupid." She flinches and he reaches out and puts his good hand on her leg. "No, not like that," he says. He rubs his thumb across the fabric of the sweat pants. They are too small for her hips and the fabric stretches around her thighs. "I didn't mean it like that. I mean—Jesus—sorry. Just come lie down," Abernathy says. "Will you lie down? I'm too tired to do the back-and-forth today. Just lie down with me and tell me what's going on."

Rhoda stiffens. She does not make eye contact.

"I'll close my eyes." Abernathy says.

Rhoda clears her throat.

He closes his eyes.

Rhoda lies back, slowly. Her face is in front of his face. Her knees touch his knees. He can feel her breath on his skin.

"Go ahead," he says, eyes still closed.

"Promise you won't hate me?" Rhoda asks.

"Why would I ever hate you?"

"For being weak," Rhoda says.

"Rhoda, you're not weak. You're a badass. You're the queen of badasses."

"Even badasses can be weak sometimes," she says.

"Not you," he says. "You're stronger than the sun."

He feels her shake her head. No.

"I'm not going to tell you unless you promise."

Abernathy laughs. "OK." He says. He puts out his pinky and she wraps her pinky around his. He feels her kiss her fist. Eyes still closed, he kisses his. They pull their hands apart. Abernathy rests the heart of his palm against her waist. He pulls her closer. Just a bit. Just enough so that he can deny it, if she were to ask. "I promise. I won't hate you. I could never hate you."

"But you promise?"

"I promise," he says.

So she tells him a story.

**THIS IS THE** story she told him:

At sixteen Rhoda had the bad luck of falling in love.

We could say a bunch of cute shit about it: love was a star that fell upon her from heaven; it burned a wide trail of light in its wake.

We could make it dark. We could say: when it hit it hurt; she burned too; it wasn't beautiful; love didn't wrap its starry arms all over her; it didn't imbue her with warmth or celestial understanding; love moved through her with violence.

We could be irreverent. We could say: love was phoenix shit; love was ashes shit; after the flames of love subsided, Rhoda was reborn; instead of shedding her body to the flames and emerging all red-winged and fire-kissed, replenished, or whatever—she emerged ugly; she emerged desperate.

But why say any of that? It's all too complicated and overwrought and only partially true.

It would be much simpler to say that when she should have stopped, she kept going.

His name was Derek.

She cornered him at a party. She was sixteen. He was twenty. He sat at the edge of a fireplace holding a red Solo cup. He was too old to be there. He wore his dark hair long. He had a sleeve of tattoos. Most were stupid, but some, Rhoda thought, were pretty good. Classic. A dagger. A heart. A candle being held up by a hand.

A romantic, Rhoda remembers thinking. A man with a soul.

He was talking casually with some boys from her high school. Seniors. Rhoda interrupted the conversation. She stepped right between the boys and Derek.

She was feeling bold. She had just gotten her first tattoo. A stick-and-poke on her upper thigh that she wrapped in cling film as soon as it was done. Real idiot shit.

That night, beneath her skirt, it stung.

The tattoo was a tiny black horseshoe, meant to give her luck.

As an adult, if Rhoda wanted the tattoo to be at all recognizable, she had to spit and rub her skin hard with her thumb.

"Hey," she said to Derek, interrupting the two boys mid-speech. "Are you as bored as I am?"

Derek had a stupid name, she remembers thinking. Just like her. Which, thank God, she thought, as she looked down at his pale face and dark hair, because if he were this beautiful *and* had a great name, it would be too much.

The boys behind her started to protest. She ignored them.

Derek, disinterested, looked up from the hearth.

"You're still trying then?" he asked.

Defiant, Rhoda looked him in the eye, chin firm. "Yes," she said.

He snorted. "Why?"

"Dude, come on," said the boys behind her. "You can't be for real."

She was feeling bold that night. Maybe it was her, who saw through him. Maybe they saw through each other.

"Come outside with me," she said with a smile, "and I'll tell you."

"You want me to," he said. It wasn't a question.

"Yes. And you will."

He gave her a sidelong glance.

She was a scrappy sixteen-year-old with long black hair, middle-parted. Big black boots. Tiny pleated black skirt. Her favorite musician? Evanescence. She wore colorful beads around her neck. She had spent an hour smudging eyeliner against her lower lashline. All her underwear was still little kids underwear. Most of the white panties were covered in cowboy hats, or shooting stars, or little hearts. The type of underwear she buys Timmy now.

"Will I?" he asked.

"If not now, then later. You'll come. In every version you come."

She gave him a wry grin.

He rolled his eyes.

"How do you know?" he asked, lazy. Like he was asking her for the weather.

The boys behind her were loudly complaining.

She put her finger beneath Derek's chin. She turned his face so she could whisper in his ear.

"Because we're meant to be together," she said, completely fucking winging it. "Because I saw you, and I loved you immediately. Because," she said, "I say so. Because I get my way."

His eyes flickered to her eyes to see if she was serious.

She was serious.

Sometimes, now, she wonders why the fuck she did that.

The rest was typical teen shit. All wet mouths and heavy pressure and thrust. When the test results came back her parents weren't pleased. They were so worried she would abort that they locked up all her shit in a safe—birth certificate, driver's license, social security card—and installed alarms on the doors. According to her dad, she wasn't allowed out. Her mom didn't exactly ask her to stay inside, but she didn't say, "You can leave your room," either.

It sounds, in retrospect, like so much chaos, but at the time it was her life. No matter how shitty a life is, it's always normal to the person living it.

By the time Rhoda was showing, she hadn't left her room in nine weeks and had missed a third of her senior year.

It was Derek's dad, Rhett, who came and got her. Just by himself one day. He showed up and said, "She's coming with us."

Rhoda's dad was sitting on his recliner. He didn't get up. He eyed Rhett and said, basically, that it was no skin off of his back.

Derek was waiting in the car. When he saw Rhoda, he cried. He put his head in her lap. She rubbed his ear. It was all very tender.

Five months later, in the backyard where she first fucked him, Rhoda married Derek. A month after that, she had their son. The labor took four hours. Only Derek's mother was in the room with her. The other woman watched as her grandson crowned.

Epidural moving swiftly through her, Rhoda remembered thinking: *If, with my vagina, I am crowning him, does that mean he is a king?*

There was a lot of blood.

She named him after Derek's father, Rhett.

He was a beautiful baby. A boy.

**AT THIS POINT** in the story, Rhoda has to take a break.

"You don't have to tell me this stuff, you know," Abernathy says, uncomfortable. His eyes are still closed. He's greatful for it. He doesn't know how to react to a story like this.

"I know," Rhoda says. She turns so her back is to his chest. He pulls her close and she no longer smells like pine. She smells like his shower. She smells like the outside. She smells like rain. "I guess I want you to know me."

"I know you," Abernathy says, though now he isn't so sure.

"The real me," Rhoda amends. "The actual me."

Abernathy doesn't want to argue with her. He makes small circles on her stomach with his hand until she is ready to go on.

**FRESH OUT OF** her body, her son was ten pounds. As big as her torso. If she held him up by the armpits, his chubby body stretched and stretched.

The first few weeks were meant for marveling, and marvel she did. Rhett had gummy little eyes that would flick open to look sleepily around the room. He loved to eat, and latched fiercely. When smiling came, it was easy.

If we're going to go back to saying cute shit: looking upon him, Rhoda felt like a small part of her heart had split off and was now burning within him, too.

When Rhoda was nineteen, and Derek twenty-three, Rhett Sr. was ill. To give her parents-in-law time together, by themselves, before it was too late, she and Derek moved into a shitty apartment with a leaking ceiling and a nonexistent kitchen. Most days she ate rice. They used cloth diapers (she despises, to this day, cloth diapers). Rhoda made Rhett's food by mashing together boiled carrots and peas.

Derek worked a lot during this time and Rhett was mostly colic and fuss. During nights, Rhoda worked as a maid, with an old high school friend and her grandmother. Rhoda liked to clean. She liked to see the big condos with the wall-to-wall glass showers. She loved to wipe the marble counters down with the spray that smelled like oranges and she loved to fold the towels and put them in the linen closet. She loved that they had linen closets.

During that time, her feet always hurt. That winter, when Rhett Sr. died, her feet hurt so bad she had to wear sneakers to his funeral.

Though she didn't speak to anyone, or acknowledge Rhoda in the pews, Rhoda's mom came to the funeral, too. It was the last time Rhoda would see her.

At twenty, Rhoda got her GED and her sweet, slow baby finally learned to walk.

Rhett Sr. left a bit of money. Not too much, but enough for a small house, in the slums of the outer city, paid for with $3,000 down and a mortgage from the bank. It was a low ranch house, bright white with mold on the corners outside. Four windows out front. Not a single plant in the yard. They fixed it up themselves.

During that time of construction, Derek liked to smoke cigarettes on the porch while holding his son. When Rhoda walked in on these moments, she felt like she was the intruder, observing the lives of strangers. Derek and his son looked so much alike. Black wavy hair. Soft searching eyes. An inner calmness and humor. An unknowability. Derek used to hold Rhett on his hip and stare out the window. In a low voice, he would give running commentary on the people driving their cars down their street: where they were going, how they were getting there, and with who.

Meanwhile Rhoda spent her time coaxing her son. Holding him up. Helping him stand. Trying to let go. But every time she let go, he would cry out, look terrified, reach out for her as he wobbled unsteadily back and forth.

It was weak of her, but as soon as he called for her, she was there. She never let him fall. Maybe this is why it took him so long to learn, on his own, how to walk.

At twenty-two, Rhoda was perfectly, astoundingly happy. She now thinks, unironically, that this was the happiest time of her life. Pregnant again, she wanted a baby girl. A baby girl is what she got.

Even though Rhoda had not spoken to her mother since those first few weeks at Derek's parents' house, she gave her daughter her mother's name: Thelma. Bulky names were a family tradition. They called her Timmy for short.

Seven months later, her mother died in a head-on collision and Rhoda was not invited to the funeral.

Cheesy, maybe, but it hurts too much to describe without the blunting of old sayings. Rhoda can only come at it sideways, never straight on.

When her mother died, Rhoda hollowed. Like they had taken more than just her child out of her, when they reached in and split her open. They had taken the dark star of her heart, too. She felt lost without it. Displaced. She no longer orbited her family with ease.

In the months following her daughter's arrival and her mother's departure, Rhoda often found herself "coming to" while standing at a sink, or holding a toy, or folding a pair of tiny shorts. Sometimes she was looking down at herself from high above, as if she was an audience member in her own life.

One night Rhett walked in as Rhoda held Derek. Derek was crying. Weeping, really, if we're telling the truth. Her husband hid his face from his son.

Rhett, now three, stood in the doorway, holding his own hand, staring curiously at her husband, his father, a man of many mysteries whose gravity pulled them closer and closer to one another. Rhoda found herself idly wondering if she would be alone when she finally fell into him, or if her children would fall with her.

"Why is he crying?" Rhett asked Rhoda.

Derek held very still, as if that would prevent Rhett from seeing.

"He is overwhelmed," Rhoda said slowly, not knowing how to answer the question, when all Derek had said before he began to cry was that he felt like Rhoda was far away. He could barely feel her.

Rhoda waited, then, for her husband to answer, but he said nothing.

Finally, Rhoda said, "He loves your sister. And he loves you. And he loves me. That is a lot of love. But it is also a lot of responsibility. He is surprised by how much he can hold at once."

That year Rhett took to hovering at Rhoda's skirt line. Quietly reaching out for her hand. Rhoda could not always lift him up. From the ground he watched his father, who doted on his new sister, with a wary eye. He frequently seemed confused. He held on to the hem of Rhoda's dresses as if any moment he could blow away.

She often wondered if her first born sensed something she didn't.

During this time Rhoda was desperate for any touch from Derek. If he walked into a room she would seek him. Each night she would lay on her stomach. She liked it when he whispered, "You are here with me, you are here with me, you are here." Only in those moments, would it feel true.

"I love you," he would say. "I chose you. You are mine."

And she would believe him. She never doubted him. She always believed him, because for him it was true.

It was herself she was beginning to doubt.

If twenty-two was the best year of her life, her twenty-third year was her worst.

Her father always told her that Death comes in threes. He would say it often. Death comes in threes, Rhoda. When her neighbor died, Death comes in threes. When her chorus teacher died, Death comes in threes. When her dog died: What did you expect? he had asked. The dog was the third. At least now we're free of it.

RHETT WAS A beautiful, complicated child. He was content in a way that Rhoda has never felt. He was friends with nature. He gravitated toward objects that sounded like bells, or wind chimes. Animals loved him. His favorite food was blueberries. He called her Mimi, instead of Mommy, or Momma, or Mom. He called Derek Pop. He called Timmy princess. He used to bring his stool over when she was washing dishes and hold up a towel from the bath.

"I will," he would say.

He liked to press his shoulders to her hip at the sink.

She should have done the math. If first there was Derek's father, who died from a cancer that ate up his gut, and then there was Thelma, who bled out across her steering wheel after being T-boned on her way to choir practice, of course—of course—there would be a third.

Nobody cheated death.

Not even her son.

Rhoda was in the yard, watching Rhett. Derek was at work. Timmy was fussy that day. Rhoda was worried she was coming down with something. Her stomach was upset and Rhoda kept having to go back into the house and change her. The worst moment of her life happened while she was wiping her daughter's ass.

Rhett was pulling dandelions up from the yard. He was talking to them. Rhoda could hear him from the window.

"You can be called Dylan, and you can be called Jaime, and I'll call you Matt, like my friend."

While listening to the quiet hum of her child's monologue, she examined a small patch of scaly red skin around her daughter's left leg. Her daughter was much more fragile, she remembers thinking, than her son. As a baby, Rhett hadn't suffered. He never had sinus infections, or baby acne, or diaper rashes. In the last minutes of her son's life, she stood over her daughter worrying that she was doing something wrong. She worried that she needed to change the detergent. She worried that Timmy wasn't eating enough fruit. She left her daughter babbling on the changing table and walked into the kitchen to get a soft, wet cloth.

What she should have been worrying about was her son, who, in the garden, as she wet a washcloth with warm water and soap, pulled a mushroom from the ground and placed it into his mouth.

ABERNATHY HOLDS VERY still. Every part of his body is tense.

"How did he die?" Abernathy asks. "Your son. Rhett."

They are facing each other again. Rhoda has a faraway look. Now it's she who closes her eyes.

"Allergy," she says. He watches her face. She works hard to keep it neutral. To keep herself inside herself. "It was—he ate—from the yard. It wasn't—they weren't poisonous. We made them test. Test everything. It was just, the examiner said it was just bad luck. Just really bad luck. I would have— if I was there I would have stopped him, in case they were poisonous, you understand, but I was in the backroom changing Timmy, and he was—he was allergic. To what he ate."

Abernathy reaches out to hold her hand, but she pulls back. She holds herself.

She closes her eyes. "That's all," she says. "An allergy."

"He was . . ." Abernathy says slowly, trying to understand, "allergic to the dirt?"

Her eyes flash open. "No," she says. She sounds hollow. "It's even dumber than that." Her voice cracks. She is crying. "It's so pathetic and stupid. I hate how stupid it is. It makes me mad how stupid it is." She takes a deep breath and her face is unnaturally calm again. "Our yard had portobellos. We let them grow free. Now Timmy keeps trying to find them, but they don't grow in our yard anymore. Rhett had never had— He was allergic to— He had never had them before. His airways—his airways closed up." She wipes angrily at her eyes and stares out the window. Abernathy wonders if the rain has cleared and she can see her house.

"Oh, Rhoda," Abernathy says, and reaches out again.

"Don't," she says miserably. "Don't. I don't deserve it. I wasn't myself. I should have been paying more attention and I wasn't— I didn't—"

"How could you know?" Abernathy asks.

"I should have known," she says again, but this time more to herself. "I should have known. You don't understand. I was his mother. I am his mother. Mothers know."

"Rhoda, that's horrible. No. There's no way you could have—"

"When I walked into the yard," she says, "and I saw him I called the ambulance. I called Derek and I said come home. Come home now. But it was too late. I knew it was too late. His face wasn't—wasn't moving. I went to go get, I went to go get Timmy. And we all sat together to wait. I held him in my lap. His perfect face. All three of us together. We were all together. All three of us were together but all I could hear in my head was my dad. He was just saying it over and over again. 'What did you expect? *At least now we're free of it.*' I thought that. *At least now we're free of it.* I thought that about my own son."

Her eyes are red-rimmed. Angry. She holds all of it, just there, beneath. But then her gaze flashes and she is gone again. All of her. All of her had been put away.

"Rhoda, that wasn't you," Abernathy says quietly. "That was just—that was just your brain. That wasn't you thinking that."

"That's what Derek said," she says. "I tried to leave him and Timmy. I didn't—" Her voice broke. "I didn't deserve them."

She starts to cry and this time Abernathy doesn't try to hold her.

"This is what your dream was about?" he asks. "The dream you thought was real?"

She shakes her head. "I told you," she says. "I told you: you don't *know* me. You don't know me. I'm so much worse than you thought."

Abernathy lies there with her, whispering things to her, sweet things, affirming things, "I am not going anywhere" things, nothing things, but Rhoda doesn't say anything else. Soon her breathing evens out. She is sleeping. Beneath her lids her eyes move back and forth. Abernathy watches her. She is thirty-six, he realizes, but she is very young. They are both very young. Maybe people are young forever, but it's only in sleep that we can see.

She must be dreaming, Abernathy thinks. He tucks a piece of hair behind her ear. He lets his thumb linger. And then he moves his hand away. He hopes it is a peaceful dream.

He holds his hands to himself and lays still for a time until slowly, very slowly, he sits up in bed.

Slowly. So slowly. He gets up.

He gets dressed.

He finds himself at the door to his apartment. He watches Rhoda, asleep on the bed. *She contains life in her*, he thinks. *Infinite life.*

He slips on his shoes.

The rain has stopped. Abernathy steps out. The air is heavy with water. He just needs a second, he tells himself. He just needs to clear his head.

## 23

THERE IS A VERSION OF Abernathy's life, maybe, where instead of leaving, he puts on his suit before getting back into bed. In this version, he and Rhoda wake in the morning together. In this other morning, Rhoda turns to face him, wearing his clothes. Her eyes are crusty. Her voice is hoarse. She lets out an "*Oh God,*" and laughs. She is embarrassed. He turns to her, in his dream suit, crinkling.

They hold eye contact.

The moment is broken when she says, "That thing is hideous," and he says, "I know."

Just like that, it is over. They don't talk about her son. What's worse, to always bring up the memory or to never bring up the memory? At least now they would know. Now they would know they can trust each other. Now they could begin.

"Are you feeling better?" he would ask, as he stands and begins to dress.

She would shrug.

She would say in a joking voice—a voice full of bravado and cheer—that sometimes she feels like life is crushing her and she won't make it out alive.

The two of them would then laugh about this, because it's true.

After a moment's pause, Abernathy would tell her (in a voice that she can pretend not to hear, if she wishes to pretend) that seeing her that upset made him feel both too small and too big and, at the same time, not at all big enough. He didn't know what to say or how to feel. He was starting to think he was bad at feeling.

It would be a stupid confession to make. But he would reason, that she showed him hers, it would only be fair for him to show her his, no matter how feeble and limp.

Rhoda might look at him across the torn quilt, on this other morning, and reach for him, and pull him back onto the bed, wrapping him close.

"Yeah," she might say into his chest, "Same," but it would be something better, something more Rhoda-y. Something both witty, and distant, and clever. Something that would be personal only in the conversation they were having beneath the conversation taking place.

And maybe Abernathy would, in that moment, feel unselfconscious enough to tilt her chin up and move closer. Closer. Until she presses the stupid visor button on his stupid suit. He would want her to choose to. He would want her to reach in.

It would be the dumbest first kiss of all time, but it would be theirs.

The kiss would tell her without telling her that he sees her, he's with her, he has no answers, either, but he likes it when they are in the same place.

This is, however, not what Jonathan Abernathy does.

THAT NIGHT THE walk away from his house is long, and meandering. He passes a series of small tenement houses, a dollar store, and an ugly food chain and then there it is, right in front of him, winking at him like it knew he was destined to arrive there all along: the Archival Office lights are on.

At first, the doors do not open for him.

Abernathy cups his hands to the glass and uses his palms like binoculars. There is no one at the front desk. The lights are turned low—one flickers feebly in the corner. It is very early in the A.M. The night is balmy and full of June-ish dew. Things are sparkling and clean after last night's rain. Abernathy can faintly hear muzak.

He swipes away the fog of his breath as it crowds the automatic glass doors. He knocks. But there is no one here. And though it is June, the moisture in the air makes him shiver. He has, once again, underestimated the potency of a 4:00 A.M. spring chill.

He thinks something particularly rude about himself and is almost shamed into turning to head back the way he came, down the meandering roads whose occupants are not always friendly to pedestrians, back to his house, where Rhoda lies in wait, probably not yet realizing he has gone. If he manages to return before she notices, he tells himself, perhaps he can pretend like he never left.

He has almost done it—almost decided to cross into the white lines of the parking lot—when he hears the whoosh of the Archive's door and feels air conditioner on his back.

Only the tail of his jacket catches as he sprints through the closing glass.

Abernathy is not proud of the decision he makes. But he is, however, relieved.

The very simple question he should be asking: From whom is he running? And to what?

The office is as dental-y and doctor-y as ever. He's not sure why he expected it to be different, maybe because it's he who feels different, standing bluntly within so much bureaucracy. Despite the early-morning chill, a potted plant waves under a vent circulating air. The only other movement comes from the flickering halogens. Not a single soul is here besides himself.

"C'mon," he mutters, pulling at his jacket. The left cuff is stuck in the glass mouth of the door. "Please? I'm having a shit day."

The universe, of course, does not give a fuck.

"I'll come back for you later," he whispers in defeat as he slips one arm from the coat and then the other.

At the sight of his jacket hanging limp and green in the middle of the doorway, Abernathy has the urge to kick at the door, to scream, and rage, and storm around, and break things.

Deep breaths.

✓ You are good, *he tells himself.*
✓ You are breathing.
✓ You are alive in a world where trillions have already died.

✓ You are complicated. You are a mystery. You are unknown to yourself.

✓ One day, you will do better.

(*Though today*, he adds, *is not that day*.)

Now that he is further inside, he feels despicable.

He walks to the other side of the room and presses his nose to the plexiglass barrier that separates the secretary's desk from the waiting room. He sees nothing extraordinary behind the glass. No indication at all that Kai had even been here in the first place. What actually takes him by surprise is his reflection.

If upon his first visit he appeared pigeon-like, wide and gray all over with desperation, he has now achieved a depressing storkliness, if storkliness meant looking as if you'd lost fifty pounds during a period of duress and were then microwaved back to life and plopped upright in a foggy pond.

With disgust he turns from his visage—always a disappointment to himself and never a gift—and steps around the plexiglass to try the door. He is overcome by the urge to do something *good*. Something *helpful*. The door opens.

Abernathy steps into the room.

It is much warmer here. Set to motion sensor, a yellow bulb flickers to life at the desk. The energy is friendlier, more welcoming. His reflection watches him from the interior, too.

The urge to do something good, brave, foolish, bold—it doubles.

Why had he done it? Why had he left?

Kai's office chair swivels as he sits. He opens her drawers.

Maybe Rhoda was right: it had been too much. He could not hold it. He had to set it down.

But how embarrassing that is—attempting to hold something and realizing it is too heavy to carry.

A normal person who has (in a moment of extreme self-loathing) decided to search for information on a missing colleague instead of confronting their fear of intimacy might first be inclined to search the filing cabinets on the far side of the room. Abernathy is sympathetic to that course of action.

However, his mother had been something of an office worker herself, so he spent many evenings huddled under her desk, wedged between the space heater and her feet. From his experience, the really personal stuff—the stuff that is important—that stuff is always kept crumpled and crammed at the back of drawers.

Plus, it's easier to feel heroic while sitting here, swiveling.

He opens both the left, the right, and the middle all at once.

Staples. A stapler. Paper clips. Scissors. A tray for all the used bobs and ends. A bright pink handheld flashlight. A used tissue. A few folded notes shimmy forward as a petite green nail polish container rolls to the front. Press-on rhinestones.

Kai has been here.

(Is this what the inside of Rhoda's desk looks like, too?)

(Does she have a picture of her son at her desk?)

(Does she have a picture of her son in her home?)

The notes don't have much on them. Call so-and-so. Make an appointment on the fifth. A not-bad doodle of Penn hanging from a tree. On one of the notes— one stuck at the veeeeeery back corner—there is a number with a heart neatly drawn alongside it.

Abernathy pauses at that.

Perhaps it would be best, he thinks, as he dials the number, to leave it alone.

Outside, the sun rises among the car hoods. It is early enough that he expects to get a voicemail recording that gives him a name. Then maybe he could just go home.

(Is Rhoda waking up? Has Rhoda woken up? Is Rhoda awake?)

Outside the window is dazzling chromatica and darkness.

A young woman picks up, breathless. "Kai? Kai? Is that you? Where have you been? Did Penn—"

"Sorry," says Abernathy, slightly panicking. "Wrong number."

"Wait—" says the woman. "I know where you're calling from. Tell me— what's happened to Kai?"

"I—"

"You have to give me Kai," she repeats.

Abernathy holds his breath.

She says, "I deserve to know."

Abernathy doesn't know what to say.

"I thought maybe—" says the caller. "But no. She wouldn't do that. Has she woken up? Are you helping her? Do you know where she is? Have your people—"

Abernathy feels as if he is being pushed underwater. Out of breath. Not so sure, any longer, which way is up.

Who is this woman?

What does she mean by "woken up?"

Is there actually something going on here?

Is Abernathy, right now, doing more than playing pretend?

They are silent on the phone together.

Abernathy attempts to do a sort of breaststroke toward serenity, despite drowning in panic. He asks, "W-what do you think happened to her?"

"You tell me, asshole. You're calling from the office in the outer city."

The woman has a point.

"Look," Abernathy says, not sure what's going on. What he knows is pretty simple. It isn't much: there's this thing called a dream archive; Kai ran into her doppelgänger that had, somehow, gone bad, and this upset her; Abernathy keeps finding himself in the same dreams, being dreamed by the same people; Kai had hinted things weren't exactly sunshine and roses—but when was anything ever really sunshine and roses, like, actually? He hasn't seen her since, not really; and—she's been acting mega fucking weird.

None of this amounts to much, admittedly, but before Abernathy can confess any of it, the power flickers out in the office. The phone line goes dead. There's not even so much as a dial tone for comfort.

Abernathy is alone.

It is silent.

He is in the dark.

It takes a moment for his eyes to adjust. The few pale wisps of outside sunlight barely penetrate the Archive's window. At least the halogen has stopped warbling. Abernathy returns the phone to its cradle. He grabs the flashlight that rolled forward from the back of the desk and, without much thought, without much reflection at all, with only the desire to run from himself, to avoid his life and insert himself in another, he heads toward the carpeted stairs.

As he descends, light bobbing, he makes up his mind.

He's going to the archives.

He's going to check Kai's box.


THE BASEMENT IS darker than the office. Collapsed folding chairs rest in two wheeling banks parked on either side of the room. Otherwise, the vast carpeted floor is empty. Abernathy feels the urge to lay in the middle and look up at the Styrofoam tile ceiling, as he did when he was a child attending church with his mom. In retrospect, he spent a lot of his childhood laying or sitting on floors. Something he never really does, now. If his mom were here, she would remind him that it was by the grace of God that he stood here, swerving his light through all this emptiness and then she would tell him he needed to get his ass home.

Abernathy thinks he sees movement in the corner. He pauses. He has almost managed to lose himself in the moment and forget about Rhoda.

Perhaps she is already awake.

In the basement he points Kai's pink flashlight, but the beam does not spread across the wall.

Low to the carpet, smeared against the baseboards, there is a dark and jammy blackness. To Abernathy it looks almost as if the blackness is cowering from—and avoiding—the light.

Abernathy walks toward the shadowy thing.

As he does so the circle of his light grows larger upon the wall. The black speck remains in the middle.

He is six feet away.

Five feet.

Four.

In the middle of all that yellow is a small cowering thing.

Above him something clangs and Abernathy turns off his light. He dives behind the wheelable row of folding chairs in the corner out of blind, straight-up fear.

Abernathy's breath is loud. He has to hold his hand over his mouth to even hear anything.

Is it a person? Has someone arrived? It probably looks pretty sketchy for him to be here alone. And he left his jacket at the door, so anyone who entered would realize there was another person here. That feels pretty stupid, now, in hindsight.

Abernathy is so busy kicking himself that it takes several more clangs before he understands that, despite it being June, the noise comes from the heaters kicking slowly to life. Bureaucracy at work.

When he turns his flashlight on again, the cowering thing is gone.

Is he seeing things?

Well, why wouldn't he be?

He has stayed up all night. He is exhausted. His feet hurt. He is working all the time, and when he is not working, he is on the phone with the IRS, with the court systems, with the credit companies and the student loan people, all of whom want something from him, like money or time, that he does not have. The onus is on Abernathy, however, to prove that absence, yet to prove the absence takes resources. How does one even prove the absence of something? How do you explain a Catch-22? Can anyone without money prove something happened? Creditors act as if their paid harassment will somehow material-ize paychecks in Abernathy's name. But he was not a pale king. He was nothing. He was no one. He was a broom of the system. No wonder he is see-ing things and being paranoid. It's exhausting to use every one of your waking hours explaining how poor you are to people who either (a) don't believe it or (b) are intimately acquainted with the experience and therefore don't really give a shit; they are desperate to meet their quotas and keep their jobs, too.

(Plus, he did just stay up most of the night, talking to—)

Abernathy calls Kai's name again, sweeping his light across the space. It smells like a church gathering room: old perfume long sunken into the carpet, the ghosts of inescapable women rising faintly as he walks, the after-smell of a hundred bodies and citrusy disinfectant layered over top.

Abernathy can almost see his mom as she was in his youth, shaking hands of the ladies around her, pinned brooches shimmering at the breast line. Little miniaturized flower sculptures of wreaths or post-9/11 American flags.

(What would he do, if it were his son who had died? How would he feel?)

Abernathy is ready to give up. To call it a day.

Cowardice and sad nostalgia work hard within him.

(Who was Rhoda, anyway? And what did he owe her?)

It all makes Abernathy think of how many people he can't seem to hold on to. Would his mom—would anyone—be proud of what he has become? Probably not. But then that begs the question, was it enough to merely survive? Abernathy can barely manage to maintain a base-level existence. His whole goddamn life is what, really? Not much. Not anything. Stupidity. Cowardice. Self-loathing. When you hold it all together and try to get a look at it, there's not even that much to see.

Is there worth in the things you cannot see?

Abernathy is considering going upstairs. Swiping that Post-it with the number on it. Heading back home, where he would, what—exactly? Apologize to Rhoda, if she were still there? Admit that he was? What? Was there any way to say it that wasn't stupid and played out as hell? He could get poetic, maybe. Tell her that fear often grows large within him, kudzu-like and invasive, until it overtakes him completely? But that sounds even fucking dumber. He tries to be different. A better him. He really does. It's just, he hasn't managed yet. He always runs away.

His stomach is starting to hurt with how complicated everything is. How . . . you know . . . complicated life is. Rhoda would what? When he got there? It was already too late. It hadn't begun and it was too late. Years of friendship thrown away on an impulse. What possessed him to do it? Why had he run? Why were his motivations and actions always so stupid to him? Why so confusing, when he is the one living here, in his body, being the person doing the things that cause him pain? Why is he the way he is.

Abernathy kind of feels like he's about to start crying. Which is a weird feeling. And a stupid one. (Has he called himself stupid enough times? (No. Never. (He is being stupid now.)))

It's not good for Abernathy to think thoughts like these, really, because it always leads to him spending two weeks in bed, losing his job, getting fired, feeling exhausted, not being able to stand up, barely being able to feed himself. It's a pathetic, overblown (stupid) response he feels, and yet each time he bows to it, at its mercy. You know: that embodied kind of sadness nobody believes exists until it happens to you. Where even (stupid shit like) breathing is a particular and labored pain. Where the idea of how corrupt he is crushes his actual (stupid) self until he can't see past the idea into the actuality.

And then the idea becomes real, inescapable, a fright barrelling toward you until it's so real you're suffocating under it, even more idiotic, even more cowardly, even worse.

That's what happened at his last job. It started taking effort to stand up and it was impossible to exert all that effort all of the time. Who was he, he began to wonder, and why was he doing things? Who was he doing them for? How did one exert power over oneself to overcome such vapid, unimportant questions? Were other people getting caught in these traps? Was it just him? One day he just couldn't leave his bed. The next day he was fired.

The amount of money he lost from that one day was incalculable. It took him months to find work again after that. He's still trying to course-correct from that one day of exhaustion.

Was it the universe, he wondered, getting back at him for something? Or was it something worse? Did God hate him? How did he escape it? What if there was no escape?

Being here, looking for Kai, thinking about Rhoda, it's opening that cycle of thought for him. That (horrible) (embarrassing) (shameful) (idiotic) cycle where he is suddenly aware of the Pointlessness of All Things.

That "what does it matter" feeling.

Shouldn't he give up on this?

He calls Kai's name one more time. He is at the carpeted stairs. His jacket awaits him, surely missing him by now, all lonely and trapped between the door where it sits in limbo: neither inside nor outside, not going anywhere at all. He's going to go to a diner, he thinks. He's going to drink a cup of coffee, he thinks. He's going to go be around other people and tell himself that he is no more of a failure than anyone. He's going to sit there and think of nothing, no thoughts, no self, no contemplation, all impulse, until he's ready to go back to Rhoda and face the version of himself that she now knows.

At this diner he will drink that coffee until he can tell Rhoda he likes her too much, he's never felt this way before, and he's scared. It feels more like drowning than he thought it would.

He does none of this.

He takes a step onto the stairs, but stops.

Here's what he should have realized: He left her when she needed him because her need terrified him, and he could not sit with that terror. He was not strong enough. Even though he knew she doubted her own strength, he left her alone to carry the weight. He left her alone. He left her fear so that he would not have to sit with his.

Coming from behind the long hallway door, he hears a voice calling his name.

*Jonathan Abernathy.*

*Jonathan Abernathy.*

*Jonathan Abernathy, are you there?*

Dark room. Dark carpet. Dark heart beating all loud and gross inside of him. Is Abernathy scared?

✓   Yes, Abernathy is scared.

But of the two—between the dark hallway calling his name and the bed where the judgment of the woman he loves waits (*loves*? (Fine, he decides. Yes, he decides. Loves))—he is less scared of the hallway than his life.

Besides, he tells himself. Kai is also his friend. And wherever she is, won't she be scared, too?

He stands at the step, looking at the faint outline of the doorway, already knowing, before he does it, that he will go into that (stupid) hallway which is (stupidly) long in search of (stupid) Kai who doesn't even like him, the odds of her even being there incredibly slim if existent at all.

Yet, from the hallway, there it is. Someone calling his name.

IF POSSIBLE, THE hallway stretches in front of Abernathy like a long dark snake. He holds the flashlight with resolution. The beam extends to a fine pinprick, growing so small it disappears before it encounters a wall to refract upon. The voice sounds very far away.

*Abernathy*

*Abernathy*

*Jonathan Abernathy, are you there?*

Abernathy shakes a little bit, in his knees.

The walls are ornately trimmed and decorated with painted portraits of previous dream officers, each holding their helmet.

Nothing to do but press onward.

And onward.

Onward some more.

Abernathy walks for so long, he turns back to check his progress and can no longer see the door he came through, or the door he is headed toward.

In front of him, the hallway stretches out, no end in sight.

He no longer hears the voice. No one calls his name.

No matter. When he begins to move forward again, a smooth black door to his left appears. The door was not there before. A silver doorknob beckons him.

He puts his ear to the door. The metal is cold on his skin. "Kai?" he asks. "Hello, Kai? Are you there?"

No answer.

It is hot in the hall. Slightly stuffy in a warm, comforting sort of way.

Abernathy feels a dark drowsiness sweep over him. His limbs are heavy as he opens the attic door.

The smell is overpowering: garlic and warm heat rising through baseboards.

It is gloomy in the attic, but in a comforting way, like curling up at the window to read against the rain. The only light comes in from an unwashed window that frames an empty field. Abernathy hesitates at the door's arch. But then, there it is. The smell of his mother's perfume as she climbs the attic stairs to retrieve him for dinner. This is the duplex on Perry Street where Jonathan Abernathy spent fourth and fifth grade.

The floorboards of the attic creak when Abernathy steps onto them. How could he not step onto them? Jonathan Abernathy thought he would never step onto these floorboards again.

Shrill bells of warning are going off in his head: Go back! Turn around! Beware! He should listen to his gut, because what comes next is nothing but heartache. But the attic looks more real than he remembers and that is more intoxicating to him than anything the world could ever offer. His own memory of the attic is so often returned to that the recollection itself has become thread-bare. Certain particulars have split off. There are holes.

Not so, here.

The cot in the corner is stacked high with books: Ray Bradbury, Philip K. Dick, Dumas's musketeers and vengeful counts. Jules Verne and his multitu-dinous journeys to the middle of the earth. James Baldwin, Harlan Ellison, and Shakespeare. So many men, all full of suffering: Charles Dickens, Leo Tolstoy, Mr. Dostoyevsky. The jackass brotherhood of Hemingway and Fitzgerald. Bukowski. Heller. Nabokov. Conan Doyle and Louis Stevenson. Raymond Chandler. Aldous Huxley. Edgar Allan Poe and Mark Twain and Herman Melville. Vonnegut. Douglas Adams. Pratchett. William Faulkner. Salinger, the gifted son of a bitch.

There were others, too, that he read secretly. Only at home, in the attic, where no one could see. Authors whose names were such an embarrassment he didn't dare say them. O'Connor and Hurston and Welty. Austen and her characters who bowed to no man. Morrison and Angelou. Harper Lee. Le Guin. Butler. Mary Shelley's Frankenstein, who was more of a monster than the being he created. Brontë, whose Heathcliffe contained enough multitudes to carry a bibliography all his own. Piles, and piles, and piles of beat up softcover mysteries whose authors would die in obscurity. One lonely copy of the diary of Sylvia Plath.

(Plath? *Really?*)

((Yes. Dammit. Plath.))

When he was younger, his parents didn't allow him to read anything that wasn't what they called "An American Classic."

In another corner, Christmas ornaments patiently wait inside cardboard boxes labeled in his mother's hand. Plastic bins of used fabrics and other hobbies his mom attempted to begin but could not finish crowd the room.

And on the floor, scrawny and nested amongst bunnies of dust, a flashlight in one hand and a bent-spined copy of *Ubik* in the other, it's him. He is a child and he is reading.

Abernathy had forgotten that he used to like that sort of thing. He used to like to read.

What he had loved as a boy, more than anything else, was a really, really good story.

Like any person, he liked to be told a tale.

Abernathy, now older, and jacketless, steeped heavy in oncoming heartbreak, doesn't understand that he has found his way into his own dreams and that he should, at all costs, turn back. We aren't meant to watch our dreams unfold from the outside. From the outside, where one is an observer and not a participant, the details are meaningless.

Abernathy, instead, steps into the shadows of the attic. He hides in wait. He knows that his mother is ascending the ladder. She is about to open the attic door.

Abernathy can't help but feel that if he could get one last glimpse of her, one last glimpse of who she had been . . .

The attic latch lifts slightly, begins to pull up.

From where he stands, he can only catch a sliver of her face, backlit with the yellow light of the hall, the corner of her hair, and the most meager glimpse of her forehead.

If he can just move a bit to the right he would better see her. He needs to see her. If he sees her, all will be fixed. He knows this somewhere deep within himself. Seeing her will fix him.

She stands on the ladder, calling his name. He knows she is calling his name, to come down to dinner before his father arrives home from work (always in a bad mood), except Abernathy cannot hear her over the talking.

Two dream officers have arrived. They are unhousing their gear.

His child self ignores his mom and pretends he is not there. He lies very still, holding the book rigidly upright to cover his face.

Abernathy wants to shake him. He wants to grab himself by the shoulders and shake until the ungrateful cretin knows what he will one day lose.

The lead officer who has just entered the dream is Jason. He snaps on a glove. The auditor alongside Jason raises her visor, looks around in distaste. The auditor is the fast-food worker from the informational video. The one who doodled beside him about government indentured servitude.

Jason sighs. "I thought I got rid of this dream. Back when I started, I was in and out of this one at least once a week." He hands the girl a clipboard. "Look around you, try to figure out what it is that's causing distress. Mark that, then afterward I come in—or my team—and we remove it."

"What do you mean you'll remove it?"

"You know what, hon, it's not worth explaining. Too complicated. Better for you to just watch."

Jason turns on his pack.

Abernathy stumbles forward in horror. He tries to grab hold of Jason. He cannot. It is as if Abernathy is not there. His hand passes through Jason's body and Abernathy topples through the girl, whose only response is to yawn.

Jason holds the vacuum hose in his hand and kicks open the attic door where Abernathy's mother stands below, on the ladder.

Abernathy picks himself up from the attic floor. He attempts to step in front of Jason. Abernathy can see the top of his mom's head below as she lifts a ringed hand to raise the door no longer there.

Abernathy is not above pleading.

"Look, " he says, "you don't understand. I'm one of you."

First his mother's hand disappears into the hose. And then her arm. And then it's as if she is mist being vacuumed from the air. She is gone before he can see her face.

When Abernathy looks down at the ladder, there is no one there.

Just that forlorn and forsaken beige carpet.

"Right then," says Jason. He re-hoses his vacuum. Claps his hands, one against the other. Turns to the trainee as he steps back from the ladder. "You understand now, how it must be done?"

"Oh," says the girl. "They disappear just like that?"

"Just like that," Jason says. "Actually, sometimes they fight it. Not many, though."

"Do they ever escape?"

"No," says Jason. "Never."

"Where do they go?"

"They're only dreams."

"Yeah," says the trainee, "but where do they go?"

"What do you mean?"

"They have to go somewhere, don't they?

"Huh," says Jason, giving her a funny little frown, "I don't think I've ever been asked that."

"Well, do you know?"

"Sure I do."

"And . . . ?"

"And," says Jason patting the girl on the back, "that bit of information is above your paygrade, sweetheart. Just remember—all you have to do is write down the irritant on the paper, and then my team and I will handle the rest."

Abernathy stands in the slanted attic room, frozen as Jason catapults himself and the young service worker from the dream. His younger self remains reading at the windeye, oblivious. Sickly looking. Too childishly skinny and bony to do anyone any good. Standing at the attic door, Abernathy looks down into one of his many childhood homes. He steps back from the gap, only to realize he is holding a box. A cardboard box with his name on it. His box, which is lidless. The lid is on the floor. The tile floor of the archive.

He is not in an attic at all.

Abernathy looks up from his black tadpole, now the size of a small fish. It swims languorously from one corner of the box to the other. He can't remember how he arrived in the archives or how long he's been here. He tries to think hard on it. He feels there is something he must hold on to. It is at the edge of his vision. If he could just turn fast enough, he could catch a glimpse of it as it closes an attic door.

But before he can grab hold, he's lost it. Nothing is there.

When he looks up from his box, he is alone. He is alone in the archive of dreams.

## 24

**THERE IS A STRETCH IN** time where Abernathy feels like his body has been sold to the highest bidder. While he remains trapped inside it, his body works. His body lugs itself from one job to the next. As soon as he wakes, his body begins to move. As soon as he finishes work, his body drags itself to sleep again and up again and to work again. He is nothing. He is an onlooker. His dream load has increased and so have his day shifts at the stand. Jonathan Abernathy is tired, and hurting, and exhausted. He is hopeless. He is achy. He is fucked up. But he is also alive. And because he is alive, there are people he owes.

Throughout this time he thinks of Rhoda. Almost obsessively he thinks of Rhoda. He thinks things like: what is Rhoda doing, how does Rhoda look, what is Rhoda thinking? Is Rhoda talking to her boss right now? Is Rhoda holding Timmy? Does Timmy still allow herself to be held? Does Timmy know about her brother? Is this why she's so obsessed with mushrooms? How does her obsession make Rhoda feel? Is Rhoda doing work in her yard, weeding them away right now? If Rhoda is thinking things, is she thinking of me? Is Rhoda mad?

By the time Abernathy finishes his *Armillaria tabescens* sculpture, it is the final gasp of summer. When Rhoda opens her door to him, she seems displeased.

Rhoda wears a loose black tank dress. She has cut her hair again. He hasn't cut his own. His hair has grown to his shoulders. The air is hot and dry. The grass is very brown.

Rhoda greets Abernathy with a cold "It's been a while since I've seen you."

The last time he saw Rhoda was the night she came over. He has been thinking about it nonstop since.

He follows her inside and delivers his sculptures to both Rhoda and Timmy with a "ta-da" and lots of impressive hand waving. Mostly for Timmy's enjoyment, but for Rhoda's, too, if she happens to be watching. Timmy has gotten taller since Abernathy last saw her, but she still finds delight in the token. Rhoda looks beautiful, as always, cutting like a knife through the world as she retreats to the bathroom to get ready for work.

"Mom has been letting me stay home alone," Timmy says. She lies on the carpet and examines the small cluster of blooming friendship mushrooms. She tries to hide it, but Abernathy can tell she sounds proud that she is allowed to be by herself.

"Oh—is that true?"

"Yeah! It's cool."

Abernathy doesn't say here that he is surprised. His mind can't help going to Rhett. After something like that, would he leave his child alone? He will miss being Timmy's babysitter. He will miss their special time together lounging around and hunting for fungus in the yard. He does not say: What am I supposed to do with my time now? Instead he asks, "What do you get up to?"

"I read?"

"It doesn't get, like, scary? Without me?"

Abernathy is mostly teasing, but also doesn't want Timmy to forget that he enjoys coming over, too. It is not just Abernathy fulfilling his neighborly duty when he arrives to watch Rhoda's ward. The ward herself is actually pretty cool.

Timmy gives him a hesitant look that Abernathy can't read. She says, "It's OK. If anyone comes, I have a baseball bat."

Abernathy tries to remember his first time staying home alone and if he felt proud. But he was alone so frequently as a kid he can't recall when the first time was. His mother never seemed worried about things like leaving him to himself.

Rhoda gathers her hair into one of those clips that Abernathy loves. A lot of strands wisp out the back. He goes to join her at the mirror and tries to catch a strand between his fingers, but she shrugs him off and moves to the kitchen. He tries not to take this personally. Instead he watches her, trying to put his finger on how she wants him to approach her. He follows into the living room and sits on the couch. She goes to the restroom mirror again. He can tell something is wrong by the steady way she looks into the mirror instead of at him. Her cold gaze meets her cold gaze.

Abernathy sits on the edge of the couch and raises his voice so he can talk to both Rhoda and Timmy about how busy he's been. How all-encompassing work is. How he finally feels like he's getting ahead.

Rhoda doesn't even make little sounds to show that she's listening. Timmy gets up and goes into the kitchen to get a glass of water.

Abernathy tells them about his coworkers—he works with all sorts of officers now that he no longer works with Kai. He tells Rhoda about Kai, specifically, leaving out her name so that he can bring it up that he knows her later, once this miscommunication is over. Not a lie by omission. Just an omission of convenience.

"She's a hard-ass," he explains. "But, ultimately, she's good."

"Right," says Rhoda. "Sounds like a real party."

"It kind of is," Abernathy says, even though that couldn't be further from the truth. Working with Jason sucks. And he hasn't seen Kai since the time in the mansion with the parquet floors. Still, he says, "We are all a big family."

Rhoda stiffens. "You make a habit of joining families, then?"

To this Abernathy confesses, but tries to be funny about it: he can't think of the last time he had friends. Like, real friends. It comes out like, "It's been a long time since I've been around anyone who actually enjoys my personality," but less lame and more funny. Or, at least he thinks he's being funny.

Rhoda at the mirror is silent in a terse, maybe even hurt way, which Abernathy pretends not to notice, mostly because Rhoda's coldness is starting to confuse him. The closer he gets to her, the more transparent he expects her feelings to be. The opposite, so far, has proven to be true.

Abernathy had been so excited to see her, to apologize, to own up to his mistakes, but now he can't figure out how to fix whatever it was he broke.

Timmy comes back from the kitchen. She sits next to Abernathy on the couch and tells him she's not as interested in mushrooms, now that she's older (her eyes, at this, dart to Rhoda. Does she know the cause? Is she old enough now that she can know?) but she likes his sculptures all the same. She pats his knee while she says it. It's good she likes them, because Abernathy worked really hard on the sculptures, even if it took him a long time. He even took them to a local pottery place to have them kilned. It took a lot of money to get to the pottery place (he had to take a cab). But once he got there, they told him that actually, this type of clay could be baked in a regular oven. Then Abernathy had to explain he didn't have an oven, just a microwave and a hot plate. He ended up paying the pottery place prices to use their kitchen. Then he had to pay for the cab to come back. It was too far away to walk.

Abernathy stops watching Rhoda (stoic, beautiful, severe, unknowable in her existence) at the mirror because Timmy is explaining that she is going to name one of the mushrooms after him, Abernathy. But then she changes her mind. Returning Abernathy's name to him, she decides to call the gifted sculpture Captain Mushy the Tenth instead.

Like Abernathy said to Rhoda— Things are looking good! Abernathy finally has a handle on his life! His other coworkers respect him, now that he is working with them more frequently. And thus, his life is a life that others can peer into and say: Wow, what envy this induces in my heart!

Silence from the bathroom and the mirror. At the sink, Rhoda applies mascara with precise, hard-mouthed swipes.

This is all wrong. This whole interaction is wrong and not what Abernathy thought it would be. He stands and moves toward her, but before he even finishes saying her name, Rhoda says, "Don't," in a warning tone.

Shocked, Abernathy stops. He sits back down.

For the rest of the visit, they both pretend they are comfortable. They eat dinner together. They drink wine. Timmy tells them about school (it sounds awful).

After Abernathy gets home from his sculpture delivery, he lays down to sleep and breaks into a panic he didn't realize he had been holding in. He can't breathe. His eyes sting. His chest contracts. His life is suddenly too heavy to carry and he has no idea how to set it down.

Then, as quickly as it started, the attack is over.

Wretched and wracked, grubby with the salt of his own tears—as if nothing out of the ordinary has happened and this were an everyday occurrence—as if he contained no thoughts at all, Abernathy closes his eyes and falls into work.

THE DREAMER OF tonight's dream is incapable of moving. She must wait in her driveway as her husband runs over her with their new car. Dark hair. Tattoos with faces. When the husband has finished running her over, he pulls out of the driveway, drives down the street, loops around, begins again. She looks like Rhoda.

Abernathy tries to think how many of the dreamers looked, to him, like Rhoda. The woman in the field. The woman with the child in the mud. The woman on the swing. One of the dancers who stared through the crowd as he and Kai were forced to waltz. The girl in Kai's dream who is pregnant and scrubbing the floors.

Abernathy hovers at the garage where the woman in the driveway cannot see him. He drops his sheet to the floor. It disappears before it touches the toys. He kicks a Barbie convertible and it rolls beneath a shelf. The dreams no longer feel real to him. The officers will soon remove any discomfort. Tomorrow Rhoda will wake up, go to work, be fine.

She doesn't need to know.

It's better if she doesn't know.

The man from the bus—Penn—arrives instead of Kai or Jason. Abernathy misses Kai. She's gone for weeks. But anyone is better than sniveling Jason, so Abernathy takes what he can get.

Trying to make small talk—and assuage his own curiosity—Abernathy asks Penn if he's seen her. Kai.

Penn rolls his eyes. "Kai's sick," he says.

Abernathy's face must give off the fact that he doesn't believe this, because Penn looks him up and down before laughing. "You should be disappointed, bud. The rest of us aren't going to put up with your 'oh poor me I'm new and sensitive' bullshit."

Penn says this all with a sinister goodwill, but he stops chuckling when he sees the woman crawling up the driveway.

Her husband's already driven off. The woman is on the concrete alone.

"You've gotta be fucking kidding me," Penn says.

"Tell me about it," Abernathy replies.

Abernathy and Penn watch as the Rhoda look alike tries to drag her body into the garage. As Penn's eyes fall upon the woman, his expression hardens. Abernathy can understand why. Abernathy feels sorry for Rhoda too. It's an awful dream. It's not economical to feel sorry all night long, either for himself or for the dreamers, but he *knows* this is Rhoda. She's told him this was her and that this is a dream she has. Of course Abernathy is here feeling bad. The two men stand in the shadows and watch the woman slug and crawl and pant. Watching her is the only way to pass the time. She twists and she turns, in pain, and both men think: *she is beautiful.*

They have to wait for her husband to come back to remove him.

They kill the time admiring her determination. Her body. Her will. Her life.

Abernathy has to give it to her, in what seems to him to be a pretty much hopeless situation, Rhoda *is* determined. Abernathy would not be so determined. He would have given up a long time ago, stopped crawling, lie there waiting to die.

Rhoda is silent as she pulls her crushed legs behind her. Abernathy is thankful they have the power to siphon her husband away.

"You know," Penn says. They can hear the truck's rev around the corner. Rhoda increases her struggle to make it into the house. She's starting to, out of the corner of her eyes, cry a little. As she should. She will not make it. If it were Abernathy, he would be crying a lot. "I think you're wrong on this one."

"Right," Abernathy says. He is speaking in a flat monotone. "How could it possibly be *the truck coming to plow through the dreamer*? Not enough emotional connection there for a removal. Nothing bad about that at all."

"However you want to internally justify it," Penn says. He sounds hollow. Flat.

"OK," Abernathty says, snapping at Penn. "I get it. No one likes me. Everyone thinks I'm an idiot. I can't read a dream for shit. Ha. Ha. You've had your fucking joke. Just remove the fucking truck."

The man shrugs. "Sure. Whatever." His look is cold. Abernathy has this feeling like he is falling backward, toppling over himself, tumbling deeper, deeper, deeper into his life.

"But," says Penn. His voice is stony, and resolved. "The man stays. He's not going anywhere."

The truck speeds through the corner. Rhoda looks into the garage. She's not looking at them, exactly. She can't see them. That's clear enough. She's looking toward safety. As she looks at them without looking at them, Penn strides into the driveway to squat in front of her.

It *is* Rhoda. There's no way it's *not* Rhoda. It can't be Rhoda, right? But all the same, it must be.

Abernathy does not understand Penn's actions. How is this helping? If it is Rhoda—and Abernathy is correct in thinking it really is her—Penn's being more of a dick than Abernathy initially thought he could be.

The truck screeches into the yard. The driver is hidden by the glinting sun. Abernathy gets this sinking feeling he can't shake. And then the sun moves into the cloud and Abernathy sees that the driver of the truck is Rhoda's ex-husband. Rhoda's ex-husband, Penn.

*Oh*, Abernathy thinks in slow motion. *Penn must be his last name.*

Dream Penn parks the truck. He steps out, onto the driveway. Officer Penn stands in the driveway as he stood in her doorway—he's got his foot jammed. He will not allow Rhoda to close this door. He won't allow Rhoda to close the door on his family, or their relationship, or their son, and he'd be damned if he'd let some asshole like Abernathy come in at the last moment and attempt to close it for her.

What *is* Derek Penn thinking as he squats down to lift up his dreaming wife?

Abernathy doesn't know. He steps toward them to do something, do something, somehow do—he doesn't know what. He is in the driveway. He is watching his coworker—Penn, Derek Penn— reach out to touch Rhoda on the shoulder while his other hand goes to his belt. Rhoda looks pissed. Rhoda looks absolutely burning mad. Abernathy is going to do something. Abernathy has got to act. Rhoda looks up at Penn. She must see him. Does she see him?

Even if she does, it's too late. Jonathan Abernathy is pulled back, into a silver elevator. *La la la*, the jingle rings. He has plenty of time to stand there in shock, looking at himself looking at himself. When the elevator finally slows the contraption gives a faint *ding*.

"Destination," says a nondescript voice, "Home."

The doors open and with a blink Abernathy wakes in his bed.

The streetlamp outside casts dull yellow light onto his ceiling. OK. Ok. ok. Big breaths. He can still feel the truck. He tries to calm down. It was definitely her. It was definitely Rhoda. He is suddenly ready to ask himself the big questions. The questions that should have been apparent to him from the start. If that was Rhoda, then—

How many of the dreams he audited have been Rhoda's dreams?

What was it, exactly, that he had been taking?

Should he cross the street? Should he wake her? Should he confess it all, no matter the cost?

Abernathy is paralyzed with indecision. He lies there, staring at his ceiling in horror, until another light joins the street light casting a shadow across his walls. He is too terrified to look outside for the simple reason that if he looked outside he would see who the light belonged to. And if it was Rhoda's light, if Rhoda was awake in her room, if Rhoda were looking into his, if Rhoda could see him—

IN THE COOL light of the morning, Timmy reads a book on her porch. Fog swirls against the damp cuffs of Abernathy's pants as he waves and calls out, "Hello to Mushy the Tenth!" Timmy does not look up.

A man holding Timmy's tiny suitcase steps out of the house, without locking the door, and scoops Timmy up with one arm. This is impressive. Timmy is getting tall.

Timmy just keeps reading as the man carries her to the car. Fall is soon coming. Tucked in the beak of her father's arms (it is, in fact, the arms of her father), Timmy holds her body straight in protest. She holds the book in front of her face.

Penn sets the suitcase on top of the car. Opens the car door. Sets Timmy inside.

Abernathy knows him by his swagger. By his shoulder's determination. By his steady, never ending pull.

But where is Rhoda?

Why isn't she pushing back?

## 25

ABERNATHY BLEAKLY STEPS INTO THE suit with very few psychic complaints. Just a dull, throbbing sense of obligation. A desperation for praise or friendship or growth. He hasn't realized it yet, but he is lonely. Couples kissing. Couples fucking. Couples breaking up. Rejection. Dismissal. Refusal. Rape. He siphons it all away. In the most intimate rooms of another's interior, Abernathy gains very little emotional insight about himself.

In the megadome of his own thoughts, he tries his best. Rhoda has not spoken to him (really spoken to him) since the gift. And though Kai has not returned, he repeats her mantra: at best his work as an auditor could be described as unintuitive or sloppy. At worst a company liability. He keeps her in mind as he goes. He wants to stay hired long enough to scrape together this month's rent.

✓ Jonathan Abernathy you can do this!
✓ You got this!
✓ Life bows at your feet!

Here's the question he should be asking himself: Where did Kai go, and am I going there?

Here's the question he *is* asking himself: Am I good enough? Do others enjoy my company? Have I ever had a friend?

At the end of a night's cycle, Abernathy steps into a dream he has been in before. He is in the serene field. Grass sways. Mushrooms cluster. Cows chew cud. A woman with short black hair is at the swing. He steps toward her into a puddle of mud. His white boots go *schlick schlack*. The mud begins to double. Triple. Rising quickly around him, black guck. Like the dream with the dead child, yet instead of a train engine, he hears the rumbling of a truck as it rounds the corner. This dream is several dreams at once. Dreams he has already traversed. He fills out his sheet with haste and drops it into the swaying grass. The paper and the grass are quickly overtaken by the dark mud. Yet the sheet doesn't disappear. He fills another: *black guck, mud rising, truck coming across the horizon with promises of doom, a rope like a hanging*. The mud is at his calves. The paper floats.

He struggles toward the tree. The woman on the swing turns as if she senses him. It's Rhoda. He misses Rhoda. Is this really Rhoda or is someone else dreaming of Rhoda? Who, here, is the dreamer? He is terrified of being judged by her. She stands out of her swing. The mud parts for her. Whose dream is this? Who dreams of this? Before she can speak, her body morphs. Her hand becomes his hand. Her face becomes his face. Her shoulders and heart and hair and mouth and teeth become his. Her eyes are the eyes of the man in the mirror he despises.

Quite sensibly, Abernathy begins to run.

It's only, he runs for so long and so hard that when he looks up he is surrounded by blackness. No grass. No mud. No tree or truck. No ceiling. No floors. All emptiness. True nothing. He is in a black and distant whispering. He stops running to catch his breath, look around, find a way out. He can only see his hands just centimeters away from his face. He is bodiless, or at least he feels bodiless. He runs his hands up and down until he can feel his stomach rising and falling. He gasps stupidly for breath.

It is not the blackness he is scared of. The blackness itself is seemingly inevitable and final-feeling.

It is his thoughts that terrify. They expand inside him, uncontrollably. As they fill him he begins to feel like someone else, something else. A worser, darker, angrier version of himself. His thoughts are the thoughts we all have, except they are now the only thing he can feel: *You are worthless you are miserable you are good for nothing you are lazy you are unreliable you are incorrect you are stupid you are goddamned and you goddamn those you love you are not good you are soulless you are cursed you are void—* It is not the thoughts themselves that have power. Rather it is the feeling of the thoughts, the strength of the stream which Abernathy cannot escape. There are no external stimuli here, in this darkness, and so who knows how long he is standing there, trying to push back the flood raging through him. He does not, for the most part, even think he is an idiot! (Right?) He thinks he is, maybe, trying his best at all times and his best does not match up with other people's best. ((Right?)) But actually, no, that's not it. That's a stupid thing to think.

It becomes apparent Abernathy does not actually believe this: his non-idiocy. He only tells himself this like you would tell a child a story to calm them down. Prepare them for bed. Prepare them to go alone into the dark. Everyone else's best is better and more exemplary than his best. This is because, he thinks, he is incapable and incompetent when it comes to being alive. There it is. There's the truth. He is an incompetent. The king incompetent of the incompetents.

And then comes a knock. Someone is knocking. And he remembers these are all just thoughts.

He tells himself: *Jonathan Abernathy, you are good! Wipe your eyes! Slap yourself on the cheeks! Hock a loogie into the oncoming darkness and say: NOT TODAY! TODAY I WILL NOT FALL BENEATH!*

He stumbles and stutters through the black toward the knocking, groping along the emptiness with his hands stretched out. He gets close, but then walks past it, so that the knocking sounds far away again. He retraces his steps, walking backward carefully without daring to turn around. He runs his hands up and down the emptiness until he feels metal. He is holding a door knob. He turns the door.

Kai unfolds from the doorway, stumbling out and straightening beside him. Kai! Beside him! He can barely see her in the soft and loamy gloom. She seems like she is angry, but as she looks around her face softens. He has never been as grateful to see anyone as he is to see Kai.

She isn't wearing her suit. She wears simple black slacks. A gold bracelet. A black shirt. Gold hoops. Her hair is up and still so, so red. She puts a reassuring hand on his back.

"We were worried about you," she says, which confuses him. She adjusts her glasses. Her nails are set. Isn't she the one that's been gone?

"These dreams give me the creeps," she says. She does look a little scared. She reaches down and pulls her suit out of the floor. She steps into it. Zips up. She turns her pack on without catapulting Abernathy out.

The whispering has grown louder.

"No criticism?" He laughs. "Nothing personally I did wrong?"

Kai begins to vacuum up the darkness. "Is there—" She hesitates. The darkness is crumpling. The whispering turns to screaming. She has to raise her voice. "Anything you've forgotten, Abernathy? Is there anything bothering you?"

"What?" he asks, thinking of Rhoda all alone in his house. "What are you talking about?"

Kai is clearly uncomfortable. "You need to wake up, Abernathy."

"Ha, ha," he says. "Very funny."

"Remember the archives?" she prods him. Her face flickers. She is herself, but for a moment, he sees *his* face reflecting back to him. Speaking to him. Telling him something he must already know.

"When you take something important from someone," Kai-as-him tells him, "if you siphon it out of them, it doesn't go away. It becomes something else."

"When you get back," she says, and she is Kai again, looking around uneasily—"ask yourself: Where have I gone?"

The screaming of a truck catching the curb has stopped. The dream is an endless whispery gray. Before Abernathy can ask her where she's been, when she'll return, what's going on, he's awake. He's awake in his bed and he's starving.

He stumbles toward his alarm clock. It's feebly ringing. He stops at the date. Two days have passed.

Alone in his apartment this makes him laugh.

Is this where he's been? In his apartment, asleep?

He laughs and laughs and laughs.

No one—not a single person—had noticed he had gone.

Whether she was real, whether she knew something he did not, whether she got her freedom and escaped her dream cycle, whether it was only himself he saw in that darkness—Abernathy will never see the real Kai again.

## 26

RHODA IS ON THE DECK with her hair half done. Her dress, unzipped, flaps like wings against her shoulders as she marches through the yard. The leaves are barely starting to turn. Abernathy debates whether he should call out hello from his lounge chair on the driveway, but remembering Penn's arrival at the beginning of the month he hesitates.

He is not usually outside at this hour. He is trying to catch sun after doing prep work at the stand this morning before the trick-or-treaters get there and destroy everything with their tiny little hands. Lately, with Rhoda, he is trying to play it cool. In response to him playing it cool Rhoda mostly ignores him. She is either ignoring him now or she doesn't hear him. She circles the yard once, twice, looks under the deck where Timmy collects mushrooms. Rhoda looks confused, like she can't remember why she's here.

Beneath the deck there is only the deck. No child wriggles through the mud.

It's starting to get cold outside. Abernathy is wearing layers. Rhoda is wearing none.

"Looking for Timmy?" he calls. "You're going to catch a cold."

She stops her circling to look at him.

"What?" she says.

"Are you looking for Timmy?" he asks.

She looks confused and turns away from him.

"Are you *crying*, Rhoda?"

She puts her hand to her face. Looks at her wet fingers. Her brows tick inward. "I feel sick," she says. "I can't remember why I came out here. Maybe it's to say hi to you. Not that you care whether we speak or not." Weak smile. She doesn't mean it.

"You haven't said hi to me in a while," Abernathy admits.

She stiffens, then turns. "For good reason."

"And what reason is that?" he asks to test her. He has a theory that she can't remember. She can't remember what he took from her dreams.

A blank look comes over her face. "I can't—" she says, and for a second he thinks she's going to say *Remember. I can't remember.* But midway through the sentence she seems to change her mind. "I can't get into this with you right now. OK? I'm busy as fuck." She gestures to her dress, half-zipped. Her back is a black-and-white tapestry of flora and fauna tattoos.

Abernathy ignores this comment. "Last time I saw Timmy she left with her father. A couple of weeks ago. I wondered where you were."

"I don't know what you're talking about," she laughs. "Are you trying to make me feel better by confusing me? If so, it's not working." She frowns at him, then looks away.

Abernathy sits up. "What?"

"You know what, I slept past my alarm. I was having the weirdest dream." She gives him a quick, furtive look. "That's it. Sorry for interrupting you in"—she waves her hand—"whatever it is you're doing. I would say let's talk later, but obviously you don't like to talk much anymore at all so—"

"Rhoda, hold on," Abernathy says. He gets up from the lawn chair and goes to the fence. She is already at the screen door. She closes it without looking back.

Abernathy waits, but Rhoda does not return.

When Abernathy gives up to go inside, only his alarm clock greets him from atop the microwave. He doesn't understand what's going on between him and Rhoda. He suddenly doesn't understand her at all. He stares at the alarm clock for a long time. There's a picture of a woman smiling next to the clock, thumbtacked to the wall. She is young and arm and arm with Abernathy's dad, who he never really got along with that much.

Abernathy doesn't remember a lot about his childhood—his dad killed himself when Abernathy was in middle school, and then he was all alone. Looking at this picture only reminds him of how alone he actually is. He can't even remember how long it's been there or why he put it up. Looking at the woman and his father, Abernathy feels a sloshy dread. He throws the picture away.

Of course he does. He doesn't remember what his mother looks like.

Should he go back to sleep?

He wants to, though it is only noon.

Now it is noon o' one.

LATER THAT NIGHT he spends maybe too much time awake, thoughts racing, until he steps into the elevator and it deposits him in a small, orange-lit conference room. He hates office dreams. They're endlessly dreary and self-important, qualities he fears he shares and thus finds insufferable in other people. Quickly he looks around the room for his clipboard.

He's surprised by the four managers—men in crisp black suits—seated behind him at a long table. Abernathy is afraid, but thankful, at least, that Kai is not here for this. If she were, she would be zeroing in on his most private insecurities, casting little judgmental side glares at him as he fumbles his way into the room.

Appear to be confident. Appear to be competent. Appear to be good.

"Abernathy, finally. Why don't you take a seat." A big, important-looking man in a black suit sits at the head of the table. He motions to a chair that appears.

Abernathy sits down absolutely sure he is 100 percent fucked.

Abernathy tries to think of his best qualities and how he might frame them in a way that makes him seem indispensable.

He can think of none.

The manager leans forward and a plate of cookies appears in his hand. "Macadamia nut? Chocolate chip?"

Abernathy hesitates. Is this a test?

He chooses chocolate chip, the reliable cookie that can be depended upon in emergencies to cheer up the masses.

"There's no need for your nervousness," the man informs him. "Your name was put forth for a promotion. The board is impressed with your work ethic and is offering you a raise in title and salary."

Abernathy chokes on his cookie. One of the men leans over to slap Abernathy on the back. A crumb is expelled from his mouth and in midair, the crumb changes to a pigeon.

"A promotion?" Abernathy asks once he's caught his breath. Astonishment is one word to describe how he feels. Disbelief is another. It's as if someone has sucker punched him with a bag of gold. Not one of the men has a shadow.

The man wants to know—how does middle management sound?

One pigeon multiplies into forty, and above them, in the rafters, there is song.

MANAGERS, ABERNATHY IS surprised to learn, are paid more. Waaaaaayyyy more. Having never been asked to manage anything in his life, Abernathy is astonished. He signs the liability form without hesitation. All he can think about is the money: Bathing in money? Spending money? Hoarding money? Maybe Rhoda, next time he sees her, will let him spend some of his money on her. If she won't let him spend his money on her, perhaps she will let him spend it on Timmy? All money seems good to Jonathan Abernathy.

A pin comes in the mail. It is a pin to pin on his suit, on the right breast, where everyone imagines the heart to be. His official number? Dream Officer the Two Hundred and Sixth. Dream Officer 206, officer of dreams. Officer Jonathan Abernathy, the Two Hundred and Sixth, how do you do.

Abernathy decides he will not quit the hot dog stand. Despite his oncoming windfall, he will not quit as he waits for his managerial liability paperwork to be accepted, nor when he is officially inducted. The happiness at the prosperous turn of his future prospects makes the idea of working at a food stand not so soul crushing. Not so *death at the slow hands of capital.*

Jonathan Abernathy is transformed, overnight, into the type of man who works hard to get ahead. A bootstrappy man. A man whose bootstraps are so lusty and vigorous any doomed soul could lift themselves from the crushing depths of unemployment into a powerful life of purpose and intent. It is he, this year, who is full of holiday cheer.

Yes, sir, Jonathan Abernathy is sure of it: here his future comes.

There is only one piece of paper left to sign. He must await its arrival by post. Today it is Black Friday. He waits for his future at the hot dog stand, where they are beset with a line.

The small, four-walled cart is tiny, tight. The more humid the stand becomes, the less erect the paper hat grows upon Abernathy's head.

Abernathy is always waiting for his future, but this time feels different. Breathing in the steam of processed meat, Abernathy knows that this time will bring change.

Adam is crammed into the box with him so Abernathy must lean against the anterior wall, next to the stove, occasionally burning his arm, in order not to brush against his colleague. His hand has pretty much all the way healed, except for a small black speck, but the same is not true for his other injuries. Abernathy's only been at the stand for a year and yet his lower forearm is covered in burn marks that look like crosses. The still-healing scars pucker like ass skin so that his arms look as if they are covered in tiny butthole crosses of the Lord.

Today the customers come nonstop. They want to buy, buy, buy.

Adam is flying, preparing seven hot dogs at once. He wields the ketchup like a sword and some spills onto Abernathy's apron. But where there was previously only the inhospitable landscape of resigned despair, there is now a seed of hope! The hope is a strange, weird, glorious thing sprouting inside him. Its growth now colors the world.

At the sight of the ketchup, Abernathy laughs.

Adam looks at him funny.

("What the fuck is wrong with you?" "Nothing, man. Not a single goddamned thing." "OK, well, focus, in that case." "Focusing." "Douchelord." "Chode.")

When a man does not tip on his order, Abernathy thinks calm, angelic thoughts full of grace and empathy. The customer is no longer a curmudgeon, but rather a struggling upstart like Abernathy himself who must save every penny to better build his life.

When Adam bumps him against the stove Abernathy thinks: *Aha! With what gusto the working man labors to receive his wage! An honorable dedication to which we can all aspire! A resolute determination which keeps us in the game for yet another turn of the moon! Thank God!*

It is fun to think this way.

Is this what a future does? Because make no mistake, Jonathan Abernathy's hope has come from his newly created future. His current gig has transformed from a symbol of personal failure into a door which he will force open in his quest for freedom. The tedium of this labor is now a mere symbol of his willingness to work hard! To give it all he's got! To tackle the American dream with verve and gusto! To pin his hardships to the wet cold pavement of life and say: I WILL DEVOUR YOU WHOLE.

"Abernathy!"

In fact in ten years this would all make for an astonishing story. One to tell at a dinner table where his many loved ones gather nightly and say: SIR! TELL US BUT HOW! HOW DID YOU ENDURE!

Abernathy will put down his fork, dab his lip, smile patriarchally and say: OH CHILDREN. THE ONLY WAY ONE CAN ENDURE IS TO ENDURE. Knowing smile. Loving glance all around. Wisdom received. And he, the holder of resilience's great secret.

"Abernathy!"

"What?"

"Pass the sauerkraut, Jesus. Where are you today?" Adam holds a hot dog in its tiny cardboard boat. The inside of their cart is a mess. A pink-faced customer stares with dead eyes through the stand's service window, not so much seeing as autopiloting. The customer gazes at Abernathy and Adam through a thick pane of workplace exhaustion. She is surrounded on all sides by other customers. The customers, poor fools, look as if they have been worked to death.

Daydream interrupted, Abernathy feels righteous sympathy. "Right," he says. Here are people who are hungry! And who—were it not Abernathy—is meant to feed them?

Abernathy tops the customer's hot dog with the energy of a man destined for greatness, for he knows himself now to be a man destiny-ed. Surely everyone here can see that.

## 27

ON OFFICIAL LETTERHEAD SENT THROUGH the U.S. Post, Abernathy is invited to managerial training.

He arrives with gusto. The swooshing office doors part for Jonathan Abernathy as if he is Moses and the doors are the Red Sea. He has come to save the life of his people (in this metaphor, his people are himself and his many past attempts at employment). His first day in his new position will surely be, as they say, a cakewalk. A walk in the cake.

He arrives at the plexiglass desk and introduces himself as Jonathan Abernathy, the two hundred and sixth officer. Feeble tinsel decorates the wall. A wreath hangs at the door. Shoulders back, grin on, chest out, his pin glints above his imagined heart. Jonathan Abernathy appears to be confident. He appears to be competent. He appears to be good. He wears his sixty-six-dollar suit. Just as Abernathy supposed; he has developed appearances and, in the process, solved his life.

He says none of this at the intake desk. What he says is a tidy, noncommittal "Hello."

Can he see his reflection in the plexiglass?

No, he cannot.

An old-fashioned woman rises from her desk chair without fuss or fight. With a sigh, she leads Abernathy from the waiting room to the slow-gathering managerial class waiting in the basement below.

Abernathy is five minutes early. He looks nice! He looks good! He fits in! The way the pants swish-swish as he walks across the carpeted floor is an experience of bliss, a joy that Abernathy knows one only has a handful of times in one's life.

The receptionist is no Kai, but she brings him water, smiles in a tired way, and bows her head as she exits the basement. It feels good to be respected and served. Abernathy stands next to the festive pastries (wreaths, christmas trees, Star of David–shaped cookies) holding his tiny cup of water, more pleased than the most pleased man in the universe.

The cut of his suit! The gleam of the pastries! The way the light flickers as if trembling in anticipation for the rest of his life!

Things, finally, as they should be.

The managers file in slowly. Almost all of them are men wearing suits, like Abernathy. He wonders if they, too, opened a fresh lint roller just for this. Abernathy watches with a studied air of haughty ambivalence (the opposite of how he feels) as other new members of the managerial class are led down the stairs and deposited in the room one by one, their suits wrinkled around the collar—same as him.

Now that Abernathy thinks about it, almost everyone who files into the room looks like him. Guys with previously stooped shoulders, chips on their back newly removed but still felt, a little greasy but with a glint in their eye which indicates they always knew they were meant to be here but are still startled by the course of events all the same. All of these guys are managers? The information session looked a little more democratic than this. Abernathy looks around for Kai, but no luck. The only two women wear boxy clothes, have their hair pulled back, are in suits that disguise their hips.

A few men come over and shake Abernathy's good hand with respect.

"What's up, man?"

"Nice to meet you."

"Pleasure's all mine."

"Just came in this morning, really an honor."

Their touch electrifies Abernathy. The firmness! The authority! He forgets, immediately, his previous observations on their likeness and instead is filled with powerful fantasies of being accepted into this group of men, welcomed into them, held as important by them, embraced bodily into them.

Perhaps they all, at one point, hug? Their faces all pressed together, each of them inhaling a tiny circle of communal air. Their air circulating in Abernathy's body. His air circulating in their body. The social desire to join such a group is so strong Abernathy finds himself grinning as if he has just imbibed intoxicant. He is shaking hands. So many hands. He doesn't even like shaking hands, normally. He sweats. But his desire to be accepted is so great he ascends his social anxiety. Does he tell his jokes with calm, self-assured dignity? Yes, he does. Does he sip regally from his tiny glass of water? Indeed. His sips are the tiniest, most dignified sips any man could aspire to take.

The other men congregate around a three-tier muffin holder and begin telling stories of dreams they've audited. After several men share their stories (harrowing! astonishing! great bravado!) Abernathy tells the story of he and Kai suctioning up a whole slew of kids: the way they folded into themselves and disappeared. How morbid that was, kids folding in half. It's not that funny a story, actually, more of a harrowing tale, but lots of people laugh. Lots of people think Abernathy is funny. Lots of people think this is good.

There is chatter. There is camaraderie. Abernathy belongs.

That is, until Jason arrives in a beige suit. Jason acts like he doesn't remember Abernathy and has never worked with him before. He even introduces himself again (even though Abernathy shakes his hand and says, "We've completed a few audits in our time together" and Jason says, "Have we? You all look the same in the dreams to me" (The groups laughs at this)).

Jason then tells a story that confuses Abernathy. It's a quick one. Abernathy follows the beginning: It's a perilous dream, an attic dream in some beat-down house. Clutter and grime everywhere. Jason is there with a new recruit, a girl who doesn't know what she's doing. It's an ugly attic, the attic of poor people, full of poor people stuff like lots of moth-eaten paperbacks. *Genre*, you know. Literal cobwebs. In the dream, someone's mom is ascending a ladder to let herself in.

"And then this kid—the dreamer—starts screaming at his mom." Jason says. "Telling her to turn back and run from us," Jason says. "I look to see who 'us' is, and I realize this kid is a grown man looking at *me*. Me and the new girl! He's telling his mom to run from *us*. Not every day a dreamer can see you like that."

"Whoa," someone says.

"I have goose bumps."

"Just goes to show you," Jason says, "that in this line of work it never gets boring, huh, man? " Jason shakes his head and slaps his hand onto Abernathy's back.

Abernathy looks around to figure out what his reaction to the story is supposed to be. Is this story funny? Abernathy has no memory of his own mother and thus believes he never knew her—although he would have liked to —and to him it seems sad, the dream and this kid.

All the managers are laughing, and so Abernathy joins in.

The men quiet down. There's murmurings. Some "Yup." Some "Been there, man."

In a cool and collected voice, in his most sophisticated-because-he's-not-that-interested-actually-he's-just-polite-and-secretly-judgmental voice, the voice that all men have, the pretend voice, he asks—"So what did you do then?"

"Oh," Jason says, taking his hand from Abernathy's back to rest on his stomach. He chuckles. "Get this: I packaged the whole dream. The dreamer disappeared. Must have somehow got him, too."

The men laugh and nudge each other.

"Been there."

"Done that."

"Must have been a helluva trip."

"And I'm sure someone somewhere gave a piece of their mind about the ethics of that!" Hahahaha.

"Well it's all about expediency boys, bag 'em and tag 'em. Get it done."

"That's right."

"Couldn't have put it better myself."

Abernathy really doesn't get it this time, so he waits until the time for affirmation and companionship is over, when they all stand contentedly shaking their heads with the end of the story 'get a load of this guy' back and forths.

"I'm sorry," Abernathy says, still smiling, still channeling their mirth so they don't sense his ignorance, "Let me get this right: you *packaged* the whole dream?"

A couple of men share looks. Abernathy realizes he's misstepped somewhere, gone wrong somehow. Though he's not sure where that may be exactly. Maybe the way he said packaged? Or his inflection on *whole dream*? Men are very sensitive to any kind of perceived aggression. This is why Abernathy often makes himself small.

"Sure did," Jason says. A little bit of hostility now, which is surprising, because most of the time Jason is just snivelly and annoying. "Got a problem with it?"

The other guys look at Jason. Look to Abernathy. Look back at Jason.

"No, dude," Abernathy says, forcing a tone of good will and good feeling. At his edges, he senses that it's time to put on his disguise, a disguise which fundamentally perverts who he considers himself to be. A disguise of bro-y-ness and gusto. It is a slimy disguise. He does not like wearing it.

"It's just," he says, disguisedly, "what a *fucking* feat, man. I don't think I've packaged a whole dream—maybe, like, ever."

The guys around him relax, laugh.

"Well, I got lucky," Jason says. "My manager wasn't too strict. Some of them can be real cunts."

"Tell me about it."

"My manager once railed me after packaging company memories. Just bent me over on the spot in front of district. As if I could have known they were important!"

Packaging seems to mean sucking up all the bad bits. Packaging a dream, Abernathy guesses, means hosing the whole damn thing into your pack. Abernathy didn't even know that you could bag the whole dream instead of specific elements.

Abernathy shows he understands this concept and is not just hearing it for the first time by saying, "Right, right."

"But now that there's change in our division leadership—" Jason wiggles his eyebrows.

"Way better."

"Yeah."

"Better for the company line, really."

"Better for us!"

The men laugh. They have brown hair or lightly black hair or ashy blonde hair. They are not *fit* but not *not* fit. Their skin tones range from pale and sunless white to maybe-white-maybe-something else, but that's about it.

"To us!" one guy proposes, holding up his water.

The other guys say, "Hear, hear!"

The women participate, too. But they seem to be faking in the way that Abernathy's faking. They won't look him in the eye.

"Yeah." Abernathy laughs. "Yeah."

Abernathy raises his water to their tiny waters. They all drink.

"Anyway," the man who apparently packages whole dreams says, "it's all about efficiency. The new boss doesn't care what you bag as long as you're hitting quota."

"Amen."

"Anything that looks impressive to the client, that's what he cares about. The numbers."

"It's that truth that does it for me."

"I did a night where I audited like fifty dreams: just boom boom boom." The guy snaps at each *boom*. "Back to back. Had a couple of doubles where the same dreamer was present. Really fucks you up,"—he taps his head—"you know up here."

"I'll average about sixty a night on a good night."

"What about you," Jason says, looking directly at Abernathy. "What do you pull?"

Abernathy knows this is a power play and so tries to look unperturbed, confident, but mostly he feels sick and a little worried. He hits about ten to twenty dreams most nights. And he never does them like these guys do them. Kai only allowed him to package one or two elements of each dream. Anything more, she said, destabilized the worker. Since her departure, he's kept up the practice. He didn't know there was another way.

Kai used to say the worker they audited was top priority, always, but it seems like these men disagree.

Abernathy misses Kai, but, thinking she had returned to some extent, that he would see her again, he also resents her for putting him in this position. Why hadn't she shared the standard term of engagement everyone else seemed to operate on?

"Me?" Abernathy asks.

"Yeah, you."

"Oh, well on a good night, Jesus—" Abernathy exhales through his nose as if he's counting. Are they lying? How could someone possibly audit this many dreams in one night? Should he say fifty? Or forty? Though maybe forty is too low. He has no eye for metrics.

Before he can answer, the secretary returns. She stands next to the stairs and asks them to welcome the director.

The group—about fifteen or so men, two women—leave the refreshment table to gather in a crescent moon around the stairs. The women don't make eye contact with the secretary. The men turn up their faces as if they are astronauts looking, for the first time, upon Earth. Jason stands on his tip toes to see who will be greeting them. Abernathy cranes his neck. No luck. He can't see shit. But wait—there it is. The sound of footsteps descending. Here he is. The reason they are all here.

The group sees the director's feet first. Then his knees. Very nice knees, by all accounts. The men who comprise the crescent of onlookers hold their breath. The director comes slowly down the stairs, out of the shadows, into the basement's fluorescent light. Abernathy awaits him eagerly, the man who has the possibility to change his life.

When the director steps from the stairs into the room every man in the basement claps. Every man except Abernathy. How can Abernathy clap when the man in question is Derek Penn.

PENN LEADS THE group of shuffling men down the ever-expanding corridor. He walks with something of a prodigious pace. Abernathy gets the feeling that Penn thinks this whole thing is funny. Particularly funny to Penn are the men lagging behind him, desperate to be something to somebody, and maybe in the process escape their miserable lives. Or at least that's how it seems to Abernathy. The managers are like shuffling ducklings, bumping into each other and the wall as they try to get ahead, to the front of the pack, where they can be seen, noticed, approved.

"Gentlemen," Penn says, stopping abruptly.

Abernathy is pushed forward and backward as the group careens to a halt.

The space is tiny. The group fills the two small alcoves on either side of the hall. Miraculously, Penn now stands in front of a door holding a key.

"What I have to show you—it's of the greatest importance. The most secret heart of the secret hearts of what we do." No smile, but nods to various men in the audience as if to assure: they do in fact exist and their existence is personally meaningful to him, Penn, not to mention the company.

There is tittering among the men. Jason stands a little straighter. Straightens his collar. Abernathy is both disgusted by this and pressured into performing this way himself. Does Jason not realize that Penn is not a good person? Abernathy knows this already, right? Yet Abernathy feels his shoulders settling into the ramrod position of his childhood, as if he were holding a broomhandle behind his neck.

Penn asks, softly, "I can trust you, can't I, gentlemen?" He smiles and opens the door. "Wait wait—don't answer." He laughs at his own joke. "Of course I can. I hired you."

At first the men rush the door, but the door is more slender than it appears. The group must go single file. There is jostling, but eventually a single line does begin to form. As each man gets to the door he must turn sideways and stoop.

Abernathy is pushed and cut in front of and when things settle he finds himself at the back of the line, behind Jason. Jason turns and gives him a wan smile (he knows who Abernathy is, and remembers working with him, Abernathy is 99.99999 percent sure). Abernathy returns the smile with enthusiasm, mostly to mask his dislike. As if his eagerness could somehow make up for Jason's disdain.

Before Abernathy can shuffle through the door, Penn lays a heavy hand on his shoulder.

"Abernathy, isn't it?"

Abernathy looks at the hand on his shoulder. "Uh," he says. "Yeah. Yes. Hello, Penn. Long time no see."

Jason hovers in the doorway looking angry (jealous, more likely) as Penn smiles. "You can go on through, Mr. Kiln. I just want to have a conversation with Mr. Abernathy for a moment."

Jason looks unbelieving, pissed, astonished that it was not he that was being chosen as confidant numero uno. Jason stalls for a moment, hovering inside the doorway, then stoops sideways into the room. Penn's hand still rests upon Abernathy's shoulders. Just sort of sitting there. Heavily. Sitting on his shoulder heavily. Abernathy can't stop looking at it. The hand. Abernathy keeps thinking: *Your son is dead. Your son is dead. Your son is dead.* When Penn starts speaking, Abernathy has to drag his eyes away from Penn's (freakishly symmetrical) cuticles.

"Having a nice time so far, Ab?"

"Uh—me? Am I—?"

Abernathy looks around for anyone else who might be called Ab—but no it is just the two of them in the long dark hall. He must be Ab. This is the first time he's ever been called Ab. Candles intermittently flutter on the wall. Penn's face is cast into shadow. The shadow itself seems to wriggle. It is unclear if the shadow moves on accord of the guttering candle light or the general spookiness of the hallway. Really, at this point, either could be true Abernathy would not be surprised.

"Yes," Abernathy says. "Having a very nice time. Thank you."

"Are they treating you well?"

"Yup," he says. He is uncomfortable being alone with Penn. He's not sure where this is going, so he decides to play it safe for now. "It's all daffodils and sunshine," he says, smiling, laughing a little. "Ha ha."

"Right," says Penn. Tight smile. Steel-wool eyes. Eyes that could scrub Abernathy out of existence if they wanted to. Eyes that have seen things.

"Right!" says Abernathy.

Penn's voice is soft, yet powerful. "You understand why you're here—Abernathy—don't you?"

The hallway is drafty. Abernathy can hear wind whooshing through it. It's such a long hallway. It's hard to know where the wind is in its journey. Penn's hand is still on Abernathy's shoulder.

"Yes . . . sir," Abernathy says slowly, trying to give himself time to think.

"Why is that."

Is it just Abernathy or are the shadows on Penn's face growing longer, wider, deeper, blacker?

"I'm sorry?" Abernathy can't tell if Penn is asking him questions or just making interrogative statements.

"Why are you here."

"Here as in . . . ?"

"Why are you at this training."

"I'm here . . ." Abernathy says ". . . because of dedication . . ." He can't see Penn's face, so doesn't know if this is the right direction. ". . . my dedication and efficiency in helping America's middle class navigate the intensity of their . . . professions?"

"No."

"No?"

"No. That is not why you are here."

Abernathy says nothing.

"Your answer is fundamentally incorrect."

"Ah."

Now Penn is silent.

"Why is that . . again?" Abernathy asks.

"You're not talented. You're not smart. And you're not particularly hard working."

"O-oh?"

Through the doorway the men chat and laugh. The light seems warm and inviting. Abernathy wants to go home.

"Frankly, I don't think you could find your way out of a paper bag if you had to."

"Right."

"Make no mistake: You are here because I will do everything in my power to protect my wife. That is the only reason."

". . ."

". . ."

Abernathy gives into the silence first and confesses, "I don't understand."

Penn closes his eyes. The shadow on his face flickers and grows darker. He takes a deep breath and opens his eyes. "My daughter and my wife—they are . . . precious. There is nothing," he says, looking at Abernathy, "*nothing* more important to me than them."

With Abernathy, Penn makes intense, uncomfortable eye contact.

"Ah."

"Do you understand?"

"Y-yes?"

"Because of your decision," Penn says, "I was able to give my wife what she has long," here he takes a deep breath, "*yearned for.* While she . . . is . . . processing things, Thelma will continue to live with me."

"Thanks to . . . me?"

Penn steps closer. There is so much eye contact happening. Like, a suffocating amount of eye contact. Penn presses his hand down upon Abernathy's shoulder.

"And if you do anything to jeopardize that," Penn says, "if any of your actions lead to my daughter being taken away from me"—though his face is now inches away from Abernathy's face, though he is whispering, though the light now falls behind him, the shadow across his face has not moved—"or to my wife becoming unhappy . . . Do you understand? You are not here because you are talented. Or smart. Or good. You are none of those things. You are here so I can watch you. You are here to service me."

Abernathy stands very still.

"So I'll ask you again: Do. You. Under. Stand."

The pressure on his shoulder is so great, like Penn is trying to push Abernathy to his knees. Abernathy is loath to admit it, but he does crumple just a little. Just a bit.

"I understand," Abernathy says.

He does not understand.

"Say it again."

"I understand."

How could he understand? He has never been married. He has never had children. He has never given himself to another person and he has never had to go through the grief that comes when your gift is returned. How was he supposed to know, then, that when Penn spoke of giving his wife what she often yearned for, he spoke of giving her the freedom from himself, from her daughter, from her son. He was giving her the relief of being, at least for now, someone else. Someone to whom horrors had not happened. Someone on her own.

Abernathy has no way of understanding that. All Abernathy sees is an ex-husband who is terrifying, who won't let go, who has taken his daughter from her mother's care.

Abernathy cannot conceive it, because Penn is both. It is very hard to hold two truths at once.

"Good." Penn picks Abernathy up by the elbow. Penn dusts Abernathy off. Penn shakes Abernathy's hand. The shadow on Penn's face is gone. "Shall we go in?" he asks, perfectly cordial with not a hair out of place. They do. As they enter, Penn laughs and smiles widely, chuffing Abernathy on the back with his hand as if they had, the two of them, just shared a great joke.

The room is all warm tones and carpet. Penn keeps his hand on Abernathy's back as the two of them circle the managers sitting around a long, oval table. Penn gestures that Abernathy should sit at his right and an officer scrambles out of the seat. Abernathy lowers himself slowly into the butt-warmed leather.

The other officers are looking at Abernathy as if he is the smartest, most talented, most loved man in the world. Which, to be fair, is something Abernathy is desperate to be.

"Gentlemen," Penn says. He stands at the head of the table. A young man slowly circles the group, refilling their water. Penn is smiling. The young man is not. "Welcome to the first day of your life."

## 28

TWO MEN IN DREAM GEAR enter the conference room. They carry something heavy between them, the object obscured by the angle of Abernathy's seat. Their steps are lumbering, as if the mere act of walking under the weight of the object is agony.

The escorts set the box at the middle of the table, on the edge. The mahogany table begins to tip. The escorts then press their fingers alongside the underbelly until they find the button they are looking for. The button is pressed. The box is whirred as if on a small conveyor belt to the middle of the table where it rests in the center of an inlaid circle.

The new managers watch in anticipation (Abernathy included). The inlaid circle clicks. Rises. The managers can all see the box now. It is a small cardboard letterbox, as are all the boxes in the dream archives. A simple cardboard box with a fitted lid.

The men who brought the box into the room leave the room.

Penn sits back in his chair. He leans back with his elbows on the rests, his hands steepled in front of him. His fingers rest lightly on his lips. He allows the managers to observe the box in silence.

The unhappy young man tasked with refilling their waters stands in the corner of the room, still holding the pitcher.

Penn lowers his fingers. He smiles, though it does not reach his eyes. Perhaps the suspense is personally amusing to him. He sits forward, elbows on the table.

*His mother's name is Janice*, Abernathy finds himself thinking. *His child is dead. His dad was called Rabbit. Rhett.*

"Who here can explain the role of an officer?" Penn asks.

Abernathy knows enough now to know this is some sort of trick. He keeps his hands in his lap. His eyes, too. His cuticles are not very symmetrical at all.

The other managers must feel the same as he does. They, too, don't speak up.

Penn turns to Abernathy. Abernathy glances up from his lap. He tries to formulate an answer in his head but all he can hear is static noise. The faint buzz of his processing power abjectly failing.

Penn shifts his gaze lower down the table, to Abernathy's right. "Jason, why don't you fill us in."

Jason coughs and sits a little straighter. "Of course, sir." What follows is straight out of a handbook. Though what handbook that is or when they were supposed to have read it, Abernathy knows not.

"The job of an officer is to ensure the proper removal of obstructive dream matter. This aids the client in their personal productivity. Officers must conduct themselves safely and professionally when handling nightmare-grade material in order to ensure the continuation of America's global lead in productivity."

Abernathy nods. Yes, that sounds exactly right. Why hadn't he thought of that and answered so? He is not the only one nodding. Most of the managers nod or smile along. Some look toward Penn before mirroring their agreement.

Penn, smiling to himself, takes a long sip of water from his tiny cup. "Well done," he says to Jason. "That's what we have told you. A dream officer packages elements of the dream for safe disposal. Once those elements are packaged, the worker's performance should improve, thus fulfilling our contractual obligation. You're correct."

The men look relieved, nodding and smiling to one another.

"A hell of a job it is, too," says a man at the far end of the oval. The rest of the men laugh.

The suspense of the meeting wanes. At their own peril, the managers begin to forget the cardboard box at the center of the table.

"And so it is," says Penn. He nods along with the officers, playing up this jovial atmosphere. "But," he asks, holding up a slender finger, "what do you think happens to those elements—once we take them away? Once they are packaged."

The men in the room share confused looks. "We dispose of the matter?" one officer offers.

"When we deposit our packs at the end of the shift?" adds another.

Penn nods thoughtfully. "I see my question is too difficult for you gentlemen."

The two women exchange a long look.

Penn stands. It seems he does everything with leisure. Penn stands *leisurely* and *leisurely* walks behind Abernathy, along the table of managers, to the middle of the table where the box sits.

"I see no one here fully grasps the extent of our operation," says Penn. "And this is suitable, of course. How could you. But I was hoping, by now, that at least one of you had the initiative to discover the financial imperative which allows you to be here."

Penn looks around. The managers look ashamed. Many look at their laps, where they, too, clasp their hands at their thighs. Even Abernathy looks down again, but he does so as if he is in prayer. As in prayer, he keeps one eye raised to watch Penn deliver his sermon.

"What we collect, gentlemen, is the unwanted subconscious. It doesn't come easily. This is where your talent comes in. You collect the best material. That which you manage to collect, we package, bring into our world, and turn it into pliable matter, which we then," he says matter-of-factly, "sell."

Penn flicks the top of the cardboard box off. The clatter of the lid on the table surprises the men. Abernathy is not the only one to jump.

The men are no longer looking at their laps. They are looking at the box. The open box. Nothing has happened. It is still just a box. But now the box is open.

Penn walks—*with leisure*—back to his seat where he sits and leans back, the whole masquerade of employment and payment so neatly folded into his life that he no longer thinks of himself as separate from this job. He is this job. This job is power. And he wields his power with the greatest mastery. As if it is his right. This, Abernathy realizes, is his goal.

"Ask yourself—what do we do with these nightmares? Where does the runoff run off to?"

The room is quiet. The open box sits at the middle of the table. Abernathy is not sure, but the box seems to tremble slightly. Just *slightly*. Vibrating. He thinks of the dream hall and the jammy black tadpole at the corner of his box swimming against the edge. Does this box hold something like that?

A dark, shadowy hand rises from the box and grips the side. Another hand. And now there are arms rising to the corners of the box, gripping the sides. The arms push themselves out. The box tips over. A dark shadow pulls herself from the cardboard opening, onto the table where she lays on her stomach, panting. She is shimmering into existence. Her body is the body of a woman, solidifying. Her hair covers her face. She is wispy and hollow around the edges as she actualizes, as if she is a mirage.

She begins to materialize. And then she becomes whole.

Were she not to have just emerged from a box one-eighth her size, the men would not now sit in shock, holding their breath. She looks that real. As it is, they did see her emerge from the box. Several men roll back from the table. Abernathy himself feels the need to put between himself and this woman as much distance as possible. She looks sick. She coughs. She lifts her head and she is smiling between lank strands of hair. Arching her back, she stands.

She wears jeans—low rise—and a polo shirt. Except for the surreality of her appearance and the black whorls escaping along her edges she looks as if she could be any woman. Any normal woman at all.

In quick, jerking motion she looks at Jason, who sits next to Abernathy. The two men have put about a foot between themselves and the table. She begins walking toward them, eyes on Jason, taking stuttering steps. Her knees buckle as she walks, as if it is her first time using them. She pushes her hair back from her face.

There is a scream. The water pitcher drops, shattering on the floor.

Everyone in the room jumps. Except for Penn. Penn sits coolly. Penn sits *at his leisure*. Abernathy turns. The water pourer in the corner has covered his eyes and cannot bring himself to look at the woman. Abernathy realizes the woman is not looking at Jason. The woman is looking directly behind him, at the water pourer. She pushes Jason and the manager on his other side apart as she steps from the table onto the company carpet. Both managers visibly shudder. The water pourer holds his hands out in front of himself. He is trying to talk, but fear has caught his voice. "S-s-s-stop."

The woman is close to him now. She reaches out to tuck a strand of hair behind the boy's ear. The boy collapses in a dead faint on top of the glass pitcher which crunches beneath him. Water spreads across the carpet.

Are they related? It's hard to tell. The woman could be the boy's mother from the past, his sister, his babysitter, himself in the future.

Yes, there is blood.

The officers who brought the box come back with their packs whirring. The woman turns toward them, but she must deem them harmless because she begins to expand, growing taller and wider, curving her body over the boy.

From where Abernathy sits at the woman's back, it looks as if she's trying to grow large enough to envelop the water pourer whole. Turning away from the officers is a mistake, at least on the woman's part. The taller one starts to package her. Black wisps break from her body and are sucked into the hose of the demonstrator. It takes several minutes of choked silence to capture all the black whorls. Some float to the ceiling and get stuck, like balloons, but soon the woman herself is gone. When the last of her is cleaned up, a demonstrative officer presses the button at the edge of the table and the box whirs back to the edge, no longer heavy with that nightmarish black matter. The officer carries it under one arm as if it is merely an empty cardboard box and not the container of horrors.

The two demonstrators leave the room yet the managers are no longer seated at the table. All of them have stood, in an effort to get away from the shadow-y creature. They now line the walls where they remain, looking dazed.

No one helps the boy bleeding out on the carpet. His blood coagulates with the water spilled from the pitcher. Delicate sliced lemons float on the red.

Penn speaks. "We sell the matter we collect to the highest bidder," he says into the silence. The managers turn slowly to him. "This is your priority. The subsidies which we offer to corporations are merely the beginning. Our money is made packaging nightmares, which can, for the right price, be unleashed."

## 29

A COMPANY ALWAYS HAS MULTIPLE revenue streams. If you can't easily identify at least two, it's likely you're one of them.

What happened after the water pourer's display?

Abernathy stumbled from the meeting with resolve hardening in his heart. He walked home in the raucous silence of early spring: birds careening, trees growing new leaves so the wind has something to whistle through, the last patches of snow crunching beneath his boot as faint sounds of play happen across the vertebral yards connecting the outer city.

Abernathy had a lot of questions:

- How long does it take to accumulate enough dream matter to make a nightmare walk in reality?
- How are these nightmares controlled?
- Does this have something to do with Kai?
- Who buys this dream matter and why?
- Does this have something to do with Rhoda?
- Who the fuck is Derek Penn?

There was even a moral moment, as Abernathy walked home, where he held the terrified water boy inside of him and tried to honor him. He earnestly did attempt to imagine giving up the job at the archives, not to mention all the hope it affords him. For a few mood-swinging days, Abernathy thinks he can do it. To do what Kai warned him to do. To quit. He is going to quit.

He thinks this and thinks this and thinks this until his paycheck comes. When his paycheck comes, he stops thinking.

On his last birthday, his paycheck is more money than he has ever received at once, almost $1,000. And with this $1,000 (earned fairly over the course of March, thank you very much), Abernathy's life begins to change. Combined with his $180 a week from the hot dog stand (for those of you doing the math, that's $1,360, or $2,720 a month, $32,640 a year, pretax), Abernathy can afford to eat better and his skin clears up. His skin clears up and his mood shifts. His mood shifts and he can get out of bed. He has energy. He has desires. He wants to do things. The hope and happiness that comes with meeting your basic needs is almost enough to forget the original managerial meeting, and Rhoda, and Penn, and Rhett, and the creature—among all those waiting and watching men—that climbed out of that wretched box.

Abernathy knows that some people cannot live off of this amount. That to some people this is nothing. But suddenly this amount of money makes the world seem navigable, experienceable. He is capable of meeting the world with joy and harmony instead of spite.

The truth of it—which, if he works hard enough, he can capture in his periphery—the real truth is that he would do just about anything to stop feeling dread.

He will hem and haw. He will worry. He will pretend to be a good person caught up in the perils of his own decision-making. But in the end, in his heart of hearts, one hundred times out of one hundred times he will make the same choice. Leaving this job would mean stepping from precarious stability into the unknown.

Abernathy *hates* the unknown.

What Abernathy does not hate is the checks.

All companies are evil, Abernathy reasons after depositing the check. And how many people—*really*—could have someone out there, willing to buy their terror? Hardly anyone, he tells himself. Certainly. Even if someone were to buy that runoff material, what could they do with it? The demonstration must have been an exaggeration. Penn makes everyone uncomfortable by being too intense. Hasn't Abernathy seen this? Hasn't Rhoda told him this? The man is a walking and talking black hole. Everyone and anyone is in danger of falling in. But isn't Abernathy's job fundamentally the same in the face of this information?

At night he travels around saving people from themselves.

For the first time:

- ✓ Yes, he is starting his journey to financial security,
- ✓ Yes, he feels like a success, and
- ✓ Yes, he wakes up each morning feeling hope.

Does he sleep at least eight hours a night?

- ✓ He sleeps fourteen.

The night of his final birthday, Abernathy is in the middle of putting on his white suit when a deep panic overtakes him. He sits on the edge of his bed, heart cavorting, pulse stuttering. He has two legs in the crinkling plastic. He wears no shirt.

Kelly—his landlord—has guests over. Abernathy hears them talking through the air vent. Kelly is laughing. Whoever the guests are, they speak in low, hushed tones. Soft, ambient sounding music trickles down to him.

Is it her friends?

God, he has no idea.

How the fuck is everyone living such large, complicated lives all at once all the time?

Abernathy's thoughts are weird and moving really fast. He tells himself he is excited. That's all. One thought keeps hitting him on the inside. *oh god*, he thinks, all lowercase and desperate, like a private whisper. *oh god oh god oh god.*

He sits on the bed, half-dressed. If he didn't know any better, Abernathy would suspect the wet, hot, desperate feeling creeping through him to be a type of despair.

But what could he possibly feel despair over? He's alive, isn't he? That's more than most people can say.

If he were a different type of man, an unselfconscious man, he would feel compelled to drop onto his knees and bang his head against the concrete until he bled. He almost feels moved to action now, but instead he just sits there in the silence. At the edge of his thoughts, not quite graspable, he wonders: When has he ever been moved to take action against or for anything?

The last few nights waiting for his officerial duties to begin are swinging moods. Manic, uncontrollable happiness followed by crying spells. Heaving. Pacing. Collapsing despondency. Explosive joy. He feels Kai's eyes on him from wherever she is. He spends a lot of time at his window, watching Rhoda's house. But Rhoda does not come out. Rhoda does not say hello.

Is Abernathy thinking of the water pourer? Does he consider that in many versions of this story he himself has once been the water pourer, standing at the edge of the room in pain while those who make decisions avert their eyes? Not really. He is mostly thinking of the constant low-grade panic of his life before this job. The feeling of not being good enough. That knee-jerk knowledge that he is not meant to live in the current iteration of this world. He is simply not capable of existing how others exist. The state of being poor and knowing you're poor and knowing you'll be poor forever is not a state he ever wants to go back to. Being poor is okay if you don't realize it, he thinks. His dad, for example, single and sad, didn't realize he was poor up until he did. And then he died. Abernathy has known of his own impoverished state for years, and yet he keeps living, (stupidly) hoping to one day be able to leave what he has always known.

But what happens if he gets there, and it's even lonelier than he was told?

Abernathy zips into his suit, lies down in bed.

Above there is laughter. Amongst the dulcet tones of landlord camaraderie, Abernathy swings into slumber. Kicking and falling back into it. Tired in every part of his body, including his face.

His last thought before he descends?

He misses his dreams.

At least in his dreams he found reprieve.

## 30

**WHAT DOES IT MEAN TO** be successful? People ask themselves this question to the point of obsession. They believe it is their mission in life to "succeed," as if life is something to be climbed on top of and bested.

**ABERNATHY IS ONE** such person.

**THOUGH, OF COURSE,** like most people who are afflicted by preoccupation with success, he remains oblivious to the true pleasures in life. As such, he is willing to sacrifice them.

# /// IV ///
# JONATHAN
# ABERNATHY
# WAKES

## 31

IN ABERNATHY'S SLEEP, HE ARRIVES in an orange conference room not unlike the room they met in during his training. Long conference table. Lots of chairs turned this way and that. Shitty carpet that somehow actually looks kind of nice. (No bloodstain, he checks.) It's official-looking. A group of officers are already here. They are laughing. A few shake Abernathy's hand. He grips their grips with grins and pleasure, his woes banished for now. Even the dark spot on his hand has gone. *See?* he thinks. *This is good.* Despite any potential misgivings they may have had, the other officers, too, chose to stay. Look at all that smiling! Would everyone be smiling if there were dire consequences to their actions? Surely not. Abernathy smiles, too.

If you drink from a water cooler in a dream are you really drinking? Abernathy pours himself a tiny cup and idles near a tall window. An otherworldly sight looms below.

"Lavender fields of France," Penn says. His voice, as always, is firm. His tone is disinterested and polite. "We collected this memory from a man who grew up farming them. He later immigrated." Penn takes a step forward. He is now standing against the window as well. He cuts an impressive figure. "The man was dreaming about the murder of his uncle, which happened as he was plowing the field. Even though the dreamer was quite old, he kept returning to the field in his dreams. A nightly obsession. One of my first assignments. Every night: Lavender fields. Lavender fields. Lavender fields. It got to the point where if I saw the color purple I felt like murdering someone myself. I decided to help us both out. I took the whole thing."

"It's very pretty," Abernathy says.

"If you look at the top of the hill, you can see some of the flowers covered in blood. Do you like it?"

Abernathy searches for the rust stain almost automatically, before he realizes what he is looking for. There it is. At the top of the hill a small crumpled patch of flowers have buds rustier than the rest.

Abernathy knows he should be scared. He suspects Penn is trying to scare him. But is it working?

As if on cue, the man rests a heavy hand on Abernathy's back. Abernathy can feel it through his plasticky suit. Abernathy doesn't know if he feels scared, necessarily. He mostly feels sort of, like, resigned. Like the constant dread that doubles when Penn is around is almost becoming normal. Like a tide that ebbs and flows depending on the time of the day. It is better to feel dread often, rather than always—isn't it? Abernathy has already resigned himself to the trade off. He forgoes his financial instability and constant anxiety and instead accepts a shitty boss who he, somehow, both hates and empathizes with. What worker hasn't made the same sacrifice?

"How did you transport the field?" Abernathy asks, genuinely curious. "Did someone package the whole thing and then you unpackaged it outside this window?"

"Secrets of the field." Penn says, deadpanning. The guy is like fifteen years older than him, so Abernathy tries not to roll his eyes too hard at the pun. Penn takes his hand off Abernathy's back. "I think you'll like the recruit I've paired you with, Ab. She has a certain . . . similarity . . . to your mentor."

"Kai?" Abernathy asks. "Do you know what's up with her? I've been worried."

Penn laughs. Shakes his head. "Nothing for you to worry your pretty head over," he says, patting Abernathy's hair. "What I like about you is your attitude. You may be astonishingly stupid, but your outlook on life is so limited it gives you a cheery optimism. Cheers me right up."

Penn turns from Abernathy and claps his hands together once, then spreads his arms wide. "Gentlemen," he bellows, which quiets the room. "Any moment now your auditor should be filing their observations. You'll notice a button added to your utility belt. When your auditor's paperwork has been properly

filed your button will vibrate. It is a transporter. There are two. The top button will transport you. The bottom will transport your auditor. Please check
in with your auditor before transporting them. Dreams can be dangerous places
to be. We want you to be safe. Understood?"

A chorus of "Yes sir!" "Yes sir!" "Yes sir!"

"Now as you know—" Penn stops. Abernathy's hand is delicately raised.
"Yes, Abernathy, do you have a question?"

"Just one, sir."

"Well," says Penn magnanimously lethal into Abernathy's silence. "Go
ahead . . ."

Abernathy is thinking of the great blackness which consumed both Kai
and himself. How he was lost within it for days. How Kai spoke as if she, too,
had shared the experience. Abernathy asks, with as much deference to authority he can muster (a lot of deference), "What happens if your auditor gets lost? . . .
Sir?"

The managers share a confused look. "Lost?" they seem to be asking.
"How can auditors get lost?"

"As always, Abernathy, your imagination is impressive." Penn laughs. The
rest follow. "A very good joke."

"But sir—I—"

"Now," interrupts Penn, just as the button buzzes and the men tense in
preparation for their first day as the head of the beast. "Go forth. Collect the
debris of the soul."

ABERNATHY STEPS INTO a small field. No lavender flowers, just nubby grass.
On one side of him the sun sets. On the other side children spill from double
doors into the ring of a bus port. Abernathy snatches a piece of paper from the
air as it floats down to meet him from above.

It is a detailed report, as far as reports go. Instead of listing merely "children"
or "bullying," his auditor writes, in looping cursive with a fierce diagonal slant:

> *cluster of five children—boy wearing redshirt, boy with adult woman's*
> *face, teacher trapped in boy's body, boy with bowl cut, boy with*

*chipped tooth—cause emotional and physical distress to object of*
*dreamer's affection, a young girl. suggested solution: package face of*
*teacher trapped in body of boy. location: swiftly moving at far right*
*of crowd toward the edge of the bus rotunda, jests growing more*
*boisterous as distance is formed between target and school ground.*

Abernathy reads the paper twice. The first time in disbelief. The second in disdain. He feels something new. Not a frequent occurrence for him. He . . . feels outrage? Thoughts like: *Who does this auditor think she is? To come up with a solution for him?*

Then, more quietly: *Is this how audits are supposed to be done?*

Astonishingly, Abernathy finds himself angry with the auditor because of her competency. Or at least someone's incompetency. A niggling feeling at the edge of his mind suggests it may be his own ability that he is unhappy with. He is, after all, only here because of his unintentional cover up—a betrayal of his only friend, a grieving mother estranged from the only family she has, at that. No, that's not right. Not a betrayal. He would never *actually* betray Rhoda. It was an accident. Right? Still, he'd never thought to write a report like this in his time. But, his introspection is not internalized. His realization is lost. As he takes wide strides across the dying soccer field, into the shade of the bus awning the only thought he takes away from his musing is: *Who does this auditor think they are?*

A school looms like a prison behind the children. The dream smells overwhelmingly of Axe body spray and bus fumes.

"I've been waiting for you," says the auditor—which, hey! is not how things are supposed to go. Abernathy is supposed to say that to *her*. She pushes off of a metal pole and stands straight, crossing her arms.

She is young. She has a round face and big eyes and she wears her hair in braids. She has one of those pixie, heart-shaped faces that look ethereal and a bit otherworldly.

Abernathy squints at her. There it is again. The thought. *Who does she think she is?* But then Abernathy recognizes her: she is the fast-food worker! The one he met during Holiday training. Her goggles are pushed into her hairline, which is exposed because she hasn't put on the hood of her suit (against regulation). No doubt about it, this is the teenager he sat next to at intake who scribbled about indentured servitude. She must be nineteen or twenty. Incredulously young. Things have changed since that day in the basement. For example: he is no longer excited to chat. For example: she has aged.

The children near them swap secrets in whiny pre-teen voices, gossiping about friendships and romances and other petty school dramas. They seem not to see Abernathy or his new auditor. They have no idea what awaits them. Not the slightest hint that their friendships are fleeting, their wills to live soon to be devoured, a working world waiting to swallow them alive, their children, though they are just children themselves, already doomed to die. They have no idea that they will struggle to meet even their most basic needs as they hurtle through a marketplace inhospitable to human functions and that they will be fated to take this inhospitability personally, as we all are, as if it were their fault they could not simply work harder, faster, longer. The collapse of their personhood is only a few scant years away, yet these lanky adolescents remain oblivious. All of them, every single one, will have to sell their life to someone, for something. They appear now, before such a collapse, to be happy. Which, to Abernathy, is particularly a depressing contrast.

Abernathy desperately clings to his own crumbling self in the face of such bleakness.

"Here's the situation as I see it," the auditor starts, though Abernathy doesn't recall asking her opinion. He squints at her as she talks. She makes broad hand gestures, sweeping his attention to the group of students that have already begun to surround the young girl on the far side of the bus lot.

The auditor seems to be saying, "Blah blah blah, compared to me you are a failure who cannot perform even the most basic of human skills, blah blah blah."

Which—Abernathy wants to know—who died and made this girl the expert?

Abernathy stares at her for a few moments as if he does not understand her. He lets a long silence stretch between them like a cord: to develop intimidation, to establish authority, mostly to buy himself time to figure out what he's supposed to say. He wants to do something cooler than this, than staring, but his hands are already in his pockets and he is already leaning back languorously against a support beam with a sly, performative disinterested-ness—as they do in TV Shows and Movies. He is: *THE GUY ABOVE IT ALL*. He is: *THE COOL ASSHOLE*. He has: *SEEN IT ALL*. There is not much else he can do to signal the fact that he knows what's up beside stand and lean and stare. Meanwhile, in his pocket, he nervously crumples her audit sheet in his fist. He feels as if his blood is pumping two million miles an hour inside him.

Is he sad?

The girl stares right back.

Why would he be sad?

She is calm. She is cool. She is disaffected. Perhaps she is a bit contemptuous. His TV intimidation is not working, and no wonder, he hasn't been able to even afford TV in years. All he knows is that, in this moment, he cannot be the first to break eye contact or be the first to speak up.

The children are laughing. It feels like they are laughing at him.

He misses Kai. In a moment like this, what would she do?

He breaks eye contact to turn and activate his pack. The girl watches. He decides to, like Jason says, package them all.

Abernathy siphons away the children mulling at the edge of the bus rotunda who speak so candidly about their friendships and the way their feelings affect their tiny stupid hearts. They are dragged into the blackness by the power of his hose. This gets a rise from his coworker. The auditor shouts out. She looks shocked. She looks angry. "What are you doing!" she demands.

This is good. What Abernathy is going to say next is even better: "I'm doing my job," he says (he sounds very cool, he thinks, very management), "why don't you try to do yours?"

The auditor steps toward him, hand outstretched as if she were to stop him. She can't. She doesn't realize how serious he is. Abernathy has sacrificed too much to be here. Abernathy deserves to be here. Abernathy is done being dragged through the mud. Abernathy will no longer be told what to do. Abernathy will solve problems—his way. This girl has no chance but to do as he says.

He smiles at her as he presses the bottom button on his pack. His belt vibrates. He sees why Kai did this all the time. It is so simple. So effective. The auditor is gone.

Abernathy sweeps the whole area. His pack hums but not from strain. It's like his pack is happy. Abernathy takes away the children and their stupid, petty dramas. He takes away their stupid friends and their stupid hopes and their stupid dreams. As he packages, Abernathy's own feelings of loneliness and incompetence diminish. Rhoda who? Childhood who? Parents who? He is packaging the dream in record time. He will show the other managers. He will show Penn. He will show them all: anyone who ever doubted him or hurt him or fired him or thought he was doomed. Every child goes quietly until he gets to the boys who surround the girl on the sidewalk.

He siphons away the laughing and they climb into his pack eagerly, whooping as if they are descending basement stairs into a kegger.

He is reminded of Kai, whose laughing children fought against her hose until their last folding breath. In contrast, these children climb in with joy. It has to mean something, right? Surely it is some type of universal measurement of Abernathy's competence and goodness.

The girl on the sidewalk? She is on her knees. Her hands cover the back of her head as if she is in a tornado drill protecting her brain from potential damage. Those boys are gone. But it doesn't matter. Abernathy siphons her away, too.

Being a manager means Abernathy now manages people. Here he is managing.

It is just him, standing at the bus rotunda listening to the chirping spring birds, and the dreamer who is on her back, panting, black eye forming. Blond hair sprawled out around her. Abernathy recognizes her. It is his landlord. It is *Kelly*. She is young. Her fight no longer exists. She will remember no one. She will need no one. No one can hurt her. Surely she will be happier now that all this pain and suffering has been taken from her. Abernathy is doing her a favor. Stepping into the next dream, Abernathy can feel it.

ONCE HE THINKS HE SEES Rhoda opening her door across the drive. The dusk is setting. The light grows long on the walls surrounding him. Peering across two kissing and empty driveways, he realizes it is not Rhoda he sees moving across the drive, but his own shadow flickering in his periphery against the sill.

Abernathy turns so as not to look at it.

The days sit on top of one another, crushing one another.

The last time he spoke to someone he did not work with or serve—what did he say?

THE NEW AUDITOR IS A fumbling idiot, always searching, frequently apolo-
gizing. When she talks to Abernathy, she stoops.

Late from the stand, tired already, Abernathy stumbles into the dream.
"You moron," he says as greeting. "You great bumbling buffoon." He suctions
up mermaids brushing their long hair on a rock and catapults the auditor
into the next dream where he travels to meet her in the backseat of a minivan.
It's the children, not the stoplight, he informs. It's the crumbs on the floor, not
the homework in the front.

Not that he knows, really. It's not even that he dislikes the auditor, it's just
he's found he must establish an air of authority otherwise fall victim to extreme
episodes of unprecedented self loathing. He wonders if Kai knew what she was
doing. For the most part, all Abernathy does is guess and hope he's right.

Anyway, what really matters is that he now speaks with the appearance
of authority, exactly as his first dream auditors suggested. When he speaks
with authority, the new idiot auditor must listen.

It's true that speaking to the new auditor in this way has effects on Abernathy. In committing to his job and the mistreatment of those below him,
Jonathan Abernathy starts to believe *he is good at things*. Which, in turn, as
perverse as it may sound, makes him respect himself. As he starts to respect
himself, Jonathan Abernathy also starts to like himself. People (strangers) start
to like him, too. The grocery store clerk talks to him as he buys beautiful, golden
apples with shiny white organic stickers, bushy lettuce heads free of bugs, big
natural jars of peanut butter which one must stir before they eat. Abernathy

cannot afford many of these items, but when he does splurge the feeling buoys him for weeks. He keeps the jars, perfectly rinsed, lined atop his lone shelf as a reminder of his wealth. He drinks out of them, their labels long gone so that their glassy bodies stamped with the raised names of brands he can now afford are visible always. These brands are a little comforting reminder that he is doing well. That all is okay. That he does not need anyone else (Kai, Rhoda, Timmy—even Kelly, or Penn). That worry is far out on the horizon, a long way from shore. That he is safe.

It is as if Abernathy has returned to college and is once again protected by that thin veil of potential which can grant someone so much invisible power. It's not until such veils are lost that you realize what such a veil gave you: hope, a future, a chance to change your path, optimism in the life destined to come. Which is to say that when others believe you to have potential they create opportunity for you. Without others, there is nothing. Without belief in ourselves, we cannot acquire the belief of strangers. Without the belief of strangers, we have no institutions. Without institutions, we have nothing to measure ourselves by, and the question becomes: Why believe ourselves at all?

Abernathy joins the new auditor in the next dream. He's been here before. They are in a field. A small wobbly path leads bucolically to a woman swinging from the branch of a large, knowledgeable-looking tree. The tree's roots are dotted with red-and-white mushrooms. Brown shelves of fungus sprout from the trunk. Moss hides yellow caps beneath its green carpeting.

He tells the new auditor she is stupid. "It's the rope, not the cows." (There they are, grazing in the field, their heads dipping below the waterline of wheat.) But the auditor grabs the silver paper and shakes it with vigor. "I said it was the fucking cows so it's the fucking c—" He voids her from the dream and looks up. The sky is full of pigeons.

Jonathan Abernathy reminds himself: appreciate the beauty around you.

He tries to appreciate the beauty around him.

Birds. Birds. Birds. Birds circling the cattle gods beneath.

Being a manager is all managing, no respect. Jonathan Abernathy wants to know: Where is the respect? He has been through so much. Does he not, finally, deserve to be respected? He misses Kai and her infinite wisdom. Rhoda and her sullen expressions. Timmy and her fungal obsessions. At least he no longer works with Jason. The pigeons are circling in figure eights. First he sucks up the cows, then, feeling superstitious, the birds for good measure. A few escape. He lets them. He wonders over Kai. His wonder is fruitless.

It can take us years to realize that we have seen a person for the last time. In some cases, this is because the soul of the person has departed, but their body remains and keeps going about its business. This is what happened to Abernathy's mother, though since Jason packaged Abernathy's childhood dreams, Abernathy no longer remembers her or the way she was. Sometimes it is because we expect to meet the person again at some point in the future and the future never comes. This is what happened to Abernathy's father. And then, sometimes, it is because a life has ended, but the news does not reach us, and so their life goes on unfolding quietly within us even after it has ceased unfolding for them.

The next audit note arrives. Abernathy allows the sun to play across his face before reading.

He has always liked this dream. In this dream, the weather is nice.

**THE NEXT DREAM** is the same as the first dream he ever visited. A drowned thing floats, bloated, in the mud and a mother, Rhoda, circles around it calling out for help that will never come.

Abernathy suspects, now, that the child is Rhett. A gentle giant.

Today, in the dream, the mud is not yet a river. Rhett does not float anywhere. In a small clearing, a pool of muddy water forms a perfect circle. In the center of the circle there is a door.

The new auditor is sitting on a stump, jiggling her crossed legs with impatience. Though they have worked with each other for weeks at this point, Abernathy refuses to call her by her name. "Auditor!" Abernathy says. "Look sharp!"

She rolls her eyes. "Would it kill you to call me Eleu?"

Abernathy explains, "If I were to call you by your name it would insinuate that I intended to continue our professional relationship."

She snorts.

Abernathy glances at her report again.

"Right," she says, "as if I would want to continue to work with *you*."

*marshland. muddy pond, skeletal trees, dusk. dreamer is absent. in the middle of the pond stands a door. too few elements to make a thorough audit. deference to the officer on duty.*

"Well?" she says. She doesn't stand up but instead gestures widely. It is indeed dusk in the dream. The sun perpetually setting. The mud pit is surrounded by swampy marshland. The grass and clover gradiates out from beneath the water. Yellow swamp russulas, green brittlegills, king pine boletes and gray milkcaps and honey pinkgills sprout against the treeline. The center of the pond ripples as wind moves across it. "What do you recommend we do, Mr. Big Shot?"

Though her face is neutral, Abernathy can tell the auditor is laughing at him. Fucking with him. Telling him: *Do my job if you think I'm so shitty at it.* He crumples her report, drops it into the pool. Without saying anything, he walks around the pit. He is unhappy with her, yes. He is trying to display his power, yes. But, most of all, he is scared.

Unlike her, he knows the horrors this dream can hold.

He remembers the field being ravaged by rushing water. A dreamer swimming in circles as she tries not to drown. A train that never comes. A child, gentle, and bloated, and sweet, in the middle of it all. Abernathy listens: but there are only the crickets, the wind, a distant rumbling. The rumbling sounds more like a thunderstorm than a train. Or the sound of a car as it drives down a distant highway.

Abernathy is lonely.

"Should we package the sky?" Eleu muses. She tilts her head back and lets the wind play across her exposed throat. "Perhaps the sky is menacing the trees. Or no, better yet, forget the sky entirely. Perhaps we should package ourselves. We're the intrusion, aren't we?"

Eleu casts him a sly look. Abernathy ignores her.

Abernathy walks the perimeter of the pond again. Trying to be calm, cool, collected. Kai is not here this time. The officers are not joining to laugh. The back side of the door is the same as the front. It looks familiar. He gets the feeling that were he to open the door it would swing both ways. He asks the auditor, "And you haven't seen the dreamer?"

"Or maybe," she says lightly, "we would be better off siphoning the oxygen away. Surely we can both agree oxygen is the cause of the issues here. How we may do that, I'm not sure. I will leave the logistics to you, O' wise one."

Abernathy steps into the mud. He sinks in. It comes up to *just* below his knees. To walk to the door he must lift one leg up high and then plunge it forward, lurching through the muck.

"Or," the auditor says, totally exasperated, "we can do that. Great. Makes complete sense."

In front of the door the mud reaches his thighs. The door is elevated above the mud. Like in childhood, he is eye level with the doorknob, a perspective we don't realize we lose as we grow taller.

"Eleu," Abernathy interrupts, "*Where* is the dreamer?" Abernathy needs to know before he opens the door. He presses his ear to the wood and, yes, there it is, the rumbling happening just beyond the frame.

Eleu lets out a long exasperated sigh. "Now you say my name. The dreamer is in the woods, sleeping."

Abernathy slushes his way out of the mud. "I need you to take me to her," he says.

"Her?" She says, eyebrows raising.

"Yes."

"Say please."

"*Now.*"


THE DREAMER IS asleep, just as Eleu said.

Abernathy bends down to the dreamer's level. Dripping with pond scum, he's careful not to get any algae on her. This time, finally, he knows who it is.

Eleu leans against a tree with her arms crossed. "I've never seen someone asleep in their own dream," she says. "Normal? Or weird? What do we think?"

The dreamer is on her side, her knees at her chest, teal rain boots still on, just as she was in the dream with two Kais. He can't see her face. She is shivering. Her hair is plastered with sweat to her forehead. She mumbles in her sleep. Her hand grasps her hand. **SHIT**, says one. **LUCK**, says the other.

"So are we going to do something about this," the auditor asks, "or just stand around with our dicks in our fists?"

Abernathy turns the dreamer so she lies flat on her back, mumbling her children's names in her sleep. He rests a gloved hand on Rhoda's forehead. Through the material he can feel she is running a fever. Her cheeks are hollow. A dark, splotchy pink.

"You go ahead," Abernathy says to the auditor.

"Now hold on a second." Eleu pushes off from the tree. "I have every right—"

But Abernathy has already sent her forward, into the waking world.

He is alone in the dream with Rhoda.

Abernathy lowers himself onto the forest floor. He doesn't know what to do, or how to react, so he pulls Rhoda close and he tells her a story. In the story she is rich. She does not have to work. Timmy is with her. Rhett, too. He'd be, what, fifteen? Sixteen? All three of them stand in the yard, laughing, sun setting as Timmy rolls through the grass. Standing next to Rhoda, she can have whoever she wants. If she wants no one, she can have no one. If she wants him, he will be there. If she wants Penn, Abernathy will be her friend. If she doesn't want to be his friend that's OK, too. In this story, it is implied that the next day will always be better. Each day better and not worse than the last. Every day, continuing for ever and ever. For ever and ever until she and her children are happy. Happy and old.

Eventually the dream begins to ripple. Grass grows. Rhoda's breathing becomes even. He pushes her hair back from her forehead. He wipes the sheen of sweat from her brow. Flowers sprout from the mud. It is time for Abernathy to wake up.

## 34

SUMMER! BIRDS SING. TREES FLOWER. Breeze sweeps through the neighborhood intending to be enjoyed. Yet Rhoda's house does not prosper from the season. Beneath her deck mushrooms grow wild. Scraggly weeds spread like a blanket across the yard. Abernathy has not seen Timmy's face in months. Picking his way across the flowerless walk, Abernathy knocks on Rhoda's front door.

He waits for a moment. As embarrassing as it is, it wasn't until the previous night, standing in Rhoda's dream, that he realized how much time had passed since they last spoke. He hasn't faced her since giving her (what he now suspected was) the world's worst gift.

He had not seen her for lack of desire. In his life, he has not been moving forward. Merely standing still. He has not realized that time, though frozen for him, continued for others. While Abernathy was stuck determining what to do next, Rhoda had moved on.

He still feels the same way, but would she?

Abernathy knocks harder. No answer. Perhaps she is in the back, he reasons, getting ready to work. He tries the doorknob without luck.

As he crosses the driveway to head home, Abernathy tries the garage. There's no car in the driveway. The metal door is rusted. He pulls on the handle and the garage door rises easily, squealing as it lifts. The garage is dark and full of boxes. It is much colder than the yard.

Abernathy steps over a dusty bike, around a box of books. He knocks on the garage door that leads into the house. The door swings open, unlocked.

The house is dark and full of shadows. The living room empty. The kitchen, stark. For the first time, he sees not a single pile of laundry. He thought the laundry would last forever. Its absence is a shock.

"Rhoda?" Abernathy calls. She doesn't answer. He steps inside.

Every curtain is drawn shut. Most of the furniture is gone. It still hasn't been replaced since Rhoda sold it earlier this year. There is only a lone folding chair, placed in front of the TV.

Abernathy shuts the door carefully behind him. The house has an empty feeling that Abernathy finds hard to bear. His body is tight and cold all over at the thought of Rhoda living here, alone.

The house is a small ranch house. A half bath sits next to the porch door. But there is, he knows, also a hallway. And down that hallway is where Rhoda and Timmy sleep.

Abernathy stands at the mouth of the hallway. He is trying to picture Penn living here with them. He is trying to picture Rhett, on the floor, in the kitchen, or, better yet, Rhett, at the TV, large face turned upward and watching. Had Penn been different, at one point? Kinder and softer and maybe more whole? Would going farther into the house be OK? If Rhoda were to come home and find him in her house alone how would that feel to her? Probably bad.

Conversely, what if something were wrong?

Her hallway is carpeted. Abernathy can't see much except that it's not a long hallway. Surely there's no harm in walking down it. He takes a few steps, experimentally. He immediately steps upon a pile of letters. A trail of envelopes leads to the end of the hall. They have been opened and immediately discarded. He picks the letters up as he goes and stops at the door he knows to be Timmy's. It's closed. He places his hand on the knob and turns, but the door is locked.

Abernathy follows the remaining mail. The trail ends in a small pile at Rhoda's bedroom door.

The pale light of the living room is just enough to see that the letters are bills. Payday loans and mortgage bills. Abernathy stops reading before he can see the rest. He shuffles them and places them in a respectful pile in the corner of the hall. This time he knocks first.

"Rhoda?" he whispers. The door is open just enough to see that the inside is dark black. He pokes his head in, trying to put on a mask of cheeriness in case something is totally wrong.

"Rhoda," he calls. "Hellooooo?"

There is no answer. He steps into the room. The heat isn't going, nor is the air, so the house is exceptionally quiet. He has never been in Rhoda's room before. It's not what he expects.

The floor is carpeted, covered in little piles of clothing and mail. The bed takes up most of the room. Next to the bed is a small nightstand that's been shoved into the corner and acts as an altar to many different water cups, all of different sizes and water levels. At the end of the bed is a desk covered in different lipsticks and makeup. A laptop is perched on a pile of books. A large photograph is turned face down. The chair can only be pulled out so far before it hits the wall, which for some reason depresses Abernathy. At the window, which is high up, tiny and oblong, two children's beach towels have been nailed to the sill to block the light.

The bed is covered in a nest of blankets, all of different colors and textures. He can't tell if Rhoda is in bed or not. One of the blankets is a ratty green quilt. One is a child's blanket covered in fuzzy fire trucks. The room is so dark he can't tell if the trucks have faces. A group of pillows are spread haphazard across the bed, no rhyme or reason to their organization or positioning. He reaches out his hand to touch the pile, to wake Rhoda, if she's there.

"Abernathy!"

He jumps. His knees hit the bed frame. The bed frame hits the side table. The water glasses rattle and one almost falls.

At the door, Rhoda is shadowy, standing in her work clothes. Cream blouse. Long black skirt that covers her knees. Nude heels. Hair back. She looks— totally normal. Which surprises him. Abernathy feels wobbly like the water glasses. As if he might fall, too.

He places his hand over his heart. "You scared me!" he says, trying to laugh through his embarrassment.

She crosses her arms over her chest and frowns. "What are you doing in my house?"

"I was worried about you," he says, pushing his hair back. It's grown quite long. She raises an eyebrow. He blushes. "I haven't heard from you in weeks."

"I could say the same for you," she says, crossing her arms. "Though I would probably say months, in place of weeks." Underneath an apathetic tone there it is: a faint smile of relief. She is touched. Right? She must be touched.

"Ha, ha," he says. "I guess we've both been busy, huh?"

She steps out of the doorway, into the hall without answer. He follows, looking back at the towels she nailed above the windows. No chance light could penetrate that.

ABERNATHY CHOOSES THE lone barstool tucked beneath the counter. It seems like a better choice than the lounge chair in front of the TV. He rests his elbows on the skinny island, head in one hand. Looking at Rhoda, he smiles, trying to project a total ease which he doesn't necessarily feel but which he has perfected in managerial training. Shoulders back. Eyes a little sparkly. Smile just faint upon his lips, as if he knows he shouldn't be smiling yet cannot help himself in her presence.

"Tea?" she asks. She holds up two boxes: decaf black or ginger green. Abernathy chooses ginger green.

Rhoda fills the pot, opens the kitchen curtains, turns on the burner. He waits her out. This is another managerial tactic he has seen other men use. Don't speak until spoken to, then dominate.

This does not work as well as he hopes. Rhoda can hold long periods of silence. As the tea boils she does not speak a word. She clicks around the tile and stands at the other side of the island, across from him. She takes one heel off, massages her ankle, takes off the other heel and does the same. At her hand is a butter knife, which she grabs and uses to open the mail. One at a time, methodically, she opens each letter with barely a glance at the envelope.

Abernathy sits in silence. The longer he sits in the silence, the tighter the silence feels. He tries to look devil-may-care. He looks into the distance, squinting a little in what he hopes is a moody way.

It doesn't work. She doesn't speak. So, he begins. "Rhoda—"

The tea kettle sounds its alarm. Rhoda doesn't hear him.

"I don't do this very often," she says as she sets the hot tea in front of him. "Do you take it with anything?"

"No," he says. "No." So much relief in his voice that she gives him a queer look. He thought something would be wrong. That she would be disfigured or something and he would be to blame. Maybe there would be a black spot on her palm, slowly spreading across her body, desperate to consume her. But everything seems very normal. Abernathy bends forward to pull the tea toward him. Rhoda still smells like musty lilac and pine.

She turns back to the window and they resume their silence. This silence does not feel so oppressive, now, and Abernathy tries to stop acting like someone he's not. His shoulders slump. He stops forcing a smile. The tea steams gently. Rhoda closes her eyes as the sunlight falls across her face. The smell of ginger and lemon. The faint hint of bodies being lived in. Abernathy takes the opportunity to look at her. Really look at her. Dark under eye circles. Cheeks sinking inward. Hair escaping her low bun. Cuticles bitten to hell. Her hand trembles slightly as it rests against the counter.

The two neighbors drink their tea in silence. She doesn't ask him again why he's in her house. He wouldn't know how to answer, anyway. Would he tell her that he's missed her? That he's been worried? That he's been busy? That he's been a horrible friend? That he's sorry? That he wasn't ready to meet her where she was? He's scared to bring this up, because what if he brings this up and he discovers that not only has the whole thing been his fault, but there's no way to fix it.

It is not until Rhoda leads him to the door that Abernathy finally breaks. "Are you feeling OK, Rhoda?"

He stands on her front porch. Hands in pocket. One of those days where the weather is perfect, the sun is beautiful, nature is singing. Rhoda leans against the doorframe as if standing upright is too much energy.

"I've been waiting all this time for you to apologize to me and this is what you decide to say?" He can't tell if she's joking. "You haven't talked to me for almost a year. You broke into my house."

"I don't know if I would call it breaking in—"

"What would you call it then?"

"Checking in on a friend?"

"Oh, are we friends now? You could have fooled me."

"We'll always be friends."

She looks away. "Yeah, OK." She says, "I'll remember that next time I wake up in your bed alone."

"That was—" he says.

She holds up her hand. "I really don't want to hear it."

"Can you just let me say—"

She scoffs.

"Rhoda," he asks gently, he has to ask it gently, "where's Timmy?"

"Now you're really evading."

"You don't know what I'm talking about," Abernathy prods, his suspicion growing larger. He has suspected for a long time, but he does not want it to be true. "Do you?"

"OK," she laughs. "Evade the question. Fine. No, I don't know anyone named Timmy. Is this someone you're seeing?"

"What?" Abernathy asks.

"This is so low," she says.

"I'm just trying to ask: Do you know who Timmy is? Do you remember telling me about Rhett?"

Rhoda laughs. "Cute," she says. "I should have figured you were just like the rest of them. Make me seem crazy so you don't have to answer for yourself. Men love to do this. I don't know why I thought you would be any different. I may not be sleeping that much with all the extra shifts at work, but do you really think I would fall for this? You don't have to try to make me jealous, Abernathy. You can just say you're fucking sorry."

Abernathy searches her face. He can't tell if she's being serious. She's smiling slightly, but he thinks she's serious and she's smiling because she's nervous. Her eyes are glassy and she seems hurt. His shadow on the floor is rippling, but he can't tell if it's because the curtain on the wall is fluttering in the draft or if it's because of something else.

"You got me," he says, holding his hands in mock surrender. He presses on gently. "I came in because I was really worried about you. I miss you. I don't know how to apologize to you, OK? You're kind of a scary person."

She snorts.

"You are."

"Whatever," she says.

And he asks the question, the one he doesn't want to know the answer to. He asks the question because he knows his actions, that day with Penn, on the driveway, is the cause.

"Rhoda, why aren't you sleeping?"

Her face pulls together. She's surprised and her surprise means that her mask of disaffectedness falls a little. She seems moved. Behind Abernathy a car sputters through a stop sign. Wind moves through leaves. Children talk to their neighbors.

"I'm not sure," Rhoda says. Then very quietly, she confesses, "I guess I'm scared."

"Scared?" he asks. "You?"

"Well," she says slowly, almost as if she's just figuring this out herself. She pulls at the cuffs of her shirt. "Lately I've just been . . . worried."

"About?"

"I don't know," she says, defensive. She shifts her eyes away from his.

"You can tell me," he says.

She scoffs. "And you've made yourself so trustworthy."

He's silent.

She continues. "It's like, well—it's stupid really. I know it can't happen."

"What can't happen?"

"You know," she says. "I dream about *you*. And the funny thing is, I know you aren't dreaming of me." She laughs. It is a watery laugh.

"Is that what you're scared of? Me? That's why you don't fall asleep?"

"No," she says. "That's not it."

"I would dream about you if I could," he says. His voice cracks a little. At the intensity of his response Rhoda steps back.

They are silent in the doorway together. When she speaks her voice breaks, too. "I feel like every time I go to sleep I wake up and I've forgotten something. Someone important. I feel like there are these people who are in my life that I've forgotten. I know it sounds crazy—but . . . what if I'm going to sleep as me and wake up as a different person? If I wake up thinking and caring about things I would have never thought or cared about the day before, doesn't that make me a different person? What if I am going to sleep as one person, and then wake up without any idea who that person was? What if I wake up every day and forget who I was the day before?" She sees the look on his face. "I can't explain it," she says quickly. "I know it's neurotic."

"It's not neurotic," Abernathy says.

"Yeah, OK." Even Abernathy can tell she doesn't believe him. "Right."

"Rhoda," he says, "Look—"

"Just so you know, next time I see you, I'm going to fight with you. I have a lot to say to you. You're getting lucky this time because I'm tired, and—"

"I'll fight with you whenever you want," he says, interrupting her. He means it. To him, any type of talking is better than no talking at all.

## 35

**A SMALL NOTE FROM PENN** comes in the mail. The note is written on company letterhead, the handwriting slanted and hard to read. The message is simple. Hardly a line. Yet it takes Abernathy the better part of an hour to set the note down.

> *Jonathan Abernathy,*
> *remember why you're here.*

Abernathy prays to a God he does not believe in to keep Rhoda out of his life. She stops by his house with a Tupperware of steamed broccoli and chicken. He hides, like a coward, in his bathroom, holding his breath. He stands on his toilet seat and peaks out the modesty window with only the tops of his eyes to make sure she leaves.

A week passes. He doesn't leave the house unless he sees that she has been to work. If she is at home and he *must* leave, he slips through the door without fully opening it, in case the creaking of his screen door carries across their driveways.

This works for a while. Abernathy attends to boring regular dreams of boring regular people. He works conservatively. He takes away only the glaringly obvious. He doesn't challenge or exceed expectations. He doesn't stand out. He doesn't criticize his employee. He even calls Eleu by her name.

He is late to work, hovering in his apartment, too anxious to leave, when there is a prim, crisp knock on his door. Abernathy turns off the sink and answers the door in his hot dog suit. Pale blue bunting adorns his shoulders. Atop his head he wears a crisp white hat not unlike an inverted paper boat. He dries his hands on his apron as he stares at the other side of his screen door. There is no one there. A small brown cardboard box sits on his welcome mat.

He looks around for the person who delivered the box. There is no one. It is early November. The trees are a sumptuous orange. His name is scrawled in pencil across the top.

Before he can take any action at all, black smoke begins to spill from the box.

Abernathy slams the door. Locks it. Closes his blinds.

In his hot dog costume he stands still, breathing hard, with his back to the door.

Someone—something—knocks three times. Slow, even paced raps.

Abernathy slows his breathing. He tries to make himself very quiet.

The knocks come again. This time louder.

"I know you're in there!" Kai St. Clair calls from the other side, her accent unmistakable.

Abernathy does not move.

The knocks have changed. She bangs on the door with the side of her fist. "Jonathan Abernathy! Open the fucking door!"

The banging grows louder. She kicks at the door. She says, "I'll scream."

The thought of Rhoda seeing her lurches Abernathy into action. He opens the door just a bit. The smallest amount. He peeks out. "K-Kai?" he asks, "but—how—?"

She pushes the door, hard, with her hand. She forces her way inside. Abernathy takes several steps back in quick succession and falls back, onto his bed.

"There," says Kai. Except it's not Kai. It is and it isn't Kai. "That wasn't so hard, was it?"

She sets a briefcase down on his desk, knocking over a series of cups. Black wisps are floating off of her head, her hands. She waves them away like a Hollywood starlet waving smoke from the room. The wisps disappear.

This is the other Kai, the doppelgänger from the dream. She looks just like Kai, but off. Her hair, piled atop her head, is red but not red enough. The green of her nails are faded, rhinestones chipped.

Kai tucks a braid back into the pile on her head. She looks at him. "If you ever fucking ignore me again I will kill you."

"W-w-what?"

"Just kidding," she says. "Obviously." She rolls her eyes and snaps open her briefcase. She is wearing a smart black suit. Hoops glitter in her ears. Abernathy has never seen her look so put together, but so dull. "Let's get this over with," she says.

"How are you—why are you—?"

"Hand?" she says, holding out her hand.

"What?"

"Your hand, please." She makes an impatient gesture, snapping her fingers together in a signal that he should place his palm in hers.

"Yeah," says Abernathy, trying to sit up and scoot as far back as he can. His back is against the wall. "I'm not fucking doing that."

Kai rolls her eyes. "Funny you think you have a choice but OK."

She rifles through the briefcase and then pulls out a sheet of paper which she flips through quickly.

She holds his questionnaire. The very first one he turned in.

She holds it out to him.

He can see his answers.

✓  Yes, he is in financial peril.

✓  Yes, he is a former student of the public education system of the State.

✓  Yes, he feels like a failure in all things, but still somehow wakes up each morning feeling hope.

"Yeah," he says, "nothing about that says I have to do a single thing you say."

She taps the bottom corner. There it is, beneath a question about sleeping, a small box in fine print that he had checked.

*Are you willing to comply with all terms of employment?*

✓  Yes, he is.

"The terms aren't listed," he says automatically. "It doesn't count."

Kai flips the paper over. "They're on the back."

Sure enough, on the back of the paper is a faint gray wall of text.

"Go ahead," she says. "Take it." She wiggles the paper. "Read what you signed up for."

He snatches the paper from her, careful not to touch her hands where black tendrils are curling like smoke from her arms.

*Terms of employment include (but are not limited to):*

Before Abernathy can read anymore, the words begin to blur. Quickly, almost in one breath, the sentences move and coagulate to become a gray mass. The paragraphs collapse in on themselves. The mass turns black. The mass, now a black tadpole, pulls itself out of the page and scuttles off the corner, up into Abernathy's hand.

"What," says Abernathy, "the fuck."

"Oh yeah," says Kai, taking back the paper. She files it away in her briefcase. "I should have mentioned that."

Abernathy is trying to pull the black leech off of him, but it has latched onto his palm where his former cut was. The black tadpole is using his cut as an entry point into his body. It wriggles and squeezes. He is losing feeling in his arm. The tadpole disappears into the black spot.

"There," she says. She pulls out another piece of paper. "Thanks for your service. If you'll just sign here."

"Yeah," says Abernathy, squeezing his palm, the tip of the black leech's tail remains outside his body, a pimple he cannot pop. "There's no way."

Kai rolls her eyes. She snaps her fingers and the black welt grows larger. A shimmering black glove of shadow wraps around Abernathy's hand, spreading upward, up his arm. His fingers curl in on themselves against his will.

He watches in horror as his arm, capped by the shadow glove, reaches out to take the pen the false Kai offers him. He signs the paper with his left hand.

She rolls up the document and tucks it into her briefcase.

The whole process took less than ten minutes. Abernathy's front door is still open.

He officially signed his life away.

"This has been a courtesy notice," she says, as the black glove unspools again, folding back into itself. The leech is visible, bulbous, and blood-filled. It burrows into him again, until it is just a dark purple spot on his palm, nothing more than an inkstain obstructing his life line. "Sent to you by your lenders. Because you have violated the terms of your employer, your lenders will now be collecting. Per the Archival Act, you have been granted a one-hundred-twenty-day grace period to pay back the entirety of your debt or the Archival Office will be forced to intervene." The other Kai looks him up and down. Abernathy is still huddled against the wall, now gripping his left hand with his right, as if the left palm would fall off at any moment. He has not regained movement in his arm, it feels as if the limb is asleep. Pins and needles. "Should your debt not be paid back, your contract with the Archival Office will be terminated."

"Kai—what are you—what is going on? Are you still in there, somewhere? You would never do this. Talk to me."

Would she?

Abernathy's whole body tingles, is numb.

The other Kai looks at him with disgust. She is not Kai at all. She is merely the nightmares Abernathy did not have time to dream, sold off to the highest bidder.

"Still a dumbass, I see. I thought for sure by now you would have gotten that worked out."

He slurs now. "What are you—"

"A pleasure doing business with you." She says. She closes her briefcase. Abernathy feels woozy. Against his wishes, he feels a great sleep coming over him. He is so tired. Endlessly tired. Kai picks up her briefcase and steps over the threshold. She turns back to look at him, head cocked to the side.

"You know I really did enjoy it," she says. "Being coworkers."

The last thing Abernathy sees, before he drifts off to sleep, is the wisping otherness of Kai returning—right foot first—into the box from whence she came.

## 36

**IT IS RAINING AGAIN TONIGHT.** Soft welts of wetness collect at the rims of Abernathy's basement windows. He moves through his apartment with damp delay. Fingers tracing window seals, eyes scanning ceiling bumps, hands picking up glasses only to set them down again. The December chill is moving in. No matter how much he has scrubbed and picked, the black spot on his hand remains unmoving.

His thoughts are ungenerous and cruel, like a radio in the background the listener no longer notices. *My body is a poorly oiled machine. My life is a little shriveled turnip of anguish. I am unlovable and unloved. I am incompetent and unwise. I know nothing. I will never make money again. I will die destitute and alone.*

Poor Abernathy, he brushes it all away before he can feel it. He brushes sadness away before he can realize what it is he is sad about. His anger does not surface. He knows nothing of himself.

He tells himself: *All is well.* Stranger things have happened. He thinks: *My life? My life is good.*

He thinks: *I can pay them back.*

There is ever-mounting pressure in his chest, and though you might assume Abernathy would intuitively connect this mounting discomfort to the knowledge that things have gone terribly, terribly wrong—he does not. We all must deny what we can to stay alive, even if it is our denial that kills us in the end.

Abernathy thinks: *Tomorrow will be better.*

Abernathy thinks: *If I can just get to tomorrow, that will be enough.*

Poor Abernathy, as he lies down in his careworn quilts, for the last time, someone knocks. It takes some effort for him to get up.

Framed by the night, his landlord stands in his doorway. *Kelly.* Beneath the yellow light, her cheeks are bright red and her blond hair is slightly mussed. It is sleeting. Ice mixes with the furious rain. Despite living in the mother-in-law suite beneath her house, Abernathy can count on one hand how many times he has interacted with her in the last five years.

"Hello, Abernathy," she says. She is smaller than him, wider and older, too. Probably half a decade older than Rhoda. She has a deep voice. Her shoulders pull in a bit, which gives her a slightly concave, office-focused look. He is surprised that her concavity endears him. He can't remember the last time he looked at her. She looks more human than he previously thought.

"*Kelly*," Abernathy says, trying to stifle his surprise.

"I've just finished work," she says, brushing the snow mixture from her hair. She is frowning slightly as she looks Abernathy up and down. "Thought I should stop by."

"Ah . . ." Abernathy takes a sharp breath, trying to remember: Has he paid this month's billings? Is he behind on that, too, or is there another reason for her to be here, speaking directly to him? He has a hazy memory of slipping his customary check into the mailbox on his way to the stand. But, he can't recall: was that this month or the month prior? "Do I owe you . . . ?"

"No," she says. "No, actually, I was wondering, can I come in?"

"Come in?" he repeats.

"Yes," she says. Beneath the slurried light above his door, she brings a hand across her face and takes a deep, shuddering breath. "I have a bit of bad news, actually. It might be best if we sit down."

"Right," says Abernathy. He takes several quick steps back. "Right, yes, come in."

Clothes are strewn across the floor and Abernathy quickly pushes them under his bed with his feet.

Kelly looks around. She frowns slightly. Closes the door behind her, to keep out the cold. "You might want to sit down." She gestures to his bed, embarrassingly empty except for one pillow and a bag of open chips.

There is not enough space for both of them to sit without touching. He does not wish to touch her. Unlike the last time someone entered his space (he thinks of Rhoda with a twinge), Abernathy finds himself feeling like an unexpected visitor in his own room. He sits on his bed as if he were the guest. The thought of Rhoda—all prim and proper, tattooed and looking around with those eyes— makes him, like, actually, physically hurt. In comparison to Kelly and her crisp blouse, Abernathy is a wreck. Half-naked, wrapped in a quilt, hair stand- ing on end, dark purple bags practically radioactive beneath his eyes.

Kelly leans against the doorway. In the bare white light of the basement fluorescents she even looks—and this is saying something—more tired than he.

"You might have noticed the for-sale signs that have started popping up in the neighborhood," she says.

Abernathy had not, but he nods anyway. He is so shocked by the fact that *Kelly* is standing here, right here—in front of him!—that he doesn't really know what to say.

Her hair is damp and the sleet is still coming.

"And you might have noticed," she says, "an uptick in moving vans, despite the, uh," she gestures, "weather."

Abernathy tries to remember if he has seen moving vans. Maybe one, maybe two. Hardly anything out of the ordinary.

He's not following her. She's making him nervous. So he just outright asks: "Kelly—is something going on?"

Kelly looks so, so tired.

"You know," she says, laughing a little to herself. "I never thought it would happen *here*, and I've lived in this city forever. When I was a teen I watched it happen downtown. Before I married, I watched it happen on the north side. I guess I thought we were close enough out here to the suburbs that it didn't matter. That it wouldn't happen to us. I mean, who gives a shit," she says, with a watery laugh, "about the outer city? Nobody important lives here. Nobody that matters."

"Kelly," says Abernathy, "What are you—?"

But it seems like Kelly can't talk much faster than she's already speaking. She takes a long pause. "I wanted you to hear it from me first. I figured you were going to hear it from Rhoda seeing as they contacted her, too, and she

agreed. I know you two are"—here she squints and looks away, disapproving—
"*friends*. Anyways, I would want to be told outright if it were me, so I wanted
to tell you outright. I'm sorry."

"Tell me what outright?"

Kelly takes a deep, shuddering breath, as if preparing herself for something
particularly grim. "When your mom passed away, she knew about my problems with Dave. And she figured we—you and I—could help each other out,
you know? I liked working with her, your mom. She was thoughtful like
that." She looks at Abernathy now. Abernathy looks away. He thinks she must
have had too much to drink. She isn't making any sense. "You won't deny I
haven't helped you, right?"

"I don't know, Kelly." Her name feels uncomfortable. "I mean, you've been
a good landlord . . ."

"Hush," she says. "Hush. I've known you since you were how big? Do you
remember the way you used to come into the office and sit on the desks and
watch us type?"

Abernathy does not remember.

"What I am trying to tell you, honey, is that it's time for me. They made it
so I can't refuse. I wanted to refuse, I did, but even if I could, I won't have enough
to even cover the legal charges. They told us they aren't above going to court.
It's a sign, I reckon. It's time for me to move on."

"Move on?"

"Yes." she says. She folds her hands together and looks at her nails. "I've
agreed to go in on a package deal with the Donahues on the other side of
me, and so has Rhoda. We're selling, along with most of the other folks in the
neighborhood. I never thought I would see the day. But it's no use fighting it,
really." She looks Abernathy in the eye.

She says, "They aren't even building lots."

"Wow," Abernathy says.

"They want to turn it all into a highway," Kelly says. "It'll connect downtown and the suburbs so you can get from one to the other in fifteen minutes
or less. It should make the county lots of money," she adds, as if that makes it
any better. She says, mostly as a comfort to herself, "They want the tourism."

"*What?*"

"You ought to think about moving on, too," she says. "I don't think you're going to be able to find rents like this again. I heard they're going for almost a thousand a month right now—spaces like this."

"A thousand," Abernathy echoes. He pays five hundred, now. He dimly realizes he has balled his sheets in his fist. He uncurls them.

"That's right," she says.

"Well, you haven't sold yet," he says, "have you? I mean, there's still time to figure it out. There's no rush."

Kelly smiles at him, then. It is a pitying smile. Abernathy thinks, for a moment, that he does remember talking to her in an office, when he was young. There are cubicles. She always had candies. Red Hots. She wore the most insane lip liner and her hair was styled in blond and brunette stripes. If he's remembering correctly, he liked her because she was the youngest in an office full of older women, the closest to his age. But this memory feels false to him. It feels unreal. He can't remember why he would have been there in the first place. There was no reason for him to be in an office when he was younger. His dad was a bartender.

He remembers the dream where those kids were fighting in the bus port. She had a black eye, as a teenager, and he packaged everyone away. For a moment he wildly thinks that he could say something, use this against her somehow, but he can't figure out how it would be useful, or what it might mean. She looked so helpless in that dream. Surely, he should be able to do something with that?

"Did you grow up here?" he asks.

"I did," she says.

"You must have had a lot of friends?"

"I must have," she says, and her eyes go a bit glassy as she looks at his microwave clock.

"Stay," he says. "Don't—"

"I don't really have reason to stay. I can't remember why I turned down all those offers in the past. I don't really know anyone around here."

"But—"

"It's a lot of money," she says flat out. "And I need it. I'm drowning, and I need it."

"Surely your friends—"

She laughs, then. "What friends? Me—all I do is work."

That sounds familiar to Abernathy.

"I don't think I can —" he says.

She interrupts him. It's clear she's made up her mind. "I wanted you to hear it from me, that's all. We still have a couple months left. A few months. But after that, after that I don't know. You'll just have to figure it out on your own."

She looks nothing like she does in her dreams. In real life she is not tough. She is tired. She is wilting. She is going to leave.

Did he do this? He wonders. Did he take her memories and make it easier for her to go?

"And Rhoda, too?" he asks. He wraps the quilt a little tighter around himself as she opens his door. "You spoke to her?"

"Yes," she says. She is already stepping out. Into the night. Into the rain.

He shivers as the cold comes in. A bit of slurry gusts across the opening.

"But," Abernathy says, fumbling, calling after her, "what about the other people—"

"I don't have answers for you, sweetheart." She doesn't turn around. She holds her hands above her head as she steps into the grief of the sky. "I just know what I have to do for me. I'll put it all in writing. For your records."

"Kelly," he says, searching for something that will make her change her mind, knowing that nothing will, that he is powerless, that he has, somehow, contributed to this hellish turn in his life, "where will you go?"

Kelly shrugs. She cuts an impressive figure in the doorway, with the rain coming down and the porchlight on her face. "I don't know yet." She lets the screen door close. "I'm not sure. I'm not all that convinced that it matters. It seems more and more everywhere is just like everyplace else. "

DESPITE HOW AWFUL things have lately become, Abernathy's walk home from the stand is disturbingly pleasant. The afternoon weather is perfect. It is not too cold, and it is snowing. Children are out, rolling snowmen out of the white. Families putter on their porches, wrapped in gloves and mittens. They raise hands in lazy acknowledgment as he strolls past. The naked trees are capped with white powder, the breeze wind-chimes across their ice with beautiful discordance. For a second, Abernathy's face grows hot with the unfairness of all this beauty. His nose burns. He thinks he might cry.

Wherever she is, can Timmy hear the trees singing, too?

A few houses before Kelly's, a woman sits in a wheelchair on the porch. A plaid blanket is draped over her lap. Her gloved hands rest on the wheelchair's arms as she watches young men move her furniture out of her garage, into a small moving truck parked in the drive.

As he passes the house Abernathy mutters a "Happy holidays" and keeps walking. He gets to the end of the drive when he hears his name.

Eleu appears in a bright yellow puffer jacket, holding a box against her hip. "Abernathy? What the fuck? Do you live around here?"

"Oh, darling, must you?" asks the grandmother.

"Sorry, Nan," she grins, sheepish. "I mean: Abernathy! Whoa! Do you live around here?"

The sidewalk snow crunches beneath his feet as he comes to a stop. The men moving furniture grunt. Billows of steam come out of their mouths as they lift a plaid sofa into the open bed of their truck.

"Do *you*?" he asks, shocked.

"Are you going to introduce me or am I just going to sit here as ornamentation," the grandmother asks. "And you," she calls to Abernathy. "No need to stand on the sidewalk. Come up here and let me get a look at you."

"Abernathy, this is my grandmother, Florence." Eleu says as he crosses the snow-covered yard. "Nan, this is Abernathy. We . . . work . . . together."

Seeing Eleu in real life is incredibly disconcerting. She looks weirdly normal. This sounds dumb—even in Abernathy's head—but suddenly, to him, she looks real.

"Why do you say it like that?" her Nan says, swatting her arm. "The way you say it work is a death sentence. When I was your age we were proud to go to work."

Eleu and Abernathy exchange a look.

"I live right down the block, next to Rhoda," he says, to change the subject.

"She's a sweet girl," says the grandmother. "It's very nice to meet you. Eleu never tells me about her work life, no matter how much I want to know."

She offers her hand and he takes it. They shake.

"Nice to meet you, too," he says. And then adds, to be polite, "I've heard a lot about you."

"You work with my other granddaughter, too, do you?"

"Your other granddaughter?" he asks, then looks closer at her face. He recognizes her. "You're Kai's grandmother?"

Eleu groans.

The grandmother turns toward her. "Don't go groaning at me, ma'am." She says, now to Abernathy, "The way this one goes about it I should be ashamed of her. Is that what you want of me, Leu? To never mention her name again?"

"That's not it, Nan, and you know it."

"Well then what is it, girl, speak up."

Eleu shakes her head.

"I like Kai," says Abernathy. "Is she here?"

He hopes the real Kai is here. She might know what to do about everything.

The grandmother looks at Eleu with a quizzical look. "Is she here?" she asks. "Is she *here*?"

"Now, Nan, don't go getting worked up."

"No," Florence says to Abernathy, giving him a proud, dignified look that makes her seem much younger. "She is not here. She is serving her time. She was wrongfully convicted."

"I see," says Abernathy, not seeing at all.

"This one acts like I should be ashamed. Why should *I* be ashamed?"

"I didn't mean anything by it," Abernathy says.

"See, Nan, this is why I don't want to talk to people about Kai. It's complicated."

"Just because your cousin is complicated doesn't mean you should pretend like she doesn't exist."

"You're right, Nan," she says.

"That's right," the old woman agrees. "I always am."

"I see where Kai gets it from," says Abernathy.

At this both women grin.

The men moving the furniture take a break at Florence's request.

"You'll come in and have a cup of cocoa?" she asks him. "The other men are going to. It would make an old woman happy."

"Oh, I don't know about—"

Eleu shakes her head.

Florence gives him a stern look.

"All right," he says. "I guess just one."

The inside of Florence's house is much smaller than Rhoda's. Everything is very old, including the wallpaper, but clearly well cared for. He and Eleu hover in the empty kitchen while Florence wheels around, doling hot chocolate out of a thermos into paper cups. She ribs the movers, joking and easy with them, and they rib right back. They are all big men. Wide as they are tall.

"It's weird seeing you outside of work," Abernathy says. He itches the gauze on his hand absent-mindedly. "You seem more . . . I don't know . . ."

"Cool?" Eleu asks, with a smile.

"Ha. No."

"Wowww."

"More real," he says. "You seem more real."

"You know what your problem is, Abernathy?" She doesn't sound hateful, like Penn, or exasperated, like Kai, or even melancholic, like Rhoda. She sounds thoughtful, not like she has a personal opinion, but rather like she is musing out loud and he just so happens to be the subject of her fleeting thoughts. It doesn't matter to her one way or another, how he feels. She's not casting judgment. She's not being cruel. She is merely observing aloud. Sort of like how the trees do not matter to the wind. The wind will move forward regardless of whether the tree is there or not. It is up to the trees, how they respond.

"What's that?" Abernathy asks.

"You hate yourself," she says. "It's really obvious and really sad to watch."

"Yeah," Abernathy says. He doesn't even try to deny it. Usually he would deny it. It's a pathetic thing not to deny. "It is sad to experience, too."

She pats his forehead in a friendly, pitying way. It is awkward and funny but it also makes him feel seen. He suddenly thinks of his family, but the thought is slippery, and before he can hold on to it the thought is gone.

They watch Florence reach up and pull one of the big movers down to her level, so she can squeeze his cheek.

"Eleu?" Abearnathy asks.

"I love that you use my name now," she jokes. "It makes me feel so fancy. What a promotion!"

"I'm sorry," he says. "I'm really sorry."

"What are you sorry about?" she asks. He feels, suddenly, like she knows. She knows that Kai is gone. She knows he has been marked. She knows he chose himself and his interest over everything. Right? She must know.

"I have not been good to you," he says. His voice is strangled.

"Took you long enough to realize."

He clears his throat and continues, "Lately," he says. It is a stilting, awkward confession, because it is the truth. And Abernathy is not used to acknowledging the truth. "I have not been good to anyone in my life. I am a black hole," he says. "People's lives disappear into mine."

"Oh yeah," she says, "I have noticed that about you."

Jonathan Abernathy is not sure how to describe the sound that comes out of his throat. Perhaps strangled. Or wet.

Eleu is silent for a moment. She is thinking. "Florence thinks that life is a gift. I'm not so sure about that. Whatever it is, at least it's interesting. Any little bitch can whine about it while it's happening," she says, shoving his shoulder, "but the thing is: it's not over until it's over. No matter how old, we're always becoming ourselves."

Abernathy grunts.

"Do you hear me?" Eleu asks. She flicks him on the shoulder. He flinches. "It's you who decides who you become, loser."

Abernathy bats her hand away. "Do you believe that?"

He expects her to take the easy way out and say that yes, she does think he is a loser. Instead she is surprisingly sincere. "Yes," she says, holding his eyes. "I do. Your life is in your hands. I think you keep trying to get other people to take responsibility, but ultimately what you do is up to you."

They both turn back to Florence. She wraps her hand around one of the young men's biceps. He's grinning. From her wheelchair, covered by her plaid blanket, she gives his arm a squeeze.

## 37

HE DREADS FINDING HIMSELF AGAIN in Rhoda's subconscious.

He has already taken away the memory of her only daughter.

He does not want to take anything else.

Abernathy has just catapulted Eleu into the next dream. He's still siphoning away teeth as they fall from the sky when Eleu's note arrives: *circle of mud with creepy door. train noise. dreamer in the forest. suggested action: door removal*

Abernathy has to sit at the base of a tree as soon as he finishes reading. Teeth rain down upon him. In the distance his dreamer, an older woman, wanders from one pile of fallen teeth to the next. She holds one tooth up to her mouth, then another. Clearly, she is looking for the right one.

Abernathy rests his head in his hands. His breath comes in short little bursts as if he were a child. Before he can really rev up, into a panic, Abernathy feels a tap on his shoulder. It's the dreamer. She holds a tooth out to him, as if it will solve his problems.

He looks at her. Before he understands what he is doing, he turns his pack on. He takes the teeth for himself. He takes the ground. He takes the trees. He takes the sky. He takes the dreamer's clothes. He takes the dreamer's dignity. He takes and he takes and he takes. He takes it all until all the sound is pulled away and everything is gone. Teeth stop falling. All is silent. The color fades. His pack hums on his back. Calm fills Jonathan Abernathy from head to toe.

Into all that emptiness, he calls an elevator.

. . .

**THE LIFT LETS** him out at the perimeter of the forest. A white, wooden door rises from the wet lake of mud. He catapults Eleu from the dream before she can acknowledge his arrival.

His walk through the forest is quiet. A note from Eleu arrives from the next dream.

*AND THIS AFTER OUR TALK?*

He throws it away. Another immediately arrives.

*COWARD.*

Abernathy finds Rhoda in the forest. She is on the ground blindly feeling her way from one root to the next. She's in search of something. Abernathy has a good idea of what. Timmy and Rhett are not here, but he helps her up from the forest floor anyway. Where her eyes should be are two holes of shadowy blackness. Rhoda does not recognize him. Probably for the best.

Arm in arm, the two stroll. It feels nice to touch her. At the muddy heart of the dream he leads her to a stump and she sits.

"Stay here," he says. He can't tell if she can hear him. Though like all dreamers, she acclimates to her new situation without inquiry. Jonathan Abernathy wades into the pool of mud alone.

The mud is up to his knees, the trek slow going. He gets to the door and hears an engine.

Here's how he figures it, and he's not all that wrong: the dreams of Rhoda are interconnected. Now that she can't remember her daughter, the membranes of her dreams are becoming more porous, allowing one dream to bleed into the other. Whatever Penn stole from Rhoda's dream after Abernathy left has contaminated all the other parts of Rhoda's mind. It was too big of a thing to take.

The door swings inward, but instead of opening into the other side of the swamp, it opens into Rhoda's garage. A garage filled with children's toys. In the middle of the concrete floor there is a nondescript brown box.

Waist-deep in the mud, still on the side of the forest, Abernathy stares through the open door into the room.

Before lifting himself into his neighbor's garage, Abernathy tells himself something even he knows is an obvious lie:

*Jonathan Abernathy you are kind.*

*You are good.*

*You deserve.*

The concrete floor of the garage is cold. The door is open and frames the driveway. It is early spring, late winter. The weather is cold and a wind is blowing through the driveway's empty trees. Nothing has yet had time to bloom. There's another Rhoda, in the driveway, using her elbows to pull herself toward the house. Abernathy hears the truck rumbling toward them. Rhoda, as always, is determined. She cries angrily, but she does not give up. Abernathy turns his back to her. Instead he approaches the small cardboard box at the center of the garage.

Abernathy thinks of Penn (and all his swagger). Abernathy hopes Penn is not thinking of him.

The box rattles, as if the rumbling noise is coming from within. Abernathy squats and takes the box lid between his hands. As soon as he touches the box, it quiets. In the distance, despite the chill, there are birds. Abernathy sets the lid on the floor. A small black shadow wriggles inside the box like a fish tailing its way from side to side. The shadow is the size of Abernathy's two fists, but now that he has opened the box, the shadow grows.

The thing expands upward until it is half his height.

Abernathy stands and stumbles back.

As the shadow lurches into being, it begins to form a body. A child's body. As it solidifies, chunks of shadow fall from it to reveal a flesh underneath. The flesh ripples to form shoulders, hands, a face which holds a mouth which in turn begins to cry and split in two. It is Timmy. She is older. Next to her is her brother, stuck forever at six. They stand in the box wailing. What remains of the shadows cling to them like leeches.

Abernathy rushes toward them. He has missed Timmy's shaggy hair cut and lopsided ears. He fumbles at his pack, but before he can siphon away the remaining shadows they double and swell. Black wisps drip from her head, and shoulders, and arms. Rhett is already collapsing in on himself. Just as Timmy materializes, she begins to disappear again. First her hands, then her arms, the impenetrable darkness grows around her, swelling and expanding to wrap her within a cocoon. Abernathy only manages to activate his pack after the shadows have overtaken most of Timmy's body. Only her eyes remain, looking at him. She is bewildered. She is suffocating. She must wish he were her mother. She must want him to help. With a wink her eyes are gone. The shadows have her. The being collapses, back into the box. It shrinks down. The memory of Timmy and Rhett swim back and forth against the walls of the cardboard, barely the size of a fish.

Rhoda still pulls herself up the driveway, but a different Rhoda now stands behind Abernathy, dripping mud onto the floor. She has climbed through the pond, into the garage. Her eyes are clear, no longer shimmering black pools. She is not looking at the box which contains the shadowy memory of her children. She is looking at Abernathy.

Abernathy wakes, tangled in sheets. Cold sweat. Breathing heavy. The plastic of his suit is sticky and damp. He's awoken three hours before the end of his shift. His alarm clock blinks with red disdain. No amount of lying or denial or self-aggrandizement could protect him from what he just saw.

Rhoda's look was a look of hatred.

It is 4:00 A.M.

He knows what he has to do.

## /// **38** ///

ABERNATHY DRESSES IN THE DARK. He fears that any light will act like a beacon across the drive. Bumping knees into the bedframe, slamming into a cabinet, Abernathy hops into his shoes one foot, then the other, tugging their mouth over the tops of his feet and lacing on the fly. Acutely Abernathy feels time passing. He feels the months of time he's already wasted suddenly crushing him. He has wasted many months. His birthday is soon to arrive, but by the time that it comes it will be only another day. Another time. He will not be in this world to greet it. With his marked hand he fumbles with the lock on the door. The gauze makes it hard to get a grip. Once outside he crouches around the house, keeping to the shadows. He does not want Rhoda to see him as he hits the street with a run.

Abernathy is not fit, but he runs hard through the city outskirts, street after street until he arrives.

Amongst rows of storefronts, the service office sits in the dark waiting for him.

He crosses the parking lot quickly, panting. He cuts through the morning fog as if his body were a knife. Only then does he allow himself to take a breath, hands on his knees, humbled against the sliding doors, praying that they will whoosh open for him.

Does he realize this is the third year he has worked at the archives?

No, he does not.

It is early-early. No one is inside. Abernathy is no longer thinking. He has entered a slippery state. Logical thoughts do not occur to him. When he moves into the office it is only his body he feels: gut drop, numb chest. His actions carry him forward without conscious allowance from his brain. Why is he here? To do something. To help somehow. To alleviate the sick, crushing feeling of *having done wrong*. His blood inside him is rushing so quickly he feels like he is drowning in it. Drowning in being alive.

Through the waiting area, down the carpeted stairs, into the gathering room that reminds him so much of a church. Behind the folding chairs he opens the door.

The hall stretches out in front of him, seemingly folding and unfolding ahead, more dreamlike and unreal than ever. Jonathan Abernathy takes it at a jog, the muscles in his calves spasming with effort. As the hallway seems to curve, he has the curious feeling that he is in a funhouse, walking on the ceiling, dodging through mirrors, running from himself.

Each time Abernathy walks the hall it seems less substantial, as if he himself were becoming more dreamlike as, in turn, the hall becomes more real. As he moves forward, reality slipstreams around him, fast and loose. He prays under his breath for a door only to run face-first into a wall which has seemingly risen from nowhere in the dark.

He falls back, skidding across the carpet.

The impact causes his nose to bleed. Abernathy can taste the blood in his mouth and feel the wetness against his chin. He uses his shirt to stop the flow, exposing the soft hair of his belly.

In the moment of his careening, eyes closed, a door appears in the wall.

Now, to make himself open it.

THE ARCHIVE OF Dreams is silent. There are no windows, yet sunlight suspends dust motes in tiny rivers of light. Abernathy's footsteps echo solemnly as he crosses the tile floor. Dread begins to take shape within him. He can feel Penn's note opening inside of him: *don't forget why you are here.* What is his job? Not what he's doing now.

But through Abernathy's inaction, through his desperation, he can finally admit what he has suspected all along: he's caused something horrible to happen. Specifically, he has taken memories that did not belong to him, and he has stolen them, in order to anasthetize workers who were more preoccupied with their personal lives than their jobs. Jonathan Abernathy is not able to articulate this knowledge. He doesn't know—exactly—what the Archive is or how it works or who invented it or why. He only knows that he has fallen into this . . . this *thing* . . . this massive thing that has used him by hiding within a guise of opportunity. While part of this office, Jonathan Abernathy has hurt people he will never know. Worse than that, he has overwritten Rhoda's conception of her own life in service of his own.

The Archive of Dreams is quiet. Lonely. Rhoda's box sits on the shelf. Unlike the boxes on either side, hers is not covered in dust. The cardboard looks newly folded. He lifts it gingerly from the shelf. It is *heavy*. He can't hold it with one hand and his other still holds his shirt to his nose. Abernathy staggers a bit beneath the weight of the box, first backward, then sideways. He half-drops, half-sets it upon the tile floor. The fall cracks the tile, a rift splits from the center to the edge.

The box is fine, sitting upright as if unmoved.

Before he opens the box, Abernathy takes a few laps around the room to calm himself. *Be calm*, he thinks. *Calm*. His shirt is covered in blood. He pinches his nose.

*Jonathan Abernathy you are kind.*

*You are competent.*

*You are well respected by your community.*

*People, including your family, love you.*

He knows now, what he did not before. It feels good to pretend.

His nose stops bleeding. He can feel the blood heavy in his stomach. His shirt is ruined. At the box he kneels.

The cardboard is vibrating almost imperceptibly. Underneath the sound of the tiled room, there is a hum. On either side of the lid he rests his hand. The box quiets. It is warm, as lights are when unplugged. He can feel the electricity of it. That it once was connected to a power source but has since been removed.

Abernathy wants it both ways. Sitting on the floor of the dream archives, it's early enough in the morning that he can maintain his delusion: the separation of his personhood and his employment. That he can be a moral person in one and not the other. That what is "right" does not apply in settings where money is traded. That he can indeed compartmentalize his life into two discrete units which don't apply force against the other. He can both free Rhoda's shadow *and* he can do so without his employer finding out. Thus maintaining his means of livelihood *and* upholding his moral obligations. He will face, he believes, no repercussions. He will maintain, he believes, his employment with an organization who steals from their workers in order profit from them. He can work for a company who sells fear *and* he can be a good friend, a kind person, a nice guy.

The sick, dropping feeling as his stomach gives way. The loudness of his pulse. A dizziness as he sits on the floor. The trembling of his hand as it rests on the lid.

IF THE SHADOW in the box was once a tadpole, swimming from side to side upon first viewing, it is now the size of a catfish curled around itself as if asleep. As the light falls upon it, the dark thing shudders and begins to uncurl itself. The movement is confused, not as fluid as it was in the dream. The shadow is too big for the box and as it unfurls the blackness slips from its container to slide across the floor. Abernathy stumbles back, into a shelf. The impact shakes the boxes above him.

The shadow emerging from Rhoda's box is a slick black thing. Wet like a newborn. Abandoned on the tile.

Abernathy wonders if he should touch it or help it somehow, it looks so hopeless. But then the shadow begins to grow legs. If it was a fish in the box, it is now an ungainly evolutionary creature dragging itself from the depths of the sea. The monster—it looks like a monster—slips and slides across the floor as it attempts to gain purchase on the tile. The shadow is weak, but its slick body sprouts arms, nubs that stretch darkly out to place themselves upon the tile. On all fours the shadow raises itself and begins to grow. Abernathy cowers in front of it as it lurches. As it rises. The thing lifts its arms off the ground and pulls itself up so that it is standing. A torso begins to take shape. Now there is a head.

Abernathy drags himself across the shelves, barely breathing, so as not to draw the shadow's attention to him. It is not looking at Abernathy. It is too preoccupied with being born. Its dark head turns to one side. Then the other.

It has heard him.

On shaky legs, it begins to move.

It is still growing.

It is human-shaped.

It is taller than him.

It is expanding.

It is near.

"S-stop," says Abernathy. He sounds like the water pourer. He holds out a hand. The shadow is so close. "Please, s-stop."

The shadow stops. Quivering in anticipation, black tendrils rise from it like smoke. It is not the shape of a child as it was in Rhoda's dreams. It is a large, lanky thing, barely human, still growing, though now more slowly, toward the ceiling. It is the dark shape of a subconscious forced hastily into a human-body. Together the two beings, Abernathy and the shadow, stand in the archive breathing the same air.

The dream shadow is panting like an animal as what might be its chest rises and falls in quick collapse.

Abernathy is doing the opposite. Abernathy is holding his breath.

He exhales in a gust and the shadow seems to turn its head to better hear Abernathy speak.

"Can you—" Abernathy says. The shadow leans closer, it is almost the size of two Abernathys. "Can you hear . . . me?"

The shadow does not have a face, but Abernathy feels that it is attuned to him. Tentatively, Abernathy reaches out a hand. The shadow reaches out an arm—what could be an arm—and allows Abernathy to touch what may be its hand. Not wet at all but *dry*. Cool with warmth pulsating underneath. He thinks of Rhoda and how this . . . *thing* . . . *this memory* . . . could possibly find her. Will he have to walk it out, bring it home? Beneath his fingers the blackness jolts. Shudders. It begins to color and shift form. It grows darker, deeper. It begins to expand rapidly, shooting upward to grow even taller. Its head hits the ceiling. The boxes shudder. The creature stoops over Abernathy, towering over him. The shadow fills the room.

Yet Abernathy feels as if the shadow is peering at him in recognition.

An opening stretches out where a mouth might be. The shadow is curled against the ceiling and sides of the room of the archive as if the small basement room were now its box, the roof its lid.

Now curled around Abernathy, it fills the room with unrepentant darkness. Abernathy cowers among the shelves. Or what was once the shelves. The entire room is black. Abernathy is a tiny speck in an endless, empty expanse. It is then, from all around him, that the darkness speaks. The darkness sounds like Rhoda. An all-powerful, all-knowing Rhoda.

*YOU HAVE AWAKENED ME.*

"I w-w-want to return you to my friend."

The darkness' laughter is a dark billowing thing: wind rushing through a barn at night. *I AM WHERE I HAVE ALWAYS AND NEVER BEEN, IN THE PLACE FROM WHICH THERE IS FEW RETURNS.*

The laughter is a gale pushing Abernathy's body backward, but when it ends, so too does the wind. Abernathy has found himself in the dark and endless eye of a hurricane.

"No," Abernathy says. "I'm s-sorry, that's not right. You belong to my friend."

*I BELONG TO NO ONE.*

"You belong to Rhoda—"

*I AM EVERYTHING AND NOTHING. I AM DREAMING. I AM CONSCIOUSNESS. I AM DESIRE. I AM LACK. I AM MEMORY. I AM FORGETTING. I AM LIFE ITSELF. LIFE ITSELF DOES NOT BELONG TO ONE BEING.*

"That's"—Abernathy clears his throat—"that's very nice. You are a very formidable LIFE ITSELF," Abernathy says. "And I would—would never th-think of containing you. But maybe there's some place you are not?"

*I AM IN ALL PLACES.*

"I beg your pardon," Abernathy says tentatively. The darkness around him ripples. "But there is one place that I can think of that is not as formidable as it once was."

*I AM IN ALL PLACES.*

"E-e-even in the mind of my friend? Rhoda?"

LIFE ITSELF says nothing. It seems to recognize this name, but as a horse recognizes upon its body a fly.

"Yes!" Abernathy says, doubling down on this recognition. "You were once in her dreams and I"—he takes a deep breath—"I stole you."

*DO NOT LIE TO LIFE ITSELF. LIFE ITSELF IS THE LIE.*

In the rumble of this statement Abernathy loses his balance and falls to his knees.

"Y-you're right," he says. "You're right. I'm sorry. I stole you from the mud. I stole you from the cows. Someone else stole you from a driveway. In the driveway, you were a child's body. It was wrong of us, and I'm sorry."

*I CANNOT BE STOLEN. I AM ALL THINGS.*

"Y-yes." Abernathy agrees. "But, When I reduced you, my friend couldn't remember herself. I did that to her, and I'm sorry for it."

Abernathy is wondering where he went wrong. Was it when he touched the hand of the darkness that made it swell to such heights? He knows nothing about the archival officers, what they do or how they control the dreams. He is just a manager! A *dream* officer. He has very little to do with the archives. And before his promotion he was even lowlier—the lowliest—an auditor!

But, all he can think about is Rhoda pulling herself up her driveway. Timmy standing in the mud. Rhett on the kitchen floor. The way Penn must have looked, when she pulled his collar down, and whispered in his ear. He wishes the darkness would return to them. He wants it badly. He feels it in his blood.

*AH*, murmurs LIFE ITSELF, as if it too can see what Abernathy wants. *YOU ARE RUMINATING ON THE 104,567,012,936TH ITERATION OF THE HUMAN EXPERIENCE. YOU HAVE LESSENED ITS CONCEPTION OF ITSELF.*

"Yes!" says Abernathy, though he does not quite understand what LIFE ITSELF means. "Yes!"

*THIS IS A MATTER TO BE RESOLVED IN DREAMS.*

LIFE ITSELF folds rapidly into its center, shrinking and pulling itself into a human body. The body shudders. Black wisps tendril from it. For a moment, Abernathy thinks he sees a memory of Timmy warbling inside the body of the darkness, like she is pressing up against a fogged glass, holding the hand of her mother's only son. Then the darkness collapses into itself, sucked as if through a hose until all that's left is a pinprick. There is a deafening sound, like a train or a hurricane or a truck as it plows through a yard, and the pinprick is gone.

The darkness has disappeared. Abernathy finds himself no longer in the dream archives. Instead he stands at the hallway's main door, in the basement gathering room. The lights are off. The door is closed. There is no knob.

Abernathy hopes it will return to Rhoda.

Through the greeting room, up the stairs, and into the waiting area he goes. As he exits he waves a shaky hello to the secretary who climbs into her car. Abernathy is covered in his own blood. The sun is setting at the place where the parking lot meets the horizon. In the light, Abernathy realizes he is wearing his favorite jacket. He can't remember where he found it, when he lost it, or how he put it on.

## 39

RHODA CALLS HIM AS HE arrives home. He answers. He listens. He nods. He tries to talk, but she interrupts. She says her final word. He hangs up the phone.

His four months are up. The black spot on his hand grows. He does not have the money. But, perhaps, he's made things right.

Does Rhoda remember?

Yes. Finally. She does.

Staring out the window, Abernathy thinks he sees a figure at the fence line. A man in a suit who looks disturbingly like himself. The sight of himself at the fence line is terrifying. Abernathy blinks quickly and when he opens his eyes again there is no one. The fence line is empty. Only a small patch of bulbous white-caps, climbing up the metal lattice.

Abernathy retrieves the spare key to Kelly's car from beneath her bumper.

This is what he and Rhoda have decided: Abernathy is going to borrow and/or steal his landlord's car, depending on how you look at the phrase "borrow and/or steal."

He is worried, if he says this out loud, that his black mark will hear him and spread once again, over his body. Or, worse, that Kai will appear. He believes his nightmares have been let loose by Penn. If Penn were to hear what he and Rhoda were planning, he would not like it at all.

But after seeing what happened to Rhoda, Abernathy understands now what had escaped him for so long. There is no coming back from this.

In the driveway, Abernathy unlocks the car with ease. He puts the car in neutral, opens the car door, and pushes. It's a tiny car, but it's still hard to move. It takes him twenty minutes of slow, steady praying to get onto the street.

Rhoda's house is empty. The lights are not on. The moving vans have already come and he missed it. He has missed so much. Inside her house, nothing is left.

Now in the street, Abernathy gets the car started just fine and then he is cruising through the night to the outdoor mall's parking lot where Rhoda is waiting for him.

It feels incredibly good to be driving. A type of freedom he hasn't felt since childhood. Night stretches out in front of him. Velvety air envelops him through rolled down windows. Stoplights turn over as he approaches, so that the whole ride is just ease and vibes. Soft cricket sounds. Downy silence of folks asleep in their houses. Everyone in the world resting and him just driving through it.

Is he nervous?

Yes. He is.

In the parking lot, he catches Rhoda in his headlights. Her car is full of boxes. Suitcases. She wears her hair back, tucked under a ballcap. The brim's shadow falls over her face.

Rhoda slips into Kelly's car easily. If she recognizes it, she doesn't say. Abernathy tries to help her get situated. She lets him, a little, before taking the seat belt from him and shrugging off his hand. "Let's go," she says. This is a very Rhoda-like response. Brusque and unreadable.

The consistency of it brings Abernathy joy.

He looks at her: sloping eyebrows, unreadable expression, glinty eyes, tired ears and shoulders and neck and mouth. It's clear that she remembers all of it now. Her children. Abernathy in her dreams, fiddling with her life. Her husband. When was the last time Abernathy saw her? He is filled with watery feelings that slosh around inside him. Regret? Adoration? Self-hatred? Love? He has no idea. He starts the car despite it all.

"I thought you were going to fight with me," he says as they pull onto the highway.

She turns to the window. "I don't have anything to say."

"Say something to me," he says. "Please. Anything. Tell me you hate me. Tell me you wish I was dead."

She says nothing.

Abernathy wants to tell her about his life since she last saw him: about how, when he is awake, he feels tired and sluggish. He has to take frequent moments of rest. He is always leaning against things. He is always having to sit down. He has betrayed everyone he has ever known, he used to think he had a good reason for it, but now he doesn't know. His hours asleep get longer and longer while his pay remains the same. He wishes he could dream of her and Timmy. He dreams of other people's people instead.

He wants to tell her that all this would be fine, except each night he steps from one dream to the next and wonders: What's the point of this? What's the point of all of it. Rhoda seems like she might know the point, which is why he wants to tell her that he has a hard time being alone in the blackness, in the howling wind, he has a hard time being alone in general and that sucks because he's almost always alone. He's sorry for leaving her alone. He's sorry he wasn't brave. He is trying, now, to be brave. He has, in his myopia, ruined lives. His life. And others. He wants to tell her that he's sorry for leaving her. He wanted to take it back immediately, but he kept waiting for the right moment and the right moment never came. It was always too awkward, and too hard. He thought Kai was so cynical, at first. He used to tell himself that whenever he got to her position, he would have a different attitude. Things would be different. Now she seems reasonable. Kind. Measured. The only one with her priorities straight, and she was gone. Just totally gone.

It's only now, as his sleep elongates, has he realized where she has gone, and what it is The Archive takes. His body is betraying him for it. It is falling deeper and deeper into sleep. Soon he knows he will not wake up. He will join Kai. He will be there, in the darkness, full-time.

He wants to tell Rhoda that he feels as if he has signed his whole life away for a paycheck that, when it comes, doesn't really buy all that much. Now he worries he might have sold not only his life away but the lives of the people he loves, too. Her life. His mother's life. The life of his father. There's no time for other people. There's barely enough time for himself.

Abernathy wants to tell Rhoda all of this so he can beg her to tell him one thing, anything, about herself. What was her divorce like, he's sorry he never asked before. What happened, between her and Derek, after Rhett passed away?

He's sure it must have been hard. Beyond hard. Has she loved anyone since? Was Penn, at one point a different person to her? Was Abernathy? Was she ever in love with either? Really in love? He is in love with her. He finally has realized it: he is in love with her.

And did she really manage to save up? Does she need any more? If he can help, he wants to help. Does she still dislike her job? What's something her boss did today? Actually, forget about her boss, what are her secretest, most-innermost hopes for her life? It's okay if she doesn't have any, but if she does Abernathy would be honored to know. How can he get her to trust him again? And what did Penn say to her in the dream, when Abernathy left? The real ex-husband Penn or the dream ex-husband Penn, whichever's words hurt her more. Does she hate him, Abernathy? Will she always? He might not have known how to help. In the dream and in the later. He sees now he was wrong then. He's sorry now. He was so tired, and so scared, but he sees now, that this is no excuse. She is tired and she is scared, too.

But, true to her word when they spoke on the phone, Rhoda does not want to be friends. They arrive in Penn's neighborhood without exchanging a single word. The houses, in his division, are nice.

Finally speaking, Rhoda asks him to park Kelly's car several blocks away.

Abernathy is happy to do this. He sidles up next to a mailbox. She gets out without saying anything. She walks through the headlights toward her daughter. She looks determined and, maybe, also, scared. There is a second where she almost looks back. There is a second where Abernathy almost gets out to help. The second passes. Rhoda moves forward. Abernathy stays in his seat.

When she called, what she asked was simple. Pick her up in a car that can't be traced back to her. Help her get her daughter back. Help her leave. He owes her that.

Abernathy is alone in the car while he waits for her to return with Timmy. Or, he thinks he is alone. His eyes drift toward the rearview mirror and he catches the gaze of another him who sits in the back seat. In the front seat, Abernathy jumps. He almost slams on the horn, but diverts his hand at the last moment. He hits the steering wheel, hard. "Jesus," he says, clutching his heart.

In the rearview mirror, there is no one.

Abernathy turns around in his seat, to check, but there is nothing. No one. Only empty McDonald's wrappers. Popeyes containers. Gatorade corpses. Consumption bloat. Before Abernathy's blood has managed to quiet, the back door opens and he is face-to-face with Timmy. Rhoda helps her into the backseat.

Timmy is rubbing her eyes and yawning. Abernathy is startled by how much older she appears, and tries to calculate how much time has passed. He can't. She has started puberty. She is tall. She has left childhood, and he was not there to see its end. She is almost fourteen and drags an ancient mushroom plushie with her. It has a smiling face stitched into the red-and-white cap except the cap has yellowed with age, and the smile is slightly threadbare. A stuffed thing. From her childhood.

Years have passed for Timmy.

Abernathy looks at Rhoda. Years have passed for her, too.

Where was Abernathy? Had the years passed for him?

Rhoda ducks into the car to buckle Timmy into her seat.

"Are you sure this is OK, Mom?" Timmy asks, sleep still heavy within her. "Dad said it's OK?"

Abernathy does not know what Rhoda's going to say. Maybe there is nothing to say. Rhoda's ear is amazingly close to Abernathy's cheek. He can feel her blood moving through her. He can feel the heat coming from her. He can almost feel the sadness, and the resignation, and the steely reserve. Timmy deserves to know this feeling. This feeling of love. He feels sick at the realization that he almost took this feeling from her. Rhoda's hairs wisp him as she slides out of the backseat.

She never does answer Timmy's question. Yet within moments, Timmy is asleep.

Abernathy closes his eyes and tries to savor this feeling.

Then Rhoda is in the front seat. And Abernathy is turning on the car. And they are driving into the night. They are driving away.

Rhoda does not look at—or acknowledge—Abernathy for the whole ride back. She rests her hands in her lap. Turns in her seat. Looks at her daughter, to make sure she's there. She rolls the window up and down. Sighs. Looks at her daughter again, as if she could disappear at any moment. Timmy is still sleeping as Abernathy pulls into the mall's parking lot. Rhoda gets out without a word. She crosses in front of the car, through the headlights, to the driver's side where she opens the backdoor and unbuckles Timmy into her arms.

Timmy is too big to be carried like this. Rhoda stumbles beneath her weight. Abernathy hastens to unbuckle, too, but his good hand gets caught, he doesn't move fast enough, and Rhoda has already lowered Timmy into her car, into the passenger seat—surely she is not old enough for the passenger seat?—Rhoda has buckled her in.

Abernathy feels longing move through him, like lightning. Then, the thunderclap of guilt.

Rhoda stands in his headlights, her back to him. Is she hesitating? Maybe she is hesitating at the driver's side door. He wants her to turn. Turn back. Turn a little bit more. Look at him with a bit of sadness, throatiness, and maybe, also, if he's lucky, love. He loves her. He's not sure how he loves her, or if it will ever be good enough, or if it is the way other people love, or if it will ever be returned, but he does. He has, to his own surprise, gotten to know her. And in his knowing, there is an appreciation, a witnessing. He realizes, staring at her, that he has been blind to time and in his blindness he has been incredibly cruel.

She does turn. Only a fraction. He can't tell why. It's dark. It's hard to know the intentions of other people. Why they do things and what it means to them. If dreams have taught Abernathy anything, it's that. Even the most innocuous of actions is impossible to interpret. Has Rhoda seen Abernathy? Does she understand him? Does she love the man she knows and is the man she knows the man he is?

Abernathy steps out of the car. He crosses the beams of light. He wraps Rhoda in his arms.

Rhoda is very firm, beneath his grip.

Abernathy has one hand on her upper back, one hand at her waist. He looks down into her eyes. She pulls back. Away. She turns her face. What does she want? he wonders. He will never know.

Still, Abernathy kisses her. His breath upon her breath. And Rhoda, for a moment, kisses him back. It is gentle. She is warm. Her arms move to his chest, to his heart. But Rhoda doesn't linger long. The hands at his heart push him away. She pulls back. She turns. She takes a deep breath and gets into her car. He is standing right there. She gives him some type of look. The door closes.

This is her leaving.

Whatever this was, it's over before it begins.

Her window is rolled down. She is perfectly within speaking distance, yet Abernathy is frozen. His whole body is alight from where his skin touched her skin. He cannot move his lips.

She pulls out of the parking lot, flattening gravel.

She does not look back.

And what does he do?

What does he do in this penultimate moment?

What does Jonathan Abernathy do as Rhoda and Timmy drive away?

He certainly doesn't chase after the car and insist on going with them, as he desires, as he should, as he wishes.

No.

He stands alone in the darkness, the dim headlights of her car receding.

In the chill morning air, black spot slowly inking across his palm, he waves.

The alternative being too horrible to consider, he tells himself what he knows to be an obvious lie:

*Jonathan Abernathy, you will see her again.*

## 40

DRIVING HOME, ABERNATHY HAS TROUBLE staying alert. Down the freeway, beneath the lights, dozing into another's existence, jerking awake. He manages to get the car in the driveway as the sun is coming up. He steps out of the car into a field of flowers, awake, being held by his parents, awake, swimming with Timmy in the creek of his childhood, awake, blackness, awake. Is he dreaming? If he is, they are dreams of his own.

He realizes, finally, sluggishly, that something has gone wrong.

It is too late. His debts have not been repaid. His contract has been terminated. Death has come.

Abernathy struggles into the yard, where the other Kai is waiting for him. She sits on Abernathy's lounge chair, legs primly crossed as wind blows dark wisps of shadow from her body.

"Jonathan Abernathy," she says, with a small, sad smile. "Our appointment at last."

*Something has gone wrong*, Abernathy thinks. *Something is wrong.* His thoughts are slow. Sluggish. He steps away from Kai and stumbles through Rhoda's fence line into a cab. The cab deposits him inside Rhoda's house but he has no money to pay the fare. Abernathy barely has time to search his pockets because Kai is at the door. She lets herself in. Abernathy breaks away, but he feels as if he is moving through thick slabs of water. In the bathroom, a dream of Rhoda does her hair. Abernathy walks toward her, into the service office parking lot. Abernathy staggers through rows of empty cars, through the whooshing cold of the automatic doors. He is having a hard time staying present. There is no Kai at the desk. Other Kai is at the desk.

"Have you chosen to complete your payment now?" she asks Abernathy, sliding a clipboard beneath the plexiglass. Abernathy fumbles with the form. He does not have the money. He knows he does not have the money. He feels LIFE ITSELF around him. The suffocating, inevitable darkness of being the one who owes. He can hear a truck revving its engines outside. He tries to think soothing thoughts:

✓ Jonathan Abernathy you are important.
✓ You are a pillar in your community.
✓ You are fine.

There is no one at the desk when he returns the form. He must find Kai—the real Kai—and the chute that opens in the floor. He must find Eleu. And Rhoda. He must find himself. What has he forgotten in the process of collection? But, he is distracted. The truck has arrived. A dream of Penn swings down from the cabin as the office begins to fade. Gently, at first. The room is brown, soft gray, dark gray, a wisping smoking black. In the background, the faint sound of Penn laughing as he strolls down the drive to pick up his son.

The black dot has spread across Abernathy's body until he is trapped within it. Pushing against it. Straining against the shadow and the nothing like it is a sack and he can escape.

He cannot escape.

The darkness encompasses him until there is no him left to encompass.

As the darkness folds around him, what's left of Jonathan Abernathy is nothing more than a shadow. Like Kai, the body does not contain the being it once was. The body transforms, and instead of Jonathan Abernathy, there is only walking compendium of fear wearing his visage, doing as it's told.

Perhaps, one day, the body will arrive at your doorstep to collect from you.

AS FOR ME, I remain in a small cardboard box, high upon a dusty shelf, deep in the darkness of an archive you can access if you survive a long walk down an infinite hallway. I am known as the 100,030,008,0035th iteration of LIFE ITSELF. And though I have ended, it's true, also, that I have no end.

In life, I was known as Jonathan Abernathy.

Most people called me Abernathy.

There were only a few people who ever called me Jonathan. Of those people, my favorite was the 104,567,012,936th iteration of LIFE ITSELF. She was my neighbor.

When I recollect my life, I often return to my favorite memory. The 104,567,012,936th iteration of life and I are at the cabin of her childhood. Her daughter is asleep in the backroom. The lights are off and outside we can hear crickets. We have just eaten a frozen pizza. We are surrounded by dollar store candles. We are drinking very cheap wine and her socks are green. Her head is in my lap. Her hands are covered in tattoos. She has one hand on my leg, one on her stomach. **SHIT**, says the hand on my leg. **LUCK**, says the hand on her stomach.

As we sit among the dark flutters of tea candles, I trace a small symbol behind her ear with the edge of my finger. At the moment when I reach the top of the loop, right before I descend again into the infinity, she looks up at me, a smile on her lips.

In this version of existence, I call her Rhoda.

I hope, one day, we meet again.

# ACKNOWLEDGMENTS

While writing this novel, I worked in publishing. As such, I have untraditional opinions about the "Acknowledgments" page. Typically this page is a time for an author to reflect upon their lives and influences, while giving the reader a bit of insight into the author's personal thinking and writing of the text. For the close reader of acknowledgments, they can allude to the often invisible webs that link writers, readers, artists, and institutions. I think that is well and good, but I would rather my acknowledgments page give direct credit to the many talented people who assisted in the publication of this book. For every book, there is a crowd behind the scenes: teachers, editors, marketers, admins, librarians, booksellers, publishers, publicists—all tirelessly doing their jobs. Without them, you would not be reading this.

PUBLISHER: Ben Schrank

EDITORIAL: Kishani Widyaratna, Danny Vazquez, Alessandra Bastagli, Rola Harb, and Nicole Jashapara

MARKETING: Tiffany Gonzalez, Sarah Christensen Fu, Jordan Snowden, and Isabel Sanchez Hodoyan

PUBLICITY: Alexis Nowicki, Rachael Small

COPYEDITS: Janine Barlow

CONTRACTS: Stella Iselin

PRODUCTION: Lisa Taylor, Elizabeth Koehler, Alisa Trager, Olivia Dontsov, and Nishtha Singhal

SALES: Jack Perry

DESIGN: Alicia Tatone, Adriana Tonello, Rodrigo Corral, Richard Oriolo, and Frances DiGiovanni

FIRST READERS: Hilary Leichter, Margaret Meehan, Alicia Tatone, Linnie Greene, Dylan Kiely, Zain Khalid, Sara Hinkley, and Matt Cruz

BOOKSELLERS AND LIBRARIANS: all of you—whether I meet you and know you by name or not—thank you

AGENT OF SALE: Jessica Friedman

TEACHERS: Sam Lipsyte, Alexandra Kleeman, Ben Marcus, Gary Shteyngart, Rivka Galchen, Ben Metcalf, Leslie Nneka Arimah, Sean McDonald, Jenna Johnson, Michelle Foytek, Kelly Lonesome, Ellen Datlow, Will Hinton, Devi Pillai, Hilary Leichter, Sara Birmingham, Maya Binyam, Nadxi Neito and Katie Raissian, Jesse Shiedlower, Emily Hughes, Caro Perny, Renata Sweeney, Ruoxi Chen, Christina Orlando, Anelise Chen, Heidi Juliavits, Susannah Felts, Charlie Hickerson, Andi Winnette, Jordan Bass, Diane Williams, Brigid Hughes, James Wood, Benjamin Taylor, Lincoln Michel, Rob Spillman, Brian Evenson, Neil Gaiman, Kelly Link, Holly Black, Cory Doctorow, and Brandon Sanderson, Patrick Nielsen Hayden and Beth Meacham and Miriam Weinberg and Fritz Foy, Kristin Novotny, Steve Wehmeyer, Kathy Quimby Johnson, Jim Ellefson, Erik Shonstrom, Gary Scudder, Sanford Zale, Tammy Hutchinson, Warren Baker, and Tanya Stone. I am forever a student and apprentice of the arts.

AGENT: Angeline Rodriguez

On a personal note, thank you to my family for living interesting lives and being beautiful people: Leah, Keith, Maddie, Deanna and Jane and Fred, Bill and Pam and Ken, Ricky and Russell, Dylan and Connor and Tyler and Grazia and Linnie and Tyler, Maddie and Cody and Austin and James and John Matthew Addison, Connie, Juanito, Sam and Zion, Sarah and Juan—and most of all Mateo, my soulmate, whose life is a gift and an honor to share.

And a special thank you to James Dittes, my high school creative writing teacher, who saw a bratty, scabbed-over aspirational high school drop-out and dragged her rural ass kicking and screaming to ACT testing—who knew someone with fleas could get perfect scores in reading and English, despite being two weeks away from flunking out? Not me. Thank you for ignoring my protests. Thank you for sending my scores out, along with one of my essays. Thank you for paying the application fee. Thank you for the thirteen following years you spent urging me to publish. In total, the ACTs and the application cost you one hundred dollars. If you wouldn't have believed in me, I'm not sure I would still be around. I certainly didn't believe in myself. You forced me on a journey I would have never thought myself worthy of. So here it is: you were right. Reading and writing are my life.